The Selected Works of T. S. Spivet

"IT IS NOT DOWN IN ANY MAP; TRUE PLACES NEVER ARE."
-HERMAN MELVILLE, MOBY-DICK

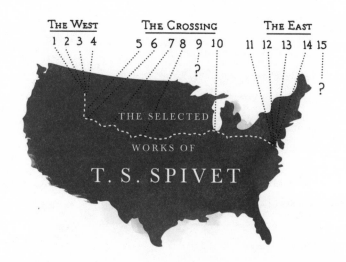

THE WEST · THE CROSSING · THE EAST
1 2 3 4 · 5 6 7 8 9 10 · 11 12 13 14 15
? · ?

THE SELECTED

WORKS OF

T. S. SPIVET

REIF LARSEN

HARVILL SECKER

LONDON

Published by Harvill Secker 2009

2 4 6 8 10 9 7 5 3 1

Copyright © Reif Larsen 2009

First published in Great Britain in 2009 by
HARVILL SECKER
Random House, 20 Vauxhall Bridge Road,
London SW1V 2SA

www.rbooks.co.uk

Addresses for companies within The Random House Group Limited can be found at:
www.randomhouse.co.uk/offices.htm

The Random House Group Limited Reg. No. 954009

A CIP catalogue record for this book is available from the British Library - - - - - ►   THIS BOOK IS ABOUT:

1. CHILD CARTOGRAPHERS—MONTANA—FICTION.

2. VOYAGES AND TRAVELS—FICTION.   - - - - - - - - - -

ISBN 9781846552779 (hardback)
ISBN 9781846552786 (trade paperback)
ISBN 9781846553325 (Limited edition hardback)

Book design and typography by Ben Gibson

The illustrations were created by Ben Gibson and Reif Larsen
except those on pages 3, 104, 171, 270, and 343, which were created by
Martie Holmer and Ben Gibson and are based on the author's original drawings

Moby-Dick map created by Ben Gibson

BUT ALSO:

3. CONTINENTAL DIVIDES—FICTION.

4. SPARROWS—FICTION.

5. BEETLES—TIGER MONK BEETLES—FICTION.

6. GIRLS—GIRLS WHO LIKE POP MUSIC—FICTION.

The Random House Group Limited supports The Forest Stewardship
Council (FSC), the leading international forest certification organisation. All our titles that are printed on Greenpeace approved FSC certified
paper carry the FSC logo. Our paper procurement policy can be found at
www.rbooks.co.uk/environment

Printed and bound in Germany by
Appl Druck, Wemding

- - ► AND ALSO: 7. WHISKEY DRINKING—FICTION. 8. RIFLES—1886 WINCHESTER SHORT RIFLE .40-82 CAL—FICTION. 9. THE SMITHSONIAN INSTITUTION—FICTION. 10. THE MEGATHERIUM CLUB—FICTION. 11. HOBOS—FICTION. 12. HOBO SIGNS—FICTION. 13. THE RESILIENCE OF MEMORY—FICTION. 14. THE OREGON TRAIL VIDEO GAME FOR THE APPLE IIGS—FICTION. 15. MANY WORLDS THEORY—FICTION. 16. HONEY NUT CHEERIOS—FICTION. 17. SMILES—DUCHENNE SMILES—FICTION. 18. LANYARDS—FICTION. 19. FOOD POUCHES—FICTION. 20. THE INHERITANCE OF HISTORY—FICTION. 21. INERTIA—FICTION. 22. WORMHOLES—MIDWESTERN WORMHOLES—FICTION. 23. MUSTACHES—FICTION. 24. PARALLEL LONGING—FICTION. 25. MOBY-DICK—FICTION. 26. MEDIOCRITY—FICTION. 27. RULES—THE THREE-SECOND RULE—FICTION.

For Katie

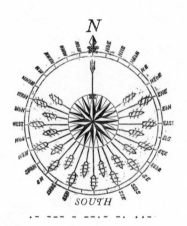

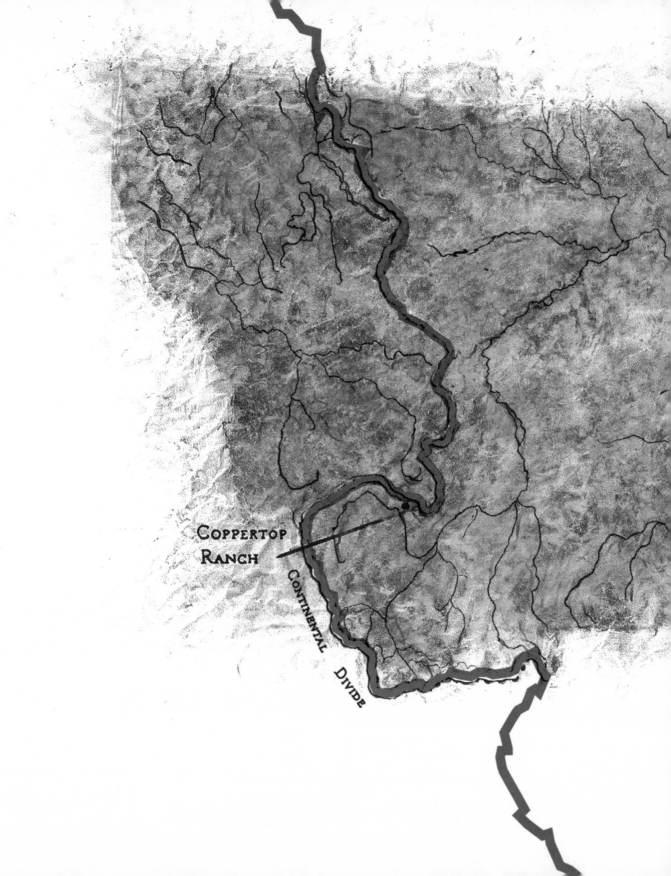

COPPERTOP
RANCH

CONTINENTAL DIVIDE

PART 1: THE WEST

Montana as Rivers

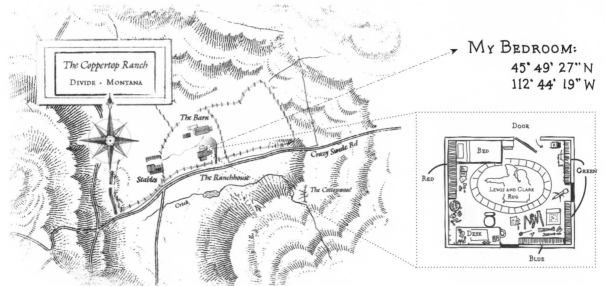

CHAPTER 1

The phone call came late one August afternoon as my older sister Gracie and I sat out on the back porch shucking the sweet corn into the big tin buckets. The buckets were still peppered with little teeth-marks from this past spring, when Verywell, our ranch hound, became depressed and turned to eating metal.

Perhaps I should clarify. When I say that Gracie and I were shucking the sweet corn, what I actually mean is that Gracie was shucking the corn and I was drawing a diagrammatic map in one of my little blue spiral notebooks of precisely *how* she was shucking the corn.

All of my notebooks were color-coded. The *blue* notebooks that neatly lined the south wall of my room were reserved for "Maps of People Doing Things," as opposed to the *green* notebooks on the east wall, which contained zoological, geological, and topographical maps, or the *red* notebooks on the west wall, which was where I mapped out insect anatomy in case my mother, Dr. Clair Linneaker Spivet, ever called upon my services.

I constantly battled the curious weight of entropy in my tiny bedroom, which was stuffed to the gills with the sediment of a cartographer's life: surveying equipment, antique telescopes, sextants, long rolls of goose-twine, jars of rabbit wax, compasses, withered, malodorous weather balloons, a sparrow skeleton perched on my drafting table. (At the moment of my birth, the sparrow had fatally crashed into the kitchen window. A stiff-legged ornithologist from Billings reconstructed the shattered skeleton, and I was given a new middle name.)

The
Sparrow Skeleton
from Notebook G214

And I think she was right. ←------------

Every instrument in my room hung on a hook, and on the wall behind each piece I had drawn and labeled the outline of the apparatus, like an echo of the real thing, so I always knew when something was missing and where it must be returned to.

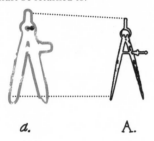

a.   **A.**

Still, even with such a system in place, things fell and things broke; piles formed and my methods of orientation always seemed to unravel. I was only twelve, but through the slow, inevitable burn of a thousand sunrises and sunsets, a thousand maps traced and retraced, I had already absorbed the valuable precept that everything crumbled into itself eventually, and to cultivate a crankiness about this was just a waste of time.

My room was no exception. It was not uncommon for me to wake up in the middle of the night with my bed full of mapping mechanisms, as if the nocturnal spirits were trying to chart my dreams.

Chart of My Dreams from Notebook G54

I had once tried lining maps on the south wall of my room, but in my excitement to organize, I briefly forgot that this was where the entrance to my room was located, and when Dr. Clair opened the door to announce that dinner was ready, the bookshelf fell on my head.

I sat on my Lewis and Clark carpet, covered in notebooks and shelving. "Am I dead?" I asked, knowing that she would not tell me, even if I was.

"Never let your work trap you into a corner," Dr. Clair said through the door. ----

Our ranch house was located just north of Divide, Montana, a tiny town you could miss from the highway if you happened to adjust your radio at the wrong moment. Surrounded by the Pioneer Mountains, Divide was nestled in a flat-backed valley sprinkled with sagebrush and half-burnt two-by-fours, a reminder of when people actually used to live here. The railroad came in from the north, the Big Hole River came in from the west, and both left heading south, searching for brighter pastures. Each had its own way of moving through the land and each had its own odor of passage: the railway tracks cut straight ahead, asking no questions of the bedrock through which it sliced, the wrought-iron rails smelling of axle grease and the wooden slats of rancid, licorice-scented shellac. In contrast, the Big Hole River talked with the land as it wound its way through the valley, collecting creeks as it went, quietly taking the path of least resistance. The Big Hole smelled of moss and mud and sage and occasionally huckleberries—if it was the right time of year, though it had not been the right time of year for many years now.

These days the railway did not stop in Divide, and only Union Pacific freight came rumbling through the valley at 6.44 A.M., 11.53 A.M., and 5.15 P.M., give or take a couple minutes, depending on the weather conditions. The boom era of Montana mining towns was long gone; there was no reason for the trains to stop anymore.

Divide once had a saloon.

"The Blue Moon Saloon," my brother Layton and I used to say while we floated in the creek, our noses pointed pompously upward, as if only gentry frequented the establishment, though in retrospect the opposite was more probable: these days, Divide was a town of holdout ranchers, fanatical fishermen, and the occasional Unabomber, not dandy fops with a mind for parlor games.

Layton and I had never been to the Blue Moon, but the idea of what and who might be inside became the basis of many of our fantasies as we floated on our backs. Soon after Layton died, the Blue Moon burned down, but by then, even up in flames, the place was no longer a vesicle of the imagination; it had become just another building burning, and now burnt, in the valley.

If you stood where the old railroad platform used to be, next to the white rusted sign that, when you squinted your eyes in just the right way, still read D I V I D E—from this spot, if you pointed yourself due north, using compass, sun, stars, or intuition, and then walked 4.73 miles, whacking your way through the scrub brush above the river basin and then up into the Douglas fir–covered hills, you would collide with the front gate of our little ranch, the Coppertop, nestled on an isolated plateau at 5,343 feet, a stone's throw south of the continental divide, from which the town had gleaned its name.

The divide, oh, the divide: I had grown up with this great border at my back, and its quiet, unerring existence had penetrated deep into my bones and brain. The divide was a massive, sprawling boundary not

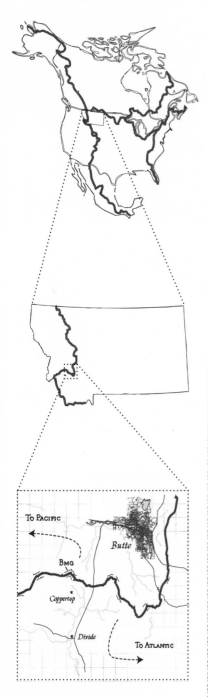

Continental Divide as Fractal ◄----
from Notebook B58

determined by politics, religion, or war but by tectonics, granite, and gravity. How remarkable that no U.S. president had signed this border into law, and yet its delineation had affected the expansion and formation of America's frontier in a million untold ways. This jagged sentinel sliced the nation's watersheds into east and west, the Atlantic and the Pacific—and out west, water was gold, and where the water went, people followed. The raindrops blown a couple of miles west of our ranch would land in creeks that percolated through the Columbia River system into the Pacific, whereas the water in Feely Creek, our creek, was blessed with the task of traveling a thousand miles more, all the way down to the bayous of Louisiana before spilling through the loamy delta into the Gulf of Mexico.

Layton and I used to climb Bald Man's Gap, the exact apex of the divide—he taking care not to spill the glass of water clutched in between his hands, while I minded a rudimentary pinhole camera that I had fashioned from a shoe box. I would take pictures of him pouring water on either side of the hill, running back and forth, yelling "Hello Portland!" alternately with "Hello N'Awlins!" in his best Creole accent. As much as I worked the dials on the side of the box, the pictures never quite captured the heroism of Layton in that moment.

Layton once said at the dinner table after one of our expeditions, "We can learn a lot from a river, can't we, Dad?" And though Father didn't say anything at the time, you could see in the way he ate the rest of his mash that he appreciated that kind of thinking in his son. Father loved Layton as much as anything in this life.

Out on the porch, Gracie shucked and I mapped. The tickers and clickers spattered the fields of our ranch with their droning orchestration, and August swam all around us—hot, thick, and remarkable. Montana

6

glowed in the summertime. Just last week, I had watched the slow, quiet spill of daybreak over the soft, fir-topped spine of the Pioneers. I had stayed up all night drafting a flip book that superimposed an ancient map of the body from the Chin Dynasty on a triptych of the Navajo, Shoshone, and Cheyenne understandings of a person's inner workings.

At the nip of daybreak, I walked out onto the back porch barefoot and delirious. Even in my sleepless state, I sensed the private magic of the moment, and so I gripped my pinky behind my back until the sun finally cleared the Pioneers and flashed its unknowable face at me.

I sat down on the steps of the porch, bewildered, and those crafty wooden boards took this opportunity to engage me in conversation:

It's just you and me, buster—let's sing a quiet song together, the porch said.

I have work to do, I said.

What work?

I don't know…ranch work.

You are not a ranch boy.

I'm not?

You do not whistle cowpuncher tunes or spit into tin cans.

I'm not good at spitting, I said. I make maps.

Maps? the porch asked. *What is there to map? Spit into tin cans. Ride the high country. Take her easy.*

There is plenty to map. I do not have time to take her easy. I do not even know what that really means.

You are not a ranch boy. You are a fool.

I am not a fool, I said. And then: Am I a fool?

You are lonely, the porch said.

I am?

Where is he?

I don't know.

You know.

Yes.

Then take a seat, and whistle a lonely cowpuncher tune.

I am not finished with my maps. There is more to map.

The first map I ever drew was from this back porch.

Hello, God By T. S. Spivet, age 6

At the time, I thought these were useful instructions on how to walk up cranky old Mt. Humbug to heaven and shake hands with God. In retrospect, the map's crudeness was not only due to the shaky hands of youth but also because I did not understand that the map of a place was different from the place itself. At age six, a boy could enter the world of a map just as easily as the genuine article.

While Gracie and I were shucking, Dr. Clair came out on the back porch. Gracie and I both looked up as we heard the old porch creak under Dr. Clair's footsteps. Squeezed tightly between thumb and forefinger she held a pin, on the end of which gleamed a bright blue-green metallic beetle that I recognized as a *Cicindela purpurea lauta*, a rare subspecies of the Cow Path Tiger Beetle from Oregon.

My mother was a tall, bony woman whose skin was so pasty that people often stared as we passed them on the street in Butte. I once heard an older woman in a flowered sunhat remark, "Such fragile wrists!" to her traveling partner. And it was true: if she weren't my mother, I would have thought there was something wrong with her.

Dr. Clair pulled her dark hair back into a bun using two polished sticks that looked like bones. She only took her hair down at night, and even then only behind closed doors. When we were younger, Gracie and I used to take turns peeking through the keyhole at the hidden scene of grooming on the other side. The keyhole was too small for us to see the whole picture: you could only make out her elbow moving back and forth, back and forth, as if she were working some old loom; or if you moved your body just slightly, you might be lucky enough to see some of the hair itself, the comb returning again and again, making that quiet thrushing sound. The keyhole, the peeking, the thrushing: it all seemed so deliciously naughty at the time.

Layton, like Father, wasn't interested in anything that had to do with beauty or hygiene and thus never joined us. He belonged with Father in the fields, punching cows and breaking broncs.

Dr. Clair wore lots of green jewelry that jingled—peridot earrings, little sapphire twinkle bracelets. Even the chain that kept her spectacles around her neck was made of green malachite stones she had found on a field expedition to India. Sometimes, with the sticks in her hair and all the quiet emerald ornamentation, I thought she looked like a springtime birch tree ready to burst into blossom.

For a moment, she just stood there, surveying Gracie with the big tin bucket of yellow ears between her legs and me on the stairs with my notebook and my magnifying-glass headpiece. We looked back at her.

And then she said, "Phone for you, T.S."

"Phone? For him?" Gracie said, shocked.

"Yes, Gracie, the phone's for T.S.," Dr. Clair said, not without some satisfaction.

"Who's calling?" I asked.

"I'm not sure who it is. I didn't ask," my mother said, still twirling her tiger beetle in the light. Dr. Clair was the kind of mother who would teach you the periodic table while feeding you porridge as an infant but not the type, in this age of global terrorism and child kidnappers, to ask who might be calling her children on the telephone.

My curiosity about the phone call was complicated by the fact that I was in the middle of drawing my map, and an unfinished map always left a little tickle in the back of my throat.

On my map, "Gracie Shucking the Sweet Corn #6," I had put a little numeral 1 next to where she first gripped the husk at the top. Then

To tell you the truth, like Gracie, I was also a bit mystified by the phone call, because I really had only two friends:

1) *Charlie*. Charlie was a towheaded boy in the grade below me who was eager to help out with any of my mapping expeditions that took him up into the mountains and beyond his family's trailer in South Butte, where his mother sat in a lawn chair all day long running a garden hose over her enormous feet. It was almost as if Charlie were half-mountain goat, because he seemed most at home when standing on inclines of forty-five degrees or more, holding his bright orange surveying pole as I spotted him from across the valley.

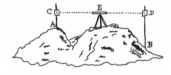

2) *Dr. Terrence Yorn*. Dr. Yorn was an entomology professor at Montana State in Bozeman and my mentor. Dr. Clair had originally introduced us at the Southwestern Montana Beetle picnic. The picnic had been dreadfully boring before I met Dr. Yorn. Our plates full of potato salad, we talked about longitude for three hours straight. Dr. Yorn was the one who had encouraged me (admittedly behind my mother's back) to submit my work to *Science* and *Smithsonian*. In some ways, I guess you could call him my "scientific father."

Jimney, the Transit.
Dr. Yorn gave me this transit after my first publication in *Smithsonian*.

JIMNEY

she yanked downward three times: *rip, rip, rip,* and this motion I had denoted by three arrows, although one arrow was smaller than the others, because that first rip was always a little bit belabored—one must overcome the initial inertia of the corn husk.   I do love the sound of ripping corn husks. The violence of the noise, the sustained popping and shoring of the silky organic threads, made me think of someone tearing up an expensive and potentially Italian set of trousers in a fit of madness that this person might just regret later. At least that's how Gracie shucked the husks, or *husked the shucks* as I sometimes called it—a bit mischievously, I might add, because for some reason it upset my mother when I bent words in this way. You couldn't blame her, really—she was a beetle scientist, and she had spent nearly all her adult life studying very small creatures under a magnifying glass and then precisely classifying them into families and suprafamilies, species and subspecies, according to their physical and evolutionary features. We even had a photograph of Carolus Linnaeus, the Swedish inventor of the modern taxonomic classification system, hanging above the fireplace, much to Father's silent and ongoing protestations. So in a way, it made sense that Dr. Clair would get annoyed at me when I said "grasspopper" instead of "grasshopper" or "ex–parrot puss" instead of "asparagus," because her job was to pay very close attention to the smallest details that the human eye could not possibly see and then ensure that the presence of a hair on the tip of the mandible or little white rear maculations on the elytra meant that the beetle was a *C. purpurea purpurea* and not a *C. purpurea lauta*. Personally, I thought my mother should be less concerned about my inventive wordplay, which was a kind of mental aerobics that all healthy twelve-year-old boys engaged in, and pay more attention to the mild insanity that took hold of Gracie when she husked the shucks, because this really ran against her general character as a bona

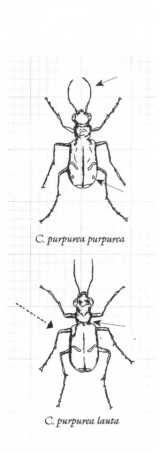

C. purpurea purpurea

C. purpurea lauta

Identification of
Cow Path Tiger Beetle Subspecies
from Notebook R23

I have not shown these drawings to Dr. Clair yet. She did not ask for them and I feared she would get angry at me for stepping into her field of expertise again.

fide adult trapped in the body of a sixteen-year-old, and to me pointed to some unaddressed wellspring of anger. I suppose I could safely say that even though Gracie was only four years my elder, she was many years beyond me in terms of maturity, common sense, knowledge of social custom, and understanding of the dramatic posture. Perhaps the unhinged look she cultivated on her face while shucking the corn was nothing more than that: a cultivation, just another cue that Gracie was a misunderstood actress sharpening her forté during one of the many mundane chores on a Montana ranch. Perhaps—but I was more partial to the idea that beneath her pristine exterior, she was actually just unhinged.

Oh, Gracie. Dr. Clair said she was absolutely dazzling as the lead in her high school's production of *Pirates of Penzance*, although I could not attend, because I was finishing a behavior map for *Science* magazine on how the female Australian dung beetle *Onthophagus sagittarius* used its horns during copulation. I didn't tell Dr. Clair about this project. I merely complained of a stomachache and then got Verywell to eat some sage and throw up all over the porch, and then pretended it was mine— pretended I had eaten the sage and the mouse bones and the dog food. Gracie was probably miraculous as the pirate's wife. She was a miraculous woman in general, and probably the most together member of our family, for when you got right down to it, Dr. Clair was a misguided coleopterist, who for twenty years had been chasing a phantom species of beetle—the tiger monk, *Cicindela nosferatie*—that even she was not sure truly existed; and my father, Tecumseh Elijah Spivet, was a quiet and brooding bronc-buster, who would walk into a room and say something like, "You can't bullshit a cricket," and then just leave, the type of man who was born perhaps one hundred years too late.

• • •

And then there was my younger brother, Layton Housling Spivet, the only Spivet boy born without the birthname Tecumseh in five generations. But Layton died this past February during an accident with a gun in the barn that no one ever talked about. I was there too, measuring gunshots. I don't know what went wrong.

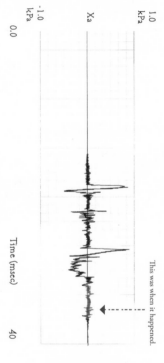

Gunshot #21
from Notebook B345

After that, I hid his name in the topography of every one of my maps.

"He's probably tired of waiting, T.S. You'd better go get the phone," Dr. Clair was saying. Clearly she had discovered something interesting in the *C. purpurea lauta* on the end of her pin because her eyebrows went up and then down and then up again and then she turned on her heel and disappeared back into the house.

"I'm going to finish the shucking," Gracie said.

"Don't you dare," I said.

"I'm going to," she said firmly.

"If you do," I said, "I won't help you with your Halloween costume this year."

Gracie paused at this, weighing its seriousness, and then said again: "I'm going to." She held up the ear of corn threateningly.

I carefully took off my magnification headpiece, closed my notebook, and laid my drafting pen on top at a diagonal so as to convey to Gracie that I would be coming back soon—that this business of mapping the corn was not finished.

As I walked past the entrance to Dr. Clair's study, I saw her struggling with the weight of some huge taxonomic dictionary, using only one hand to hold the giant tome, as the other was still maintaining the pinned tiger beetle upright in the air. This was the kind of image I would remember my mother by when and if she ever passed on: balancing the delicate specimen against the weight of the system within which it belonged.

To get to the kitchen where the phone lay waiting, I could take an infinite number of routes, each with its own pros and cons: *The Hallways/Pantry Route* was most direct but also the most boring; *The Upstairs/Downstairs Route* gave me the most exercise but the necessary shift in altitude also made me feel a little woozy. In the heat of the moment, I decided on a route I did not often use, particularly when Father was lurking around the house. I cautiously cracked open the plain pinewood door and then made my way through the leathered darkness of the Sett'ng Room.

The Sett'ng Room was the only room in the house that was distinctly Father's. He claimed it with a silent fierceness that you did not test. My father rarely spoke above a mumble, but once when Gracie kept insisting at dinner that we should make the Sett'ng Room more of a normal living room where "normal" people felt compelled to relax and have "normal" conversations, he slowly steamed over his mash until we heard a sort of muted pop-and-tinkle kind of sound and we all looked over and saw that he had splintered his whiskey glass in the palm of his hand. Layton loved that. I remember him loving that.

"That's the last place I got to set in this house and throw my boots up," my father had said, his palm slowly bleeding rivers into the potatoes. And that was that.

The Sett'ng Room was a museum of sorts. Just before my great-grandfather, Tecumseh Reginald Spivet (*see Tecumseh sidebar*), died, he gave my father a hunk of peppery Anaconda copper for his sixth birthday. He had smuggled the ore out of the mines during the turn of the century, back when Butte was a booming copper outfit and the biggest city between Minneapolis and Seattle. The piece of copper put some sort of spell on my father, for thereafter he developed the habit of slowly collecting trinkets and props from the vast stage of the open range.

On the northern wall of the Sett'ng Room, next to a large crucifix that Father touched every morning, there was a shrine to Billy the Kid, lit somewhat awkwardly by a single incandescent bulb and complete with rattlesnake skins, dusty clinks, and an ancient Colt .45 lining a portrait of the infamous prairie buccaneer. Father and Layton had painstakingly

THE TECUMSEH SPIVETS

TECUMSEH TEARHO SPIVET (1851-1917) ✳

DEAD

TECUMSEH REGINALD SPIVET (1878-1965)

TECUMSEH PERRYMORE SPIVET (1917-1978)

TECUMSEH ELIJAH SPIVET (1959-)

NOT DEAD

TECUMSEH SPARROW SPIVET (1995-)

✳ Reginald's father (and my great-great-grandfather) was actually born just outside Helsinki as Terho Sievä, which in Finnish roughly translates to "Mr. Handsome Acorn." So perhaps it was a relief for him when the immigration authority at Ellis Island flubbed his name as Tearho Spivet and a new family name was created with the false flick of a pen. On his way out west to work in the Butte mines, Tearho happened to stop off in a ramshackle Ohio saloon long enough to hear a drunk man who claimed to be half Navajo deliver a much embellished story about the great Shawnee warrior Tecumseh. It was at the part in the story when Tecumseh made a final stand against the White Man at the Battle of the Thames that my great-great-grandfather began quietly weeping, even though he was supposed to be one of those hardened Finns. In the battle, after Tecumseh was felled by a double ball shot through the chest, General Proctor's men scalped and mutilated his body beyond recognition and then threw him into a mass grave. Tearho walked out of that saloon with a new name in a new land.

At least that's how the story went—you never know with these ancestral tales.

constructed the installation. To an outside observer, it might have seemed strange to see God and a Western outlaw given equal treatment, but such was the way of things on the Coppertop Ranch: Father was guided by the unspoken Cowboy Code embedded within his beloved Westerns as much as by any biblical verse.

Layton used to think the Sett'ng Room was the greatest thing since grilled cheese. After church on Sundays, Father and he would sit together all afternoon watching the Westerns that played continuously on the TV in the southeast corner of the room. Behind the set there was a vast yet carefully selected library of VHS tapes. *Red River, Stagecoach, The Searchers, Ride the High Country, My Darling Clementine, Who Shot Liberty Valance?, Monte Walsh, The Treasure of the Sierra Madre*—I was not an active watcher like Father and Layton, but I had been exposed to these films so many times through osmosis, they felt less like feats of cinema and more like my most intimate recurring dreams. I often returned home from school to the muted rattle of guns or the sweaty canter of hooves on this strange television, Father's version of the eternal flame. He was too busy to watch during the middle of the day, but I think he took comfort in knowing that it was on in *here* while he was out *there*.

And yet, the TV was not the only thing that gave the Sett'ng Room its "room-feeling." Cowpuncher bric-a-brac abounded: lariats, bridle bits, hackamores, stirrups, boots finally worn through from ten thousand miles of pounding the plains, coffee mugs, even a pair of lady's stockings once sported by an eccentric puncher from Oklahoma who claimed they kept him riding straight. Everywhere in the Sett'ng Room there were fading and faded photographs of nameless men on nameless horses. Soapy Williams riding crazy old Firefly, his elastic frame impossibly twisted yet still

"Every room has a room-feeling." ◀---

This I learned from Gracie, who, for a short period a couple years back, became infatuated with reading people's auras. The room-feeling you got when entering the Sett'ng Room was a rich sensation of Western nostalgia that washed over you in waves. Part of it was the smell: old whiskey-stained leather, some of that dead horse from the Indian blanket, a little mildew from the photographs—but beneath all this was the smell of something like recently settled prairie dust, as if you were entering a field that a group of cowboys had just galloped through; the thrashing of hooves, the clench of sun-beaten forearms—and now the clouds of dust were gently returning to earth, the evidence of man and horse settling back into itself, leaving only the echo of their passage. You walked into the Sett'ng Room and you felt like you had just missed something important, as if the world was quiet again after a real wild time. It was sort of a sad feeling really, and it matched the expression on my father's face when he would set in the Sett'ng Room after a long day's work in the fields.

somehow clinging to the back of the bucking beast. It was like looking at a good marriage.

On the western wall, behind which the sun set every evening, Father had hung an Indian horsehair blanket and a portrait of the original Tecumseh and his brother, the Shawnee prophet, Tenskwautawa. On the mantel above the fireplace, overlooking a porcelain Nativity set, there was even a marble statue of the heavily bearded Finnish god Väinämöinen, who my father claimed was actually the first cowboy, before there was even a West to roam. He saw no contradiction in mixing pagan gods with the scene of Christ's birthing. "Christ loves all cowboys," he liked to say.

If you asked me—and my father never did—Mr. T. E. Spivet's mausoleum of the Old West memorialized a world that had never even existed in the first place. Sure there were still real cowboys in the last part of the nineteen hundreds, but by the time Hollywood began sculpting the West of the Western, the barbed-wire barons had long since cut up the plains into fenced ranchland and the days of the trail drive had been gone for a while. No longer did men with chinks, boots, and sun-worn Stetsons round up the cattle on the thorn-studded plains of Texas and drive them a thousand miles north through the flat, expansive swath of plains inhabited by hostile Comanche and Dakota before finally arriving at one of the bustling railroad depots in Kansas, where the livestock would be distributed to the East. I think my father was drawn not so much to the real cowboys of these trail drives but to that melancholy echo of the drive, a melancholy that propelled every single frame of every single movie in that collection behind the TV. It was this falsified memory—*not even his falsified memory, but a falsified cultural memory*—that fueled my father to set in his Sett'ng Room, his boots at the door, his whiskey glass up to his mouth once every forty-five seconds with a sensational degree of regularity.

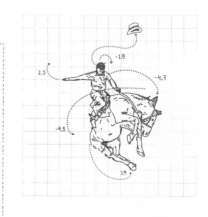

Soapy Williams as Motion Vectors
from Notebook B46

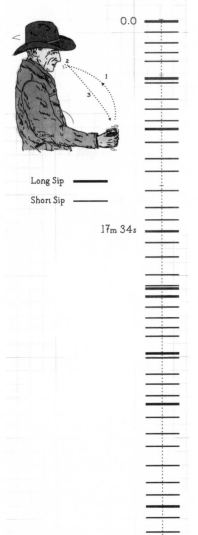

Father Drinks Whiskey with a
Sensational Degree of Regularity
from Notebook B99

0.0

Long Sip

Short Sip

17m 34s

Maybe I never prodded my father about the conflicting hermeneutics of his Sett'ng Room not just because it would earn me a first-rate whooping but because I too plead guilty to harboring some longing for the Old West. On Saturdays, I would get a ride into town and pay my respects to the Butte archives. There, I hunkered down with my Juicy Fruit and my magnifying headpiece and studied the historical maps of Lewis and Frémont and Governor Warren. The West was wide open back then, and these early cartographers of the Corps of Topographical Engineers drank their coffee black in the mornings from the back of the chuck wagon and stared at a totally unnamed set of mountains, which, by day's end, they would soon add to the swiftly expanding receptacle of cartographic knowledge. They were conquerors in the most basic sense of the word, for over the course of the nineteenth century, they slowly transferred the vast unknown continent piece by piece into the great machine of the known, of the mapped, of the witnessed—out of the mythological and into the realm of empirical science. For me, *this* transfer was the Old West: the inevitable growth of knowledge, the resolute gridding of the great Trans-Mississippi territory into a chart that could be placed alongside others.

My own museum of the Old West was upstairs in my room, in my copies of the old Lewis and Clark maps, scientific diagrams, and observational sketches. If you turned to me on a hot summer day and asked me why I still copied their work, even when I knew so much of it to be wrong, I would not know what to say to you, except this: there was never a map that got it all right, and truth and beauty were never married to one another for long.

"Hello?" I said into the phone.

I wrapped the cord around my pinky finger.

"Is this Mr. T. S. Spivet?"

On the other end of the line, the man's voice had a subtle lisp that gently folded a *thf* into each *s,* like a baker lightly pressing his thumbs—just so—into a lump of dough. I tried not to picture the man's mouth as he said this. I was a very bad phone-talker, because I was always visualizing what was going on at the other end, and so I often forgot to speak into the phone.

"Yes," I said carefully, trying not to see that cinematic close-up of the strange man's tongue slipping across his teeth as he spoke, splattering the littlest tidbits of saliva onto the telephone's mouthpiece.

"Well, gracious Mr. Spivet. This is Mr. G. H. Jibsen, Undersecretary of Illustration and Design at the Smithsonian, and I dare say it has been a chore to get a hold of you. For a minute there I thought that I had lost the connection—"

"Sorry," I said. "Gracie was being a brat."

There was a silence on the other end in which I could hear some sort of ticking in the background—like a grandfather clock with its front door open—and then the man said, "Don't take this the wrong way…but you sound quite young. This is indeed Mr. T. S. Spivet?"

In between the man's lips our family's last name took on a kind of slippery, explosive quality, like something you might hiss at your cat to get him off the table. *There must be spittle clinging to the receiver.* There just has to be. He must have to wipe at it occasionally with a handkerchief, perhaps one that he kept tastefully concealed inside the back of his collar just for that very purpose.

A Short History of Our Phone Cord

Gracie was very much in the phase where she liked to talk on the phone all night, the cord stretched taut from the kitchen through the dining room, up the stairs, through our bathroom, and into her room. She threw a fit when Father refused to install a phone in her room. Despite her tantrums, he said only, "House'll fall down if we touch that scramble," and then left the room, though no one in the room really knew what this meant. Gracie was forced to go to Sam's Hardware downtown and buy one of those fifty-foot telephone cords that can actually stretch to a thousand feet if you've got the inclination for stretching. And she did.

The phone cord, used to being stretched to impossible lengths by Gracie and her loneliness, now lay coiled and cowering on a small green hook that my father had nailed there to corral its numerous loops and curlicues.

"You could bulldog a moose from half a mile with a riata like this one," my father said, shaking his head as he nailed that hook into the wall. "Girl can't say what she needs to say in the kitchen, what's she saying anyways?"

My father saw conversing as a chore, like shoeing a horse: it was not done for enjoyment; it was done when it needed to be done.

One thing that might surprise you about Layton: he knew every U.S. president in order, as well as each of their birthdays, their places of birth, and their pets' names. And he had them all ranked according to a system that I could never quite decode. I believe President Jackson was right up there, maybe fourth or fifth on his list, because he was "tough" and "good with guns." I had always been amazed at this glimmer of encyclopedic disposition in my brother; in all other respects he was such a prototypical ranch boy, who thrived on shooting things, punching cows, and spitting into tin cans with Father.

Perhaps to prove that I was indeed related to him, I would pepper Layton with endless questions, plumbing his knowledge of the Executive Office:

"Who is your least favorite president?" I asked once.

"William Henry Harrison," Layton said. "Born February 9, 1773, at Berkeley Plantation in Virginia. He had a goat and a cow."

"Why is he your least favorite?"

"Because he killed Tecumseh. And Tecumseh cursed him and then he died a month into office."

"Tecumseh didn't curse him," I said. "And just because Harrison died, that's not his fault."

"Yes it is," Layton said. "When you die, it's always your fault."

"Yes," I said, trying very hard to stick to the adult conversation we were having. "I am quite young."

"But you are indeed the same T. S. Spivet who produced that most elegant diagram of how the *Carabidae brachinus* mixes and expels boiling secretions from its abdomen for our exhibit on Darwinism and intelligent design?"

The Bombardier Beetle. I had spent four months on that illustration.

"Yes," I said. "Oh, and I meant to say something before, but there is a small mistake in one of the glandular labels—"

"Ah splendid, splendid! Your voice threw me there for a second." Mr. Jibsen laughed and then seemed to regain himself. "Mr. Spivet—but do you know how many comments we've gotten on your illustration of that bombardier? We blew it up—huge!—and made it the centerpiece of the exhibit—backlit and everything. I mean, as you can imagine, the intelligent design people were all up in arms about this and that and *irreducible complexity*—their favorite buzzword at the moment and an absolute cussword here at the Castle—but they come in and see your Glandular Series in the middle of the room, and there it is! Complexity *reduced!*"

The more excited he became, the more frequently and pressingly his lisp seemed to insert itself into his speech. It was all I could concentrate on—the saliva and the tongue and the handkerchief—and so I took a deep breath and tried to think of something obvious that I could say to him, *anything* besides the word "spittle." Chitchat, adults called it, so I chitchatted: "You work at the Smithsonian?"

"Ah-ha! Yes, Mr. Spivet, I do indeed. In fact, many would say I practically run the place...ah, the increase and diffusion of knowledge, mandated long ago by our legislators, backed in full by President Andrew Jackson over one hundred and fifty years ago...though you would never guess it, what with this current administration." He laughed and I could hear his chair squeaking in the background, as if it were applauding his words.

"Wow," I said. And then for the first time during our conversation I was able to pry my mind away from this man's lisp and let the reality of who I was talking to wrap itself around me. I stood in our kitchen, with its uneven floors and its somewhat absurd proliferation of chopsticks, and I pictured the handset of my telephone connected through copper wires that fled across Kansas and the Midwest into the valley of the Potomac and on up to Mr. Jibsen's cluttered office in the Smithsonian Castle.

The Smithsonian! *The attic of our nation.* Even though I had examined and even copied details from the blueprints of the Smithsonian Castle, I could not quite actualize the Institution in my mind. I think one always needs the sensory smorgasbord of a firsthand experience in order to truly absorb a place's atmosphere—or, to borrow Gracie's term, to read the sum of its "room-feelings." This data could not be collected unless you were there to smell the scent of its entryway, to taste the stale air of its porticos, to let the tip of your shoe bump up against its existential coordinates, as it were. The Smithsonian was the kind of place, you could tell, that gleaned its hair-raising, temple-like quality not from the architecture of its walls but from the vast, eclectic karma of the collection that lay *inside* its walls.

Mr. Jibsen was still talking on the other end of the phone, and my attention swung back to his intelligent, slightly slippery East Coast drawl: "Yes, it does have quite a history here," he was saying. "But I think men of science like you and me stand at a real crossroads right now. Attendance figures are down, way down—I say this to you in confidence, of course, because you're one of us now…but it's entirely worrisome, I must say.

One of the most compelling pictures I had ever seen of the Institution was in *Time* magazine of all places, which Layton and I were leafing through as we lay on our stomachs beneath the Christmas tree at 6.17 A.M. We didn't know it at the time, but this was the last Christmas we would lie together on our stomachs like this.

Normally, Layton perused a magazine at a rate of about a page a second, but as he was riffling through, I caught sight of an image that made me grab his arm and halt the steady beat of page turning.

"What are you doing?" Layton asked. He got that look like he was going to hit me. Layton had a temper that our father both rebuked and encouraged in his way of saying nothing but expecting everything.

I did not answer him, however, as I was enraptured with the photo: in the foreground a drawer from a large specimen cabinet was open, displaying for the camera three gigantic dried African Bullfrogs—*Pyxicephalus adsperus*, their legs extended as if in mid-leap. Stretching back into a seemingly endless corridor were thousands of musty metallic cabinets just like this one, filled with millions of hidden specimens. The Western explorations of the nineteenth century had collected Shoshone skulls and armadillo shells and ponderosa pinecones and condor eggs and sent them all back east to the Smithsonian—by horse and stagecoach and later by train. Many of these specimens were never classified in the rush to gather them, and now they lay buried somewhere here, in one of these endless cabinets. The picture made me instantly long for whatever kind of room-feeling you felt when you walked into those archives.

"You are such an idiot!" Layton said, and tugged the page so hard that it ripped, right down the corridor.

"Sorry, Lay," I said, and let the page go, but not the image.

◀– The rip was like this except bigger and real.

Never before, not since Galileo's time…or Stokes's at the very least…I mean, inexplicably, this country is trying to roll back one hundred and fifty years of Darwinian theory.…Sometimes it's as if the *Beagle* never set sail."

This reminded me of something. "You never sent me a copy of *Bomby the Bombardier Beetle*," I said. "In your letter you said you would."

"Oh! Ha-ha! And a sense of humor! My, my, Mr. Spivet, I can see you and I will get along splendidly."

When I didn't say anything, he continued: "But of course we can still send you a copy! I mean, it was more of a joke, really, because you place that children's book alongside your illustration, and—I'm one for healthy debate and all—but this book, this children's book! It's so, so insidious! I mean, that's exactly what we're up against here. They are using children's books now to undermine the very tenets of science!"

"I like children's books," I said. "Gracie says she doesn't read them anymore, but I know she does because I found a stash in her closet."

"Gracie?" the man said. "Gracie? Is this your wife, I presume? My, I would love to meet the whole family!"

I just wished Gracie could've heard the way he pronounced her name with that curious, almost innocent lisp of his—*Graysthfie*—like some sort of insidious tropical sickness.

"She and I were shucking when you—" I started, and then stopped.

"Well, Mr. Spivet. I do say, it is quite an honor to finally speak with you." He paused. "And you live in Montana? Is that right?"

"Yes," I said.

"You know, out of some extraordinary coincidence, I was actually born in Helena and lived there for the first two years of my life. The state has always held a kind of mythological stature in my memory. I often wonder what would've happened had I stayed out there and grown up *on the range*, as they say. But my family moved to Baltimore and…such is the way of things, I suppose." He sighed. "Where do you live, exactly?"

"At the Coppertop Ranch, 4.73 miles due north of Divide, 14.92 miles south-southwest of Butte."

"Oh, well, I really must come and visit sometime. But listen, Mr. Spivet, we've got some very exciting news."

"Longitude, 112 degrees 44 minutes 19 seconds, latitude, 45 degrees 49 minutes 27 seconds. At least that's my bedroom—I don't have any of the other readings memorized."

"That's incredible, Mr Spivet. And clearly your eye for detail is reflected in the illustrations and diagrams that you have supplied for us this past year. Absolutely stunning."

"Our address is 48 Crazy Swede Creek Road," I said, and then suddenly wished I hadn't, because there was still a possibility that this man could turn out not to be ┄┄┄┄┄┄┄┄┄┄┄┄┄┄┄┄┄┄┄►

┄► and could instead be a child kidnapper from North Dakota. So I said, just to potentially throw him off the scent: "Well that's maybe our address."

"Fabulous, fabulous, Mr. Spivet. Look, I'll come right out and say it: you've won our prestigious Baird Award for the popular advancement of science."

Spencer F. Baird was in my top five. He had made it his life's mission to bring all manner of flora and fauna, archaeological artifacts, thimbles and prostheses to the Institution's great holding pens. He increased the Smithsonian's collection from 6,000 to 2.5 million specimens before he died in Woods Hole, staring at the sea, perhaps wondering why he could not collect that too.

He was also the father figure of the Megatherium Club, named for an extinct species of giant sloth. The Megatherium Club was a short-lived society that existed during the middle of the nineteenth century for aspiring young explorers and scientists. Its members lived in the towers of the Smithsonian, training under the watchful eye of Baird by day, drinking spiked eggnog and making a hullabaloo with badminton rackets in the museum's exhibits by night. What conversations must have transpired among these rabble-rousers concerning the nature of life, connectivity, and locomotion! It was as if the Megatheriums gained a sort of insatiable kinetic energy inside those great halls of taxidermies before Baird released them out into the wild, and, armed with their collecting nets and badminton rackets, they would head out west to contribute to the great roundup of knowledge.

When Dr. Clair told me about the Megatherium Club, I went silent for three days, perhaps out of jealousy that time's insistence on linearity prevented me from ever joining.

"Can we start a Megatherium Club in Montana?" I asked, finally breaking my silence at the door to her study.

She looked up at me and tipped down her glasses. "The Megatheriums are extinct," she said mysteriously.

I LIKE YOU.

Megatherium americanum
from Notebook G78

Silence, and then I said: "Spencer F. Baird, the second secretary of the Smithsonian? He has an award?"

"Yes, Mr. Spivet. I know you did not apply for this award, so this may be news to you, but Terry Yorn submitted a portfolio on your behalf. And frankly, well—up until that point we had only seen the small bits you had done for us, but this portfolio, well, we'd like to build an exhibit around its contents immediately."

"Terry Yorn?" At first I didn't recognize the name, in much the same way you could sometimes wake up in the morning and not recognize your own bedroom. But then, slowly, I filled in my map of him: Dr. Yorn, my mentor and Boggle partner; Dr. Yorn with those giant black glasses, the high white socks, the flittering thumbs, the laughter that sounded like hiccups and seemed to emanate from some foreign mechanism inside his body...*Dr. Yorn?* Dr. Yorn was supposed to be my friend and scientific guide and now I find out he had secretly submitted my name for an award in Washington? An award created by adults, for adults. I suddenly wanted to hide in my room and never come out.

"Well, of course you can thank him later," Mr. Jibsen was saying. "But first things first: we want to fly you out to Washington as soon as possible—to the Castle, as we call it—so that you can give an acceptance speech and announce what you will do with your yearlong post...I mean, you should give it all some thought, of course. We're having a gala to celebrate our one hundred fiftieth anniversary next Thursday and we were hoping you would be one of the keynotes, as your work is exactly the kind of cutting-edge—visually, well...visually charged scientific output that the Smithsonian is very keen on displaying these days. Science is really up against some giant hurdles in this day and age, and we're just going to have to fight fire with fire…we've got to do a much better job of reaching out to the public, *our* public."

"Well…" I said. "I'm beginning school next week."

"Oh yes, that. Of course. Dr. Yorn failed to actually give me your full C.V., so it's—ah!—ahem, a bit embarrassing, but may I ask where your position is right now? We've been quite busy here and I haven't gotten around to phoning the president of your university to let him know the good news, but let me assure you, it's never been a problem, even this late in the game…I assume you're with Terry at Montana State, yes? You see, I happen to know President Gamble quite well."

All at once the preposterousness of what was happening fell into place in my mind. I saw how this conversation between lispy Mr. Jibsen and myself had come to pass due to a series of increasingly serious misunderstandings, built on withheld and perhaps even falsified information. A year ago, Dr. Yorn had submitted my first illustration to the Smithsonian under the guise that I *was* a full colleague of his, and the bad feeling that I got from the lying part of this statement was outweighed by the secret hope that perhaps I was a full colleague of Dr. Yorn's, at least in spirit. And then when this first illustration—a bumblebee cannibalistically devouring another bumblebee—had been accepted, and published no less, Dr. Yorn and I had celebrated, somewhat surreptitiously, because my mother still did not know any of this had transpired. Dr. Yorn had driven down from Bozeman, crossed over the continental divide twice (once west to Butte and then again south to Divide), picked me up at the Coppertop, and taken me out for ice cream at O'Neil's in Historic Downtown Butte.

We sat on a bench with our butter pecan and stared up the hill at the silent black scaffolding of a gallows frame that marked the entrance to one of the old mine shafts.

"Men used to board those skips and be lowered down three thousand feet, for eight hours at a time," Dr. Yorn said. "For eight hours the world was hot, dark, sweaty, and three feet wide. This whole town used to be on a shift of eight hours: eight hours down working in the mines, eight hours up drinking in the bars, eight hours sleeping in the bed. Hotels used to rent a bed out for only eight hours at a time. They knew they could make three times as much that way. Can you imagine?"

"Would you have been a miner if you had lived here then?" I asked.

"Wouldn't have had much choice, would I?" Dr. Yorn said. "Not many coleopterists back then."

Afterward, we went butterfly collecting in Pipestone Pass. We were silent for a good long while stalking the flighty little lepidoptera. Then, as we lay on our stomachs, scanning the tall grasses, Dr. Yorn said: "This is all happening very fast, you know."

"What is?"

"Many people wait for this kind of exposure their entire lives."

More silence.

"Like Dr. Clair?" I asked finally.

"Your mother knows what she's doing," Dr. Yorn said hastily. He paused, staring off into the mountains. "She's a brilliant woman."

"She is?" I asked.

Dr. Yorn didn't answer me.

"Do you think she will ever find her beetle?" I asked.

Suddenly Dr. Yorn lunged out with his collecting net and badly missed catching a juniper hairstreak, *Callophrys gryneus*, the wisp of a creature drifting skyward as if giggling at his failed effort. He sat on his

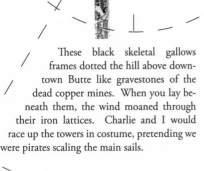

These black skeletal gallows frames dotted the hill above downtown Butte like gravestones of the dead copper mines. When you lay beneath them, the wind moaned through their iron lattices. Charlie and I would race up the towers in costume, pretending we were pirates scaling the main sails.

haunches in the rabbit brush, panting from the effort. Dr. Yorn was not an exerciser.

"You know, T.S., we can always wait," he said, breathing hard. "The Smithsonian will be around for a long time. We don't have to do this right now if you aren't comfortable with it."

"But I like drawing for them," I said. "They're nice."

We didn't speak for a while after that. We kept searching the grasses but the butterflies had gone.

"At some point we will have to tell her about this," Dr. Yorn said on the way back to the car. "She would be very proud."

"I will," I said. "When the time is right."

But the time was never right. Clear to everyone but her, Dr. Clair's unswerving obsession with her tiger monk beetle, coupled with its continued absence despite her twenty years of searching, held her career in a kind of perpetual limbo, keeping her from all the numerous systemic advancements I knew she was capable of discovering. I was convinced that if Dr. Clair had the inclination for it, she could be one of the most heralded scientists in the world. Something about the tiger monk and its stranglehold on her senses made me hold my tongue about my own blossoming career, a career that was not even supposed to be blossoming just yet but was, inexplicably, and with increasing momentum.

So the clandestine nature of our correspondence with the Smithsonian continued, and underhanded chicanery abounded: at home, my parents knew nothing; in Washington, they believed me to have a doctorate. With Dr. Yorn as my conduit, I began to submit my work regularly not only to the Smithsonian, but to *Science, Scientific American, Discovery,* even *Sports Illustrated for Kids*.

What Does a Normal Scientific Family Look Like?

I sometimes wondered how things would have turned out differently if Dr. Yorn were my father instead of Mr. T. E. Spivet. Then Dr. Yorn, Dr. Clair, and I could sit around the dinner table and have scientific discussions about antennae morphology and how to drop an egg off the Empire State Building without it breaking. Would life be normal then? Surrounded by the casual language of science, would Dr. Clair become inspired to jump-start her career? I noticed that Dr. Clair was always encouraging me to spend time with Dr. Yorn, as if she thought he could fulfill some role she was incapable of performing.

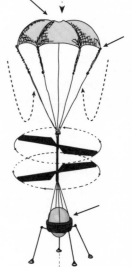

Design for Egg Drop off Empire State Building (2nd Prize at Science Fair)

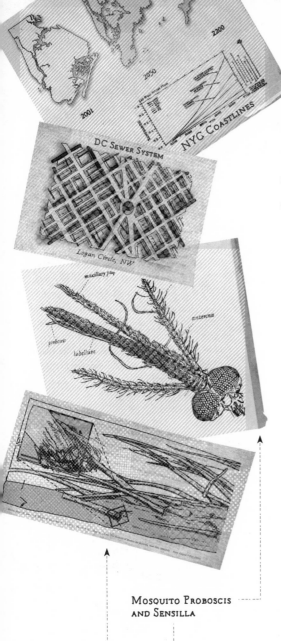

NYC COASTLINES

DC SEWER SYSTEM

Logan Circle, NW

maxillary palp

antenna

proboscis

labellum

MOSQUITO PROBOSCIS
AND SENSILLA

My projects were wide-ranging. There were the illustrations: schematics of industrious leafcutter ant colonies and numerous, multihued lepidoptera; exploding anatomical charts of horseshoe-crab circulatory systems; electron microscope diagrammatics of the feathery sensilla in the antennae of the *Anopheles gambiae*—the malaria mosquito.

And of course there were also the maps: the Washington, D.C., sewer system in 1959; a time-lapse overleaf showing the decline of Indian nations on the High Plains over the past two centuries; three contrasting hypothetical projections of the U.S. coastline in three hundred years, depicting competing theoretical outcomes of global warming and polar ice cap melt.

And then there was my favorite: the seven-foot diagram of the bombardier beetle mixing her—and it *was* a female—boiling hot secretions, which took me four months to draw, research, and label, and resulted in a terrible case of whooping cough that kept me out of school for a week.

But Dr. Yorn, once so hesitant in Pipestone Pass with butterfly net in hand, had apparently gotten excited about my potential career path and submitted my work, without my knowledge or consent, to be considered for the Baird. This seemed strangely unadult to me. I thought he was supposed to be my mentor. But, in actuality, what did I know about the often beguiling world of adults?

I didn't often remember that I was twelve years old. Life was too busy to dwell on things like age, but at this moment, faced with a great misunderstanding fabricated by grown-ups, I suddenly felt the full weight of my youth, painfully and acutely, in a sensation—for reasons I could not understand—that centered around the radial arteries in my wrists. I also realized that Mr. G. H. Jibsen, speaking from a world away, while perhaps initially suspicious of my boyishly singsong voice, now thought of me as both an adult and his colleague.

I saw myself coming to a stop at a great T-junction.

To the left lay the plains. I could put this all to rest, explain to Mr. Jibsen that when I said I needed to go to school next week, what I actually meant was that I needed to go to Central Butte Middle School and not to teach graduate students at Montana State. I could politely apologize for the confusion, thank him for the award, and explain that it would probably be better to give it to someone who could do things like drive to work and vote and make jokes about income taxes at cocktail parties. I would put Dr. Yorn in a tight spot, but then he had put me in a tight spot. And this would be the noble thing to do—the kind of thing that my father, abiding by that silent cowboy code, would do.

To the right, the mountains. I could lie. I could lie all the way to Washington, D.C., and possibly continue lying there, holing up in a hotel room that smelled of old cigarette butts and Windex, where I would produce illustrations and maps and press releases from behind a closed door like in some modern-day Oz. Perhaps I could even hire an appropriately aged actor to play me, someone who looked maybe like a cowboy, a cowboy scientist, someone who Washingtonians would appreciate as an observant man, a self-reliant man from Montana. I could reinvent myself, choose a new hairstyle.

"Mr. Spivet?" Jibsen said. "Are you still there?"

"Yes," I said. "I am here."

"So we can expect you out then? It would be great if you could make it out by next Thursday at the latest, so that you could address the gala. They would just lap the stuff up."

Our kitchen was old. It contained chopsticks and phone cords and fireproof vinyl and no answers to my questions. I found myself wondering what Layton would do. Layton, who wore his spurs indoors, collected antique pistols, and once bicycled off the roof in his spaceman pajamas after watching *E.T.* Layton, who had always wanted to see Washington, because that was where the president lived. Layton would go.

But I was not Layton and I could not hope to emulate his heroism. My place was at my drafting desk upstairs in my room, slowly mapping Montana in its entirety.

"Mr. Jibsen," I said, nearly slipping into a lisp myself. "Thank you for your offer—I am very surprised, really. But I don't think it would be a good idea for me to accept it. I am very busy with my work and, well… thank you very much anyway and I hope you have a pleasant day."

And I hung up before he could protest.

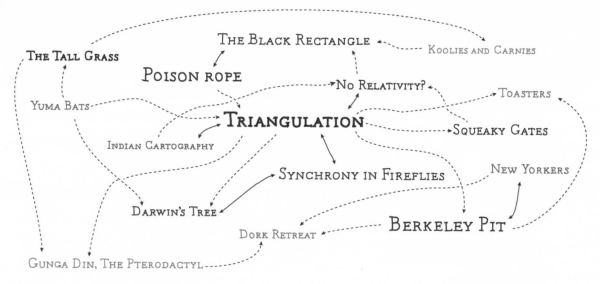

Map of August 22–23
from Notebook G100

CHAPTER 2

The receiver was placed back in the cradle, the connection from Washington to the Coppertop Ranch terminated. I imagined a woman with horn-rimmed glasses unplugging a cord from the socket in a drab little Midwestern switchboard office, the extraction causing a faint *pop* in her headphones. This woman would then turn back to her cubicle sister and continue their conversation about nail polish removers, a conversation that had lasted all day due to the constant interruptions.

On my way back outside, I paused at the door to Dr. Clair's study. She now had five gargantuan taxonomic volumes open on her desk. Her left index finger held fast to some line in one of those giant leather-bound books while in another her right index finger wildly cross-referenced this way and that across the minute taxonomies as though performing a kind of miniature tango with a company of fleas.

She saw me standing in the doorway. "I think this *must* be a new subspecies," she said, her fingers still holding their places as she looked up

She was lying. ◄╌╌╌╌╌╌╌╌╌╌╌╌┐

Gracie was going to start cooking soon. Dr. Clair always made the gesture to cook but then seemed to remember something important in her study at the last minute and left the brunt of the work to Gracie and me. This was fine: Dr. Clair was actually a terrible cook. She had gone through twenty-six toasters over the course of my conscious life, a little over two a year, one of which had exploded and burned down half the kitchen. Whenever she popped another piece of bread into the toaster and left the room to attend to something she had forgotten, I quietly went up to my filing cabinet and brought down the time-map that displayed each toaster, highlights from its career, and the date and nature of its demise.

 # 21, "The Gobbler" – Exploded 4/5/04 While Toasting Whole Wheat

I would stand at the doorway of her study and hold the map in front of my chest like some protest sign and that's about when the smoke would come wafting into the room and she would look up and smell the smoke and see me and shout *"yip seefg!"* like an injured coyote.

"It's a miracle this house is still standing with a woman like that at the chuck wagon," my father would often say.

at me. "A groove is present on the abdominal sternite that just hasn't been described before...I don't *think*. I don't think...there's always a possibility, but I don't think."

"Do you know where Father is?" I asked.

"I don't think..."

"Do you know where—" I started to ask again.

"Who was it on the phone?"

"The Smithsonian," I said.

She laughed. I did not often hear her laugh, and it caught me slightly off guard. I think my heels may have even clicked together in surprise.

"Bastards," she said. "If you ever work for a large institution, just remember that they are—by definition—bastards. Bureaucracy nullifies kindness at every step."

"What about the hymenoptera?" I asked. "They've got bureaucracy."

"Yes, well, an ant colony is all women. That's different. The Smithsonian is an old boys' club. And ants don't have egos."

"Thanks Dr. Clair," I said, and turned to leave.

"Are you two almost done out there?" she asked. "I was going to start cooking soon." ╌╌╌╌╌┐

Gracie was working on the last ear of corn when I got back to the porch.

"Gracie!" I said. "Aye! How many bad ones?"

"I'm not telling," she said.

"Gracie!" I said. "You're destroying our data set!"

"You were on the phone for like six hours. I got bored."

"What'd you do with bad ones?"

"I threw them out in the yard for Verywell."

"Them?" I asked. "Ah ha! So there was more than one. How many?"

She plucked off the last of the silk threads from the ear and dropped it into the tin bucket with the others. Inside the bucket, the bright ears of corn lay on top of one another, pointing in all directions, their perfect yellow kernels shining in the late afternoon sun like little buttons asking to be pressed. There was nothing like a bucket of uncooked sweet corn to really turn around your day. The yellowness, the fertile symbolism, the promise of melted butter: it was enough to change a boy's life.

I realized that if I was truly resourceful, I could sift through the husks and count them and then count how many ears we had and do a little deductive math to figure out how many bad ears Gracie had discovered. I cursed myself for not recording on my map from the outset the number of ears we had planned on shucking that day, though truthfully, how could I have foreseen such blatant mutiny on Gracie's part?

In the upper right hand corner of my map "Gracie Shucking the Sweet Corn #6," which now lay outdated on the porch steps, I had reserved a blank space to mark down when we discovered bad ears of corn. Before I had left to take the phone call, we had not discovered any, but I was ready for it: normally, I would draw the outline of a half-shucked ear as best I could, mark the time of the discovery, record what ilk of pest we discovered, if any—whether it be earworm or corn sap beetle or fall armyworm—and then put an X through it, to let the reader of the map know that the ear was a bad one and not to eat it. Next to this I had included historical data: I had written, quite clearly and in fractional form, the number of bad ears we had discovered over the total number of ears shucked from each of our last five shucking jamborees on this back porch.

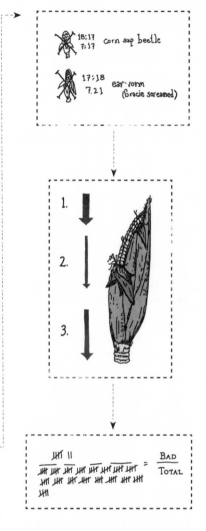

Details from
*Gracie Shucking the
Sweet Corn #6**
Notebook B457

* This crop was most excellent, I might add: only seven bad ears out of a total of eighty-five, although now this data was thrown into a cloud of confusion due to Gracie's pompous idiocy.

This data would give even the most amateur historian a good sense of the caliber of sweet corn we were dealing with here.

All of this data I had procured from consulting my library of blue notebooks. These blue notebooks contained maps covering nearly every action that had been performed on this farm over the last four years, including but not limited to: diverting the irrigation ditches, mending the fences, rounding up the cattle, branding, shoeing, haying, vaccinating, and castrating (!), breaking the cayuses, slaughtering the hens&pigs&rabbits, plucking the hackberries, trimming back the bracken, picking and shucking the sweet corn, mowing, sweeping, cleaning the tack, coiling all those lariats, oiling the old Silver King tractor, and punching the goats' heads out of the fences to keep 'em from the coyotes.

I had been meticulously mapping all of these activities ever since I was eight, as that was the age when my cognition and wisdom each blossomed from that nascent bud of childhood just enough to sufficiently grant me the perspective required to be a cartographer. Not that my mind was fully developed: I would be the first to admit that I was still a child in more than a few facets. Even now I occasionally wet the bed, and I still maintained an irrational fear of porridge. But I firmly believed that drafting maps erased many of the unwarranted beliefs of a child. Something about measuring the distance between *here* and *there* cast off the mystery of what lay between, and since I was a child with limited empirical evidence, the unknown of what might just lie between *here* and *there* could be terrifying. I, like most children, had never been *there*. I had barely even been *here*.

The number one rule of cartographia was that if you could not observe a phenomenon, you were not allowed to depict it on your parchment. Many of my forebears, however, including Mr. Lewis, Mr. Clark, and even

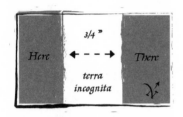

The Distance Between Here *and* There from Notebook G1

→ I think this was part of the reason why I used to wet my bed when I was younger: I did not know if the angry pterodactyl beneath my bed—who I had named Gunga Din and imagined to have white-hot pebbly eyes and a terrific beak of death—was set on killing me on any given night if I stepped out onto that chilly wooden floor to use the facilities. So I would hold it, and then I would not be holding it anymore and my sheets would be first wet and warm and then wet and cold. And I would lie there shivering but alive, gathering what little solace I could from the thought that perhaps my pee was dripping onto Gunga Din's head, making him even angrier (and hungrier) at his missed meal. However, I no longer believed in Gunga Din, so I could not explain to you why I still occasionally wet the bed. Life is filled with tiny mysteries.

Mr. George Washington (the cartographer-turned-president who could not *tell* a lie but could certainly *draw* a lie), perhaps because they were born into a world of great uncertainty, had violated this rule quite blatantly by imagining all sorts of false geographies in the territory just beyond the next mountain. *A river clear to the Pacific, the Rockies as merely a thin line of foothills*—it was so tempting to graft our desires and fears onto the blank spaces of our maps. *"Here be Dragons,"* the cartographers of old wrote in the empty abyss just beyond the reaches of their pen lines.

And what was my own tactic in tempering the impulse to invent rather than represent? Simple: every time I found my stylus wandering beyond the known boundaries of my data set, I instead took a sip from the Tab soda can on my drafting table. An addiction perhaps, but an addiction of humility.

"Gracie," I said calmly, trying to conjure an adult tone of diplomacy. "If you will just be kind enough to tell me how many bad ears there were, then I can add it to our important data set about pest management in this region. It will be a job well done."

She looked at me, flecked some more silk threads off her jeans.

"Okay," she said. "How about…ten?"

"You're lying," I said. "That's way too many."

"How do you *know?*" she said. "Were you even *here?* No. *You* were on the phone. Who was on the phone anyways?"

"The Smithsonian," I said.

"Who?" she asked.

"They're a museum in Washington, D.C.," I said.

"What were they doing calling *you?*"

"They want me to go there and make illustrations for them and give speeches."

"What?" she said.

"Umm…"

Gracie was a complex woman, and I didn't pretend to understand what happened in the black box of her head, but as she said "What?" perhaps this was the order of thoughts firing in her cortex:	I was less complicated than Gracie, but as I *ummed*, I also had a series of quick, almost simultaneous synaptic bursts:	*t* (s)
1. A strong desire to laugh in my face at the ridiculousness of what I had just said.	1. I felt uncomfortable talking about this because Gracie might make fun of me and then maybe hit me.	00:00:00.0
2. Fear that I was telling the truth and that I, her younger spaz brother, might leave Montana before she.	2. I didn't know how to explain the situation without my charts and diagrams.	
3. A hint of pride, that if I *was* telling the truth, it was *her* younger spaz brother who they wanted to come to Washington.	3. I didn't want Dr. Clair to find out about this trip just yet.	00:00:00.5
4. An element of scheming, in which she was already crafting a plan of how she might be able to come along with her younger spaz brother to Washington.	4. I was distracted because I was still wondering about how many bad ears of corn we had found today.	00:00:01.0
5. Her ever bubbling desire to be reborn as an elephant.	5. We will never be elephants. Or: we are already elephants.	
6. A strong desire to laugh in my face at the image of me giving a speech to an audience of adults with pens and clipboards in their hands when my own head barely cleared rhe podium.	6. Jibsen! The Lisp! *Good God!* The Smithsonian!	00:00:01.3

"What are you talking about?" she asked.

"Well, they want me to come to Washington and do stuff."

"Why you? You're twelve! And you're a spaz!" she said, and then stopped. "Wait…you're totally full of shit."

"No," I said. "But I told them I couldn't do it. How would I even get to Washington?"

Gracie looked at me like I had some insidious tropical disease. She cocked her head to the left and her mouth fell open ever so slightly, a tic of disbelief she had picked up from Dr. Clair.

"I can't believe this world," she said. "It's like God hates me. And so he said, 'Hey, Gracie, here's a crazy family you can live with! Oh, and you guys have to live in *Montana!* Oh, and your brother, *who is a total spaz,* is going to go to Washington, D.C.—'"

"I told you, I'm not going to Washington—"

"'—because didn't you hear? People just love spazzes! They can't get enough of them in Washington.'"

I took a deep breath. "Gracie, I feel like you're getting a little off topic.…Just tell me, *for real,* how many bad ears we had…you don't even have to tell me what kind of insects were on each one."

But I had already lost Gracie to the multifaceted behavioral phenomenon of "Dork Retreat." First, she would make this grunt that I had never heard in any other context except on a nature show when a male baboon punched his brother in the stomach and his brother made a noise similar to the one Gracie was making now, a noise which the show's narrator interpreted as denoting a "reluctant resolution to his kin's dominance." And then she would stamp off and retreat to her bedroom for long periods at a time without reemerging, even for meals, the longest of which was for a day and a half, and that was when I electrocuted her pretty good (by accident) with my homemade polygraph machine—which I wisely dismantled afterward. I managed to coax Gracie from her Girl-Pop lair only with the bribe of nearly five hundred feet of chewy tape, which I had blown my monthly USGS stipend on.

"I'm sorry, Gracie," I had said through her door. "Here's nearly five hundred feet of chewy tape," and dumped the four plastic bags on the floor.

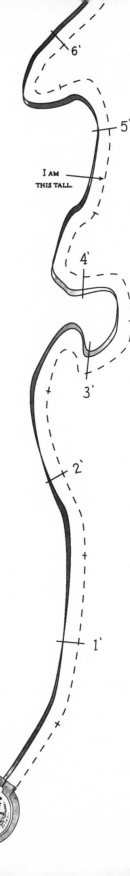

I AM
THIS TALL.

Her head had emerged a minute later. She was still pouty, but also clearly tired and hungry from her standoff. "Okay," she said. Then, dragging the bags inside: "T.S., can you just be normal from now on?"

A day slinked by. Gracie would still not speak to me, which left me no one to talk to as Dr. Clair seemed absorbed in the minutiae of her beetle problems and Father, as usual, had disappeared into the fields. For a while I pretended as if the phone call from Mr. Jibsen had never happened. Yes, yes: it was just a normal late August day on the ranch—the final haying would start soon, school was just around the corner, these were the last couple of weeks to get some good swimming in at the cutbank hole down by the cottonwood.

But Jibsen's gentle lisp followed me everywhere. That night I dreamed of a high-society East Coast cocktail gathering where Mr. Jibsen's lisp had become the life of the party. In the dream, everyone hung on his every word, as if the slipperiness of his intonation gave words like "transhumanism" their own particular kind of legitimacy. I woke up sweating.

"Transhumanism?" I lisped into the darkness.

The next day, in an effort to distract myself, I tried to start my map of *Moby-Dick.*

A novel is a tricky thing to map. At times the invented landscape provided me shelter from the burdens of having to chart the real world in its entirety. But this escapism was always tempered by a certain emptiness: I knew I was deceiving myself through a work of fiction. Perhaps balancing the joys of escapism with the awareness of deception was the whole point of why we read novels, but I was never able to successfully manage this simultaneous suspension of the real and the fictive. Maybe you just

needed to be an adult in order to perform this high-wire act of believing and not-believing at the same time.

Finally, late in the afternoon, I headed outside to clear my head of Melville's ghosts. I followed the winding path my father had mowed through the tall grass. This late in the summer, the tall grass was almost over my head. It washed against itself as the last light of the afternoon percolated blue and salmon through its gently swaying hatchwork of stems and peduncles.

There was a world inside that tall grass. You could plop yourself down in the middle of it with the scraggly stems against the back of your neck and the endless grasses rising up and jackknifing against the bigbluesky, and the ranch and all of its players would fade into a distant dream. On your back like this, you could be anywhere. It was like a poor man's teleporter. I would close my eyes and listen to the soft swish of the leaf blades and pretend that I was in Grand Central Terminal, listening to the whisper of men's overcoats brushing past one another as they hurried to catch the express back to Connecticut.

Layton, Gracie, and I used to play endlessly among these grasses. We would become engrossed for hours in games such as *Jungle Survivor: Who Gets Eaten?* or *We've Shrunk to an Inch, Now What?* (For some reason, the names of most of our games took the form of questions.) Afterward, we would come back into the house with a condition that we called "the switchblades"—where your shins were all itchy and stingy from the microscopic cuts inflicted by that clever and unforgiving tall grass.

Yet the world inside these tall grasses was not just a land of make-believe: it was the unofficial borderland between scientific observation and the practical business of running a ranch. Dr. Clair and I would hunt in its midst with sweep nets and killing jars, trying to collect blister bugs and

"Mom, can I get AIDS from grass?" Layton asked once last summer.

"No," said Dr. Clair. "Just Rocky Mountain spotted fever." They were playing mancala. I was on the couch, working on my topographical lines.

"Can I give AIDS to grass?" Layton asked.

"No," said Dr. Clair.

Tap tap tap went the little pieces into the wooden receptacles.

"Did you ever have AIDS?"

Dr. Clair looked up. "Layton, what's with the AIDS thing?"

"I don't know," Layton said. "I just don't want to get 'em. Angela Ashforth says they're bad and that I probably have 'em."

Dr. Clair looked at Layton. The mancala pieces were still in her hand.

"If Angela Ashforth ever says anything like that to you again, you tell her that just because she's insecure about being a little girl in a society that puts an inordinate amount of pressure on little girls to live up to certain physical, emotional, and ideological standards—many of which are improper, unhealthy, and self-perpetuating—it doesn't mean she has to take her misplaced self-loathing out on a nice boy like you. You may be inherently a part of the problem, but that doesn't mean you aren't a nice boy with nice manners, and it certainly doesn't mean you have AIDS."

"I'm not sure I can remember all that," Layton said.

"Well then, tell Angela that her mother is a white-trash drunk from Butte."

"Okay," Layton said.

Tap tap tap went the little pieces.

For as long as I could remember, there had always been this push-and-pull power struggle between my parents on the Coppertop. Dr. Clair had once roped off the entire hayloft right during the pupae emergence of the seventeen-year cicada cycle, infuriating my father into taking his meals on horseback for a week.

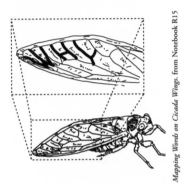

Mapping Words on Cicada Wings. from Notebook R15

Similarly, he had let the goats (knowingly or unknowingly—it was still up for debate) into the pen with all the orange halves in it, where Dr. Clair had been nursing her citrus-root weevils, just imported from Japan. Those poor, poor weevils. They traveled three thousand miles clear across the Pacific only to be devoured by a bunch of "ignor'nt" Montana goats.

That's how Father sidestepped his apology to Dr. Clair: "They're just ignor'nt goats," he said, Stetson in hand. "That's all. Just ignor'nt."

Perhaps my favorite spot of observation at the Coppertop was perched on that large fence post right in the middle of things: behind me, the tall grass and the ranch house (with Dr. Clair studying away inside), in front of me, the fields and the heifers and the goats chawing away with their little ignor'nt motormouths. Sitting on this fence post, it became evident that our ranch was, more than anything, a great compromise.

tumbling flower beetles, which would squirm and toss about so wildly when we caught them in our nets that we would both start laughing at their earnest freneticism, allowing the poor spasming beetles to make their escape.

My father did not take so kindly to the forever-expanding growth of tall grass and feisty jackbrush on our ranch. When I was younger and trying my best to be a buckaroo-in-training like Layton, Father would send the two of us to cut back the grass for a new fence or even when he just got the feeling that the wilds were encroaching too much on the ordered world of his fields.

"What—we runnin' a wilderness reserve 'round here?" he would say, and hand us little machetes to hack back the offending thicket. "Pretty soon a man'll need a periscope to take a leak."

You could tell Dr. Clair disapproved of this kind of clear-cutting—they were her local collecting grounds, after all—but more often than not, she would say nothing after we hacked away another area for Father to claim with his fences. She would just quietly return to her cluttered office and her coleoptera specimens. As her hands fluttered about, there was only a slight increase in the voraciousness of her pinning and archiving that perhaps only I, a fellow scientist, could detect.

I lay on my back in the tall grass trying to picture what it would feel like to see the Smithsonian in person, to walk down the National Mall and then come upon the turreted castle of discovery and invention. *Why had I refused such an offer?*

Suddenly, a noise in the tall grass interrupted my Smithsonian visions. My body went tense as I listened. It sounded like an approaching cougar. I flipped myself around into an impromptu attack position and readied myself. My left hand quietly checked my pockets. I had left my Leatherman (Cartographer's Edition) in the bathroom. If this cougar was hungry, I was doomed.

The animal slowly came into focus through the scrim of tall stems. It was not a cougar. It was Verywell.

"Verywell," I said. "Get a real job," and then immediately regretted saying it.

Verywell was a raggedy old flip-flop of a ranch hound. I had perused many dog books trying to trace the origins of his species, and could only produce the hypothesis that he was part golden retriever and part koolie— an Australian sheepdog that was admittedly rare in these parts—but I just couldn't see any other explanation for his wild merled coat with its swirls of grey and black and brown that looked like an Edvard Munch painting run through the wash.

Dr. Clair, the obsessive-compulsive systemic, was curiously indifferent to Verywell's background.

"He's a dog" was all she said, which was exactly what Father said the day he brought Verywell home three years ago. My father had gone to get vaccination syringes up in Butte when he saw young Verywell scampering around the rest stop on I-15.

"Who do you think could've left him there?" Gracie said, rubbing the dog's back in a way that indicated she was already deeply in love.

"The carnies," Father said.

Gracie named him in an elaborate ceremony marked by garlands and accordion music amongst the greasewood sage down by the river bottom. Everyone thought it was a good name except Father. He grumbled that Verywell was not the name of a working ranch hound, who should always be named something short and hard, like Chip or Rip or Tater.

When Layton died, Verywell went crazy for a couple of months—running up and down the back porch, constantly searching the horizon, chewing on the tin buckets all afternoon until his mouth would begin to bleed. I silently watched his torment, unsure of what to say or do.

Then one day early on in the summer Gracie took him for a long walk, a walk that could have been like any other, except she made him a garland of dandelions and stopped for a while by the cottonwood tree. The two returned with a new kind of understanding on their faces. Verywell stopped chewing the buckets.

After that, we all started using him in our own way. When you got a bad case of the lonelies, you would get up from the table and make that little click noise with the tongue, not quite as Layton had done but close enough—this meant for Verywell to come follow you down into the meadows. Verywell didn't seem to mind being used in this way. Somehow, he had made peace with losing his master. Besides, those lonely walks allowed him to work on one of his hobbies: snapping at lightning bugs, *Photinus pyralis*. During certain nights in late July the bugs would all flash in synchrony, as if following some divine metronome.

"You give a hound the wrong message with a name like that," my father said that first morning after Verywell's arrival, spooning porridge into his mouth in quick little strokes. "He'll ferget he's on the clock. Think it's vacation up here. *New Yorkers.*"

New Yorkers was a phrase my father threw around quite liberally and without any sort of context. He would tag it onto the end of sentences as a generalized indictment whenever he was talking about anything that he deemed "soft" or "fancy" or "inadequate," as in: "Three months and this new shirt done worn through. What am I paying good clean dollars fer if this thing's gonna tatter apart before I git the goddamn tag off? *New Yorkers.*"

"What you got against New Yorkers?" I asked once. "Have you ever been to New York?"

"What's the point?" he had said. "New York's where all the *New Yorkers* come from."

Though Verywell turned out to be a mediocre ranch hound at best, he became Layton's first love. The two were inseparable. Father kept complaining that Verywell wasn't worth his weight in manure, but Layton didn't seem to care about Verywell's work ethic. They spoke a language that only they could understand, a series of slaps and whistles and barks, which had their own particular cadence. Verywell would watch Layton's every move at the dinner table, and when Layton got up to leave, Verywell would follow, clicking away on the wooden floor. I think Gracie was jealous of such kinship, but sometimes you just can't argue with true love.

"Hey, Verywell," I said. "Let's go on a walk."

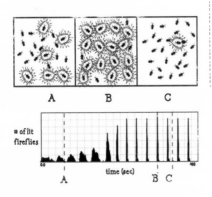

Synchrony in Montana **Photinus pyralis from Notebook R62**

But Verywell did a sort of ratter-scatter fakeout move and then barked twice, which meant that he did not want to go on a walk but wanted to play *Humans Cannot Catch Me*.

"No, Verywell," I said. "I don't want to play. I just want to walk. I have some questions I need to work out. Big questions," I added, tapping my nose.

I got up slowly, at walking pace, and Verywell moved slowly too, turning toward where we would walk, but we both knew this was all a ruse. I was trying to trick him and he knew it. He waited until just the moment when my little twelve-year-old arm could have reached out and grabbed his collar and then he bolted—*oh, he must have treasured a reason to bolt!*—and I scrambled after him. When chased, Verywell had this habit of dodging wildly back and forth, like some kind of schizophrenic running back, his hips shooting left then right then left again, and the effect was not so much to fool you as to confuse his own body so that it appeared as if he was forever on his way to tumbling head over heels. The anticipation of such an incident was part of the reason you kept pursuing him, so perhaps his antics were his way of luring you into an extended chase.

We had our extended chase. I could see Verywell's little brown-and-yellow merled tail flying just ahead of me through the bratweed and tall grass, bobbing like one of those mechanical rabbits that they hung out in front of greyhounds. Then we were bursting from the sea of tall grass and out into the open. We hit the fence line. I was running full tilt. Just at the moment I was considering doing a flying dive and tackling his haunches, I realized too late that the fence we were following was about to make a sharp ninety-degree turn in our direction. Verywell must have planned this all along. I saw it unfold in slow motion: Verywell nimbly diving beneath the bottom railing while I desperately tried to put on the brakes and

There was always that extra breath you had to take when confronted with Mr. Tecumseh Elijah Spivet. You looked at the creases of his sandpaper face, the way his salt & pepper hair poked out from under the sweat stains of his hat, and you saw the evidence of a particular kind of circular life, a life drummed out to the changing of the seasons—breaking broncs in the summer, branding in the spring, roundups in the fall, opening and closing that same gate year after year.

This was how it was here: you didn't question the monotony of opening and closing the gate. And yet I wanted to explore, to push on to the next gate, to compare how those hinges squeaked differently than ours.

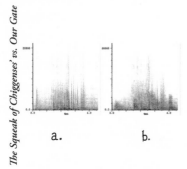

The Squeak of Chiggenses' vs. Our Gate

a.   b.

Father lived off opening and closing that same gate, and for all his idiosyncrasies—the Sett'ng Room, the strange and antiquated metaphors, his insistence that everyone in the family write letters to each other during the holidays (his letters were never more than two lines long)—despite all of this, my father was the most practical man I had ever known.

He was also the wisest man I had ever known. And I could tell—in that faint yet dead-on way that children can sometimes sense things about their parents that supersedes the usual familial reverence—that my father was probably one of the best men at what he did in all of southwestern Montana. You could just tell by his eyes, his handshake, the way his hands held that rope, not insisting, just telling the world how it was and how it would be.

then I was crashing into the fence and my momentum was carrying me up and over the wooden rails and onto my back on the other side.

I'm not sure if I lost consciousness, but the next thing I knew, Verywell was licking my face and Father was standing directly over me. Maybe I was still a little woozy, but I wanted to believe there was a hint of a smile across his face.

"T.S., what'cha chasing this hound fer?" Father asked.

"Not sure," I said. "He wanted to be chased."

Father sighed and his expression shifted slightly—a tightening of the lips, a cocking and uncocking of the jaw. Over time, I had come to translate this particular sequence of facial tics as "How is it that you have come to be my son?"

It was a difficult task reading a face like his. I had tried (and failed) to create a map of his face that properly captured all that went on there. His eyebrows were just a little too explosive and unkempt for their own good, yet they always arboretumed up and out in this perfect kind of way, hinting that my father had perhaps just returned from a long, searching ride on his burgundy Indian motorcycle. His peppery mustache was trimmed and sprightly, but not too trimmed or too sprightly so as to convey either dandy fop or country bumpkin—rather, his mustache recalled both the wonder and confidence one possesses when turning to confront the infinite skyline of the range at dusk. A scar, the size and shape of an open paper clip, marked the cleft of his chin, the white V-fleck of skin just visible enough to confirm not only my father's inevitable resilience but also that—beneath his firm grip on the saddle horn—he was also aware of his own vulnerabilities, like his weakened right pinky, the result of a bad break while fencing. The overall composition of his countenance was held together by the careful network of wrinkles that framed his face from his eyes to his jowls, these rivulets calling attention not so much to my father's age but to his work ethic and to the existence of that same gate which he had spent his whole life opening and closing. All of this was expressed in an instant when you confronted my father in the flesh, and understandably, I was worried the essence of his real-life presence might be lost in a reproduction on the drafting table.

Last year I did an illustration for an article in *Science* magazine about a new technology at ATMs and automated kiosks that registered not just the tone of the customer's voice but also his or her facial expressions. Dr. Paul Ekman, the author of the article, had created the Facial Action Coding System, which broke all facial expressions down into some combination of forty-six basic action units. These forty-six units were the essential building blocks of every human expression in existence. Using Dr. Ekman's system, I could thus attempt to map at least the muscular genesis of my father's expression, which I had dubbed the *This-Boy-Must'a-Been-Switched-at-Birth Lonesome Ponder*. To be technical, it was an AU-1, AU-11, AU-16—a raised inner brow, nasolabial deepened, lower lip depressor (and at times the expression even dipped into a little AU-17, where his paper-clipped chin crinkled up and became undulatory and porous, but this only happened when I did something very peculiar, such as attach those GPS tracking devices to the hen's necks or mount the time-lapse camera onto Stinky the goat's head that time I wanted to see what goats see).

"You want to lend me one fer a second?" he asked. "You busy?"

"Not busy, sir," I said. "What'cha need?"

"Balance the water," Father said. "Southern headgate. Stream's thirstier than a mudhen on a tin roof, but we'll squeeze 'er out this last l'il bit 'fore she dries up for good."

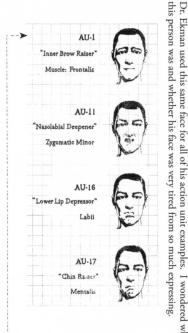

AU-1
"Inner Brow Raiser"
Muscle: Frontalis

AU-11
"Nasolabial Deepener"
Zygomatic Minor

AU-16
"Lower Lip Depressor"
Labii

AU-17
"Chin Raiser"
Mentalis

Dr. Ekman used this same face for all of his action unit examples. I wondered who this person was and whether his face was very tired from so much expressing.

This question conjured simultaneous emotions in me:

1) I was excited at the prospect of being asked to help, for aside from a few regular chores here and there, Father had accepted awhile ago that I, like Verywell, was not a creature of the ranch. During the branding, I remember looking out the window at Father working away and I wanted to put on my boots and join him, but a line had been silently drawn, which I knew could not be crossed. (Who had drawn this line? Was it he? Was it I?)

2) And thus this question also made me immeasurably sad: here was a ranch owner asking his only remaining son if he would come help him with an everyday task of the ranch. This was not supposed to happen. Ranch boys were supposed to work their entire lives on their father's land, gradually taking over foreman duties that eventually culminated in a poignant moment of passed responsibility between patriarch and son, preferably on a hillock at sunset.

"We allowed to this late in the season? Don't the other ranchers need the water?"

"Ain't no others. Thompson sold to public. No one's payin' attention to Feely. Watermen's busy fussin' over land reclamation up valley." He gestured and spat. "So you up fer it? Just want to get her shoveled out 'fore dark."

The sun was crouched on its haunches over the Pioneers. The mountains were both purple and brown, the angle of light hitting the moiré of pine and fir and bleeding out a smoky mirage that made the valley seem to tremble. It was a sight. We both looked.

"I reckon I can help you," I said, and tried to mean it.

Of all the endless chores on the Coppertop Ranch, "balancing the water"—with its overtones of harmony and synchronicity—had always appealed to me the most. Perched high up as we were in the hard, scrabbleback country—where it didn't rain much past May and most of the creeks were just tired little dribbles down the pebble-stone couloirs—we had few commodities more precious than water. Dams, canals, irrigation systems, aqueducts, reservoirs—these were the real temples of the West, distributing water by an incredibly complex series of laws that no one really understood but on which everyone, including my father, had an opinion.

"Those laws is *Rin Tin Tin horseshit*," my father said once. "You want to tell me how to use *my* water on *my* land? Then let's come on down to the crick and have a wrastle for it."

I could not speak with quite the same resolve, perhaps because I had not been balancing the water as long as he. Or perhaps it was because just over the divide, the town of Butte had a tragic relationship with its water supply that had kept me up many a late night drafting solutions at my desk, nursing a can of Tab soda.

When Father was not too grumbly, I would catch a ride with him into town on Saturdays so that I could visit the Butte Archives. The Archives were crammed inside the upper story of an old converted firehouse, and the space could barely contain the haphazard array of historical detritus stuffed into the gillwork of its shelving. The place smelled of mildewed newspaper and a very particular, slightly acrid lavender perfume that the old woman who tended the stacks, Mrs. Tathertum, wore quite liberally. This scent triggered a Pavlovian reaction in me: whenever I smelled the same perfume on other women, no matter where I was, I was instantly transported back to that feeling of discovery, the sensation of fingertips against old paper, whose surface was powdery and fragile, like the membrane of a moth's wing.

One could pore over a birth or death ledger or the musty pages of one of Butte's newspapers from yesteryear and enter into an entirely self-contained world. Traces of love and hope and despair were sprinkled throughout these official documents, and more interesting still were the journals that I occasionally discovered behind a canvas box, when Mrs. Tathertum was in one of her rare good moods and would allow me entrance into the storeroom downstairs. Yellowing photographs, banal diaries that occasionally would reveal a moment of intense intimacy if you stuck with their pages long enough, bills of sale, horoscopes, love letters, even a misfiled essay on wormholes in the American Midwest.

Sitting in this little nook on Saturdays, with sharp wafts of lavender perfume and the ghosts of inquisitive firemen tapping at my shoulder, I had come to slowly understand one of Butte's great ironies: that even though the mining companies had been sucking the mountains of their

> The monograph was by a Mr. Petr Toriano and it was titled "The Preponderance of Lorentzian Wormholes in the American Middle West 1830–1970." I was so pleased with my discovery that I secretly hid the manila folder with its contents above the cabinet in the bathroom so that I could be sure to find it again. When I returned to the archives the following week, however, the folder was gone.

minerals for over a hundred years, it was not some avalanche or widespread instability of the soil that threatened the town today but rather the *water*—the red, arsenic-laced water that was slowly flowing back into the great negative space of the Berkeley Mining Pit. Every year that crimson lake rose twelve feet, and in twenty-five years it would overtake the water table and spill down Main Street. One could see this as simply the land reclaiming what was once its own, a natural gesture toward equilibrium in accordance with the laws of thermodynamics. Indeed, over the last century and a half, Butte had survived and cultivated its persona through a booming copper extraction industry so remarkably out of synch with the sustainable world that one might say the modern-day town—nestled alongside the evidence of its historical excess in the form of a pit a mile wide and nine hundred feet deep steadily filling with toxic groundwater runoff—was now finally getting its karmic and ecological comeuppance. A couple of years ago, 342 Canada Geese had alighted on the surface of the lake and died, their esophagi burned, as if to say, *We have come here to foreshadow your suffering.* Gracie had a little ceremony for them with paper cranes and red food coloring beneath the old cottonwood tree.

This past spring, I had outlined the tenuous state of Butte's watershed in a lab report for my seventh grade science class. The report was meant only to be about the salinity of five mystery liquids and so I admit, in retrospect, it was probably not the most appropriate forum for me to ruminate at length with an extended metaphor of the arsenic-laced groundwater filling up the mining pit like blood filling a massive chest wound. I concluded my report with an underdeveloped and ultimately unpersuasive meditation on corporate social responsibility, ignoring adult ideas like "budgets" and "bureaucratic inertia" in my haste to arrive at idealistic conclusions calling for extensive government intervention. Admittedly, that

The title of the lab report was:

LAB 2.5:
THE SALINITIES OF
FIVE *MYSTERY* LIQUIDS!*

*BUT ALSO AN INVESTIGATION INTO THE BERKELEY PIT AND ITS MAJOR GROUNDWATER SOURCES AND THE GENTLE proposal of A METAPHOR CONCERNING THE RELATIONSHIP BETWEEN BUTTE AND ITS WATER SUPPLY

final section of the lab report was borderline at best, clearly written by a child who had a warped sense of the real world, but I still thought the analogical through-line was a nice framing device for my data sets. I was not a literary person and so the metaphor of the chest wound was not for flourish; rather, I had pursued it thoroughly, even examining the astonishing similarities between clotting in capillaries and underground aquifer patterns.

Mr. Stenpock, my seventh grade science teacher, was not amused. ----------▶

Mr. Stenpock was a tricky creature. A single glance would confirm this when one took in both the Scotch tape securing one hinge of his outdated aviator bifocals—which on its own would be the standard dorkdom calling card—and the fact that Mr. Stenpock always wore a noisy leather jacket while teaching, a fashion statement that tried (and yet failed) to say, "Children, I probably do things after school that you are not ready to know about just yet."

His notations in the margins of my lab report on the Berkeley Pit will help illustrate this dualistic posture of his. Next to my work on the five mystery liquids he wrote:

> Great work, T.S. You really understand the concept.
> nice illustration! ⟶

But as soon as I got to my somewhat tenuous transition to the much longer discussion of the Berkeley Pit (the last forty-one pages out of the forty-four-page report) he took a very different tone:

> This does not belong in a lab report. Take this seriously! This is not a game.

I have since coined the term *Stenpock*:

Stenpock |sten•päk| *n.* any adult who insists on staying within the confines of his or her job title and harbors no passion for the offbeat or the incredible.

If everyone was a Stenpock, we would still be in the Middle Ages, at least scientifically speaking.

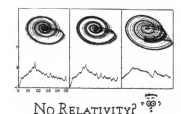

NO RELATIVITY?

No relativity. No penicillin. No chocolate chip cookies. And no mining in Butte. Thus, it was ironic that Mr. Stenpock, the source of the term, had chosen to be a science teacher—a profession that I had always envisioned as blessed with the great task of distributing wonder to children.

and

What are you doing, Spivet?
What kind of person do you think I am?!
You think I am idiot?

and

I am NOT an idiot. I will
You are way out of your league, Spivet.

I was not one to judge, but like so many Butte residents, Mr. Stenpock did not want to hear anything more about the Pit that served as an ongoing reminder of the prospective apocalyptic doom that awaited the town just down Main Street. I knew this feeling: Butte hit national headlines every other year right around Earth Day as a symbolic warning of what could go so wrong in humanity's tenuous relationship with the land. It got to be psychologically wearisome to live in the poster town of environmental catastrophe, especially because other things actually did go on here: Butte had a technical college with football games and a civic center that hosted gun shows, and there was a farmers' market in the warm months, and there were those ever popular Evel Knievel Days and Irish dancing festivals, and people drank coffee and loved and lived and crocheted just like anywhere else. The Berkeley Pit was not all there was to this town. Still, one might think that a science teacher could look beyond his provincial defensiveness and see the Pit's potential as a scientific gold mine: a treasure trove of projection analyses and case studies and extended metaphors.

Mr. Stenpock was particularly not amused by my use of him in my introduction to the Berkeley Pit section of the report, where, for dramatic

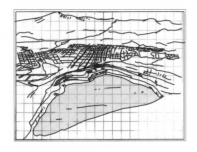

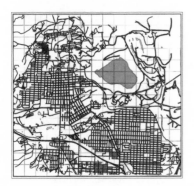

from Lab 2.5,
"The Salinities of Five Mystery
Liquids"

effect, I had outlined how if he and I froze during the instant that he handed me back the lab report, remaining immobile in this gesture of exchange for twenty-five years, eventually there would be a great rumbling and then the door of the science room would burst open and behind it a biblical swirl of red poison water would instantly soak our posters on mass and gravity and chicken eggs, and, to quote the report, "the water would burn our tender human skin on contact and ruffle Mr. Stenpock's barrette-like mustache."

"You're a smart-ass," Mr. Stenpock said when I went to talk with him afterward. "Listen: stick to your lessons. You're very strong in science, and you'll do well, and then you can go to a university and get the hell out of this place."

The classroom was empty, the windows thrown open as it was the first real warm day of spring, and outside children were laughing among the whinnying of the swings and the soft plush bounce of a red playground ball against the asphalt. Part of me wanted to join my peers, to forget about entropy and inevitability and bask in the joys of four square.

"But what about the Pit?" I asked.

"I don't give a *shittling* about the Pit," he said.

This moment of confrontation between us was frozen in my memory in a peculiar echo of the freeze-frame that I had described in my lab report. I wanted to ask what a shittling was, but frankly, I was too scared. The way he said this phrase with such an unabashed dismissiveness made me take a step back and blink and then blink again. How could a man supposedly devoted to the sciences—the life force that bound my mother to unsquirreling the natural world, the discipline that housed her inexhaustible searching, and the method of inquiry that put all of my longing and curiosity to use crafting my little maps instead of mailing bombs to prominent capitalists—how could a scientific man take such an aggressively narrow-minded stance by using this word *shittling*? Though I knew the majority of scientists were still men, I wondered in that moment whether there was something innate about the XY chromosomal makeup, whether grown men with their leather jackets and their middle-aged entropic pudginess and their half-cocked cowboy hats could ever really be open-minded, curious, obsessed scientists like my mother, Dr. Clair. It seemed that men, with their Stenpock-like natures, were rather meant to open and close the same gate and work in the mines and hit railroad spikes into the earth in repetitive motions that satisfied their desire to fix the world's problems using simple gestures done with the hands.

Mr. Stenpock and I stood facing each other in the classroom, and instead of the red waters pouring in, I had one of those rare moments of realization that tears at and eventually snaps the fibrous bonds binding us to our childhood. Despite our natural sense of invincibility, Mr. Stenpock and I lived in a narrow slice of livable conditions: a slight drop in core temperature, a nano-shift in the chemical makeup of the classroom's air, a minute change in the properties of water inside our tissues, a finger pressed lightly to a trigger—any of these could extinguish the match of our consciousness instantly, without drumroll, and with much less effort than it took to spark the flame to life. Perhaps somewhere inside of himself, despite all his gestures and verbal posturing pointing in the other direction, Mr. Stenpock was well aware of the delicacy of our time here, and the fleeting cocoon inside that leather jacket served as his personal shelter from the inevitable breaking, disintegration, and recycling of his cellular architecture.

"Are we okay?" I asked Mr. Stenpock. It was all I could think to say.

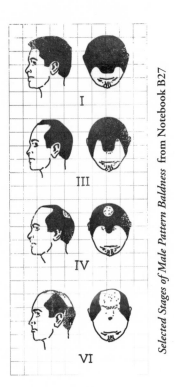

Selected Stages of Male Pattern Baldness from Notebook B27

Not All Men Are Bad

For instance: Dr. Yorn. He was a man, but he was also curious and obsessive like Dr. Clair. We once talked for three hours about whether a polar bear or a tiger shark would win in a fight (in four feet of shallow water during the middle of the day). But Dr. Yorn lived two hours away and I did not know how to drive, so I was left with cowboys and Stenpocks for my local male role models.

He blinked. The swings creaked.

Briefly—the instant passing almost before I had time to register it—I wanted to hug Mr. Stenpock, to press at his tender flesh amidst all that leather and bifocal-age.

That moment in the classroom was not the first time I became aware of our tendency to disintegrate. The first time, I had just turned on the seismoscope and had my back to Layton when I heard the *pop*—so strangely quiet in my memory—and the sound of his body first hitting the experiment table and then the ground of the barn, which was still covered in the winter hay.

I climbed into the passenger side of the pickup, struggling with the moaning hinge of the door. When it finally slammed shut, I found myself inside a cab of sudden silence. In my lap, my fingers quivered. The pickup's cab spoke only of work: in the dark shelf where the radio should've been umbilical wires twisted around each other; two screwdrivers rested on the dashboard, their heads touching in conference; everywhere there was dust and dust and dust. Nothing extra here. No hints of excess or indulgence except a miniature horseshoe that Dr. Clair had given my father on their twentieth wedding anniversary. Just the glint of that silver trinket hanging from the rearview, spinning ever so slightly, but that was enough.

The day was slipping away; the fields were settling into themselves. I squinted and saw our herd of heifers high up in a field on the public lands, just above the swath of tree line. In about a month and a half, Ferdie and the Mexicans would come around to once again bring them down from the mountains for the winter.

The roundup, the roundup: the droning of hooves on soft ground, the faint click of horn against barbed wire, the smell of dung and the heifers' skin mixed with the strange scents of the Mexicans' leather. In the morning before going to work, the Mexicans would dab the fenders of their saddles with an ointment they passed around in a black box the size of a fist. After the day was done, they would come up to the house and stand on the porch talking amongst themselves, spitting softly into the gardenias with a strange gentleness that seemed entirely natural. Dr. Clair, in an uncharacteristic display of womanly hospitality, would serve them lemonade and gingersnaps. They loved those gingersnaps. I think that's why they'd come up to the porch to talk and spit—for the gingersnaps, which they would carefully handle with their roughened fingers like treasured amulets, nibbling at the cookies bit by bit.

I found myself wondering if I would not be here this fall to see the Mexicans eating those gingersnaps, whether I would miss this ritual that marked the beginning of autumn as much as the falling of the leaves, even if it was a ritual from which I had always been excluded.

Father opened the driver's side door, got in, and slammed it just as hard as it needed to be slammed. He had replaced his boots with bright yellow waders and swung another pair across the cab for me.

"Not that you'll need 'em," he said. "Crick's drier than a mummy's pocket, but we'll put 'em on fer show." Father tapped the boots in my lap. "Fer laughs."

I laughed. Or tried to. Perhaps I was projecting, but I could see there was an uneasiness underpinning my father's motions—he was slightly uncomfortable having me in his workspace, as though I would say something inappropriate or embarrassingly un-boyish.

The old Ford pickup was blue and battered like a tornado had gotten at her (one had, apparently, down in Dillon). Her name was Georgine. Gracie had named her, just as she named everything on the ranch, and I remember her announcing this and Father nodding silently and slapping her shoulder with the flat of his palm just a little too hard. In his language this meant: I agree with you.

Father turned the key and the engine turned—once, twice—coughing and sneezing a short brittle pop before finally catching and roaring to life. He gave it some gas. I looked back through the small grimy window and saw the unfinished map of Custer's last stand on one of the walls of the flatbed. The map was a copy of the drawing by One Bull, Sitting Bull's nephew, who had depicted the battle pictorially, meant to be read from left to right.

My crude rendition was the result of Layton and me spending one afternoon together thinking we would cover Georgine with a history of the world's great conflicts. Actually, it was much more my idea, and I think Layton just wanted to get out of some of his ranch chores, because after he drew Andrew Jackson and Teddy Roosevelt shooting things (with no particular historical reference point), he then just watched me paint in the cayuses and the felled soldiers and the blood and Custer in the middle of it all and then he fell asleep until Father hollered. We never finished that map.

We bounced along the fence line. Georgine's shocks had given out long ago and there were no seat belts in the cab, so I held on to the door handle with both hands to keep from flying out through the window. Father did not seem to notice that his head almost cracked into the ceiling every time we hit a rut. Almost, but it never did, and such was the way with my father: the physical world always seemed to part and make way for his presence.

For a while, we drove, listening to the roll of the truck and the wind playing at the windows, which never quite closed all the way.

Finally, he spoke, more to himself than to me: "She was runnin' a bit last week. Snow pack still got some juice. It's like that crick is teasin' me. Just showing me what she got and then takin' it away again."

I opened my mouth and then shut it. I had several explanations for the cyclical hydrology of the creek, but then I had already shared these with my father. This spring, only a couple of months after Layton died, I had produced perhaps two dozen maps of our valley's water table—its elevations, the drainage trends, hundred-year groundwater levels, soil composition, and seepage capacity. I had come into the Sett'ng Room with an armful of these maps one evening in early April, just as the heavy spring rains had arrived and the high mountain streams were beginning to swell from the melting snowpack.

Since the Mexicans wouldn't arrive for another three weeks, I knew Father would need plenty of help getting the irrigation system up and running. While I was prepared to strap on my boots and hike out into

In this map by One Bull, time flowed from left to right. The addition of the fourth dimension as well as the looseness with which spatial coordinates were treated unnerved me a bit, but I tried to go with the flow. For One Bull, multiple points in time could exist at once.

time

This was one of Layton's contributions to the map.

In the strange aftermath of his death, with the church and the empty house and the way the door to his room stood half open all the time, this uncompleted map in the back of the pickup was the one thing that kept sticking in my mind: I wished we had taken another afternoon to finish. Another fifty afternoons. I didn't mind if Layton never picked up a brush. As long as he was sitting on the flatbed, watching me, sleeping even. That would be enough.

the fields, I had figured these maps might be more useful given my strong mind and weak hands. Layton had always been the one in the waders with the shovel, unclogging the ditches, unraveling the tarps, pulling out the boulders suctioned deep within the mud. Layton was so young and small and entirely elegant up there on his grey, almost bluish quarterhorse, Teddy Roo, and as they rode side by side, Father and he would talk endlessly in a language that I could understand but not speak:

1   LAYTON: When you bringin' 'em down?
      FATHER: Land's open....Three weeks maybe, we'll cut, load, sell about a
      quarter...size it up when she comes. You itchin' to push?
      LAYTON: Just about winter, sir. When we were punching last week...dem
5   critters scrawny as hell....Ferdie said—he says public's a bust this year.
      FATHER: No different any other. Ferdie's a wetback in a china shop, you
      ask me.

And I would ride up to join them on my horse, Sparrow (named for me and sharing many more characteristics with the bird than was healthy for a horse), who shivered and raked his head against his shanks instead of naturally falling in line with the two other horses like they did in the movies.

"What y'all talking about?" I would say. "Winter coming early?"

      LAYTON: —Silence—
      FATHER: —Silence—

With Layton gone, I found myself wondering how Father would manage balancing the water on his own. I could not simply trot up to him on my horse and replace what could not be replaced, so I did my research and drew out my water table series and entered the Sett'ng Room on that evening in April.

Father was sipping his whiskey, absorbed by the movie *Monte Walsh* on the television. His hat was on the couch next to him, as though saving the spot. He licked his fingers.

On the screen, horsemen jostled about, the hooves of their animals scratching up the land, kicking up a cloud of dust that pillowed and swirled back into itself. I watched with my father for a while. There was something intensely beautiful about the nature of obstruction in the scene, for you could barely see the riders as they danced and moved among the weary cattle, but even when they had disappeared in this sea of dust, you knew that the cowboys were in there somewhere, doing what they were born to do. My father quietly bobbed his head to this performance of horse and earth and man, as if he were watching an old 8mm home movie of his family.

Outside it was raining, the drops slapping against the porch in heavy waves. To me this was a good sign, a sign of what was to come and why these water maps might prove useful. Without saying anything, I began laying them out on the wooden floor. I used two of my father's cowgirl paperweights to keep them flat. Above me, on the screen, I could hear one of the horses blow and a man yell something indecipherable over the rumble of hooves.

At some point, Verywell came into the room, soaked. Without turning from the television screen, Father yelled, "Git!" and Verywell got, before he had a chance to soak us with his doggy-shake routine.

I finished arranging my maps and waited for a moment of quiet in the movie.

"You want to give her a look?" I asked.

Father wiped his nose and put down his whiskey. With a long sigh he eased himself off the couch and slowly came over. I watched him as

Father had a habit of periodically licking his fingers as if he were about to perform some kind task for which he needed the extra traction and dexterity. Often no task followed, simply the habitual lick and the promise of the endless chores to come, as though my father could never quite shake that tic of physical labor. Even stretched out in his favorite spot in front of the television with whiskey in hand, my father was never quite relaxed.

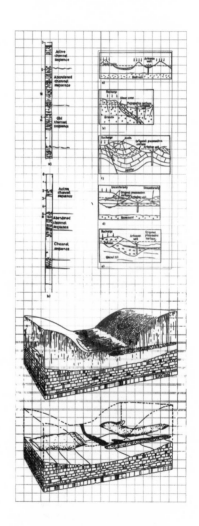

**The Water Table Series
from Notebook G56**

he glanced at the maps on the floor, stooping down once or twice to get a closer look. It was more credence than he normally gave to any of my projects, and my pulse started to pound in my neck as he shifted from one foot to the other, rubbing the back of his hand against his cheek, looking.

"What'd ya think?" I said. "Because I'm thinking we shouldn't lean so heavily on Feely. I think we actually go across the road and build a culvert to Crazy Swede and—"

"Bullshit," he said.

I suddenly remembered that I had hidden Layton's name in the borders of each one of the maps, as I had been doing with all my work since my brother died. Had my father discovered this in the dim light of the Sett'ng Room? Had I broken the Cowboy Code? Transgressed some line of silence drawn in the sand?

"What?" I said. The tips of my fingers had gone numb.

"Bullshit," he said again. "You could draw a picture showin' me how to git water from Three Forks clear across the mountains and you could make it look real purty, but that's piss in a tin can, far as I see. This kinda thing's just fancy-pants numbers and bullshit. Open your eyes a little bit and you'd see that."

Normally I would be the first to dispute this. Numbers on a page, yes, but since Neolithic times we had been marking down representations on cave walls, in the dirt, on parchment, trees, lunch plates, napkins, even on our own skin—all so that we could remember where we have been, where we want to be going, where we *should* be going. There was a deep impulse ingrained in us to take these directions, coordinates, declarations out of the mush of our heads and actualize them in the real world. Since making my first maps of how to shake hands with God, I had learned that the representation was not the real thing, but in a way this dissonance was what made it so good: the distance between the map and the territory allowed us breathing room to figure out where we stood.

Standing in the Sett'ng Room, with the rain pouring onto our pine ranch house, the drops seeping into cracks and corners, expanding the wood, running down panes of glass through the porch into the thirsty mouths of beetles and mice and sparrows huddling in convention beneath us—I wondered how I might convey to my father that I did have my eyes open, that mapping was not an act of forgery but of translation and transcendence. But before I could even begin to sculpt my thoughts in reply, my father was already returning to the couch and the springs were creaking. The whiskey was in his hands, his attention back on the television.

I began to cry. I hated crying, especially in front of my father. I gripped my left pinky behind my back, as was my wont in times such as these, and said, "Okay, sir," and then left the room.

"Your drawins!" Father yelled when I was halfway up the stairs. I went back and collected them, one by one. On the television, the cowboys had gathered in conference on a hillock. The cattle grazed lazily in the flats, showing no lingering awareness of the struggle that had just transpired.

At one point, my father rubbed his thumb around the rim of his whiskey glass, producing the tiniest high-pitch sliver of sound. We both looked at each other for an instant, surprised at its creation. Then he licked his thumb and I left the Sett'ng Room with my arms full of the useless maps.

Father hit the brakes hard. Dirt popped and pestled beneath our tires. Startled, I looked up at him.

"Them ignor'nt goats," he said, staring out the window.

I turned and saw Stinky—the most notorious goat on the whole Coppertop for getting himself stuck in the fence—and there he was, stuck in the

I remember the first time I saw Charles Darwin's notebooks. I pored over all his sketches, the notations in the margins, the digressions, all in search of the breakthrough moment, the flash in the pan that had led to his discovery of natural selection. Of course, I did not find a single moment as such, and I am not sure this is how the great discoveries were ever made, that they actually were a long series of trials and errors, corrections and redirections, where even the declarations of "ah ha!" were later revised and refuted.

There was one page in his notebooks that caught my eye, though: the first known illustration of an evolutionary tree, a few bisecting lines on the page, branching outward, nothing more, an infantile form of the image that is so familiar to us today. The image was not what stopped me, however. Above the tree, Darwin had written the line:

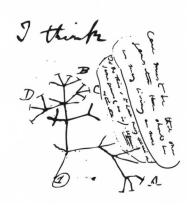

fence. Stinky's other defining characteristic was his color: he was the only goat we owned out of about four hundred that was all black, with tiny white flecks of hair all up and down his back.

Hearing our pickup come over the hill, Stinky started spasming about all pell-mell.

"The black eye of our ranch" Father called him. I called him Black Stinky Pie, or just Stinky, because he always pooped a lot when he was caught in the fence. By the look of things, this afternoon was no exception.

Father sighed loudly and cut the engine. He made a move for the door handle. Without thinking about it, I said: "I got 'im."

"Yeah?" he said. He leaned back into his seat. "All right. I'd probably kill that critter anyways. He dumber than a grasshopper and I'm sick of punching his fat head from that wire. Sonfabitch deserve to be ca-yote chow."

I got out of the cab and found myself whispering "dumb-er than a grass-popper" over and over in a singsong kind of way.

As I approached, Stinky suddenly became very still. I could see the grooves of his rib cage heaving as he breathed. His neck was cut up something terrible from where the barb had rubbed open the skin—the blood was beading and dripping off the wire. I hadn't seen it this bad before. I wondered how long he'd been there.

"It's bad," I said, looking over my shoulder.

But the truck was empty. My father had a way of disappearing for a stretch, leaving without you ever noticing, tending to something, then returning just as silently as he had left.

I cautiously stepped forward.

"S'all right, Stinky," I said. "Not gonna hurt you, just trying to let you loose."

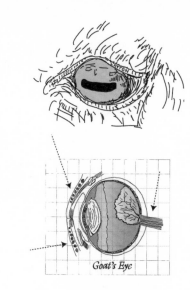

Stinky was breathing hard; one of his front legs was poised an inch off the ground, as if to kick out. I could hear the short, quick breaths slipping through the animal's wet nostrils, see the line of unchecked spittle running down into his little black beard. His fur was thick with blood. The wound on his neck opened and closed with each breath.

I looked into Stinky's eye for permission to touch his neck.

"S'all right," I said. "S'all right." His eye was a magical thing. The pupil was nearly a perfect rectangle. While I could recognize it as an eye like mine, there was something extraordinarily foreign in its bulgy unblinking-ness, in the total absence of love and loss in that quivering black rectangle of sight.

Goat's Eye

The Black Rectangle from Notebook G57

I got down on my elbows and slowly pulled down the barbed wire from below. Normally, you were supposed to just give a good fierce kick to the goat's forehead, and this was enough to pop 'im back through the fence, but I was afraid of kicking Stinky. The animal was already in bad shape, traumatized into stillness, and a kick might just cause the barb to catch the skin and slice his neck all the way up to his mouth, killing the creature.

"S'all right, s'all right," I said.

Then I noticed that Stinky was not actually looking at me. I heard a clicking noise to my left—like mancala pieces being shaken in their wooden receptacle. I looked over, and there, not more than a foot and a half from my head, was the biggest rattler I had ever seen in my entire life. As thick as a baseball bat, its head up and off the ground swaying, swaying with a heavy preoccupation, not like anything that swayed in the breeze. I did not know much at that moment, but I did know this: a rattlesnake could kill you if it bit you on the face, which was right where this one was aiming.

I saw the three of us creatures locked into a kind of strange survivalist dance—that somehow the crosshairs of fate had brought us here together in

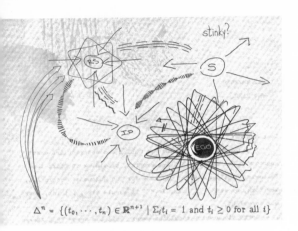

$$\Delta^n = \{(t_0, \cdots, t_n) \in \mathbb{R}^{n+1} \mid \Sigma_i t_i = 1 \text{ and } t_i \geq 0 \text{ for all } i\}$$

Triangulating Stinky and the Poisonrope ←---------
from Notebook B77

this instant of triangulation. How was each of us experiencing this moment? Was there an acknowledgment—beneath the assigned roles of fear, predation, territoriality—of our shared sentience? A part of me wanted to reach out to the rattlesnake and shake his invisible hand. I would say: "Though you know nothing more than how to be a rattler, you are not a Stenpock, and for this I shake your invisible hand."

And then the rattlesnake moved toward me, its eyes unrecognizable in their unwavering purposefulness, and I closed my own eyes thinking that this was how it was to be, that dying on a ranch from a snakebite to the face was even more fitting than a self-inflicted gunshot wound to the head by an old antique rifle in the cold barn.

I heard two shots:

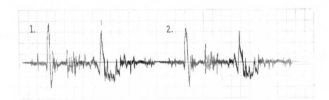

Somehow the second shot brought me back to the world of the ranch and I opened my eyes and saw that the rattlesnake's head was off, on the ground, and blood was pouring from its thick neck. The headless body was pulsing, as if it were intent on coughing up something important. The snake coiled, clenched back into itself, uncoiled again, and then was still for good.

I could feel my heart pounding and pounding and pounding and for a moment I thought that it had pounded its way to the other side of my chest and that my organs had all rearranged (*situs inversus!*) and that I would be a scientific oddity and die young in a rocking chair.

"You fixin' to kiss that poisonrope?"

I looked up. Father was holding the rifle, walking over to me, yanking me up.

"Well?" His voice was steady, but his eyes were white and moist.

I couldn't speak. My mouth was drier than a mummy's pocket.

"You stupid?" My father hit me on the back, hard, though I couldn't tell if it was to brush me off, to reprimand me, or to substitute for a hug.

"No, I was—"

"Thing'll punch you out quicker than you say Jim-Nay Christmas, and I ain't gonna be there to shoot et next time. You lucky. That's how Old Nance got on the right haunch."

"Yessir," I said.

He toed the rattlesnake carcass. "Sho. She's a big one. Maybe we'll bring that rope back to the house. Show your mudder."

"Let's leave him," I said.

"Yeah?" he said. He took another poke at the snake and then looked at Stinky, who had still not moved.

"You saw it all, huh, you sonfabitch?" he said. And then he kicked Stinky so hard in the head the animal tumbled back at least fifteen feet. I winced. Stinky sat there for a second, dazed, his tongue working the lips of his mouth with an air of lunacy.

I watched Stinky, perhaps fearful that he might keel over and die from the shock of the whole thing, but animals have a rare quality that some people—like my father—would label ignorance, but that I thought was more akin to forgiveness. As he sat there licking his lips, it was almost like I could see the tension of the previous moment's events slipping out of his body. Then he leapt to his feet and without a look backward ran up the hill, away from the madness.

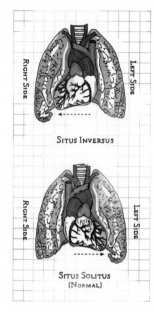

You Are One of Us
But You Are Not Like Us
from Notebook G77

This action seemed to violate rule #4 of Gene Autry's *Cowboy Code*, but then Father seemed a selective follower of both cowboy ethics and the Bible: he referenced each only when it was convenient to his actions.

1. THE COWBOY MUST NEVER SHOOT FIRST, HIT A SMALLER MAN, OR TAKE UNFAIR ADVANTAGE.
2. HE MUST NEVER GO BACK ON HIS WORD, OR A TRUST CONFIDED IN HIM.
3. HE MUST ALWAYS TELL THE TRUTH.
4. HE MUST BE GENTLE WITH CHILDREN, THE ELDERLY, AND ANIMALS.
5. HE MUST NOT ADVOCATE OR POSSESS RACIALLY OR RELIGIOUSLY INTOLERANT IDEAS.
6. HE MUST HELP PEOPLE IN DISTRESS.
7. HE MUST BE A GOOD WORKER.
8. HE MUST KEEP HIMSELF CLEAN IN THOUGHT, SPEECH, ACTION, AND PERSONAL HABITS.
9. HE MUST RESPECT WOMEN, PARENTS, AND HIS NATION'S LAWS.
10. THE COWBOY IS A PATRIOT.

"Damn ignor'nt goats," Father said, and emptied the rifle cartridges onto the ground. *Clat ta chink, clat ta chink.* "Come on now, we got our business—day's leavin'."

I followed my father to the pickup. As he coaxed that old sucker engine back to life, I was filled with a warm, burning sensation. The tips of my fingers smoldered as if thawing from an intense cold. I couldn't forget how my father had toed that snake, how he had considered it completely in that moment and then utterly forgotten it in the next. As soon as the crisis was averted, his attention had simply swung back to the task of irrigating the ditches; the assuredness of his movement essentially said: *There are no miracles in this life.*

I did not belong here. I had known this a long time, I suppose, but the tunnel vision embodied in my father's gesture crystallized this truth. I was not a creature of the high country.

I would go to Washington. I was a cartographer, a scientist, and they needed me there. Dr. Clair was a scientist too—but somehow she fit out here as much as he did. These two belonged here together, circling each other along the endless inclines of the divide.

Through the palm-smudged window of the pickup, I stared up at the soft palette of dusk. Tiny dark bodies flickered on and off across the grey, depthless sky—the yuma bats (*M. yumanensis*) had begun their frenetic dance of echolocation. The air around the pickup must have been filled with a million of their tiny radar signals. Though I flexed my ears, I could not quite comprehend the dense latticework of their labors.

We pounded along, my father's hand on top of the wheel, his weak pinky cocked slightly upward. I watched the bats crackle and plunge against the sky. Such light things. Theirs was a world of reflection and deflection, of constant conversation with surface and solid.

It was a life I could not endure: they never knew *here*; they only knew the echo of *there*.

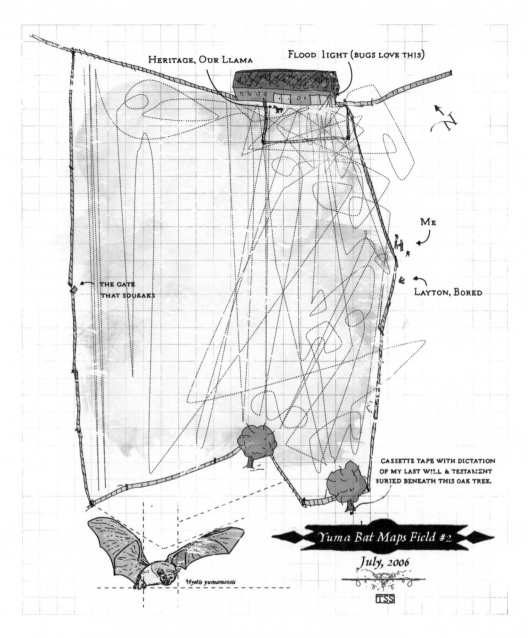

HERITAGE, OUR LLAMA

FLOOD light (BUGS LOVE THIS)

N

ME

LAYTON, BORED

THE GATE
THAT SQUEAKS

CASSETTE TAPE WITH DICTATION
OF MY LAST WILL & TESTAMENT
BURIED BENEATH THIS OAK TREE.

Yuma Bat Maps Field #2

July, 2006

TSS

Myotis yumanensis

I made this map for Dr. Yorn, who was
an amateur chiroptologist. But I also
made it for him in case I died. I wanted
him to know where my Last Will & Testament was. (I made this map before he
started lying to me.)

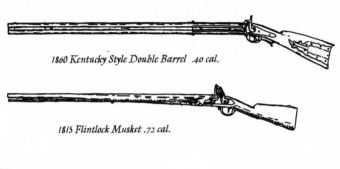

1860 Kentucky Style Double Barrel .40 cal.

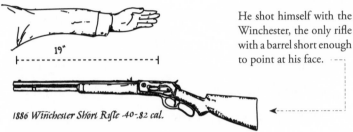

1815 Flintlock Musket .72 cal.

19"

He shot himself with the Winchester, the only rifle with a barrel short enough to point at his face.

1886 Winchester Short Rifle .40-.82 cal.

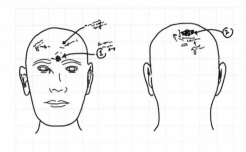

The Autopsy Report
from Notebook G45

When one of the lawyers came out to the ranch, I spotted the coroner's report on top of his briefcase. I copied this diagram while the lawyer was out in the barn with Father. Even though the coroner's template for a head looked like a tough Russian spy and not a ten-year-old boy, I think Layton would have liked being drawn this way.

CHAPTER 3

W e did not speak as we mucked the ditches. At one point Father grunted and paused to work out the lay of the land and then he pointed with his middle and index finger like a pistol to the ditch across the snap gulch.

"There," he said, firing the pistol. "Clear her out."

"Okay." I sighed and tromped on over. For an outside observer, his movements might have been part of a brilliant display of hydrologic intuition, but I no longer cared. I felt like a child actor lending some live-action ambience to a dramatically lit Smithsonian exhibit on Western Americana.

I mucked. The sound track played sounds of squelching mud, my father's sharp, guttural orders muted by the gathering of the late-afternoon

Just off to the left of the two figures, a quietly serifed museum sign was stuck in the mud:

BOY IRRIGATING DITCH ON FATHER'S RANCH — DIVIDE, MONTANA. (PRESENT DAY)

couloir gusts that blew the flaxseed and pine dust into our eyes. (Had the museum imported this as well?)

I stopped mid-shovel. The muddy canals of cold creek water flowed over and around my waders. My feet were islands. I could sense the water's chill through the rubber membrane of my boots, but everything was muted now—I suddenly yearned for the icy pinch of liquid between the soft flesh of my toes.

We rode back to dinner in silence, chunks of muck sliding down our waders onto the boot-worn floor of the pickup. I wondered if my father sensed anything was wrong. He wasn't the type to inquire about the purpose of your silence. For him, silence was a pleasure, not a sign of inner turmoil.

When we pulled up to the house, he motioned for me to get out. "Give her my regards. I got things I gots to care on. Save us a plate of grocer*ies*."

This was a bit out of the ordinary, as one of Father's formalisms was his insistence on everyone's presence at the dinner table. This mandate had loosened a bit since Layton's death, but most nights the four of us could still be found beneath Linnaeus, eating our meal in cultivated semi-silence.

Father must've caught me wondering at him, because his face briefly parted into a grin, maybe to ease the moment. I jumped out of the cab in my waders, my loafers in hand. I wanted to say some parting phrase that would cap our conversation—something short and sweet that would convey my simultaneous reverence and repulsion for this place, for him. Of course, in the pressure of the moment, I could not think of anything suitable, so I just said: "The good times."

Though my father could not have articulated what exactly was wrong with the comment, the grin vanished. There was the faint smell of oil from beneath the hood, the acrid moan of the hinge as I lightly swung the pickup's door back and forth. We were stuck there, staring at each other. He made the signal with his fingers to shut the door. I stared.

"Close," he said finally, and I closed the door. It whined and clicked shut, maybe not quite shut. I was still staring at the silhouette of my father through the window when the engine gunned and the pickup moved off down the darkened road, the two taillights burning hot, hotter, and gone.

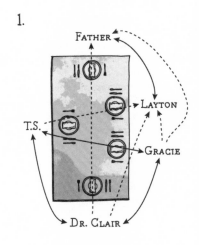

Dinner was not delicious. Canned peas, sweet corn puree peppered with those little Red Dots, and something pie-shaped in the genre of meatloaf that we simply called the Next Best Thing, because Gracie would never reveal its componentry. No one complained about the meal, however; it was not delicious, but it was there and it was hot.

We pushed the Next Best Thing around our plates. Gracie talked of pageants. Apparently, Miss USA was going to be televised tomorrow evening, which was clearly a momentous annual occasion for certain members of the Spivet household.

Dr. Clair smiled and chewed.

"Do these women have special skills? Such as painting?" She gestured halfheartedly with her fork in the air, charades-style, to denote a paintbrush at work. "Or karate? Or laboratory skills? Or are they just judged on looks alone?"

"No, this is just a beauty contest." There was Gracie's famous sigh. "Miss America has a talent section. But Miss USA is way better."

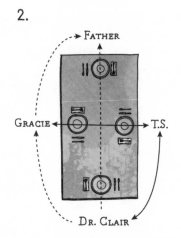

Patterns of Cross-Talk
Before and After
from Notebook B56

"Gracie, you know looks can only get you so far. I bet those women have brain rot."

"What's brain rot?" I asked.

"Miss Montana is from Dillon," Gracie said. "She's six foot one. How tall is Dad?"

"He's six foot three and a quarter," I said.

"Whoa…" Gracie said, her lips making little popping sounds as if she were counting each inch off in her head.

"Well, I just think that talent, aptitude—*scientific aptitude*—should be considered," Dr. Clair was saying.

Though Dr. Clair phrased it as a half-question, we all knew it to be true. There were many maps to document the false notes squeezed from this instrument: the nimble improvisations; the repeated middle C played for hours on end during a Dork Retreat, or one of her three dramatic breakups with Farley, Barrett, and Whit.

"Ah…Mom? That would be a science fair, okay?" Gracie turned to her, that familiar edge of sarcasm creeping into her voice. "And then no one would watch it, because it would be boring. Like my life." A mouthful of peas for punctuation.

"Well, I just think that you have more than your looks. They should have a contest that takes skills into account—like your acting ability! And your voice! You have such a beautiful voice. And you can play the oboe?"

Gracie winced. She sucked in what must have been a walnut-size pellet of air and spoke into her plate. "They *have* a contest for that. *Miss America* has a talent section. This is Miss USA." As she said each word, her fork guided a single pea around her plate in a slow, menacing oval.

Variations on Pea Anger Ovals from Notebook B72

"I just think they should encourage women to use their full faculties," Dr. Clair said in that wandery voice of hers. (Meaning: I am thinking of mandibles.) "So that they can become scientists."

Gracie stared at her. She opened her mouth and then closed it. She looked at the ceiling, seemed to compose her thoughts, and then began speaking, as if she were addressing a very young child: "Mom, I know it's hard for you to listen to me. But I want you to try: I like Miss *USA*, It's a beauty contest. The women aren't smart. They're dumb and they're beautiful and I love them. There's no science laboratory—it's just entertainment. Enter-*tain*-ment."

Gracie's preschool tone seemed to have an anaesthetizing effect on Dr. Clair. She sat very still and listened.

Gracie continued: "And for just an hour I can almost forget that I am on this wacko farm in Montana slowly dying away like a blind cat."

The blind cat comment took everyone by surprise. We all looked at each other and then Gracie looked away, embarrassed. The phrase was a strange homage to our father and yet it sounded like an ill-fitting hand-me-down coming from Gracie—somehow further supporting the fundamental point she had been recapitulating since getting her period: that this family had slowly eroded her potential as a famous actress and instead doomed her to forever be just another proverbial farm girl with a broken spirit.

In an acute display of advanced Dork Retreat, Gracie (1) produced her iPod from her pocket and jammed in her earphones—left ear, then right; (2) poured her grape juice onto the remnants of her Next Best Thing; and (3) removed herself from the scene, plate and silverware rattling aggressively in her hands.

To tell you the truth, up until the mention of the blind cat and the powerful Dork Retreat behavior, I had not really been listening to the particulars of their conversation, for this was a ritual of miscommunication they played out almost every night.

"How was working with your father?" Dr. Clair asked. Gracie was crashing around in the kitchen.

> Not that it wasn't interesting—if I were a human psychologist fascinated with mother-daughter relationships, these two were akin to discovering the Pompeii of familial female interchange. Gracie and Dr. Clair had a complex dynamic: being the only two women on the ranch, they were inherently drawn to each other, discussing such girl things as earrings and exfoliants and hair spray, conversations that created temporary feminine cocoons amidst the five o'clock stubble of a hardscrabble ranch. Still, Dr. Clair was not your typical mother in that I believed she would be more comfortable if her children had exoskeletons and withered after one life cycle. She tried, Dr. Clair, but in the end, she was a giant and tremendous *nerd*, and for Gracie, the looming inevitability of a similar fate was perhaps her deepest fear. One had only to whisper the *n*-word into Gracie's ear to elicit the most terrible of conniptions, the worst of which were assigned a year, as in: *The Conniption of '04.* Thus, based on this historical experience, n———was one of the four forbidden terms at the Coppertop.

Why these two?

I knew the facts—they had met at a square dance in Wyoming—but I did not know the internal machinations of how such a union could have ever clicked and held. Why on earth had they stayed together? These were two creatures cut from entirely different cloths:

My father: the silent man of practicality with his empty bags and his heavy hands, knotting the tackaberry buckles on those unbroken cayuses, his eyes on the horizon and never on you.

My mother: seeing the world only in parts, in tiny parts, in the tiniest of parts, in parts that perhaps didn't exist.

How could these two be drawn to each other? I wanted to ask my father this, only because I felt his thick disappointment with my penchant for science. I wanted to say: "But what about your wife? What about our mother? She is a scientist! You married her! You cannot hate all of it, then? You chose this life!"

The genesis and sustenance of their love thus got filed away with the rest of the unspoken subjects on the Coppertop, materializing only in tiny trinkets: the horseshoe ornament in the cab of the pickup, a single picture of my father as a young man standing next to a railroad crossing that Dr. Clair had pinned to the wall of her study; those quiet moments of contact that I occasionally saw them have in hallways, where their hands briefly met, as though they were exchanging a secret pile of seeds.

I hadn't realized the attention of the room had swung back to me, so I took a moment before answering: "Fine. I mean, fine. I think. He seemed angry at the water. It looked low to me. I didn't take any readings on it, but it looked low."

"How's he doing?"

"Fine, I guess. Does he not seem all right to you?"

"Well, you know him. He wouldn't say as much, but I think there's something up with him. Something's not quite..."

"Like what?"

"That man can be so stubborn when it comes to any new idea. He's afraid to change."

"What new idea?"

"You didn't marry him," she said strangely, and then she put down her fork, marking the end of that subject.

"I'm going up north tomorrow, near Kalispell," she said.

"Why?"

"A collecting trip."

"Are you trying to find the tiger monk?" I asked, and then caught my breath.

She didn't say anything for a bit. "Well…partly. I mean, I suppose. Yes."

We sat quietly at the dinner table for a while. I ate my peas and she ate hers. Gracie was still crashing around in the kitchen.

"Would you like to come with me?" she asked.

"Where?"

"To Kalispell. It would be great to have your help."

Any other day I would savor such an offer. She did not often invite me on her trips, perhaps because she felt a little threatened by me peeking over her shoulder all day, but when she needed an illustrator, I salivated at the chance to watch her at work. You could say a lot about her obsessiveness, her recalcitrance, but she was a master when she had her collection net in hand; there was nobody with better instincts, which made me fear that if she of all people had not been able to find the tiger monk after all these years, then it really did not exist.

But now, I felt like I was betraying her. I could not go with her up north, because I would be leaving tomorrow for Washington, D.C. *Washington, D.C.!* I thought briefly of confessing everything to her here, at the dinner table. Something about the peas and the meat pie created a safe forum for me to do so. Surrounded by the symbology of my family, the only family I had, I would come clean—because if I couldn't trust this woman, whom could I trust?

"There is something…I'm going—" I started, slowly, alternately pressing my pinky to my thumb and my thumb to pinky—itsy-bitsy spider– style—as was my wont when nervous.

Verywell came sauntering in, looking for stray peas.

"Yes?" she said.

I realized I had stopped speaking. And I had stopped my itsy-bitsy routine.

I sighed. "I can't come with you," I said. "I'm busy. I'm going down to the valley tomorrow."

"Oh?" she said. "With Charley?"

"No," I said. "But: good luck up there. Up north, I mean. I hope you find it. The tiger monk, I mean."

Nervous Itsy Bitsy
from Notebook B19

1.

2.

3.

4.

5.

6.

The name of the missing species sounded like a swear word when I said it. I tried to rescue the moment.

"Kalispell, Montana... *Wowee!*" I said loudly, as though delivering the last line of a poorly budgeted Technicolor commercial by the Kalispell tourist office. The line was so out of place that it actually infused a little oxygen back into the room.

"Well, it's a shame," Dr. Clair said. "Would've been nice to have you along. I'm leaving early, so I probably won't see you," she said, clearing the table. "But at some point I'd like to show you one of my notebooks. I've been working on a new project that I think you might find enlightening. She reminds me of you...."

"Mom," I said.

She stopped; she stared at me, plates in her hands, her head cocked to one side. Beneath the table, Verywell had found some peas and was slurping away quietly, like a leaky tap in a distant room.

When it was time, perhaps when it was past time, she resumed her clearing but paused behind me on her way to the kitchen. In her hands, the knives shifted on the plates.

"Safe travels," she said, and left the room.

Once the dishes were clean and dried, once Dr. Clair had retreated to her study and Gracie to her lair of Girl Pop, I finally found myself sitting alone in the dining room, facing a series of difficult, adultlike tasks.

I took a deep breath and walked to the phone in the kitchen. I picked up the receiver and pressed 0, hard, because the zero button was a little finicky on our phone. The line clicked and whirred and then finally a nice woman's voice said, "What's the listing, please?"

"I want to get ahold of Gunther H. Jibsen at the Smithsonian Museum, please. I don't know what his middle name is."

"Please hold."

The woman came back: "The Smith what? What town?"

"Washington, D.C."

The woman laughed, "Oh, sweetie. Well you'll have to call..." She clucked and sighed. "Oh, *all right.* Please hold."

I liked when she said "Please hold." She said it in such a way as to assure you that things were being done for you while you were holding, that the world was working hard to get the information you needed.

After a little bit, she came back and recited the number. "I don't know who you're trying to reach there, honey," she said. "But I would just call the main line and get them to assist you."

"Thank you, operator," I said. I felt great warmth for this woman. I wanted her to drive me to Washington. "You are doing a great job."

"Well, thank you, young man," she said.

I dialed the number she gave me and proceeded to wade through a very intense automated menu system. I went around in circles two times before finally figuring out how to get ahold of Jibsen on his personal line.

As it rang, I became increasingly nervous. How should I apologize? Should I plead a temporary sickness of the mind? A fear of interstate travel? A plethora of fellowships already offered to me? Eventually, his voice mail picked up. I should have known. It was almost ten P.M. on the East Coast.

"Um...yes. Mr. Jibsen. This is T. S. Spivet. We spoke earlier today? I am the one from Montana. Yes, well, anyways, I told you earlier that I would not be able to accept the Baird Award...but now I've managed to... um...rearrange my life and so now I *can* accept your generous offer to the

The recorded voice said, "In order to better assist you, our menu options have changed. Please listen closely." And I tried to listen closely: as she listed all my options, I even placed my fingers over the buttons that I might want to select, creating an elaborate, twisted gang sign on the keypad as my options increased, but by the time she had gotten to option #8, I had already forgotten what option #2 was.

fullest. I will be leaving tonight, in fact, so will thus be unreachable at the number you called me at earlier. So, that is to say, don't bother. But don't worry! I will be there, Mr. Jibsen, ready to give a speech at the anniversary dinner, and whatever else you should need. So…so…thank you again and have a great day."

I hung up quickly. *That was terrible.* I sat down on the stool next to the phone, deflated. I resumed a slow, melancholy sort of itsy-bitsying, staring at the door to upstairs. I was not looking forward to the next hurdle.

You see, if my father had no weaknesses, I had several, the most glaring of which was my inability to perform a mundane chore that did not usually freeze strong men with big belt buckles in their tracks: packing a suitcase. Even packing for school every day took me, at the very least, twenty-three minutes, *maybe* twenty-two minutes. Packing might seem like a normal ritual that humans practiced daily across the globe—but when you stopped to think about it, packing, and especially packing for a trip to a foreign place, required a highly developed ability to predict the implements you would need for living in an environment that you were not familiar with.

I suppose, like shoes and speech patterns and manner of walk, you can tell a lot about a person by the way he or she packs a suitcase. Dr. Clair, for instance, carefully packed her instruments of collection and dissection into a series of rosewood boxes. She always placed these in the center of her empty suitcase in a curious but meticulously lopsided diamond formation, her fingers touching the corners of the boxes as if they were living, breathing creatures with the most breakable of bones. Around this fragile heart, she then simply threw in a wild hodgepodge of clothes and curious green jewelry, treating these items with a dismissiveness that contrasted starkly with her previous attention to the beautiful boxes. Even a casual observer of this packing technique might be forced to conclude that this woman was at the very least mildly schizophrenic, and if in fact this observer were an actual doctor giving a lecture on my mother's split personality, then a slideshow of her suitcase might be the perfect diagram to begin his talk. (I would not give him my diagram, though.)

My father, on the other hand, did not so much pack for trips as just leave. When he went down to Dillon to sell horses at the rodeo, he would throw an old leather bag into the passenger seat of the pickup.

Sometimes I thought it would be interesting to compare the backpack of a cowboy from the American West with that of a monk from Cambodia. Would the similarities be superficial? Or indicative of some deeper commonality between how each approached the world? Was I just romanticizing my father's sparseness? Was his laconism a stand-in not for wisdom but for fear?

In sharp contrast to the casual hefting of a satchel through a pickup window moments before departure, when I packed for an excursion, I had an elaborate set routine, the primary purpose of which was to keep me from hyperventilating:

Its contents (which I had perused armed with a camera and a pair of tongs for a potentially dangerous mission when he was not looking) were, from top to bottom:

1) A shirt.
2) A toothbrush, the handle of which looked as if it was covered in axle grease.
3) A sheet of paper listing ten horses' names with a series of numbers after each name. (Later, I figured these must be the dimensions of each animal.)
4) A bedroll.
5) A pair of leather gloves, the left pinky torn open to reveal pink stuffing; almost like the insulation one sees in the walls of houses. This was from the fencing accident that had left the digit weakened and cocked upward.

THE FIVE STEPS OF PACKING

STEP ONE: *Visualization*

I played and replayed the scenario of the trip in my mind. I mapped out all the potential hazards of the journey, all the opportunities I might encounter where I could bring out my diagramming and notational devices, all the specimens I might want to collect, all the images, sounds, smells I might want to capture.

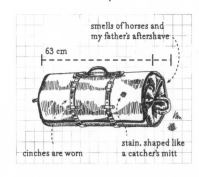

This, the Bedroll
from Notebook G33

STEP TWO: *Inventory*

Then I put all of the devices and articles I might need onto my drafting table and arranged them in order of importance.

STEP THREE: *Assemblage #1*

Having designated the items that I could not possibly bring because of finite space, I left these on the drafting table and then carefully packed the remaining essential items, wrapping them in bubble wrap and duct tape so the delicate apparatuses would not be damaged in transit.

STEP FOUR: *The Great Doubt*

Then, inevitably, just before I would zip up the suitcase, I would see the leftover pooter or sextant or 4x telescope and think of a scenario such as a woodpecker soundscaping for which I would need the seismoscope and then I would rethink the entire trip and also my entire life.

STEP FIVE: *Assemblage #2*

And thus be forced to repack it all again. And by this time I was usually late for school.

So you can imagine my difficulty packing for *this* trip, which would take me farther away from the Coppertop than I had ever been in my life. This trip, I was headed to the mecca of collections, to *La Capitale* (as I had taken to saying in my head the last couple of hours, perhaps because the accent lessened the seriousness of the venture).

I tiptoed to the base of the stairs, scanning the hallway in both directions. The growing anticipation of my imminent departure and the waves of hush-hush secrecy that I felt smoldering in my bones caused me to perhaps overreact as I hugged the wall, commando-style, going up the creaky stairs to my room. To be safe, I then went down the back stairs and up the front stairs again just to make sure no one was following me. No one was, except Verywell, and I was pretty sure he was clean. Feeling foolish, I checked his collar for cameras anyways. He enjoyed the attention of this frisking and followed me to my room.

"No," I said to him at the doorway, hand-signaling the stop sign. "Privacy."

Verywell looked at me and licked his chops.

"Not like that," I said. "No. Look—go play with Gracie. She's got the lonelies. Just listen to that Girl Pop."

The moment the latch on my door ticked shut, I began agonizing. For the act of packing I changed into an athletic costume complete with sweatbands and kneepads. This was going to be more difficult than the President's Fitness Challenge, in which I couldn't manage a single pull-up.

I put a little Brahms on the record player to calm the nerves.

With the strains of the orchestra crackling through the old speakers, I imagined my entree into *La Capitale*: arriving on the marbled steps of the Smithsonian in knee-high riding boots with four servants staggering beneath my tremendous trunks.

"*Easy*…Jacques! Tambeau! Olio! Curtis!" I would say to them. "There's a lot of important and rare equipment in there."

And Mr. Jibsen would come strolling out in a marigold bow tie, tapping a cane on the marble as though to test its integrity.

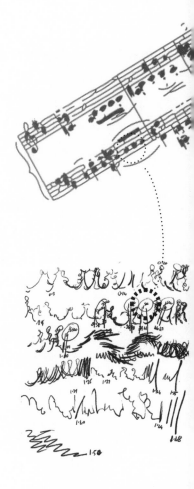

Sound Drawing of Brahms's Hungarian Dance No. 10 by New Zealand penpal Raewyn Turner

"Ahhh! My dear Mr. Spivet, *bonjour! Bienvenu à la capitale!*" he would say, the lisp now familiar and tender and in this vision…French. Indeed, in this vision, the entire Smithsonian pastoral had a curious French slant to it: bicycles were everywhere; on a park bench, a child played the accordion.

"You must be *très fatigué* from your voyage," Mr. Jibsen was saying. "And I see you packed for all occasions. *Il y a beaucoup de bagage! Mon Dieu! C'est incroyable, n'est-ce pas?*"

"Yes," I would say. "I wanted to be prepared for everything. Who knows what you might have me do in the name of science?"

But then the vision fell apart as my imaginary French Jibsen, no longer buffered by the telephone, saw the imaginary me, who had gained no years in this fantasy and was still twelve. And in the vision, I looked down at myself and my French velour traveling suit was four sizes too big, the shoulders too broad, the cuffs obscuring my hands—my child's hands—so that I could not shake Mr. Jibsen's outstretched paw, which was already re-coiling in shock. "*Oe-whee-u,*" he would say. "*Un enfant!*" Even the child with the accordion had abruptly stopped playing in horror.

Ah, yes. *Oe-whee-u.* There was still that issue.

I took all the instruments off the walls of my room and laid them out onto my Lewis and Clark rug.

I closed my eyes, pacing circles around the heap of tools, and imagined in my mind's eye the buildings of the Smithsonian and the Mall and the Potomac and the fall turning to winter turning to spring and the emergence of those fragrant cherry blossoms that I had read so much about. *La Capitale.*

Almost eight hours later, at 4.10 in the morning, I had arrived at my final inventory, which I typed up and taped to the inside of my suitcase.

I brought:

1.) Sixteen packs of Cinnamon Trident gum.

2.) Underwear galore.

3.) Only one telescope: a Zhummel Aurora 70.

4.) Two sextants and one octant.

5.) My three grey sweater vests and other things that you wear.

6.) Four compasses.

7.) My drafting paper and complete set of Gillot pens and nibs and my Harmann Rapidograph.

8.) My magnifying headpiece—"Thomas" (or "Tom" in casual conversation).

9.) Two heliotropes and the old theodolite my mother had given me on my tenth birthday. It still worked fine if you knew how to jimmy the gears.

10.) My GPS device—"Igor."

11.) Three of my blue notebooks: *Newton's Laws of Conservation and The Lateral Movements of Migrating Birds in NW Montana, 2001–2004*; *Father and the Curious Variety of His Haying Patterns*; and *Layton: Gestures, Malapropisms, Cadence*.

12.) Five blank green notebooks. G101–G105.

The Lucky Broken Compass from Notebook G32

➤ Two surveying, one directional, and one that didn't work but was a good luck trinket—Dr. Yorn had given it to me for my twelfth birthday. Dr. Yorn was actually a pretty great guy. He probably knew what was best. If he had thought that the Baird Award was a good idea, then it must be a good idea. I would make him proud of me in a way that my father could never be.

➤ Igor didn't get along with the older equipment, but he was a necessary member of the party. "One must not live in the past," a man who worked at the Butte Historical Society once said to me. I thought this was a strange thing for a historian to say, but I'm pretty sure the man was drunk.

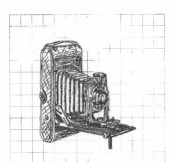

The Maximar
(I no longer trusted her.)
from Notebook G39

Considering the bird's fragility, I went to great lengths debating whether I should bring this, but ultimately decided that not bringing the sparrow was like not bringing me. The only thing that set me apart from all the other Tecumsehs before me was my second first name—*Sparrow*.

It was meant to be a Christmas card, but we never sent it out, perhaps because we realized we never actually had enough friends to warrant sending a Christmas card. Also, I don't think it was Christmastime.

13.) A handkerchief (a Berenstain Bears handkerchief).

14.) From the kitchen: three granola bars, a bag of Cheerios, two apples, four cookies, and eight carrot sticks.

15.) The dark blue parka with the duct-taped elbows.

16.) A Leica M1 and a Maximar folding plate medium-format camera.

17.) The rest of the duct tape roll.

18.) A multiband radio.

19.) Three clocks.

20.) The sparrow skeleton from the ornithologist in Billings.

21.) My rattly old Gunther's chain.

22.) A railroad atlas of the U.S.

23.) A toothbrush and toothpaste. Also floss.

24.) My stuffed animal, Tangential the Tortoise.

25.) A picture of my family in front of the barn, taken four years ago. Everyone is looking in different directions— everywhere except at the camera.

The suitcase was a half-size too small to contain all of these items.

Unfortunately, I could not part with any of them, as this short list had already been winnowed down through four laborious rounds of Apparatus Survivor. I finally managed to zip the suitcase shut by gently (and wincingly) sitting on top of the bag. As the contents settled beneath my weight, I heard several unnatural creaking noises. I imagined gears snapping, lenses shattering. But still I did not move. Instead, I eased the zipper around the beveled horn of the suitcase with small phrases of familiar encouragement.

"You can do it, friend," I said at the last turn. "Remember the old times. You still got it in you."

With the suitcase secured, grossly bulging but triumphantly zipped shut, I turned my attention to the next order of business: the small issue of how I was actually going to get to Washington.

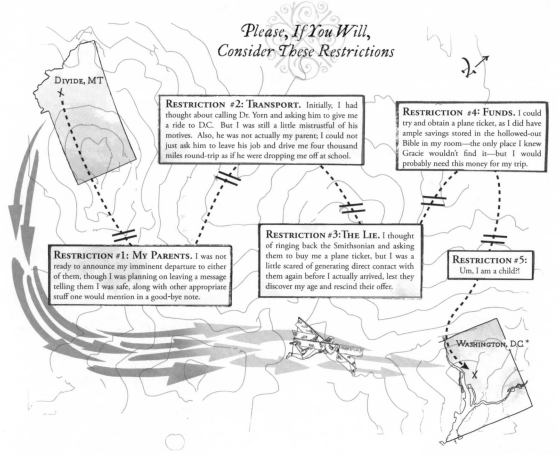

DIVIDE, MT

RESTRICTION #2: TRANSPORT. Initially, I had thought about calling Dr. Yorn and asking him to give me a ride to D.C. But I was still a little mistrustful of his motives. Also, he was not actually my parent; I could not just ask him to leave his job and drive me four thousand miles round-trip as if he were dropping me off at school.

RESTRICTION #4: FUNDS. I could try and obtain a plane ticket, as I did have ample savings stored in the hollowed-out Bible in my room—the only place I knew Gracie wouldn't find it—but I would probably need this money for my trip.

RESTRICTION #3: THE LIE. I thought of ringing back the Smithsonian and asking them to buy me a plane ticket, but I was a little scared of generating direct contact with them again before I actually arrived, lest they discover my age and rescind their offer.

RESTRICTION #1: MY PARENTS. I was not ready to announce my imminent departure to either of them, though I was planning on leaving a message telling them I was safe, along with other appropriate stuff one would mention in a good-bye note.

RESTRICTION #5: Um, I am a child?!

WASHINGTON, D.C.*

CHAPTER 4

*A Small Note to the Intrepid Traveler: This map is not meant for navigational purposes. Any attempt to use this map for actual travel will cause you to become lost in Canada.

I fetched a late-night glass of water. I took tiny little sips through the gap in my front teeth and watched the water level slowly diminish. I retrieved a raisin from downstairs, brought it back to my room, and tried to make it last for twenty bites. I stared at my suitcase.

I realized my only option. It was actually a confirmation of what I had perhaps known all along—as was evidenced by my packing of the railroad atlas—but which I had not been able to conjure in the conscious part of my cortex. Indeed, the solution for my cross-country travel was obvious, if a bit dangerous and hardly guaranteed. When I thought of it, I

I could only extract the profundity of this shift in Americans' conception of space and time from my own experience playing Oregon Trail with Layton on our Apple IIGS ("Old Smokey" we called her).

Perhaps twenty years after we should've updated our system, Old Smokey remained the computational workhorse on the ranch. Though Gracie had long ago given up on her, buying her own pink laptop that looked like a toilet seat, Layton and I didn't really mind that she was a little long in the tooth or that she was still stained with ketchup from that hot dog fight. We loved her. And we would spend hours playing a very pixelated Oregon Trail. We would always give our characters terrible names: Dickwad, Poopneck, Little Asshole Face, so that when they died of cholera, we could pretend we didn't care.

One day, and I think this was only a week before the gunshot experiment in the barn, Layton figured out that if you spent all of your money on oxen in Independence, Missouri, at the beginning of the game—forsaking food, clothing, and ammunition to buy an armada of yoked cattle 160 strong—that the game would not provide any maximum speed for your wagon but rather continue to increase your pace by 6 MPH for each oxen. Thus, you could finish the game in two days, by traveling what I figured out to be approximately 960 MPH. Naked, hungry, and unarmed, you still blasted across this continent before the cholera could catch up to you. That first time we won the game this way, we both stared at the screen, dumbstruck, trying to make room in our mental maps for a world that could include such a loophole.

Then Layton said, "That game kind of sucks now."

did a little jig on the now empty carpet, right on Meriwether Lewis's face. The reality of my impending journey suddenly set in.

"And besides," I said to myself. "If I am going on an adventure, it might as well be a proper adventure."

To get to Washington, D.C., to get to my first real job, I was going to hop a freight train. I was going to hobo it.

In some ways, I guess I was a sucker for historical myth just like Father. But whereas his Spiral of Nostalgic Unfulfillment was directed at the cinematic West of the trail drive, one need only whisper the phrase "bustling railroad town" to raise my blood pressure a notch. An irresistible montage would flash through my head: platforms filled with heavily luggaged families disembarking for a new life in the West, the hiss of steam, the smell of the furnace in the locomotive's belly, the grease, the dust, the conductor and his insurmountable mustache, the mournful expanse of sonic silence following the blast of the engine's whistle, the little man who slept all day next to the one-room station house with a yellowed newspaper covering his face, the headline reading UNION PACIFIC RAILROAD SELLS LAND CHEAP!

Okay, okay—admittedly, this sentimentalism may put me behind the times. In the twenty-first century, the term *transcontinental railroad* no longer whipped a roomful of New York dandies into a frothy expansionist frenzy as it had in the 1860s—but you know what? This kind of technological amnesia was a real shame. If I had any sort of sway with what was hip in Americans' eyes, I would try to redirect them back to the old transcontinental hubs, to the curious sigh of the steam locomotive, the tender professionalism with which that mustachioed conductor would check his pocket watch exactly one minute before the arrival of the 10.48. *The entire concept of time* had been revolutionized by the railroad: whole cities had synchronized their circadian rhythms to that lonesome whistle, and a trip across the country that had once taken three months suddenly took only a matter of days.

Was my nostalgia as misguided as my father's? His was a world of mythology, mine of empirical science. I saw my love of the railroad not as nostalgia so much as a recognition that trains had once been and still were the technological pinnacle of land-based travel. The car, the truck, the bus, these were all stunted cousins of the perfect locomotive and her clackety load.

Oh, look at Europe! Look at Japan! They had embraced the train as the conerstone of their transportation system. It carried many happy people efficiently and comfortably: on your journey from Tokyo to Kyoto, you could try to think of other perfect city anagrams; you could study the variance in topography and ecology in central Japan; you could read manga comic books; you could make maps of your journey and decorate these maps with manga comic book characters…who knows, you could even meet your future wife as you traveled in such a relaxed state from point A to point B.

So when I settled on the idea of riding the Modern American Freight Railroad, the last vestiges of this once great industry, it all seemed to fit. This was my version of the Hajj to Mecca.

At 5.05 A.M., one last glance around my room only served to cauterize my feeling that I had left something extremely important behind, and, fearing that any more delay would make me rip open my suitcase and start from square one again, I slipped out the door and down the staircase, trying as best I could to muffle the *ka-thunka ka-thunka* of my suitcase against each stair.

I recently read an article that described how the Japanese had just perfected a mag-lev train that floated a millimeter above the track using powerful repellent magnets. The elimination of friction allowed the train to reach speeds of up to 400 MPH. I wrote a letter of congratulation to Tokogamuchi, Inc., in which I also offered any of my mapping services, free of charge, for their surveying needs, because this was exactly the kind of thinking that this world needed more of: cutting-edge modern engineering combined with a deep (and respectful) historical wisdom. "Come to America," I pleaded to Mr. Tokogamuchi. "We will throw you a parade that you will not soon forget."

The house was quiet. Clocks could be heard.

I paused at the foot of the stairs and left my bag where it was. I went back up the stairs two at a time and then crept down the hallway to the last doorway. I had not opened this door for 127 days, since April 21, on his birthday, when Gracie insisted on doing a little ceremony with some sage and fake plastic beads that I knew she had bought at the dollar store. Still, I appreciated the gesture—it was much more than anyone else in the family had done. Usually this door remained closed, or almost closed, as the drafts would always unlatch the door and leave it open just a bit (which, admittedly, was kind of spooky).

I actually don't know why he had lived up there: stifling hot in the summer, freezing in the winter, with powerful wafts of mouse poop emanating up from the floorboards, the attic seemed almost uninhabitable. But Layton didn't seem to mind. He had used the extra space to practice his roping on the rocking horse. When he was alive, in the evenings you could hear the constant thump and pull of the rope echoing down from the attic.

As I climbed the last flight of stairs, I saw that red rocking horse standing in the corner same as he always did. Except for this silent creature and an empty gun rack in the corner, the room was bare. It had been cleaned out first by the sheriff and then by my mother and then by Father, who went up in the middle of the night and took back all of his gifts to Layton—the spurs, the Stetson, the belt, the bullets. Some of them ended up slowly materializing in the Sett'ng Room, in the shrine to Billy the Kid. Some of them disappeared, probably into one of the many sheds that dotted the Coppertop. Father never wore any of the accoutrements again.

I stood in the middle of the room and looked at the rocking horse. There was no feat of telepathy I could perform that would move this creature. I had the feeling that even if I walked over and administered force with my hand, the horse would not budge.

"'Bye, Layton," I said. "Not sure if you're still in here or if you've left already, but I'm going away for a while. To Washington, D.C. I'll bring something back for you. Maybe a little presidential bobblehead or a snow globe."

Silence.

"It's looking a little barren up here."

The rocking horse was still. The room was still, like a very impressive illustration of itself.

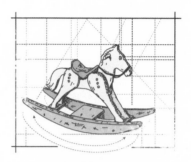

Layton's Rocking Horse
Oh. I miss him

"I'm sorry for what I did," I said.

I closed the door to the attic and headed downstairs. Halfway down the staircase, I heard a noise in Dr. Clair's study, like pebbles being rubbed against one another. I froze, foot poised in midair. Underneath the door I could see light.

I listened. There was the *tick-tock* of the mahogany Grandmeister clock in the parlor; there was the creaking of the eaves. Nothing more. This was adding evidence to my hypothesis that past midnight, sounds in old houses were no longer governed by the normal laws of cause and effect: eaves could creak on their own volition; pebbles could rub against one another.

I tiptoed to the door of her study. The door was slightly ajar. Had Dr. Clair gotten up very early to pack for her collecting trip up north? I heard the rustling noise again. Taking a deep breath, I peered through the keyhole.

The room was empty. I pushed open the door and entered. *Oh, to enter someone else's space without their knowledge!* The blood in my temples was pounding. I had been in here before, but only when Dr. Clair was present. This trespass felt desperately illegal.

The only light came from her desk lamp; the rest of the room was cloaked in dim shadows. I stared at the rows and rows of entomology encyclopedias, the notebooks, the collecting cases, the mounted dung beetles. Someday, an adult version of me would have a room exactly like this. In the center of the table sat her series of rosewood boxes, already packed and ready for her trip.

They had been given to her by a Russian entomologist, Dr. Ershgiev Rolatov, who stayed with us for two weeks a couple of years back and who I think had at least a scientific crush on Dr. Clair if not a bona fide Slavic obsession. He did not speak any English but talked incessantly at the dinner table in his mother tongue as if we all understood.

Then one night my father came into the house, thumbing the belt loops of his jeans, which always signified something was not right at the Coppertop. Later, Dr. Ershgiev Rolatov limped in through the back door with blood all over his face. His combover had come undone and stood straight up like a palm awaiting a high five. He walked past me in the kitchen without uttering a word. It was the first time he was quiet during those whole two weeks and it almost made me miss the way he would address me so sincerely in his guttural native tongue. Dr. Rolatov left the next day. It was one of the few times I saw my father reaffirm his marriage vows.

I heard the pebble-on-pebble sound again and then realized it was coming from a terrarium where Dr. Clair kept her live specimens. Two large tiger beetles were circling each other in the shadows. Then they charged, and the sound of their exoskeletons crashing together was surprisingly loud and satisfying. I studied them as they repeated this ritual several times.

"What are you fighting about?" I asked. They looked up at me. "Sorry." I coughed. "Continue your business." I left them to their negotiations.

I walked around her study. This might just be the last time I would lay eyes on this room. I ran my hands across the burgundy bindings of her notebooks. One whole section was marked EOE. Perhaps this was coding for her tiger monk notations. *Twenty years of notations.* I wondered what she had meant when she said she had wanted to show me one of her notebooks. What was her new project?

Highlighted by the glowing spotlight of the desk lamp, one of the burgundy tiger monk EOE notebooks lay on her desk. It was almost as if...

Suddenly, I heard the stairs creak outside the study. Footsteps. The panic alarm went off in my head, and for some reason—I cannot tell you why—I grabbed the notebook from her desk and fled the room. *Oh, it was a crime, I know!* Perhaps the worst crime of all was to steal a valuable data set from a scientist, for the crucial missing link might be contained within this binding—but I wanted a piece of her to bring with me! Yes, I do not deny it: children are selfish little creatures.

But as it turned out, the footsteps were not footsteps. The creak was an anomaly. The old ranch house was playing more tricks on me. *Well played, old ranch house, well played.*

There was just one thing left to do. I crept into the kitchen and tucked the letter inside the cookie jar. It wouldn't be discovered until lunchtime when Gracie had her cookies, and by that time I would have a pretty good head start.

I knew that probably Gracie would tell them about our conversation and they would eventually figure out my destination, and perhaps their phone call would even precede my arrival to Washington, in which case the scenario on the front steps of the Smithsonian could not even play itself out. But this possibility, like everything else at the moment, was beyond my control, so I filed it away under the Do Not Worry List and pretended not to think about it anymore, though the worry really just channeled itself into a sort of nervous hop-step tic I did with my right foot every time I was trying not to worry about something.

As I walked back through the Sett'ng Room to the front hall, I saw that *The Ox-Bow Incident* was playing silently on the television. In the movie, a mob watched as three bound men were hoisted up on the backs of three horses to be hung. For a minute I was transfixed by the ritual of the act: the tightening of the nooses, the firing of the shot, the whipping of

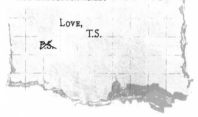

DEAR FAMILY (SPIVET FAMILY),

I HAVE GONE AWAY (FOR A WHILE) TO DO SOME WORK. DON'T WORRY. I'LL BE FINE & I WILL WRITE TO YOU. EVERYTHING IS GOING TO BE GREAT AND IS GREAT. THANK YOU FOR TAKING CARE OF ME, YOU ARE ONE OF THE BEST FAMILIES.

LOVE,
T.S.
P.S.

The Letter
torn from Notebook G54

THE DO NOT WORRY LIST

NOT ENOUGH TIME: ADULTS; TR
BEAR ATTACKS; THE END OF PER
UNTIL HE IS BLIND; GINGIVITIS;
FIRE DESTROYING ALL OF MY JOU
DR. CLAIR NEVER DISCOVERING

the horses, the invisible tumble of the bodies offscreen. I knew it was not real, but it did not matter.

Verywell clicked into the darkened room.

"Hello, Verywell," I said, watching the screen. Still, they did not show the bodies, only the three silent shadows swinging across the ground.

Hello.

"I'll miss you."

He was watching the television too. *Where are you going?*

For a moment I was suspicious that he would tell Dr. Clair if I told him, but then I realized this kind of logic was crazy. He was a dog without the faculties of human speech.

"To the Smithsonian."

Should be fun.

"Yes," I said. "I'm nervous, though."

You shouldn't be.

"Okay," I said.

Will you come back?

"Yes," I said. "I'm pretty sure."

Good, he said. *We need you here.*

"You do?" I asked, turning to him.

He did not answer me. We watched the movie a little more and then I hugged him and he licked my ear. Against my temple, his nose felt colder than usual. I got my suitcase, somehow managed to slide Dr. Clair's stolen notebook inside, and opened the front door.

Outside, there was that predawn kind of clarity, where the momentum of living has not quite captured the day. The air was not filled with conversation or thought bubbles or laughter or sidelong glances. Everyone was sleeping, all of their ideas and hopes and hidden agendas entangled in the dream world, leaving this world clear and crisp and cold as a bottle of milk in the fridge. Well, everyone was sleeping except perhaps Father, who would be getting up in about ten minutes, if he was not up already. The thought made me hurry down the steps of the porch.

The Pioneer Mountains were steady black shadows against a slowly bluing sky. The jagged horizon where the earth opened into the emptiness of the atmosphere was a boundary I had studied and traced a dozen times—it was a borderline that I encountered every time I walked out this door, and yet in this light, on this morning, that dim demarcation between black and blue, between this world and that world, looked entirely unfamiliar to me, as if the mountains had rearranged themselves overnight.

I tromped through the dewy grass. My shoes were instantly wet. Half-dragging, half-carrying my bag down the road, I realized that I could not manage this routine for the whole mile down to the tracks. I briefly considered stealing our family car, the Ford Taurus station wagon that smelled of formaldehyde and dog hair and those strawberry Life Saver mints that Dr. Clair kept stashing everywhere, but I realized this would draw unnecessary attention to my disappearance.

After thinking it over for a minute, I went around to the back porch and got on my hands and knees and there it was: Layton's cobwebbed Radio Flyer wagon, badly dented in several places (from the time he had tried to surf off the roof of the house) but otherwise in fine working condition.

Amazingly, the suitcase fit perfectly inside the uneven red walls—it was as though the dents perfectly matched the contours of the luggage.

The road down to the tracks was rough and furrowed, and I had a time with the Flyer, which seemed to always want to turn left into the ditch.

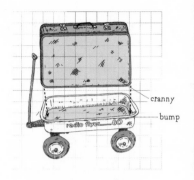

The Radio Flyer, the Suitcase, and the Aligning of the Bumps and Crannies from Notebook G101

I liked the synchronicity of Layton's gravity antics somehow aligning on this dark and chilly morning with the exact sum of my inventory. It made me miss him.

This phrase, "Wagon of Empty Promises," got stuck in my head, and as I worked my way down the road, I found myself thinking about how this could be the title of a second-rate cowboy tell-all memoir or a second-rate country album, or a second-rate anything really. Was my speech actually chock-full of these second-rate sayings? Perhaps I had grown accustomed to them because Father said many of the same things, except that when he said them, they didn't sound second-rate; they sounded just about right, like the stamp of a hoof on dusty ground, the quiet *tap tap* of the ladle on the rim of a lemonade pitcher.

"Why do you want to go in that ditch?" I asked. "You're just a wagon of empty promises."

Suddenly, car lights flared up behind me. I turned, and in that instant my heart sank.

It was the pickup.

It was over. It was over before I could even get off of our property. How was I fooling myself that I could get all the way to Washington, D.C., if I couldn't get past my own driveway? And yet, the end of my journey also brought with it a sense of great relief, as if this was, of course, how it was always meant to be—that I was never to have made it out East. I was a Western boy, and this vortex of a ranch was where I belonged.

The car came round the bend, and I briefly considered trying to scamper into the woods, as it was still quite dark out—but I had the finicky Radio Flyer to contend with and now the lights were too close anyhow, I was caught in them, and I sullenly moved to the side of the road to wait for the pickup to stop and the man inside to do whatever he was going to do.

But it didn't stop. It just went right on by. It was old Georgine, all right—I could tell by the waltzing *thrup thrup thrup* of her engine—but the thrupping never ceased, and as the pickup drove past, its interior flashed into view behind the curtain of headlights and I saw the clear and familiar outline of Father's head behind the wheel, his hat cocked low and to starboard. In that moment of passing, he didn't so much as look at me, and yet I knew that he must have seen me; there was no way you could miss an entourage like me and the Radio wagon and my bulging suitcase full of mapping equipment.

For the second time in twelve hours, I found myself staring at the two red taillights of that pickup disappearing into the darkness.

My body was shaking. I stood, hypnotized by the adrenaline rush of nearly being discovered but also by my father's baffling behavior. Why had he not stopped? Did he know already? Did he want me gone? Did he want me to know that he wanted me gone? I was responsible for his favorite son's death and now I must be banished from the ranch. Or was he just blind? Blind all these years, trying to cover it up with the familiarity of a cowboy's touch? Is that why he opened only one gate? Because it was the only gate that he could locate?

My father was not blind.

I spat on the ground. A thin, almost nonexistent bit of spittle that I had seen the Mexicans constantly conjure as they worked on horseback. The perpetual ejecting of moisture from the mouth always puzzled me, and I had come to a working theory that those droplets contained all the words that were not spoken by the spitter. As I watched my own bead of spittle slip into the crevices of the gravel road, I was hit with a second wave of realization: I had to go on. In that moment of resignation, when I had accepted my capture and the fact that my journey was over, my body had relaxed; I had let down my adventure hackles. Now, suddenly free again, facing a road that was as open as ever, I had to raise those hackles back up. I had to return to my catlike awareness, my Modern Boy/Hobo status.

I checked my watch.

5.25 A.M.

I had about twenty minutes before the train came through the valley. Twenty minutes. I had drawn a few maps showing the time it would take to walk around the world at the 49th parallel, and so had measured the length of my pace and the speed of my normal walk. My pace was about 2.5 feet, give or take a few inches, depending on my mood and desire to get where I was going. I took, on average, 92 to 98 paces per minute, covering about 241 feet.

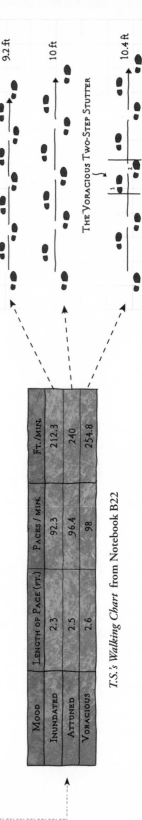

THE VORACIOUS TWO-STEP STUTTER

MOOD	LENGTH OF PACE (FT.)	PACES / MIN.	FT. / MIN.
INUNDATED	2.3	92.3	212.3
ATTUNED	2.5	96.4	240
VORACIOUS	2.6	98	254.8

T.S.'s Walking Chart from Notebook B22

So, in twenty minutes I would usually cover about 4,820 feet—not quite a mile. From my spot on the driveway, the train was about a mile away. And I was pulling this godforsaken wagon. It didn't take a genius to realize I had to run for it.

The last stars dimmed and twinkled their way out of the sky. Even as I chugged down the driveway, the front lip of the red Flyer constantly clipping the backs of my heels, I tried to turn my attention to my next quandary: how to get that freight train to stop for me. I didn't know that much about hoboing, but I did know one never got on a moving train, because no matter how slow it was going, if you slipped and fell beneath the wheels, the train did not give you much consideration. As a child I had been fascinated with Peg Leg Sam, a hobo-turned-musician who had joined an Appalachian traveling medicine show, working a harmonica with those long, knuckled fingers of his, singing strange, mumbly love songs about greasy greens and his missing leg, which he had lost riding the rails. I did not want to be Peg Leg Spivet.

The solution to avoiding a footrace with the Iron Horse came to me just as I crested the hill and arrived at the railroad grade where Crazy Swede Creek Road crossed the tracks. We did not have the red-and-white dingy gates that came down to block traffic—our road was much too infrequently used to justify such an apparatus—but what we did have was a signal light for the train. It consisted of two powerful searchlights, one on top of the other, with little brims over their tops to protect them from the rain and snow. Currently, the lights showed ALL CLEAR—a white light on top of a red light. If I could only figure out how to switch the top light from white to red, the signal would then shine DOUBLE RED, which meant absolute stop on this Union Pacific line. I looked the post up and down, half-expecting to find some kind of computer box with big buttons labeled WHITE, GREEN,

RED, but there was none. Just a cold metal post and that cursed Great White Lamp on top standing unblinkingly at attention.

As I stared at it, the light spoke slowly and carefully: *Don't mess with me, T.S. I am a white light and I am going to stay white. Some things in this life can't be changed.*

This may be true, but I also had an idea—an amazingly simple and potentially ludicrous idea. Luckily, from my work in cartography, I had found that often the best solution was actually the simplest and most ludicrous solution. In any event, there was no time for laborious debate: I now had only four minutes to enact my solution before the train rolled through. My idea, however, necessitated opening my suitcase, and after all that I had been through, this was a bit like revisiting the scene of a crime. I tried to mentally unpack the thing, mapping out where I had put each item. *Underwear in the corner, wrapped around Thomas ("Tom"), the magnifying headpiece, box with namesake sparrow skeleton above this and to the right...*

I heaved the suitcase over on its other side, the contents rattling within. The rattling did not stop when the suitcase was still again. It was a fearsome thing, this suitcase, like a prehistoric animal with a terrible case of indigestion. Going through my packing job one more time in my head, counting off the organs of this creature, I took out my Leatherman (Cartographer's Edition) from my belt, and, using the medium-sized blade, made a small incision in the top right corner of the suitcase. The leather cut easily, scoring open just how I imagine real skin would part. I almost expected the suitcase to bleed on me as I operated. I reached inside the tiny hole with two fingers, searched around for a second before I found what I was looking for, counted *one-two-three-four-five* from the right, and then pulled out a brand spanking new red Sharpie pen that I had bought just last week.

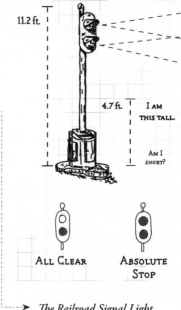

11.2 ft.

4.7 ft.   I AM THIS TALL.

AM I SHORT?

ALL CLEAR   ABSOLUTE STOP

The Railroad Signal Light from Notebook G55

Placing the marker between my teeth as if it were a buck knife, I mustered my best tree-climbing pose and quickly shimmied up the post. The metal was cold, and my fingers were instantly freezing, but I kept my concentration on the task at hand, and suddenly I was at the top of the signaling post, staring into the blinding glare of the Great White Lamp.

I held on to the pole with one hand and uncorked the cap of the pen with my teeth in an orangutanian show of skill that would have impressed even Layton. At first, the pen's ink did not seem to catch on the dimpled curvature of the top lamp, but after several tense moments of furious blank scrawl across its surface, the spongy ink tip finally caught and the ink began to flow. And boy did it flow. In twenty seconds there was already a dramatic, instantaneous shift, as though the lamp were slowly filling with blood.

What are you doing to me? the Great White Lamp cried in its death throes.

Suddenly, I was awash in crimson. It was as though, midway through its dawn rise, the sun had decided to fold in its cards, cut its losses, and descend back again into a scarlet-tinged slumber. And yet there was an artificiality to the glow of this new dawn, like the synthetic melancholy of stage lighting.

I was caught breathless, and perhaps because of this, I lost my hold on the post and fell to the ground. Hard.

Lying in the junipers on my back, winded and bruised, I stared at the red beacon before me and started laughing. I had never before been so happy to see one of the primary colors. It shone bright and steady across the valley:

Stop, it cried in its newly assumed roll of detainment. *Stop this instant, I say!*

It was a convincing act. It was as though no struggle had occurred between us—as though this light had chosen red of its own volition.

As I lay on my back, I felt a low rumbling in the ground. In my palms. In the tendons up the back of my neck. I rolled over and crawled into the cover of the jackbrush. *She was coming.*

I was so used to hearing the Union Pacific freighter rumble through the valley two or three times a day that I normally did not consciously register the sound of its passing. When you were not listening for it—when you were instead concentrating on sharpening your pencil or looking through a magnifying glass—the distant vibrations passed you by along with the rest of the sensual world that we are not attuned to noticing: breathing, crickets, the intermittent whir of our refrigerator fan.

Now, however, with my mind primed and ready for the arrival of the Iron Horse, that curious rumble grabbed ahold of every synapse in my sensory cortex and would not let go.

As the noise slowly grew in volume, I began to separate it into its respective components: the rumble was undergirded by a deep, almost imperceptible vibration in the ground (1), but on top of this—like layers of a delicious sandwich whose scrumptiousness could not be explained by just the sum of its parts—was the *clackety-clack* of the wheels hitting the uneven rail joints (2), the purring *hurra-burra* of the diesel engine's pistons (3), and the irregular *licka-tim-tam* of the clenched couplings (4). And everywhere there was the noxious call of metal scraping against metal, like two cymbals rubbed together very quickly (5), conjuring a high-pitched *hizzleshimsizzleshim-hizzletimslizzlelim*, as track and train constantly met and parted, adjusted and reacted to each other's momentum. All together, these sounds coalesced perfectly into the sound of an approaching train, perhaps one of a dozen elemental sounds in this world.

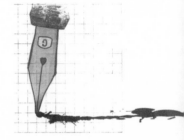

▶ *The Scratch of the Nib*

Other elemental sounds: thunder; the *tick tick tick* of the gas stove lighter; the squeak and release of the third-to-last step on the front stairs; laughter (well, not all laughter, but I guess I am thinking of Gracie's laughter, when she got into one of her giggling frenzies and her body clenched up and she became so young again); the couloir winds sweeping the hay fields, particularly in the fall, when the leaves made that soft tickling noise across the feathery seed clusters of the grasses; gunshots; the scratch of a Gillot's nib on fresh paper.

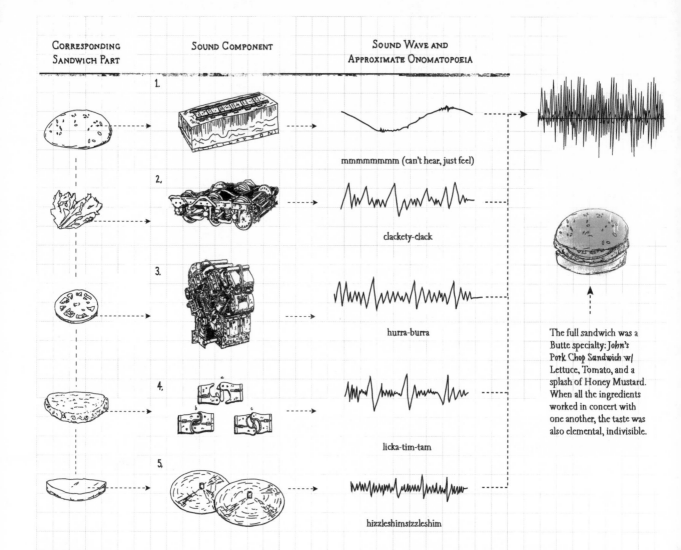

CORRESPONDING SANDWICH PART	SOUND COMPONENT	SOUND WAVE AND APPROXIMATE ONOMATOPOEIA

1.

mmmmmmmm (can't hear, just feel)

2.

clackety-clack

3.

hurra-burra

4.

licka-tim-tam

5.

hizzleshimsizzleshim

The full sandwich was a Butte specialty: John's Pork Chop Sandwich w/ Lettuce, Tomato, and a splash of Honey Mustard. When all the ingredients worked in concert with one another, the taste was also elemental, indivisible.

Freight Train as Sound Sandwich
from Notebook G101

And then I saw it: the white-hot eye of the locomotive emerging from the mist, charging toward me. That single lamp knifed open the fog and the last vestiges of dawn, ignoring the valley through which it bounded like an animal seeing only what it sees. The train hit a bend in the tracks, and suddenly I could see the endless string of freight cars behind the mustard-colored locomotive—their strange, boxlike serpentinism stretching back up the basin for as far as a boy my size could see without the benefits of magnification.

I ducked back down into the little gully next to the tracks, breathing hard. I realized that this was the first real illegal thing that I had ever done in my life.

I was all a-tingle. You could learn a lot about the integrity of your moral fiber in how you reacted to doing something naughty, and so as I was in the ditch feeling washes of adrenaline pumping through my arm sockets and out into my fingers, I was also observing myself and my reactions, as though tracking the scene through a camera perched sixteen feet above me. --►

```
EXT. TRAIN TRACKS-MORNING

WS of swiftly approach-
ing train. ECU of hand
gripping suitcase. ECU of
thin line of DROOL drip-
ping from the corner of
mouth. Zoom out slowly to
reveal reckless, wild-
eyed outlaw: T. S. SPIV-
ET. BASS and CELLOS play
three descending notes
to indicate COLLECTIVE
DREAD.
```

But there was no drool and no collective dread, because my uncanny dislocution of perspective was interrupted by my realization that the train was still approaching very swiftly, and I was suddenly gripped with the terrifying notion that it would not stop. I heard no screeching brakes, no hissing steam as I had imagined, just that slow *chugga chugga* and the cymbals rubbing against each other and the rummaging of the logs and plywood and coal and corn in all those gondolas and tank cars. And as the train approached, not more than twenty yards away now, I cursed myself for not carefully planning this out for weeks, for not scouting out the length of the train, not recording exactly how long it would take for these freighters to stop. I realized they probably had a lot of momentum behind them and they couldn't just stop on a dime, let alone to a double-red FULL STOP signal light that had probably never turned red in the whole history of the railroad.

The locomotive reached my spot in the junipers and then was past me before I could even blink. The wall of air hit me violently, rattling the loose flesh of my cheeks. My world collapsed into the sounds and sights of the freighter. What before had been a rumble that could be unpacked into its sonic particulars now was just overwhelming: pebbles and dust and grime flew into my eyes and the pounding of the wheels dismantled my ear drums and everything was rushing forward and I could feel my throat constrict. How could this gigantic behemoth of steel and smelly oiled parts *ever* stop, let alone right now? It seemed bound for eternal motion.

I recalled Newton's first law of motion, the Law of Inertia: "An object in motion tends to stay in motion until a force acts upon it."

Was my Sharpie trick enough of a force to act upon this creature? Faced with the pounding tonnage of the freight cars firing past me, I had to admit the answer was a firm *no*.

As the train continued to rush past me, I stared at those churning, rust-colored wheels, willing them to stop. Boxcars, gondolas, hoppers, tankers, flatbeds. It went on forever. The wind from the cars blew over me, and the air was filled with the smells of soot, engine grease, and strangely, maple syrup.

"Well, we tried," I said to my suitcase and its contents.

And it was just at that point that the chugging began to subside and I watched in awe as the half-mile of train gradually decelerated. The metal-on-metal screech got suddenly louder as the clanking began to ease, and then, ever so slowly, the maple syrup train came to a lilting, somewhat graceless stop, with a few final heaves from a hidden valve and chattering from the couplings before the metallic beast was finally still, breathing hard. I looked up: in front of me was a massive platform car. For a second, I was frozen with the disbelief that I had actually caused the train to stop, that a single red Sharpie had flagged down this mighty whale of a thing. The train sat there impatiently, the faint hiss of the car's air brakes just audible as it lay still and waiting with the wide open valley around us.

There would be trouble soon enough: the driver would be calling headquarters wondering what the hell was going on with a full stop signal

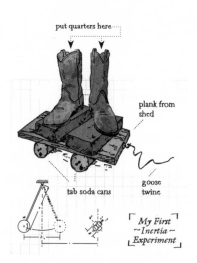

put quarters here

plank from shed

tab soda cans

goose twine

My First ~Inertia~ Experiment

My First Inertia Experiment **from Notebook G7**

It was a disaster. "Inertia is more complicated than it first appears," Dr. Yorn once said. Dr. Yorn is a very smart man.

and no approach warning from farther up the line; my little red-pen-on-white-signal trick would quickly be discovered and they would probably be piping mad, looking all over the place for a little mischief worker such as myself.

I spat into the junipers and made a little whistle through the gap in my two front teeth. This was meant to be a sort of starting gun. I then kicked into action, hauling my suitcase out from the clutches of the red wagon, which made a last-ditch effort to hold on to the bag, as if the two were old friends unable to part at the train platform.

"Bye, Layton!" I said to the wagon, and then huffed my suitcase out of the junipers and up the raised embankment of ballast. The sun-washed greenish-blue stones made little rustling noises beneath my sneakers. The noise of my feet sounded so loud compared to the relative quiet of the stopped train that I felt for sure it would give away my position.

Trying to be a carefree outlaw, I abandoned my original idea of getting into a boxcar. I figured that the platform car stopped right in front of me would have to do, at least temporarily, until I could find better accommodation. I just didn't have time to scope out each car for a suitable living quarters. But approaching the flatcar, I was suddenly faced with the four-foot height of the car's platform and the fact that my own height was just over four feet eight inches. Without thinking, I hefted my suitcase over my head, again exhibiting a display of herculean coordination and strength that shocked me even as I was doing the hoisting. I effortlessly slid the bag onto the flatbed of the car.

Alas, when I tried to do a version of a pull-up to bring my own body onto the platform (damn you, Presidential Fitness!), this legendary strength had all but abandoned me. I made a panicked kind of noise that I imagined a deer might make in the moments just before it knew it was about to be shot. - ➤

Something like:

"WEE TO WEE"

What to do with this frail cartographer's frame? I crouched on the wooden railroad tie, panting, the metal tracks on either side of me. The massive cars rose up in front and behind. From my low vantage point, I could see through the tunnel formed by all the undercarriages of the cars in front of me.

A terrible whistle, long, hard, and piercing, came from somewhere up that endless tunnel of undercarriages. The whistle sounded again. The air brakes on the platform car hissed and released. Then, with a slight jolt, the coupling above me went tense, and the carriages started to slowly roll forward.

I would be killed.

Desperately, I grasped the coupling device above my head. This was probably the worst thing to grasp, what with all the moving parts and places for my fingers to get crushed. It was greasy and slippery, but there were plenty of knobs and joints to grab on to. I kept imagining my fingers getting pulverized. Turned wide and flat like in the cartoons. *Not my fingers!* I pleaded to the coupling from below. *They are so complicated to put back together.*

I clung to the underside of the coupling as the train began to roll with increasing momentum. My feet were jogging backward against the railroad ties, and then I hoisted them up to wrap around the coupling, much as a monkey clings to the underbelly of its mother as she negotiates her way through the branches of a tall tree: needless to say, I held on for dear life. At one point I looked down, and the railroad ties were already a blur beneath me. My hands were covered in sweat and grease. I knew I was going to fall, and I played this fall over and over again through the little projector in my head, but even while accepting that I would fall to certain dismemberment, I was still fighting gravity: first one leg and then

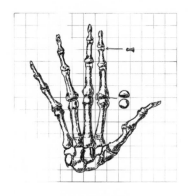

Dr. Clair's Metacarpals ◄----------
from Notebook G34

(I wanted to draw Father's hands and his bum pinky, but I did not know how to approach him for such a study.)

the other, up and over, and bit by bit, as the train gathered more and more speed and the ground became a blurry soup of wood and rail and rock, I slowly managed to claw my way an inch at a time up and then around the greasy coupling. I hoisted; I puffed; I sweated, and then I was up—straddling the coupling as if it were a saddle.

Triumph. It was the first courageous thing I had ever done in my life.

Filthy, I jumped to the platform of the car and fell on top of my suitcase. And breathed. My fingers were black with grease and throbbing with the lingering echoes of adrenaline. I suddenly wished Layton were there to share the feeling with me. He would have loved this adventure.

Lying with my cheek on the suitcase, I looked up and was greeted by the most astounding of sights. For an instant, I was extremely confused. Though I was on a train, I was staring head on at a brand spankin' new Winnebago. At first, I couldn't make the leap in categories of transportation and thought momentarily that I had mistakenly climbed onto a road or a ferry or into a parking garage, but then reason came ambling back to me. The train was transporting Winnebagos! And top-end models by the look of it. It was the last thing I expected to see on a freighter like this. Somehow, I had been prepared for basic, dirty commodities: wood, coal, corn, syrup—not this wondrous creature, this technological thoroughbred. And let me tell you: there is nothing quite like staring down the barrel of a modern-day luxury RV.

I slowly circumvented the specimen. THE COWBOY CONDO, it declared in brazen bronze lettering across the side. Behind this, depicted in soft, airbrushed earth tones, the sun set over a gleaming high-country ranch, not unlike the one I had just fled from. In the foreground, a cowboy reared his horse, his hand thrown skyward, his fingers splayed open in a reluctant gesture of conquest.

The Four Components of Adventure
by Layton & T. S. Spivet, ages 8 & 10, respectively. Now buried beneath the old oak tree along with my Last Will & Testament.

PART II: THE CROSSING

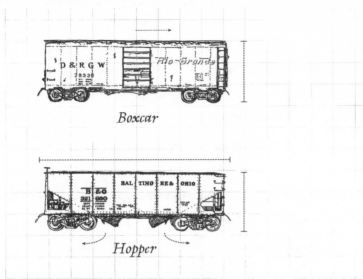

Boxcar

Tank car

Hopper

Gondola

CHAPTER 5

Most of my knowledge concerning hoboing came from second grade, when Miss Ladle read us *Hanky the Hobo*, a little yarn about a charismatic guy with curly brown hair who lived in California and soon found himself down and out. And so what did he do? He hopped a freight train, of course, and proceeded to have all kinds of delicious railroad adventures.

Though no saying was ever laminated and placed on the wall (in school, one must laminate all truisms), my classmates and I quickly created a simple equation in our heads.

In fact, we were so impressed with Hanky that we decided to do a class project on hoboing. In retrospect, it seemed kind of strange that Miss Ladle went along with this proposition, but perhaps she was from that school of teaching where you were supposed to encourage the children's interests at all costs, even if this meant doing a unit on how to break the law.

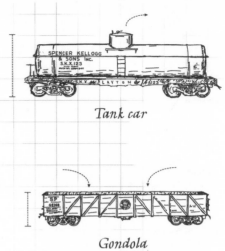

DOWN ON YOUR LUCK?

RIDE THE RAILS!

NOTHING DOING HERE

GET OUT OF HERE!

IT'S SAFE TO SLEEP
IN THE BARN

TELL A HARD LUCK STORY,
YOU WILL GET FOOD

VERY DANGEROUS MAN
LIVES HERE

Hobo Signs
from Notebook G88

When Layton saw the "Very Dangerous Man" sign, he immediately declared that he wanted the symbol tattooed on his wrist. Father did not even honor this request with a response and so Layton asked that I instead just draw the symbol onto his skin with one of my Sharpies. I began to look forward to our morning ritual, when I would retrace the faded dot-inside-rectangle onto his wrist before school. And then one morning Layton simply announced that he was finished with my services. Over the next couple of days I watched as the rectangle slowly faded to nothing.

Our class learned that during the Depression, when work was hard to come by and countless numbers of people hit the rails, hobos would simply hang around the train yards in droves. Sometimes there would be a whole gaggle of hobos in a single boxcar, maybe a mattress or two, and then they would have a *hobo party* (one group in our class staged a hobo party for their project) and they would sing songs and cook eggs and watch the countryside go by. To communicate with other drifters up and down the line, hobos would often leave *hobo signs* on depot walls or fences to indicate safe havens or dangerous spots. We learned that the train yard worker was usually a hobo's friend, revealing valuable information about where and when trains were leaving. The person you had to watch out for was the rail yard cop, or *the bull*, as they were called by the hobos. These were ex-coppers who had been discharged for their brutality, and many of them enjoyed smoking out the rail drifters and giving them a thwacking they wouldn't soon forget. As in: they killed them. (Salmon, the least well behaved but also the smartest boy in our class, did a presentation on rail yard bulls in which he started beating another kid, Olio, for a good thirty seconds before Miss Ladle intervened.)

In the story *Hanky the Hobo*, Hanky had a very exciting life running from the bulls and falling out of trains and such. And then one day while he was busy hoboing, Hanky stumbled upon a suitcase by the side of the tracks. And when he opened this suitcase, he found that it was filled with ten thousand dollars in cash.

"Ba-wing!" Salmon said from the back of our storybook nook. We did not know what that meant, but we liked it, so we laughed.

Miss Ladle continued reading: "But instead of keeping it, Hanky gave the suitcase back to its rightful owners, choosing to return to his transient life on the rails rather than spending money that was not his."

We waited for another line, but that seemed to be it. Miss Ladle closed the book carefully, like it was the top to a tarantula cage.

"So what's the moral of this story?" Miss Ladle asked us.

We all looked at her blankly.

"That *honesty* is always the best policy," she said slowly, putting emphasis on the word *honesty* as if it were a foreign word.

Everyone nodded in agreement. Everyone except Salmon, that is, who said, "But he still ended up poor."

Miss Ladle looked at Salmon. She wiped imaginary dust from the book's cover.

"Well, some poor people are honest," she said. "And happy."

Which was the exact wrong thing to say, because without ever vocalizing it or perhaps even quite realizing it, we lost a little respect for her in that moment. It was clear she had no idea what she was talking about. And this shouldn't come as any surprise, as this was the same teacher who allowed us to do an entire unit on hoboing. But my question was: where did our respect go? Did a child's respect just evaporate, or, like in the Law of Thermodynamics, could respect neither be created nor destroyed, merely transferred? Perhaps we rechanneled our respect that day onto Salmon, the cowlicked rebel who mixed his milk with his orange juice at snack time, who had challenged the system in that storybook nook, and revealed to us eager onlookers that adults could be just as stupid as kids. We respected *him*. At least until he was arrested several years later for pushing Lila off the edge of Melrose Canyon and the judge sent him up to Garrison XX Ranch for Delinquents.

As the train got cooking again—I didn't have my instruments out, but it was at least 50 or 60 MPH by the feel of things—I watched the

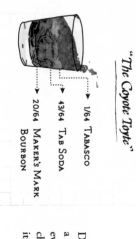

"The Coyote Toyte"

1/64 Tabasco

43/64 Tab Soda

20/64 Maker's Mark Bourbon

How to Make a Coyote Toyte
from Notebook B55

Doretta always added the Tabasco last, with a flourish, saying "And that's the good stuff" every time. It was the kind of repetitive childhood memory I came to dread, not for its content but for its inevitability.

How beautiful those purple mountains were! But they were beautiful because all the lodgepole pines were dying or dead due to an infestation of mountain pine beetles (*Dendroctonus ponderosae*).

Dendroctonus ponderosae
from Notebook R5

scenery unfold past me. I had taken this I-15 corridor many times down to Melrose to visit Doretta Hasting, a half-aunt of my father's. She was weird: she collected unexploded missiles from World War II and had a predilection for a special drink of hers called the Coyote Toyte, which contained, as far as I could surmise, Tab soda, Maker's Mark, and a dash of Tabasco. We never stayed for long on our visits, as Father always grew uncomfortable after only a little bit of chitchat. This was fine with me, for Doretta had a habit of running her hands over my face, and her palms smelled of mouse poop and moisturizer. Past her house, further down I-15, I had attended the Dillon rodeo perhaps a half a dozen times with my father, although I hadn't been since Layton had died.

As we rode south, the day opened up. It was cold with all that wind running through the flatbed, even with an extra sweater on, and so I was grateful when the first rays of direct sunlight crawled down the saddle between Tweedy and Torrey mountains, into the high grazing fields and then across the flats, warming the land as it went. I watched the line of sunlight gradually edge its way across the valley. Out of the shadows now, the mountains seemed to stretch and yawn, their grey faces turning to a deep Douglas fir green and then, as the morning pushed on, easing out into the familiar soft-eggplant hashwork of distant timber.

The wind shifted and I could smell the mud of the Big Hole, the deep, muckraking notes of silt and pollywogs and moss-covered rocks rubbed by the steady knuckles of that circuitous current. The train let out a whistle and I felt like it was my whistle. Now and then that same maple syrup smell reared up from somewhere ahead, and then always there was the smell of the train itself, the spiralic fumes of oil and grease and metal grinding and pulling and doing its work. It was a funny mixture of smells, but after a while, as always happens, this landscape of olfaction gently faded back into the canvas of perception and I ceased noticing it at all.

Suddenly I was hungry again. All the effort I had expended monkeying up signaling poles and hanging off railroad couplings had caught up with me, not to mention the multiple washes of adrenaline, which had left my diminutive biceps in a rubbery state of high alert.

Still fearful of opening my bag and risking an explosion of its contents, I again stuck my hand in that tiny hole that I had made with my Leatherman (Cartographer's Edition) and rooted around for a minute or two before locating my provisions bag and carefully snaking it out again.

I laid out all of my food. My heart sank. There was just not that much of it. If I were a hero, a cowboy, I would be able to last three weeks on this meager pile of granola bars and fruit that was before me. But I was not a cowboy. I was a little boy with a hyperactive metabolism. When I was hungry, my brain slowly began to shut down one section at a time: first I lost my mastery of social niceties, then I lost my ability to multiply, then I lost my capacity to speak in complete sentences, and so on. When Gracie rang the dinner bell, you could often find me gently rocking back and forth out on the back porch, famished and delusional, emitting little chickadee noises.

I combated this Alzheimer's-like meltdown by constantly grazing. I had a stash of Cheerios in every pocket of every piece of clothing I owned, which often led to a mess in the laundry room. Dr. Clair made me do a Cheerios check before I put an item into the washer.

Now, staring at this paltry amount of food, I was faced with a real problem of conservation. Did I go the careful route and only eat a little now, not satiating my hunger, but merely eating enough so I could still

What to do about all the pine beetles was a hotly contested issue in local politics and it was probably the only beetle that normal people were actually talking about. What was strange was that Dr. Clair had actually written her dissertation about pine beetle control in Montana, and was well on her way to being a scientific hero when she met Father at that Wyoming square dance. Once they married, something inexplicable changed inside her; she gave up her potentially useful career for the futile tiger monk beetle search.

Each spring, as new swaths of pine began turning their deathly burgundy, I fantasized about having a mother who was actually helping to fight this plague and change the world. I wanted people to drive by Crazy Swede Creek Road and point to our ranch house up in the hills.

"That's where the pine beetle lady lives," they would say. "She saved Montana."

I once worked up the courage to ask her why she no longer studied the pine beetle problem.

Dr. Clair responded by saying, "Who says that the pine beetles are a problem? They are doing very well for themselves."

"But there will be no forests left!" I said.

"No pine forests left," she corrected. "I never liked the pine. So drippy. So sticky. Good riddance, I say. Some things are just meant to die."

count to ten and point north? This seemed wise, especially considering the possibility that this freighter could keep chugging on until it got to its destination—whether this be Chicago, Amarillo, or Argentina.

Or…I could also just stuff myself. But this would mean banking on the hope that at some point a hobo concession man would come down the line of cars selling hot dogs and sizzling fajitas to all the drifters in that row.

After a moment's consideration, I selected a single granola bar—cranberry apple with mixed nuts—and reluctantly pushed the rest of my supplies (*Oh, but those carrot sticks looked so fluorescent and tasty!*) back through the little hole into my suitcase.

Munching as slowly as I could manage, allowing each piece of granola to drift around in my mouth, I sat with my back against the wheel well of the Cowboy Condo and tried to get used to this new life.

"I'm a drifter," I said in a deep Johnny Cash voice. It sounded ridiculous.

"Drift-*er*. Driffer. D'ifter," I tried. Nothing worked.

The mountains slowly began to recede from the river flats, the valley cleaving open into the great horseshoe basin of the Jefferson. In every direction, the land fled and fled and fled until it hit up against a cereal bowl of mountains that surrounded the valley: the fissured rise of the Ruby Range to the southeast, the ragtag assemblage of the Blacktails in the far distance, and, behind us, the majestic Pioneers, now fading as we hit a bend in the tracks.

To my left, distant and alone on the plain, was the great Beaverhead Rock, which had saved Lewis and Clark's expedition: on an uncommonly cold August morning, Sacagawea had recognized the outcrop as a sign that her people's summer retreat was nearby. At that point the explorers'

The Beaverhead Rock
from Notebook G101

The rock was so named because it kind of looked—if you squinted your eyes from just the right direction—like the head of a beaver. It had always looked more like a breaching whale to me in pictures, but perhaps the Shoshone, who originally named the landmark, were not aware of the existence of whales and were thus limited to woodland creatures when creating their analogies.

expedition was short on supplies and had no access to fresh horses. Their boats would be useless in the mountains—mountains that would reveal themselves to be much more extensive than Lewis and Clark had originally anticipated. Their original view saw a northwest water passage straight to the Pacific Ocean, and when this became clearly impossible, they amended their vision to a single strip of mountains that still could be easily traversed in a day or two. Like nearly all great journeys, Lewis and Clark's expedition came down to a series of hinge points in which luck and guile each played an equal part. What if they had attempted to weather the divide on their own, without the help of the Shoshones? What if Sacagawea had not spotted this landmark, grabbing Captain Clark's sleeve with those small rough hands of hers and pointing?…

I looked out through the slots of the flatbed at the rock, slowly turning as the train plunged across the landscape. I smiled. It was the same rock. Much had changed: the Iron Horse had arrived; the Shoshone were gone; cars, Sno-Cones, airplanes, GPS devices, rock 'n roll, McDonald's were all now present in the valley, but this rock was the same, as unblinking and vaguely beaverish as ever before.

Something about the geological continuity of Beaverhead Rock, which overlooked this valley just as it did when Sacagawea tugged on Captain Clark's sleeve, inherently bound me to that expedition. Headed our separate ways, we both journeyed past this stationary marker, like those pixelated rocks your wagon would periodically pass in the Oregon Trail game. The difference, perhaps, was that they had been free to travel wherever they wished, to choose any path over the continental divide and beyond, to the Pacific. Right now, bound to these rails, I had no choice as to my route; I followed the path laid out for me. On the other hand, perhaps I was just clinging to this notion of predeterminism for comfort—perhaps the route was not already laid out before me, and I was headed into just as much of an unknown as that expedition two hundred years before.

The day warmed up. The wind was stronger out in the basin, whipping up across the dry grasslands, swirling around the train, ducking through the slats. Against my back, I could feel the Winnebago rock gently back and forth, even though it was chained down to the bed of the flatcar. There was comfort in that rocking. I rocked with it. We were traveling together, the Cowboy Condo and I—we were partners.

"How you doing?" I called out to it.

"Fine," it said back to me. "I'm glad you're here."

"Yeah," I said. "I'm glad you're here too."

I took out my Leica M1, licked my fingers as my father did, and removed the lens cap. I snapped some pictures of the Beaverhead Rock. I tried to take a couple of self-portraits with me in the foreground using the camera's self-timer—with varying degrees of success. And then I took some candid shots of the Cowboy Condo too, and my feet, and the suitcase, and some artistic shots of the grease-covered couplings. I burned through two rolls in ten minutes. As soon as I got to Washington, I would make a scrapbook of my trip across America. I could edit out the bad ones later. I hated when people just put all of their photos into an album without doing a little culling first. Dr. Clair was one of these people, which was strange, because she was so particular with beetle anatomy, yet her family photo albums were long rambling affairs that occasionally included photos of strangers' children.

We went under I-15 through a tunnel and suddenly the highway was parallel to my side. Pickups rushed past. Eighteen-wheelers. RVs not too different from the one against my back. I noticed that a silver minivan had pulled up alongside the train, about even with me. Like the rest of the cars, they seemed to be going slightly faster than our train, but then their speed leveled off and we were neck and neck, as though some invisible string connected us.

In the front seat, a large bald man drove next to a lady with a magenta flowered dress and those big disk earrings. It looked like they were married. Not just because there were three girls in the backseat (there were), but because you could tell when two people are used to sitting silently next to each other for long periods of time. In the backseat, the three girls seemed to be playing some sort of elaborate cat's cradle game. One of the girls (the oldest, most likely) was very intently placing her fingers in the center of the spiderweb, concentrating on pinching two x's.

I was really enjoying watching this scene of domesticity and sibling cooperation in the back of the minivan. It was better than television. It was like peeking into a world that had always been but that I would only be privy to for a couple of seconds, like passing a conversation on the street in which you only heard one line of dialogue, but it was an extremely choice line of dialogue, like: "And ever since that night, my mother's had a thing for submarines."

Then all hell broke loose. One of the younger sisters lost her grip on the string or something equally as tragic, because the oldest threw up her hands and then pushed the girl into the window. That started her crying and then the bald father turned around in his big aviators and started hollering to them in the backseat. The mother turned around but didn't say anything. The minivan slowed down. I lost the scene.

When they finally caught up again, the minivan was really moving. I jumped up from my seat on the wheel well, and, abandoning all caution, stuck my head out through the slats to get a better look. Each girl had retreated to a corner of the van. The younger one, who had screwed up

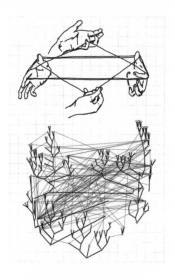

Gracie & Me Play Cat's Cradle During the Blizzard from Notebook B61

(With all possible moves mapped out from this starting position)

the cat's cradle game, was staring out the window in my direction, clearly pouting, tears glinting on her cheeks.

As the van moved past, I waved. She must have seen the motion, because she looked up, confused, her eyes searching. I waved again. Her face lit up. I felt like a superhero. Her mouth literally fell open and she pressed her face to the glass, then turned and yelled something to the rest of the car—I could almost hear it now, but by that point the minivan had already moved too far ahead. I did not see it again.

Then the train heaved and the sound of the wheels shifted and we gradually began to slow. We were coming into Dillon. I decided that the best thing I could do was get out of sight, as quickly as possible. But where to hide? Remembering that Dr. Clair had once told me: "Don't get too fancy"—advice I am not sure that she herself heeded—I went to the most obvious place I could find: I tried the driver's side door of the Winnebago right above my head.

Of course it was locked. Who would leave it unlocked?

The train came to a hissing, abrupt halt. I stumbled and fell. I suddenly felt very exposed up on this flatbed. The movement of the train had provided me security, but with it now standing still, I was a sitting duck.

Up ahead, through the slats, I could see the train yard and an old-fashioned depot. Men were coming out to the train to talk with the engine driver; I could hear them yelling something. Panic began to rise up in me. This had been a terrible idea. I should just abandon the train altogether and find some other means of transport.

Maybe I could get in the trunk of the Winnebago?

"Winnebagos don't have trunks," I said to myself. "Only a child would think that."

Dillon, the County Seat from Notebook G54

Dillon was a nowhere kind of town—the kind of town whose most notable attribute was that it was the county seat of Beaverhead County. Anytime you used the term *county seat* in a boastful way more than twice a week, you knew there was not that much to boast about. Of course, Father would have argued otherwise. For him, the Dillon rodeo was the Broadway of all man-and-beast competitions. And so I had come to regard the town as a magical place when I was younger, until I was able to finally look at a map and see Dillon for what it really was.

I ran around the vehicle, looking for something, anything: a sidecar, a canoe, a tent—any kind of recreational accessory that could temporarily conceal me from the rail yard bull with his stick and his monocle and his nose for blood.

Nothing. Didn't these things come loaded with special options?

The voices up the line were louder and I peeked over the edge and saw two men with clipboards walking down the train toward me. One of them was uniformed and he was huge, almost a foot taller than the other man. He looked like he belonged in a circus.

Great, I thought to myself. *They hire giants now. Okay. Be calm. Wait for exactly the right moment, then kick him in the gonads and run. Run to a gas station and pretend your family left you behind on a road trip. Get some Kool-Aid and dye your hair. Get some makeup and change your complexion. Buy a top hat. Speak in an Italian accent. Learn to juggle.*

The men were three cars away. I could hear the chop of their voices and the sound of crunching gravel.

"What should I do?" I whispered to the Winnebago.

"Call me Valero," the Winnebago whispered back.

"Valero?"

"Yes, Valero."

"Okay, Valero, what the heck should I do?" I hissed.

"Easy," Valero said. "Don't panic. A cowboy never panics, even when the chips are down."

"I'm not a cowboy," I whispered. "Do I look like a cowboy?"

"A little," Valero said. "You don't have the hat, but you're dirty like a cowboy and you have that hungry look in your eye. You can't fake that look, you know."

"Really?" I said.

The voices of the men now came into earshot. They must be at the next car.

All right, what would a cowboy do? Desperately, in a last ditch effort, I tried the passenger side door of the Winnebago. At first it seemed locked too, but then I heard the latch release and the door swung open cleanly. I exhaled, a short puff of an exhale. Who had left this open?

Whoever you were, thank you, Mr. Factory Worker. Gracias and adíos.

As quietly as I could, I picked up my heavy suitcase, and lugged it through the yawning portal of the Winnebago, closing the hatch behind me slowly slowly slowly. When the door finally clicked shut it sounded much too loud: the scene in the movie where the villain's eyes leapt toward the hiding place of the hero. I was sure to be caught. I did not take the time to bask in the luxury of the Winnebago's interior that now surrounded me. I ran past the canary-colored couch and made a beeline for the bathroom in the back, next to the mirrored bedroom with the king-size bed featuring a Technicolor rendition of the Tetons on its spread.

BATHROOM

=

SAFETY

I closed the bathroom door behind me. Perhaps I was merely following another age-old adage that you learned as a kid.

In the claustrophobic world of the bathroom, I tried not to breathe. This is difficult when you are breathing hard. Even though their voices were muffled through the walls of the Winnebago, I could hear the men coming closer. Then they stopped. Someone leapt onto the platform of the flatbed. A drop of sweat rolled down the center of my forehead, along the bridge of my nose, and out onto its tip, where it paused like a ladybug contemplating flight. I could see the droplet if I went cross-eyed, and for some reason, in my delusional, adrenaline-pumped state, I found myself believing that if the drop fell to the ground, the giant rail yard bull would hear its *kerplink* and instantly know my location.

The platform creaked as the man walked around the Winnebago to the passenger side. Just then, I noticed that the bathroom door had what looked to be a peephole. In that moment of self-induced cross-eyed asphyxiation, I did not go through the usual line of questioning as to why a bathroom would have a peephole in it and what kind of disturbing domestic scenes could play out from the inclusion of such an option—rather, I was concentrating on that little blip of sweat on the end of my nose and on the difficulty of being a mammal and not breathing. I merely thought, *Oh good, there is a peephole so I can see if the people who want to kill me are going to kill me.*

I put my eye up to the hole. The drop of sweat fell to the floor. I almost gasped, but not because of the droplet's descent. It was what I saw through the peephole: a huge railroad cop—and I mean *huge!* Tall *and* fat. His face was pressed up against the tinted glass of the Winnebago's side windows. He cupped his hands above his eyes in order to see inside. And on the floor, directly in front of his huge head with those gorilla palms of his, was my overstuffed suitcase.

The bull stayed at the glass for a minute more. At one point he wiped the glass with one of those palms. His hands were enormous! I imagined a tiny sparrow perched on his fingers.

The Giant & the Sparrow
from Notebook G101

After wiping the glass down with his hand, the bull peered in again. I waited for him to spot the suitcase, waited for the change in his expression: *What's this? Hey, you'd better come up here…*

What was taking him so long? Was he a narcoleptic? Was he considering buying one of these for his gigantic wife, calculating the dimensions? Either spot the suitcase and come kill me or get on with it! But don't stall the action like this! After what seemed like an eternity, he finally pulled his massive frame away from the window and disappeared from my view.

"Valero," I whispered. "Are you there?"

"I am here."

"That was a close one, huh?"

"Yes, I feared for you. But you are a skillful terrorist."

"Terrorist?" I said. But I did not feel like getting into a debate with a Winnebago about the definition of terrorism. If he thought I was a rogue, fine.

The longer we were stopped in little old Dillon, the more I thought that perhaps they were not going to let the train leave the station without finding the culprit who had vandalized their signal. On the other hand, maybe it just took that monstrosity of a man a long time to check every car with the engineer guy. Just when I was considering the suddenly attractive option of getting off the train, walking to town, getting a milk shake and then hiring a cab to take me back home, I heard the air brakes release and felt the train jolt forward.

"You hear that, Valero?" I said. "We're on the move again! Washington, D.C., here we come!"

I stayed in the bathroom, counting to 304. This seemed like a good, safe number.

I emerged from the bathroom into the plush elegance of the Cowboy Condo. For the first time, I was able to soak in my new digs. A bowl of plastic bananas sat on the fold-up dining room table. All the TVs had large translucent plastic stickers on their screens depicting a cartoon cowboy on horseback against a Monument Valley–type of landscape. A big dialogue bubble over his head read "It's an American Winnebago!"

The interior of the Cowboy Condo smelled of that new car smell mixed with a slightly sweet and alkaline cherry cleaner, as though the janitorial staff had been a little too generous with their application of the

---

Why 304? ◄

In truth, I was not sure why this number seemed reasonable to me. Why 304 and not just 300? We create informal measurements like this in our heads all the time, so much so that some of them had become popular and surprisingly steadfast rules of thumb: the 3-Second Rule for the amount of time food could lie on the ground and still be deemed edible; or the 10-Minute Rule for the amount of time a teacher was allowed to be late to class before you could walk out and have recess. (This only happened once, with Mrs. Barstank, but she was rumored to be an alcoholic and was fired a month into the school year, much to our dismay.)

Father said that if a horse couldn't be broken in the first two weeks, then he couldn't be broken at all. I wondered if my mother had some length of time in the back of her mind about how long she should search for the tiger monk beetle. Twenty-nine years? One year for every bone in the human skull? One year for every letter in the Finnish alphabet, the language my ancestors had abandoned for the American West? Or had she set no informal time period? Would she search until she could search no longer? I just wish there was something I could say or do that would bring an end to her perquisition and prompt her to join the world of useful science again.

fluids. Standing on the polyester rug, taking in my surroundings, I was struck with a sense of the uncanny: there was something familiar and safe about the room, yet something also incredibly foreign and constructed. It felt like stepping into the kitschy doilied living room of a strange relative I had heard about but never met before.

"Well, Valero, this is home. Nice place." I tried to be sincere. I didn't want to offend.

Valero did not answer me.

The train pushed onward. After a while, the mountains narrowed into a steep-cliffed canyon and the railroad tracks climbed the tight slot next to the Beaverhead River. Our pace slowed and the grinding noises got louder as the grade increased. I looked out the windows of the Winnebago, trying to see the top of the mountains on either side.

And still we pushed up and up. A red-tailed hawk swooped down into the rippling rapids of the river. It was gone for a full two seconds, completely submerged in the cold mountain water. I wondered how it felt beneath the surface, a creature trained for the air but now surrounded by liquid. Did he feel like a clumsy visitor as I did when I was underwater, staring at the minnows that lurked like flecks of light on our pond's bottom? And then the hawk was already tearing back up into the air, droplets exploding off its pumping wings. There was a tiny silver fish in its beak. A perfect slip of a thing. The bird circled once and I strained to watch it move against the cliffs of the canyon, but it was already gone.

Without knowing why, I began to cry. I sat on the canary-colored couch in the sterile Winnebago propelled by a freight train and sniffled away. There was no sobbing, nothing girly like that, just this slow release of something small and sad lying at the bottom of my rib cage, caught between my squishy organs. I sat there and it came out. It was as if I were letting out the stuffy air from a room that had been kept locked shut for a long time.

Eventually, the grade outside leveled out. The view opened up to the vast, undulatory expanse of the Bitterroots—such old, contrary mountains, like a gathering of ornery uncles who smoked cigars and recounted quasi-believable stories of rickets and wartime rationing over long, drawn-out games of poker. The Bitterroots were stubborn, but they were oh so sublime in their stubbornness, and they flowed past the window like the backs of whales in slow motion. I really wished the Shoshone had known about whales. They would have named everything after them: Whale Mountain #1, Small Whale Hill, the Whale Saddle.

We crested the pass, and I felt as if I were on the top of a giant roller coaster waiting for the great pitch downward.

I tentatively stuck my head out the door of the Winnebago. Again I was greeted by the terrific clatter of the train. Inside it was muffled, but out here I was confronted with the clanking gears and the moving and jolting of all those little mechanical parts that pushed the train onward. Always the moaning and screeching of the metal, whining, *must we? must we? must we?* like a thousand tiny birds racked by insufferable pain.

The air that rushed across my forehead was cold and thin. I could smell the clean, clear scent of the Douglas fir forests that swept upward from the tracks. This was the high country. Open country.

The significance of our cresting dawned on me as the train seemed to gather its breath at the top of the pass.

"Valero!" I said. "It's the divide! We're passing over the divide!"

This divide was much more dramatic than the kinder, gentler slopes near the Coppertop. This was Monida Pass; this was the kind of place that had seen a lot of hot action, at least geologically speaking. Great batho-

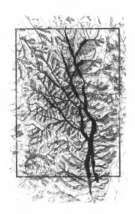

Drainage Patterns in the ◄ - - - - - - - - -
Stubborn Bitterroots
from Notebook G12

Every mountain range I have ever met has had its own mood and demeanor.

lithic slabs rising up and splitting apart over millions and millions of years, continental plates heaving and hoeing, beds of indignant magma bubbling beneath the bedrock, molding the stunning topography of western Montana. *Thank you, magma,* I thought.

I breathed in the air and almost missed a sign as the train chugged past.

I smiled. If the continental divide was the ultimate boundary between the West and the East, perhaps only now was I officially entering the West. Our ranch was just south of where the continental divide looped back west to include the great thumbprint of the Big Hole Basin in its Atlantic drainage. This meant the Coppertop was actually located just east of that symbolic dividing line. Which meant....

Father, we are Easterners! I wanted to shout out. *Pass over some of that New England clam chowder! Did you hear that, Layton? You would've been an Eastern cowboy! Our ancestors never actually made it to the true West!*

But at least here, at the jack-pined apex of this pass, the Rockies wide open all around us, two boundaries—one physical, one political—merged into one. And for me, the continental divide had always had a quiet significance of division that could not be argued with. Perhaps it did separate the true *Far West* from simply *the West.* It seemed symbolically appropriate: before I could go East, I needed to pass through the Far West.

I tried to take my camera out of my bag and snap a picture of the continental divide sign for my scrapbook, but, as with most pictures, the image was gone before I could get ready for it. I feared that my scrapbook would only be populated by shots taken just after the fact. How many snapshots in the world were actually just-after shots, the moment that elicited the shooter to press the button never captured; instead, the detritus just following, the laughter, the reaction, the ripples. And because the

Coppertop as Eastern Ranch?
from Notebook G101

I was reminded of a line from the classic Arthur Chapman poem:

Out where the world is
In the making,
Where fewer hearts
In despair are aching,
That's where the West begins.

These few criteria might have been all well and good for a poet, but what about for an empiricist like me? Where, really, was that magical line where the promise of the West began and the smugness of the East ended?

The Moment Just After
from Shoebox 3

A photograph of Layton
in midair jumping onto
a squirrel (taken only a
second too late).

photos were all that remained, because now I could only look at pictures of Layton and not at Layton himself, gradually these echoes of the moment replaced the intended moment itself in my mind. I did not remember Layton balanced precariously on the red Flyer wagon on our roof, but the resulting fall, the bent wagon, and Layton on all fours trying to hide his pain by resting his forehead on the ground, because he never ever cried as long as I knew him.

It was already dark when we pulled in to Pocatello—THE CITY OF SMILES—a well-lit sign announced. I had read once that it was against the law to look sad in Pocatello, but I felt very sad, partly because food was becoming an increasingly major issue. I had seriously underpacked. Without even realizing it, I had already eaten my last carrot stick. *Good-bye, carrot sticks, we hardly knew you.*

I decided, or rather my stomach decided, that I would venture out into Pocatello and buy a cheeseburger and then run back, as quick as I could, before the train pulled out of the yard. The whole expedition would take fifteen minutes maximum, depending on how close the nearest McDonald's was, which I imagined to be very close. Freight yards and the Golden Arches went hand in hand. As a sign of just how confident I was as to the brevity of my trip, I left my bulging suitcase and all of my worldly possessions inside the Winnebago.

But I did bring along five items. A cartographer cannot go out into the world completely unarmed.

Tentatively, I eased open the hatch of the Winnebago. The rubber lining of the door made an unsticking noise as the seal was broken. I stopped and listened. I could hear the irregular rattle of a hammer working over some piece of metal. The road running alongside the railroad buzzed now and again as a car's headlights floated by. The hammering stopped for a moment. Everything was still. And then the rattling started again, this time with the comforting release of an already familiar sound.

I carefully lowered myself down the little half-ladder off the flatcar. If only I had spotted this half-ladder before, instead of trying to Balkan-gymnast my way up the couplings! The rungs were cold and greasy against my hands. *Damn these pulpy cartographer's hands!* White as willow wood, they had seen more action today than during an entire year on the ranch. I was a dandy fop no more.

My train was parked between two other trains on a siding, and on either side of my car loomed the black hulking silhouettes of sleeping boxcars. I took a left and walked quietly between the trains, north, in the direction of where I imagined a McDonald's might be. I was without divining rod, but most boys my age were blessed with a sixth sense for locating where the nearest fast-food sprawl was.

I had not gone more than the length of three cars when I felt a hand on my back. I jumped what seemed like three feet in the air, dropping my compass and notebook. *Damn you, unconscious reflex system!* I turned, expecting to see a gun pointed at my head and wild police dogs straining at their leashes, savoring a chance to rip out my pancreas.

Instead, there was a little man standing before me in the dim light. He was only a couple of inches taller than me. The man was wearing a baseball cap and holding a half-eaten apple. He had on big puffy cargo pants with many pockets, the kind Gracie wore a couple of winters back. On his back, he carried a pack from which various sticks and poles pointed out in all directions.

"How, how," he said, taking a bite from his apple in the most casual manner. "Where you going?"

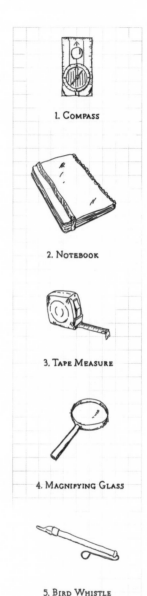

1. COMPASS

2. NOTEBOOK

3. TAPE MEASURE

4. MAGNIFYING GLASS

5. BIRD WHISTLE

Inventory of What I Brought to the Pocatello McDonald's from Notebook G101

"Me? Hey leeto wheeto shnuckoms," I said, my pulse still racing. I had no idea what I was saying.

He didn't seem to hear me. "I just called these in. This one's to Cheyenne, then to Omaha." He thumbed to the train I had just come from. "And this one's down to Ogden and Vegas." He pointed to the train to our left, then seemed to realize I had not given an actual answer to his question. "Where you headed?"

The vision of police dogs straining at their leashes had dissipated enough that I could manage rudimentary English: "I am...Washing... D.C.," I mumbled.

"D.C.?" He blew out a low whistle through his lips, took another bite from his apple, and then looked me up and down in the dim light. "First-timer?"

"Yes," I said, dropping my head.

"Hey, no shame in that!" he said. "There's a first time for everyone. Two Clouds." He held out his hand.

"Two Clouds?"

"That's what they call me."

"Oh," I said. "You're an Indian?"

He laughed. "You say it like they do in the movies. I'm Cree, or at least part Cree...my father was white, Italian," he said. "From *Genova*." With an accent.

"I'm Tecumseh," I said.

"Tecumseh?" He hooked a skeptical eye at me.

"Yeah," I said. "It's a family name. All the men are named Tecumseh. I'm Tecumseh Sparrow."

"The Sparrow?"

"Yes," I said. Somehow, talking made the whole situation less scary, so I kept at it. "My mother said that at the exact moment of my birth, a sparrow came crashing into the window of the kitchen and died right there on the floor. Although I don't know how she could have known it was right at the exact moment of my birth, because it wasn't like she birthed me in the kitchen. So maybe she was lying. Anyways, Dr. Clair sent the body of the sparrow to a friend in Billings who was a specialist in mounting bird skeletons and he gave it to me as a gift for my first birthday." *And I have the skeleton on the train right now,* I wanted to say, but didn't.

"You know much about the sparrow?"

"Well, not too much," I said. "I know they are very aggressive and kick other birds out of their nests. And they are everywhere. I guess sometimes I wish that I wasn't named Sparrow."

"Why?"

"Maybe I could have been a whippoorwill or a kiskadee."

"But you were born a sparrow."

"Yes."

"And not just a sparrow, but a Tecumseh Sparrow."

"Yes. You can call me T.S. for short."

"Do you know the story of the pine tree and the sparrow, T.S.?"

"No," I said, shaking my head.

He took one last bite of his apple and gracefully tossed the core over one of the trains. I could watch him throw apple cores all day. He wiped his hands on his shirt and looked at me square in the eye. "Well, it was one of the stories that my grandmother told me when I was a child." He paused, wiped his mouth on his sleeve. "Follow me," he said.

I followed him over to a boxcar, beneath one of the bright yard lights.

"Won't we be seen?"

He shook his head and then put his hands up near the door of the boxcar. I thought maybe he was trying to conjure the door open, because his fingers were wrapping around themselves in strange ways. I waited.

"You see it?" he said.

"What?" I asked.

"The shadow," he said.

And, of course, there it was. A perfect sparrow flying across the rusted wall of the boxcar.

He took his hands away and the sparrow disappeared, the wall returning to its previous state of rusty emptiness.

He closed his eyes for a second and then began speaking again, his voice now deep and sonorous. "Once…there was a sparrow who was very ill. He could not go south with the rest of his family and so he sent them along, saying that he would find shelter for the winter and meet them in the spring. The sparrow looked his son in the eye and said, 'I will see you again.' And the son believed him."

Two Clouds was very good at becoming a papa sparrow looking his sparrow son in the eye. He continued:

"The sparrow went to an oak tree and asked if he could hide in his leaves and branches for the winter to keep warm, but the oak refused. My grandmother used to say that the oak trees were cold, hard trees with tiny hearts. My grandmother…" Two Clouds stopped and seemed to get lost for a second. He shook his head.

"Sorry," he said. "Well, after this the sparrow went to a maple tree and asked the same question. The maple tree was kinder than the oak tree but it also refused to shelter the bird. The sparrow asked every tree he came to if they might house him from the deadly weather: the beech, the aspen, the willow, the elm. They all said no. Can you believe this?"

The Shadow of the Sparrow
from Notebook G101

"Can I believe what?" I asked.

"No," he said. "Don't answer the question. It is part of the story."

"Oh," I said.

"Well, the first snows came," he said. "And the sparrow was desperate. Finally, he flew over to the pine tree. 'Will you house me for the winter?' the sparrow asked. 'But I can't offer you much protection,' the pine said. 'I only have needles that let in the wind and cold.' 'It is all right,' said the sparrow, shivering. And so the pine agreed. Finally! And do you know what?"

I bit my tongue. I did not answer him.

"With the tree's protection, the sparrow survived the long winter. When the spring came and the wildflowers bloomed in the hills, he was rejoined by his family. The son was overjoyed. He never thought he would see his father again. When the Creator heard this story, he was angry with the trees. 'You did not shelter a tiny sparrow in need,' He said. 'We are sorry,' said the trees. 'You will never forget this sparrow,' the Creator said. And after that, He caused all the trees to lose their leaves each fall... well, almost all of the trees. Because it was kind to the poor bird, the pine tree got to keep its short little needles all winter long."

He stopped. "What do you think of that story?"

"I'm not sure," I said.

"But it's a good one, right?"

"Yes, you told it very well," I said.

"Actually, I am not sure if the story is really about a sparrow or a different bird. I have a bad memory these days."

We were silent for a bit, thinking of birds amidst the clanging of hammers and sighing of trains. And then I asked: "Do you ride these rails a lot?"

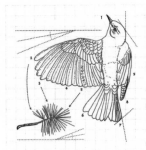

Mapping Two Cloud's Story from Notebook G101

Later, after I had some time to do a few quick calculations, I found that the insulating properties of pine needles would not have saved the sparrow. It was a good story, but Two Clouds's grandmother had told him lies.

"Ever since I ran away from home. And that was…well, I'm not sure, really. Years are a bit useless out here. You pay attention to the season rather than the year."

"Where are you going?" I asked.

"Well, I'll tell you what—Vegas sure has a nice ring to it. I normally just hit the tribe casinos, because if you play the Indian card, they throw you a couple of free rounds. What goes around comes around," he said, making a strange little gesture with his finger. I nodded knowingly, as though I understood. "But I haven't done the Vegas thing in a while. Just pumping those nickel slots, you know? Waitress gives you free whiskey long as you're feeding the meter."

I nodded again, smiling, as if recalling my days at the casinos.

"The best part about this job is you get to see some crazy things on the road. I mean, I've seen it all. I once met a family of alligator wrestlers down in Florida, four generations or something crazy like that. I even saw a flock of birds devour a man alive in Illinois, no joke. There's a shitload goes on in this country no one ever reports on the radio.

"Hey, man, that reminds me. You got any extra batteries?" he asked. "My radio went dead last night and I was just *dying* today. I gotta have my talk radio…hate to admit it, but I got a *big* soft spot for Rush."

"Sorry," I said. "I could give you a compass."

He laughed. "Do I look like I need a compass, kid?"

"No," I admitted. "How about a bird whistle?"

"Let me see it."

I showed him the bird whistle. He turned it around in his hands and then made a quick whippet of a noise, bringing the slide rapidly up and down with his pinky pointing outward. He grinned.

"I can have this?" he asked.

"Yeah," I said.

"What can I give you in return?"

"Well, can you tell me where there's a McDonald's around here?"

"One right at the intersection up there," he said, pointing north. "It's where the hammers go on break. I know all them Pokey hammers— Ted, Leo, Ferry, Ister, Angus. Good guys, same as you and me. Bull's not even that hard. O. J. LaRourke. We call him *the Juice.* He loves it when we call him that. *The Juice.* He also likes his pornography, so we have a nice agreement worked out."

Fear Not, Children, There Is a McDonald's in Pocatello **from Notebook G101**

"Thanks," I said, backing away. "Hey, do you know when this one leaves?"

"Hang on," he said. Humming, he took out a cellular phone and dialed a number. After a second, he glanced up at the train and punched in some numbers.

"What are you doing?" I asked.

He shooshed me with his finger. We waited, and then his phone beeped. "It says it departs at 23.12. You got some time."

"How do you know that?" I asked.

"The Hobo Hotline."

"The Hobo Hotline?"

"Oh yeah, you're green. I forgot. Well…you see, times have changed a bit since the old days. Hobos've got technology now too. There's a guy in Nebraska with access to the mainframe—works for UP, supposedly— but no one really knows, it's all hush-hush. Well, he set up a little service for drifters, where you dial up the hotline and punch in the call numbers on a car"—he pointed at the side of a boxcar—"and then the service will tell you when and where that car is going. Pretty handy."

"Wow," I said.

"I know," he said. "Things move on. People get smart. Indians had to get smart or we'd be dead."

He reached into his pocket and fished out a pen and a scrap of paper. He wrote something on the paper and then handed it to me. "Here's the hotline. Use it if you get in a jam, but if you're discovered by anyone, burn that piece of paper…or better yet, eat it."

"Thanks!" I said.

"Hey, no problem. Thanks for the whistle. Us drifters have to look out for each other."

I was one of *us drifters* now.

"Hope you find your way," he said. "The sticky part will be in Chicago. That's a big town. Can be ugly. Make sure you grab a blue-and-yellow CSX freighter. Those are heading east. Use the hotline, or if you don't have a phone, just ask. Most hammers are nice, especially if you buy 'em a beer. You…look a little young to be buying. How old are you?"

"Sixteen," I said. I felt a telltale tingle of pain in my jaw. My molars always ached when I lied.

He nodded, unsurprised. "That's about how old I was when I started this business. My grandmother died and I just split. Still feel like a kid in some ways. Don't lose it, that's my advice. The world'll do its best to shit on you, but if you can hang on to that little scrap of sixteen for the rest of your days, you'll do all right."

"Okay," I said. I would do anything this man told me to do.

"Two Clouds," he said, holding up two fingers.

"'Bye, Two Clouds."

"'Bye, Sparrow. Hope you find your pine tree."

As I walked down the line, I heard the soft rise and fall of the bird whistle receding into the darkness.

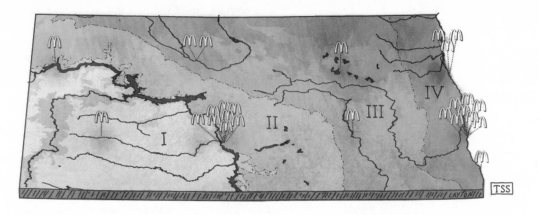

Map of North Dakota Showing Ecoregions, Surface Water,
and Locations of the Twenty-Six McDonald's

~ for Mr. Corlis Benefideo ~

ECOREGIONS

I NW Great Plains
II NW Glaciated Plains
III Northern Glaciated Plains
IV Lake Agassiz Plain

CHAPTER 6

Pasty   Samosa

Dumpling   Knish

---

*T*hank thee, McDonald's, for thy blessed trident of light.

    Dr. Clair would never let us eat at the Mickey D's on Harrison Avenue in the Flats, though I did not have a clear handle on her reasoning for this embargo: she would readily allow Layton and me to chow down next door at Maron's Pasty Shop (pronounced **pas•**tee), a blue-and-white-checkered hole-in-the-wall that actually served much more intense artery-clogging fare than its corporate neighbor.

    Now, when I once pressed Dr. Clair on the criteria for the Mickey D ban, she simply proclaimed, "There are just so many of them." As if this made sense. Though her logic was elusive, she was also my mother. One job of a mother was to make rules and one job of a child was to follow these rules, however nonsensical they were.

    As we ate our pasties inside Maron's, I stared across the parking lot at those two plastic arches, more yellow than golden, really, but nonetheless excruciatingly enticing. I would study the young kids tumbling down

> ▶ **Pouch as Food**
> from Notebook G43

    The pasty had been imported by Cornish miners: potatoes and meat with a healthy dollop of gravy neatly folded inside a doughy pocket. The containment of all that goodness inside such a sturdy pouch made a convenient meal for the mine workers to clutch in their grubby paws. The "pouch as food" had been independently discovered by civilizations across the world, further evidence for the natural selection of simple, versatile ideas. I mean, admit it: people were not that different when it came to the desire to hold and eat their food at the same time.

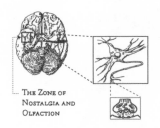

The Zone of
Nostalgia and
Olfaction

the slides in the McPlayground, the pickups and minivans endlessly churning through the semicircle haw of the drive-thru. The place had a magnetic pull on me that superseded reason. I realized that this pull was not unique to me, and was in fact present for most twelve-year-olds in the country. However, unlike my peers, I was compelled to document the componentry of this tractor beam with my scientist's eye even as it was propelling my muscles to walk into the comforts of its reds and yellows and oranges. I had read once that these colors were supposed to increase your appetite (survey says: *yes*).

I was no advertising expert, but in observing my own behavior in the vicinity of McDonald's, I had mapped out a working theory about how the place penetrates my permeable barrier of aesthetic longing, in a trio of multi-sensory persuasion:

Nº1
THE SMELL

The smell of the fry-o-lator doing its wonderful work on those tasty french fries. This smell was not always present, but children have been exposed to this smell enough that they are able to conjure it in their olfactory cortex whenever they see a McDonald's. The smell itself had been carefully designed and artificially synthesized in a smell and taste factory on the New Jersey Turnpike to maximize its desirability. They must have used the same smell molecules that are in bacon because bacon triggers similar re-actions in me, turning me into a googly-eyed hungry boy.

Nº2
THE NOSTALGIA

The presence of both the playground and the small toy in the Happy Meal. While I knew that I was too old to play in the tiny covered slides, just as I was too old to get excited about a crappy figurine with no moving parts (though I once received a Beetlebot, which still resides in my medicine cabinet), both of these elements worked on my already burgeoning sense of nostalgia for a time when I hadn't been too young for these items. That was why these elements were so infectious: they acted as a memory flag to lure us back to a simpler time before the onset of adolescence, when the quiet weight of adulthood was not waiting around the corner. The twisty slide and the promise of a crappy figurine was a way of rebelling against time.

Nº3
THE ARCHES

The Golden Arches called upon an elemental symbol that went well beyond the simple recogni-tion of a brand. In Shoshone myths, all life originated from the Sky World, drawn as a giant arch above the Earth Mother riding on the back of a turtle. There were also the aortic arches in our heart (the origin of the heart symbol), through which all of our blood was replenished. Even nature formed arches through erosion and special layerings of rock strata, as could be seen in Arches National Park. Though I had never been, I did draw a small diagram about counter balance in the park for SCIENCE magazine, who, like the rest of the world, did not know that I was only twelve and still treasured my Happy Meal Beetlebot.

Maybe because I was now officially a runaway, *The McAwesome Trident of Desire* was working its full effect on me as I entered the McDonald's abutting the Pocatello rail yards. Sometimes when Dr. Clair drove us down Harrison Avenue in the Flats, I would get a very sad, sinking feeling as we passed strip mall after strip mall, but any sort of guilt as to the disintegration of America's wilderness into temples of convenience vanished quickly under the Trident's magical spell.

Now, in the City of Smiles, 250 miles south of Butte, I approached the pictorially rich menu glowing above the counter. Once I found my target, I pointed. I realized too late that I was actually pointing at the menu with my tape measure. The woman behind the counter turned around and looked at where I was pointing, then looked back at me. "Cheeseburger Happy Meal?" she asked.

I nodded. *Dr. Clair, you cannot stop me now.*

She sighed and then tapped at the big grey box in front of her. A small green screen on the box said "Average serving time: 17.5 seconds."

After assembling all the needed parts of the Happy Meal, she said, "That's $5.46."

I realized that my hands were full of my compass, notebook, tape measure, and magnifying glasses, so I had to do some hurried rearranging in order to produce a ten-dollar bill from my change purse.

"Where are you going with that stuff?" she asked in a flat monotone as she handed me the change. I wondered if I was cutting into her 17.5-second average.

"East," I said mysteriously, and took the big Happy Meal bag from her. Our transaction caused the bag to make little crinkling sounds. I felt very adult.

Redbeard: Pensive, Off-Center
from Notebook G101

The Morse Code Message
from Notebook G84

Before I slipped back into the night through the automatic doors, I quickly checked to see what toy had come with my Happy Meal. Inside a sealed plastic bag was a crappy, nonmovable pirate figurine. I unwrapped it and ran my thumb over the pirate's face. There was a kind of comfort in the toy's crappiness—particularly in how the Chinese machine that colored these figurines had painted the pirate's pupils just off the bulge of where his eyes should have been, so that it seemed as if he was looking downward, with a mournful pensiveness that was decidedly unpiratelike.

Walking back into the night, basking in that unvarying, more yellow than golden luminescence from the arches above me, I was reminded of a lecture I had attended at Montana Tech right before Layton died. It was the first time I had ever recalled the lecture, which was strange, because I left that event convinced I would never forget what I had just witnessed.

I had caught a ride into Butte with Father to listen to an eighty-two-year-old man named Mr. Corlis Benefideo give a presentation about his North Dakota map project. The lecture was sponsored by the Montana Bureau of Mines and Geology at Montana Tech, and it must have been very poorly advertised, because there were only six people in the audience besides myself. I had only heard about the lecture through Morse Code on my Ham radio the night before. The lack of attendance was particularly astounding considering the mind-blowing quality of the work that Mr. Benefideo displayed for us over the course of his talk. He was at the end of a twenty-five-year-long project: a systematic record of North Dakota through a series of maps that demonstrated a totally comprehensive understanding of the history, geology, archaeology, botany, and zoology of the land. There was a map showing the subtle east-west oscillations in migratory bird patterns over the last fifty years, another illustrating the relationship between wildflowers and bedrock formations in the southeastern flats of the state, another showing the murder rate against the frequency of use of all seventeen border crossings to Canada. Everything was done in minute pen-and-ink brushstrokes, such that he had to show us a detail slide for each map, and at this power of magnification a whole other world was revealed.

In a very soft voice, Mr. Benefideo told us that there were over two thousand of these maps, that this was the degree of depth with which we should study our land, our states, our history, and that ideally he would love to do a whole series for every state, but that he was about to die and he was hoping the next generation of cartographers would take on this task. When he said this, I thought he was looking right at me, and I remember feeling this intense hum in the room.

As I walked back through the darkened streets of Pocatello, I recalled an exchange between one of the few audience members and Mr. Benefideo after his lecture had concluded.

"All these maps are gorgeous, of course," the audience member said. He looked like one of those young, hotshot outdoorsy geology graduate students. "But what about the *now?* Why is this field so rooted in the last century? What about mapping McDonald's or wireless hot spots or cell phone coverage? What about Google mashups? Democratizing GIS for the masses? Aren't you doing a disservice by ignoring these trends? By not mapping them? By not...*you know?*"

Mr. Benefideo looked at the man, not quite angry, but not quite interested either. "You have my blessing to pursue those maps," he said. "Google smash—?"

"Mashups, sir. People can now make maps very quickly of their favorite climbing spots in the Tetons, for instance. And then drop these on the Web for their buddies to snipe." This man was very pleased with

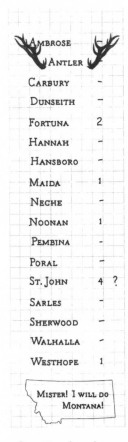

AMBROSE ANTLER		
CARBURY	-	
DUNSEITH	-	
FORTUNA	2	
HANNAH	-	
HANSBORO	-	
MAIDA	1	
NECHE	-	
NOONAN	1	
PEMBINA	-	
PORAL	-	
ST. JOHN	4	?
SARLES	-	
SHERWOOD	-	
WALHALLA	-	
WESTHOPE	1	

MISTER! I WILL DO MONTANA!

Notes from the Benefideo Lecture from Notebook G84

his map of climbing spots, apparently. He turned around and smiled and rubbed his hand over the top of his head.

"Mashups," Mr. Benefideo said, turning the word around in his mouth to see if it fit. "By all means, make your mashups. They sound…entertaining. And I am much too old now to understand the technology."

The geologist rubbed his head again, smiling at the few other audience members, satisfied at his technological know-how. He was about to sit down when Mr. Benefideo began speaking again.

"It is my belief, however, that there is much more to understand about the genesis of our food's ingredients—their relationship to the land, the ingredients' relationship to one another—before we can even begin to understand what the impact of McDonald's has been on our culture. I could take a sheet of paper and draw the outline of North Dakota and then draw a point for each McDonald's in the state and even post this on the Internet, but for me, this would not really be a map—these would only be markings on the page. A map does not just chart, it unlocks and formulates meaning; it forms bridges between here and there, between disparate ideas that we did not know were previously connected. To do this right is very difficult."

Possibly it was because I had not quite learned to overcome the McAwesome Trident, but I did not have the same problem as Mr. Benefideo in including the modern artifacts of progress into my maps. I would trace the nineteenth-century footpaths of the fur traders, yes, but I would trace them in relationship to the orientation of major shopping malls.

That said, Mr. Benefideo's emphasis on the older techniques of mapping, using your hands, and an array of analog tools with gears in them, and pencils and pens and compasses and theodolites—made my fingertips quiver with excitement. Like him, I made maps without the aid of computers or GPS devices. I was not quite sure why, but I felt much more like a creator this way. Computers made me feel like an *operator*.

"You're old-fashioned," Dr. Yorn once told me, laughing as he said this. "The world marches onward, you were born after the Internet, and yet you insist on using the same drafting methods that I used in graduate school in the seventies."

Though I know he hadn't meant to, Dr. Yorn had hurt my feelings when he had said this. So when I heard Mr. Benefideo's talk, I was finally able to let that breath out: here was a man who possessed one of the most meticulous empirical skill sets I had ever encountered and yet who also shared my old-fashionedness. After the lecture was over, I waited until the room had cleared before I made my way up to him. Mr. Benefideo had small circular glasses that partially obscured his tired, reddened eyes. There was the tiniest hint of a white mustache beneath a nose that jogged slightly to the left. He was rolling up some of his maps next to the lectern.

"Excuse me," I said. "Mr. Benefideo?"

"Yes?" he said, looking up.

There was much I wanted to say in that moment: about how he and I shared an unbreakable kinship; about how he might be the most important person I had ever met, even if I never saw him again; about how I would remember this lecture for the rest of my life—even about his glasses: I wanted to ask why he chose such small, circular lenses.

Instead, I said, "I'll do Montana."

"Good," he said without hesitation. "That's a hell of a tough state. You've got seven Level Four ecoregions there in twelve degrees of longitude. But only thirteen border crossings. Make sure you leave yourself plenty of time. That was my problem. The wick just ran out of wax."

The Resilience of Memory

A week after the lecture, Layton would be dead. In the swirl of events following the accident in the barn, I forgot all about the lecture. I suppose even these torqued moments of import could disappear if they happened to occur next to the black holes of our lives. And yet the synaptic composition of a memory was such that it could weather the pull of the black hole and reappear months later, just as the image of Benefideo's circular frames now snagged upon the baleen of my recall as I ate my cheeseburger in Pocatello.

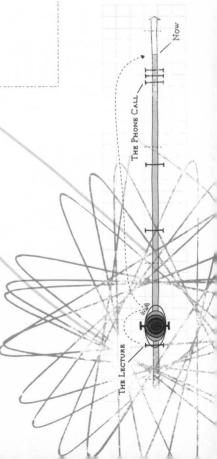

. . .

I checked my watch. 2.01 A.M. The Cheeseburger Happy Meal was now only a distant memory. I cursed myself for not also ordering a breakfast sandwich for the morning. I had returned to the yard after my meal and looked for Two Clouds, but he and the Vegas train were gone. I carefully boarded my car again, slipped back into the safety of the Cowboy Condo, and waited. It was well after midnight when the train finally started up and left the Pocatello yards. The difference between the predicted time of departure by the Hobo Hotline and the actual time of departure suddenly made me question the trustworthiness of the service. Who was this guy in Nebraska? Was he just making up a bunch of numbers? Was my train headed west to Boise and then Portland?

After a while, I gave in to the slow, inevitable progress of the train. I would go where it went. There was no changing that now. Portland, Louisiana, Mexico, Saskatoon—I was there. Accepting the inevitability of my destination brought a certain peace to my body. I realized how tired I was, how this had been the longest day of my life. In a bold display of territoriality, I sleepily put my nonmovable pensive pirate figurine onto the large flat dashboard of the Winnebago.

"Protect me, Redbeard," I said.

I did not remember lying down on the king-size Teton bed, but a while later I found myself flying off the bed when the train jolted to a sudden stop.

I looked out the windows. A sea of orange lights twinkled against a light rain. I checked my watch. 4.34 A.M. This was probably Green River, another Union Pacific hub. I wondered what people were doing right now in this twinkling city of orange lights. Most likely sleeping, but perhaps there was some little boy wide awake in his bedroom near the train tracks, wondering what it would be like to ride a freight train across the desert. Part of me wanted to switch positions with that boy, to take his spot at the darkened windowsill of his bedroom, to let him go on the adventure into the unknown and leave the wondering to me.

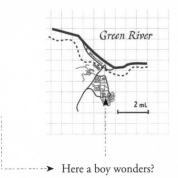

Here a boy wonders?

The train pushed out and I watched the wet lights slink away into the vast darkness of the desert.

I couldn't get back to sleep. The night slipped by. It quickly became clear that I would never be able to sleep in uninterrupted eight-hour periods on this freight train but only in short, irregular bursts. There was just too much starting and stopping, too much noise, too much rocking back and forth. The brakeman was driving this thing to get where he was going, not so that I, his covert passenger, could catch some peaceful shut-eye. I had once mapped out how dolphins sleep with only half their brain at a time, a practice that allows them to swim and breathe underwater without drowning. I attempted the dolphin technique by trying to sleep with one eye open, but this only made my eye sore and gave me a full headache on both sides of my brain.

Finally, after some sleepless pacing, I decided that it was time: I needed to venture into my suitcase. The Winnebago was almost completely dark, except for a few strange flashes of light coming from somewhere in that great desert. I turned on a flashlight and propped it up so that its beam shone directly at the suitcase. I licked my thumb and finger and then proceeded to slowly unzip the zipper, wary of the suitcase exploding my wares all over the interior of the Cowboy Condo. Upon lifting the lid, however, I was amazed to see that everything was intact, despite the wild ride of the last twenty-four hours. My theodolite was fully operational.

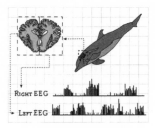

Unihemispheric Slow-Wave Sleep in the Bottlenose Dolphin **from Notebook G38**

Sleeping with one eye open? Brilliant. I still harbored a suspicion that dolphins were actually smarter than humans and were merely waiting for us to destroy ourselves before taking over the world.

Igor still made his little bleeping noises when I turned him on. All was well, it seemed.

And then I saw Dr. Clair's notebook. A wave of guilt poured over me. What had I done? I might have ruined her career with this theft! Would she notice the missing notebook before she noticed her missing son?

I picked up the notebook and examined its covering by the beam of the flashlight. Perhaps I could make up for my transgression by helping her in my own small way to solve the mystery of the tiger monk beetle.

I opened the notebook. On the inside of the front cover she had taped a Xeroxed cutout from what looked like an old diary:

As usual, Miss Osterville was up earlier than most of the men, taking readings and marking in that little green notebook of hers. She is a <u>curious</u>, obsessive kind of person, unlike any woman I have ever known. One might think she was born inside the body of the wrong sex. I am not sure the others quite know what to think of her.... but it is not for lack of knowledge or skill—she may be the most competent scientist among the group, though I would never ~~aloud~~ announce such an idea out-loud lest Dr. Hayden go into one of his fits.

Miss Osterville? The name was familiar. On a loose piece of paper tucked inside the first page, Dr. Clair had written:

Only mention of E O E by name during entire Wyoming Survey. From the journals of William Henry Jackson, the survey's photographer in 1870. Hayden once describes "the lady" and her "muddy gowns," but does not elaborate. I often wonder what I am doing lurking in this world, when the data sets are so weak. This is not science. I have Englethorpe's book, a few diaries, the Vassar archives, not much else – why am I compelled to speculate? Have I any right to do so? Would E O E approve?

And then it came to me. EOE. Emma Osterville! Of course. She was my great-great-grandmother, one of the first female geologists in the entire country. I didn't know much about her story, but I knew that somehow she had ended up marrying Tearho Spivet, who in 1870 was working as a signalman at the Red Desert refilling station in Wyoming. After they were married, they had moved up to Butte, where he worked in the mines and she had apparently abandoned her career to raise a family in Montana. Which was the beginnings of *my* family, I suppose.

Dr. Clair had talked about Emma Osterville on a number of occasions. "The first woman to ever marry a Spivet," she had said. "Now, *that's* an achievement." Indeed, she spoke so often of Emma Osterville that I realized she had eased me into the erroneous belief that somehow Emma was Dr. Clair's great-grandmother instead of Father's.

I had always been bothered by the part in Emma's story where she gave up her life's work after only a couple of months of working on Hayden's Survey. Something strange had happened in the Red Desert such that she had been compelled to leave her position on the survey, a position she had somehow earned in a historical climate that simply did not accept the notion of a woman as a "competent" scientist. She was on track to be a pioneer of feminism, to be the first female geology professor in the country, to tear down the daunting barriers of sexism erected in her field, and yet she abandoned this dream to marry an illiterate Finnish immigrant who barely spoke any English. *But why?* Why would she give it all up—the early mornings spent filling her little green notebook with those exact notations; the showing up of men more famous than she; the envy, the influence, the territories to be mapped? Why would she give it all up to move to Butte City in Montana and become a miner's wife?

I turned to the first page. Dr. Clair had written:

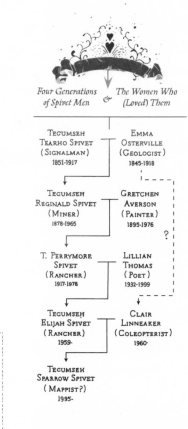

Four Generations of Spivet Men & *The Women Who (Loved) Them*

TECUMSEH TEARHO SPIVET (SIGNALMAN) 1851-1917	EMMA OSTERVILLE (GEOLOGIST) 1845-1918
TECUMSEH REGINALD SPIVET (MINER) 1878-1965	GRETCHEN AVERSON (PAINTER) 1895-1976
T. PERRYMORE SPIVET (RANCHER) 1917-1978	LILLIAN THOMAS (POET) 1932-1999
TECUMSEH ELIJAH SPIVET (RANCHER) 1959-	CLAIR LINNEAKER (COLEOPTERIST) 1960-
TECUMSEH SPARROW SPIVET (MAPPIST?) 1995-	

They Are Both Female Scientists, They Must Be Related

Why do we make these illogical associations in our mind? No one ever said, "Emma Osterville is Dr. Clair's great-grandmother," but I had come to vaguely believe it, simply through frequent association. I suppose children are particularly susceptible to such irrational connections: with so much unknown, they are less concerned with the sticky details than with trying to create a working map of the world.

*She was not born am_
*would grow up to briefl_
*eventually die in. She_

**The EOE Notebook
Stolen from Dr. Clair's Study**

As I began to read Dr. Clair's note-book, I realized how personal some-one's handwriting actually is. I had never thought of Dr. Clair as sepa-rate from the way that she wrote: those *E*'s that looked like half *8*'s had always just been a part of her. But sitting on this train so far away from the cocoon of her study, I now saw that my mother's writing was not a given, but the result of a life lived. These familiar flicks of the wrist had been honed by a thousand little in-fluences: school teachers, childhood poetry sessions, failed scientific ven-tures, maybe even love letters. (Had my mother ever written a love letter?) I wonder what a handwriting expert would say about my mother's writ-ing. I wonder what a handwriting expert would say about *my* writing?

The Beginning ? ⟶ 1845

And then:

She was not born amongst the high Rockies that she would grow up to briefly survey, measure, marry, and eventually die in. She was born in Woods Hole, Massachusetts, on a small white houseboat moored in the middle of the Great Harbor, a quiet swath of water sheltered from the high wind and waves of Buzzards Bay by the thin arm of Penzance Point, where the retired sea captains had built their houses on the bluffs.   Her father, Gregor Osterville, was a fisherman—a fisherman from a family that had been patrolling these waters in weather-beaten skiffs for over a hundred years, back when the cod still ran thick.

Her mother, Elizabeth Tamour, was a tough woman, the sort who could marry a fisherman and never complain once about the almond-colored stains that the salty air would leave on the linens, the constant smell of fish skin beneath her husband's fingernails when they lay together in bed at night listening to the lap of the waves against the walls of their house.

The contractions came suddenly. It was an overcast day in July. She was sweeping the splinter-prone deck of the houseboat and sud-denly it felt as if a hand had reached up inside of her and squeezed some fleshy organ between thumb and finger. *Hard.* Then harder still. The broom almost fell overboard, but she maintained her grip on the wooden shaft and placed it carefully on the lip of the doorway. The houseboat rocked ever so slightly, as it always did.

There was not enough time to get to the mainland. Gregor had just returned from the docks; he washed his hands in the sea with some soap and set about the task of delivering his daughter. Forty-five minutes later, he took out one of his fish knives from the box and cut the umbilical cord. He caught the placenta in a porcelain bowl. After handing the tiny child, now blanketed and bleating, to Elizabeth, he went outside and dumped the contents of the bowl into the ocean. It floated on the surface like a crimson jellyfish before sinking into the deep.

Sometime during the middle of that first night, Elizabeth—who did not love the sea but loved her husband; did not love the fish they ate every night on their lonesome floating room but loved the way his hands gutted and cleaned the white-fleshed cod in quick, assured motions—looked down at her baby under the matchbox glaze of moonlight, looked at Emma and silently wished that this pink puddle of a creature, with tiny fingers furling and unfurling like minnows, would not grow up in such a place. The child was destined to know only the slow rock of the houseboat, so that the stillness of land would always unsettle her; she was destined for her playground to be the slippery basalt tidal pools by the Point; humming into hermit crab shells; friendships formed, secrets whispered beneath overturned skiffs on the wet sand beach; always the smell of rotting fish, of festering seaweed; the constant guttural grumblings of the men who caught and split the fish; the slap of wet wool; the circling of the gulls with their unblinking eyes; the long, flat winters; the longer, flatter summers.

That night, perhaps touched by the elusive melancholy that always comes upon mothers in the silent, teardropped wake of childbirth, Elizabeth wished Emma away from the one room that they now

> Reading this very graphic description of childbirth made me realize: just as Emma had come out of Elizabeth, I had come out of Dr. Clair. *Weird.* It sounded very strange when you put it that way. She was not just an older woman who happened to live in the same house as me, but also my *creator.*

floated in together. She could hear the sea slap at the wooden sidings. They were alone. Gregor was already up and out, patrolling the waters.

Elizabeth got her wish. That first winter—the winter of 1846— was a mean one. Meaner than anyone could remember, it was so cold that the canal into the Little Harbor froze solid, and one by one the fishing boats burst and splintered against the ice slabs. Then the storm: a hundred-year storm at the end of February. Two days and two nights of zero visibility and lashing winds that brought down the church steeple right after teatime, though no one was taking tea in such weather. Sometime during the second night, all the houseboats—save for one—were blown out to sea.

Luckily, Emma and Elizabeth were staying at her sister Tamsen's house in town that night, where they had spent much of that winter. It had become clear that the single room floating on the water was no place for such a tiny, fragile child. Baby Emma seemed to be a baby without bones— when Elizabeth held her daughter, it was as though she were melting into the space between her elbow and belly, so that Elizabeth had to periodically check to see if Emma was still there, to see that she had not evaporated into thin air.

This is no place for a child, Elizabeth whispered to Gregor as they lay in bed only one week before the storm. Above them, the wind pressed at the weathered joints of the ceiling. Emma quietly suckled on a bottle in her crib at the foot of the bed. Elizabeth nudged her husband, but he was already asleep. When home, he was either sleeping or getting ready to leave.

Or for a woman, Elizabeth almost said aloud, but she did not. Elizabeth was a hard-nosed woman, harder than most, and she prided herself on how her sister and she had chosen different paths: Tamsen lived in town and had married a banker. A soft banker, with soft banker hands.

Unlike Tamsen, Elizabeth had always had an itch for adventure. Several years ago, she had come across a guidebook in the post office outlining the virtues of the wide open Oregon Territories and a place called the Willamette Valley. "A great journey brings great rewards to the intrepid pioneer," the guidebook said, providing enchanting pastel vistas of the frontier that awaited her beyond the mountains. Thereafter, Elizabeth had imagined herself as one of those pioneer women emerging into the Valley—setting up a little cabin by a creek, chopping down Douglas firs while her husband was away, and shooting a bear with the heavy-handled Winchester when the black-eyed creature wandered into her garden.

Though she had not made that great journey across the mountains, in a way she felt as if she already lived in a kind of frontier right here in New England, only forty miles south of where she had grown up in New Bedford. When the wind picked up and rubbed her skin through the walls of the houseboat—despite the corset, the double dresses, the sweater, the shawl—she felt as far away from land as if she were homesteading in the mythical Willamette Valley. The Indians of the West were replaced here by the roll of the waves: occasionally vicious, always present, always moving. And gold nuggets were replaced by the fish that the men caught and threw into the wooden bins on the docks, the cod lying in heaps, gasping.

But she loved Gregor. She had loved him from the moment she saw him on Ennis Street back home in New Bedford—and so how to describe the feeling when she looked out across the Great Harbor on that morning? The snow was still falling, but she left the sleeping baby behind and trooped out anyway, in boots that laced to the knee and were not meant for such elements. Her hands were wrapped five times around by a scratchy red woolen scarf she had borrowed from her sister.

She scanned the harbor. The sea was churning but not overly so. Snowflakes fell lazily, without any indication of the night's destruction. The familiar dozen or so black boxes that gave the Great Harbor its peculiar character were gone, save for one, but that one was not her own.

Instantly, a vacuum of air formed in Elizabeth's throat. It was as if her lungs had vanished from this world along with those dozen homes that once floated on the sea. She could feel her fingers begin searching the layers of the woolen scarf, desperately, as if she might find her house, her lungs, her breath, her husband, inside that small, coarse space.

I stopped reading and flipped through the rest of the notebook. The entire thing was filled with writing about Emma Osterville! Not one sketch of a tiger beetle, no charts of field data, no itineraries of collecting trips, no itemized taxonomies. Nothing scientific at all. Just this story.

Had I picked the wrong notebook? Was this an outlier? The book she let off steam with by musing about our ancestry? But then I remembered that the entire collection of burgundy notebooks, perhaps forty or so, were all labeled EOE. All of them devoted to Emma? Was this what she had been doing all these years? Had she not been searching for the tiger monk at all? Was my mother not a scientist but a *writer*?

I read on:

Later, when she was old enough to remember what she could not remember, Emma would replay what must have been her father's last moments over and over in her head: he, moving calmly from window to window, checking the latches, tending the kerosene lamp that swung this way and that under the lashings of the wind. And at some point in the night, the sound must have changed, as the howling nor'easter finally got what it demanded, finally, through a constant, persuasive tugging, coaxed away that last board, and the house ripped from its mooring. A tiny pinpoint of light skittering like a leaf across the churning sheet of the Great Harbor, past Juniper Point, past the Great Ledge, out into the Straits beyond.

Emma, of course, did not remember what she had not seen, but Elizabeth would later tell Emma of all this and of him, of his hands and how they held the cod just so as he unzipped the silver belly, how he jammed the crooked stub of his left thumb into the gills, the thumb withered from a childhood accident with a horse. And she would tell Emma of how he was a great collector of all that came from the sea: sand dollars and sharks' teeth, sea glass and rusted fish hooks, even a musket, which he said the British had dropped on their way to losing the American Revolution. And the inside of their houseboat had been stuffed with this collection, so that when the wind blew hard, rocking their little home up and down, this way and that, the iridescent seashells would make little tapping noises on the mantel, as if applauding their own display.

Pieces of the houseboats washed up all that spring: a headboard, a drawer, false teeth. Not much was found of their own houseboat, as if it had been blown farther out than the rest. Bodies, too, were

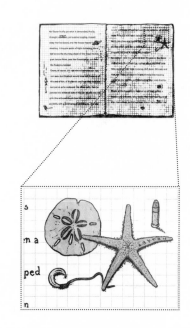

"He was a great collector of all that came from the sea."

Without knowing what I was doing, I found myself drawing a little illustration in the margin of her notebook. I know, I know—it was terrible. This was someone else's property. But I just couldn't help myself.

Father and his pinky; Gregor and his thumb—did *all* rugged men have some kind of Achilles heel? Like superheroes, they could only maintain their hardened nature by also nursing a secret weakness...

Did I have an Achilles' heel? Okay—I know I wasn't that tough. Maybe my whole body was an Achilles' heel and this was why Father looked at me with such suspicion (AU-2, AU-17, AU-22).

found: John Molpy up in Falmouth, Evan Redgrave off the coast of the Vineyard. Elizabeth kept waiting. Part of her held onto the slimmest hope that he had survived; he was a strong swimmer and perhaps he had found shelter in some distant cove; he was resting now, and soon he would backstroke home, up the little canal to the beach, where she would greet him, scold him, bring him his tea, hold that thumb of his inside the quiet of her palm.

Then one morning Elizabeth opened the door of her sister's house to find that someone had left a waterlogged copy of *Gulliver's Travels* on their doorstep. It was Gregor's. Gregor could read, which was rare for a fisherman at that time, and he owned only two books: the King James Bible and Swift's tale of adventure on the high seas. She picked up the book with thumb and forefinger, as if it were the carcass of an animal from the deep. The pages were discolored and bloated; only the front half of the book remained, the rest gone. She wept. It was proof enough.

Once, walking through Boston Common when she was ten years old, Emma asked: "Which did he prefer? The Bible or *Gulliver's Travels*?"

She herself had just discovered the pleasures of reading, and she loved the image of those two lonely volumes sitting above her father's bed. If she closed her eyes and waited, she could see the shelf and the books and the tiny shells, balanced, waiting for the next wind.

"That's a tricky question," Elizabeth said. "Are you trying to get me into trouble?"

"Why is that a tricky question?" Emma asked. They were walking on the path together, but Emma was rather dancing, running out in front and turning to face her mother every time she asked a question.

"Well, to tell you the truth," Elizabeth said, "I did not see him open that Bible once. Perhaps at Christmas...but he probably read *Gulliver's Travels* a hundred times. It was such a strange book, but he loved those names. He would read it aloud over dinner and we would laugh at the names: Glub-dub-dribb and the Houyhnhnms and the—"

"The Houyhnhnms?"

"Those were the horses that were smarter than even the humans."

"Oh, but can we read it tonight?"

"Yes, I suppose we can. I am not sure if we even have a proper copy to—"

"Is it true?"

"Is what true?" It was spring, the daffodils were out, the scent of sycamore and fresh mulch all around them.

"Do those places exist somewhere? Did Gulliver actually go to those places and see the Houyhnhnms?"

Elizabeth did not answer but rather nodded vaguely, as if she did not want to confirm or deny any of it, as if the impreciseness of the gesture would allow her to drift onward in that narrow space of existence between what is and isn't.

Somewhere, a woodpecker clustered together a string of short, staccato taps and then fell silent. They circled the pond twice without speaking before leaving the park to purchase a brand-new copy of *Gulliver's Travels* at Mulligan's Fine Books on Park Street. The bookshop smelled of tomato stew and mildew so Emma plugged her nose using both of her thumbs until the transaction was complete.

Then I saw it.
In the margin,
my mother had written:

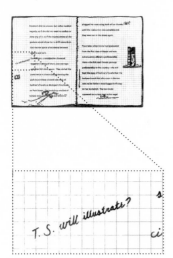

T. S. will illustrate?

She wanted me to illustrate? My eyes filled with tears. I must have somehow already sensed her wish for us to collaborate. To collaborate! (Or: to *clobber-eight*.) It wasn't exactly science, but it would have to do. I snuggled up on the couch with the notebook and my flashlight and some Gillot pens. As I read on, it was as if my mother was changing before my eyes, as if for the first time I was seeing her in her most private moments. I was peeking through the keyhole.

I kept reading:

Years later, when Emma had graduated from the first class at Vassar and was subsequently offered a professorship there—the first such female geology professorship in the country—she still kept the copy of *Gulliver's Travels* that they had purchased that afternoon in Boston next to her father's waterlogged half-copy on her bookshelf. The two books appeared so curious next to her regal taxonomies, atlases, and geological textbooks that more than one of her already skeptical scientific colleagues made passing jokes as to the real owners of the pair. Most of the jibes involved lusty, ephemeral seafarers who had passed through her waters and left the Swift novel and a broken heart in their wake.

She never answered as to the true significance of the books, but secretly in her heart she assigned a mystical symbology to that pair of Gullivers. Her possession of the twins was sentimental, she knew, and it ran counter to her empirical, Humboldtean character, but she could not escape the feeling that the initial, elusive push on her course to becoming a surveyor (born inside the wrong sex) could be traced back to her father's nighttime studies of Gulliver and his travels.

Many a man would ask Emma—at dinners in Poughkeepsie, at the libraries down at Yale where she completed her dissertation, at the Academy of Natural Sciences conference in 1869 where her professorship was announced to the scientific community, to hostile silence—how she had happened to fall upon science as a profession. They usually used this exact wording: "fall upon science," as though it were an accident, some sort of sickness that had claimed her against her will. Certainly she had not come to her present standing as a surveyor and drafts(wo)man through the standard channels, thirty miles downriver at West Point, whose top graduates would go on to conquer and name the great expanse of the West.

Emma could remember when she first heard the seductive images of the West conjured around a mantel in Cambridge. Caught in the mild depression of a childhood lived without roots or father, Emma had grown into a melancholy, quiet sort of child who stuck to her books and mumbled between sips of soup.

Emma and Elizabeth had moved up to Powder House Square, where Elizabeth worked in a flower shop with Josephine, a distant cousin. Emma began attending a seminary for young women on a scholarship that she had won despite suffering from a migraine during the entrance exam. The migraines would continue to plague her the rest of her life. She was successful at school, clearly capable of copying her lessons, but she showed no enthusiasm for any subject in particular and her acquaintanceship was limited to a younger girl named Molly—

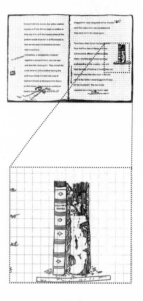

"The two books appeared so curious next to her regal taxonomies... that more than one of her already skeptical scientific colleagues made passing jokes as to the real owners of the pair."

Oh how I loved this. For a minute I schemed about getting two copies of the book myself and then letting Verywell go at one for a while to mimic the effects of the sea. But then I remembered that I wasn't headed in the direction of home or Verywell. I suddenly missed the curious shelving patterns of my room, those old planks from the barn groaning under the weight of the notebooks. Shelving is an intimate thing, like the fingerprint of a room.

Fig. 1: **From Layton's Book**

Fig. 2: **From My Book**

Yes! *The First Thanksgiv-ing with the Pilgrims Coloring Book*! Layton and I had both been given this book several years back by our half-aunt Doretta Hastings. We had both failed in using the book properly: Layton couldn't color inside the lines, and in-stead of coloring the pictures I wrote out their measure-ments and asymptotes. Be-neath her table, had Emma drawn the asymptotes as well? No, this was asking too much of her. We were differ-ent creatures.

who was strange, it was known, and who would take Emma out by the sycamores and sing to her in peculiar languages while working sticks into her hair.

And then Tamsen and her husband came up to Boston one week-end and invited Elizabeth to join them at a fancy dinner party near Harvard College. Josephine could not take care of Emma, and so, after repeated warnings about good behavior, Elizabeth brought her along to the party. Initially excited at the prospect of attending such an occa-sion, Emma became instantly bored and retired to a position under the dining room table with a color stencil of the First Thanksgiving. Her plaid dress itched something horrible. For some reason she happened to pause in the middle of her coloring work to listen to the man holding court in the den.

Perhaps it was the burlap texture in the speaker's voice as he de-scribed the mysteries of the Yellowstone Valley, the geysers and the boiling rivers, the giant mountain lakes and the rainbow-colored earth; the smell of sulfur, pine, water moss, moose dung. He described all of this with the kind of longing and hyperbolic terms that one used when discussing an eccentric yet perhaps slightly famous uncle who had not been in touch with the rest of family for some time. His speech was peppered with strange scientific words that hung in the air like little exotic birds. She could not quite see the speaker through the lace hem of the tablecloth, only his cigar and the brandy snifter which he swung around as he spoke, but in some ways the facelessness of the tale was better this way: the mythical place captured her imagination in much the same way as the Houyhnhnms first did, the talking horses who were smarter than even the humans. She wanted to see the yellow stones, rub them against her cheeks, smell the sulfur for herself. It all seemed so incredibly far from her position under a table in a parlor in Cambridge, imprisoned inside a plaid dress that kept pinching at her armpits. Perhaps the Houyhnhnms could take her there.

Something clicked. A spring popped loose, a gear shifted a notch, and the whole contraption inside her that had lain still for so long now began to move, ever so slowly.

Four months later, on a nasty April day, Emma stood shivering outside the flower shop, waiting for her mother to move the flowers back by the furnace, where it was still warm. Even though she had been forbidden to enter the store without Josephine's permission, the chill from her wet socks was such that she was about to walk inside and inquire as to what was taking her mother so long, when a very tall man, dressed in a walking cape and holding a cane, strolled up to her. She blinked, twisted her toes inside her shoes.

He bent down so that he was at eye level with her.

"Hell-oo," he said in an affected British voice, lingering on each syllable. "I'm Mr. Orrrr-win En-gele-thorp-ee. And I've been looking forward to meeting you."

"Hello," she said. "I'm Emma Osterville."

"Indeed," he said. "Indeed. Indeed." He looked up at the flower shop, and then at the sky and then further up at the sky behind him, so that Emma was worried he might topple over backward. Then he swung his head back down again and spoke in a private sort of whisper: "You know this weather is nothing compared to April in Siberia."

Another marginal note:

a certain illicit joy — no burden of proof.

Normally I'm as big a fan of proof as the next guy, but seeing my mother jot this note gave me a delicious shiver of danger...

Yes, Mother, I thought. *Do not worry about that little ugly gnome called Proof. Proof, which has suspended your career and left you wallowing in the moors of obscurity for twenty years now.*

"Proof can go to hell!" I yelled, and then felt bad for having said it. My words hung around in the empty cabin of the Winnebago.

"Sorry," I said to Valero. He didn't respond. I bet Valero didn't believe in proof either.

Emma giggled. This man's voice, his countenance, all seemed entirely too familiar.

"Siberia," he went on, "is not a place for children. Except of course if you are born there to the Chukchees. If you are a Chukchee child, then it is just about right."

The feeling of familiarity parted into recognition. In an instant, she connected the man now crouching before her with the memory of the brandy snifter swinging back and forth through the lace scrim of the tablecloth; here, cloaked in the whimsy of a man crouching on one knee, was the gravitas of that voice which had so enchanted her. His face was long and angular, with a nose that seemed to travel vertically rather than outward from his visage and a jawline which culminated in a pointed chin. His mustache was unkempt, dark, and bristly; Mr. Englethorpe appeared unconcerned with its attempts to migrate upward and outward from the confines of his upper lip. His gabardine overcoat, though free from any blemish, was tailored slightly too short, as though its creator had forgotten to carry a zero. Yet any air of inattention was countered by the rich black leather gloves that covered his hands and the polished whiteness of his ivory cane, which he used to make gentle semicircle patterns in the mud as they spoke. But it was his blue, almost grey eyes that seemed most peculiar of all to Emma, for they were unerringly bright and curious: his first gesture of looking above and behind his head at the sky was not out of the ordinary; she could see now that he was constantly alert, watching their surroundings, mentally recording every detail which transpired around them. *The patterns of puddles along the troughs of the cobblestone street. The slight dragging motion of the man's walk across the way. The four pigeons pecking*

"The slight dragging motion of the man's walk across the way."

I noticed things like this too, particularly limps and lisps and lazy eyes.

Did this make me a bad person? Father said we should never look down on anyone with a medical condition that God gave them, but was *noticing* a condition and then obsessively trying to *not* notice this condition "looking down on someone"? Was I a bad person for staring at old man Chiggins's limp and then shutting my eyes so that I would not stare? Knowing God, I was probably guilty of something.

at the trail of seed from the miller's wagon that had just rattled by. This was a man who could have walked clear across the West and noticed every stone and twig, every bend in every stream, every steppe and precipice of every mountain.

Elizabeth emerged from the flower shop and appeared startled by the sight of Mr. Englethorpe. She froze for an instant before coloring and allowing a smile to slip across her face. Emma had never seen such a strange set of behaviors from her mother before.

"Good day, sir," Elizabeth said. "This is my daughter, Emma."

"Oh!" he said. He took four steps backward and then came forward again and crouched next to Emma, just as he had before.

"Hell-ooooo," he said again, with an even more exaggerated Anglo accent. "I'm Mr. Orrr-win En-gele-thorp-eeeee. And I've been loooking forward to meeting you."

He winked at her, and Emma giggled.

Elizabeth didn't seem to know what to make of this. She made a gesture as if to go back inside the shop and then stopped. "Mr. Englethorpe has just returned from California," she said pointedly to Emma.

"California!" he said. "Can you imagine? And now I have had the recent pleasure of meeting your mother." He stood up and turned fully to Elizabeth for the first time. The scene of the street shifted, tinted, came into focus again. Emma watched the two people orbit each other, almost imperceptibly. The gravitational pull between them was invisible to the eye, but all those present on that chilly cobble street in Somerville—even the pigeons pecking at the last of the miller's grain—were very much aware of its existence.

As it turned out, he was not British or even as polysyllabic as he put forth that day, but his name was Mr. Orwin Englethorpe and he was a recent acquaintance of her mother's. How they had met was unclear—perhaps that night in the den, surrounded by stories of distant valleys, or perhaps it was earlier in the flower shop, or perhaps through an unnamed friend—no one would quite say. Emma would later find all of this secrecy extremely frustrating.

Elizabeth, for her part, was charmed, overwhelmed even, at the attentions of such a man. Mr. Englethorpe had been around the world—to California and back, to Paris, to eastern Africa, to the tundras of Siberia, to Papua New Guinea, which sounded less like a place and more like a fancy dinner platter to Emma. Mr. Englethorpe stood before her with the scents of distant lands floating about him, the sands of red deserts, the dew from equatorial jungles, the pine resin of high boreal forests.

"What do you do?" asked Emma outside the flower shop that first time she met him. She had remained silent the entire time that her mother and Mr. Englethorpe had been talking.

"Emma!" Elizabeth hissed, but Mr. Englethorpe waved her off with a gloved hand.

"The little lady clearly has a curious mind," he said. "And deserves an answer. I am afraid, however, that there is no easy answer. You see, Miss Osterville, I have been spending a good deal of my life trying to figure out that very question. One day I might answer you and say I was a prospector, and a poor prospector at that, and another day I

might say curator, or collector, or mapmaker, or even"—he winked at
Emma—"pirate."

- ➤ "He's a mapmaker, Valero!"
I said.

Emma withdrew back into the shop, amidst the safety of the lilies.
She squeezed her left thumb with her right hand. She was in love.

Valero said nothing.

"And a pirate!" I said to
Redbeard.

Silence.

I didn't care if my friends
weren't talking. I had found
the river's source.

Three rainy weeks later, Emma would accompany Elizabeth on
the first sunny day of May to see Mr. Englethorpe's residence. They
arrived at an address on Quincy Street in Cambridge just near the beautiful expanse of Harvard Yard.

At first, they could not believe their eyes. They stood before a
huge white mansion with fourteen windows, Emma counted, across
the front of the house alone.

"Fourteen!" Emma said. "You could fit a regular house inside that house. And then a smaller house inside that house. And
then—"

"This must not be right," Elizabeth said. Next to the gate a small
yellow sign hung: AGASSIZ SCHOOL FOR GIRLS.

"Mommy," Emma asked. "Is he a teacher?"

"I don't think so," Elizabeth said. She took out the slip of paper
Mr. Englethorpe had given her and found some further instructions in
small print: *follow the path around back to the carriage house.*

The large front gate did not squeak as they gingerly pressed it
open. Somehow both of them were expecting it to let out a sharp, grat-
ing whine that would arouse the suspicions of the neighborhood, so
when it did not, they suddenly felt even more wary of their intrusion
into an unknown world. The gravel path had been recently raked and

edged. A piece of gravel had escaped into a mulch bed and Emma ran over to pick up the limestone bead and place it back on the path.

The front door to the giant house suddenly opened. They froze. A young girl emerged, younger than Emma. She took the steps two at a time before she saw the two women standing on the path. The girl looked at them, wrinkled her nose, and said, "You won't. Professor Agassiz won't let you." Then she unlatched the gate and disappeared into the street.

Emma started to cry. She wanted to leave immediately but Elizabeth calmed her and convinced her that the girl must have confused them with somebody else and that since they had come all this way, they may as well try and find Mr. Englethorpe.

And her persistence paid off: as they rounded the corner of the large house, they were suddenly surrounded by an explosion of flowers—gardenias and purple-frosted rhododendrons, lilacs, and fuchsia stargazers, their lithe, tangerine aromas hitting Emma and Elizabeth in waves. Their feet seemed to pluck at the gravel beneath them. Once behind the house, they saw fully the extent of the garden. It was guarded on all sides by a row of dogwoods, and in the center a pond was flecked with pockets of yellow-fringed orchids, lilies, azaleas. Four cherry trees clustered in one corner of the garden surrounding a little wrought-iron bench. They came to an elephantine weeping willow, which they had to duck beneath as the path hugged its base.

"This is like a book!" Emma said. "Did he make this garden?"

"I think so," Elizabeth said. "He knows all the fancy Latin names of the flowers when he comes into the shop."

"Is he Latin?" asked Emma.

Elizabeth turned to Emma and grabbed hold of her wrist. "Emma. Don't ask any more questions. This is not the time to ask questions. I don't want you to ruin this too."

Emma yanked her wrist free. She scrunched up her top lip and worked it with her teeth. The tears came faster than she could wipe them away.

Elizabeth did not say anything more, and Emma sniffled as they crunched along the path.

And then they were at the side door of the carriage house. A small stone on the end of a string drifted ever so slightly across a brass plate in the middle of the door. The plate was etched with a little crescent where the stone had swung against it. Elizabeth looked at the stone and the plate for a second and then knocked on the door with her hand.

There was a silence, and then a sound of heavy footsteps, and Mr. Englethorpe opened the door, sweating, as if he had been running for a great distance. Framed in the doorway, he appeared even taller than Emma had remembered. He surveyed them both, pressed his index finger to his lips.

"Gracious! Mrs. Osterville and Miss Osterville," he said, smiling at Emma. "Welcome, welcome. Such a pleasure."

His smile pulled the vessels of mother and daughter back against each other, the gap disappearing as he reached for their walking coats and continued to exude the energy of one who had simply not been given enough time on this earth to achieve all that he wanted to do.

They followed him inside. He paused in the entranceway, hanging their coats on two pegs that looked like jawbones. Elizabeth began to recoil, but he turned to her.

"Next time, Mrs. Osterville," he said. "I must—"

"Please," she said quickly, a little too quickly. "Call me Elizabeth."

"Elizabeth. Yes," he said, trying out the name. "Well, next time, Elizabeth, I must insist that you use the stone to announce your arrival. Occasionally I have been known to become so enraptured in my work that I don't respond to any normal human knock. Dr. Agassiz had the current apparatus installed upon repeated frustrations trying to rouse me from my—experiments."

"Sorry," she said. "That, that…thing scared me a bit, to tell you the truth."

He laughed. "No need, no need. Such inventions are meant to enable us, not to hinder us. We should not be afraid of our own creations—skeptical, perhaps, but not fearful."

"Well, I will use it next time."

"Thank you," he said. "We wouldn't want the two of you standing in the cold for hours, would we?"

Emma nodded. She was nodding at everything that his voice said.

They settled down for tea. Mr. Englethorpe served them in an elaborate five-step process that involved, among other things, lifting the teapot higher and higher as he poured until the last of the hot liquid was traveling some three or four feet in the air before splashing all across the cup and saucers and the table.

In the margin, Dr. Clair had drawn a little doodle:

Just a few overlapping circles, most likely of no significance, but there was a quiet beauty in seeing the pen absently work the margins of the page as the mind whirred and tumbled somewhere far away. Doodles were fertile ground; they were the visual evidence of heavy cognitive lifting. Although this was not always true: Ricky Lepardo was a doodler and he was not a heavy cognitive lifter.

Emma watched in fascination and then looked at her mother. Elizabeth sat perfectly still.

As though finally recognizing the strangeness of his actions, Mr. Englethorpe said, "It's much better for the tea. Cools it, aerates it, reminds me of the falls in Yosemite. I learned this in Papua New Guinea. This is how a local tribe serves their cocoa tea. Powerful stuff."

As they sipped and chatted, Emma watched her mother work up the nerve to ask about the owner of the main house. When she did, it was said in a whisper into her tea, as though to no one in particular.

Mr. Englethorpe must have heard her, for he smiled and licked his spoon. He gazed out the bay window of the carriage house.

"The property belongs to an old friend who collects things like I do. I daresay he is a trifle more intelligent than I and quite beyond a trifle more organized, but we see eye-to-eye on many things. A few, we disagree on. You are of course familiar with Charles Darwin's theory of natural selection?"

Elizabeth blinked.

Mr. Englethorpe looked shocked then laughed, suddenly. "Well, of course you aren't. Goodness, look at me…I have been spending entirely too much time with the stuffed-finch crowd. One has to remember that the Megatherium boys are not the norm. No—I am not sure Darwin's ideas have quite managed to pierce the mainstream yet—despite everything written in Washington, the church still has too strong a grip on the hearts and minds of the people—but I have no doubt that he will. And Dr. Agassiz and I disagree desperately about his importance. You see, Dr. Agassiz is a deeply religious man, perhaps too much so, and this partiality to Scripture clouds his acceptance of new ideas.

Which shocks me, really—not that I am an atheist, no, but science is a discipline of new ideas! New ideas about the origin of old creatures. And so how such an utterly brilliant man—I mean, everything I know I owe to that man—how can he be so bullheaded as to reject the biggest revelation of our time just because it calls into question some of the tenets of his theology? I mean, is he a scientist or is he a—"

Mr. Englethorpe suddenly stopped himself and looked around. "Apologies," he said. "You see, I can get quite heated about these kinds of things and it all must be dreadfully boring to you."

"It isn't," Elizabeth said politely. "Please, go on."

"No t'isn't!" Emma said, overeagerly. Beneath the table Elizabeth slapped her thigh.

Englethorpe smiled and sipped his tea. Emma watched him. His nose was just faintly hooked, giving his face a slightly elongated shape. Framed by long, almost feminine eyelashes, his eyes had an unabashed kindness and a deep knowledge about them that was gentle yet hypnotic. It was as if he were taking apart everything in the room, inspecting its contents, and then arriving at some little joke in his head which made sense to only him .

He put a thumb and forefinger to his lips and then pointed to a slender white orchid on the windowsill. The flower was perfectly silhouetted in the light; six wispy whiskers spiraled from its single cupped petal.

"Observe this *Angraecum germinyanum* from Madagascar. You see that the petals have developed into long tendrils over time. God didn't make them like this. Why? You might ask, Well, this central tendril is not like the others. It is a tube which contains the nectar of the flower.

A moth must come and stick its nose down the tube and then fly to another to pollinate it."

"A moth with a nose that long?" Emma asked. She could not help herself.

Mr. Englethorpe raised an eyebrow. He got up and left the room. Presently he returned holding open a great book. There was an illustration of a hawk moth, with its long, coiled nose.

"Imagine four flowers," he said. "Each has petals of a different length. Along comes a nasty predator who is looking to eat the nectar. He takes a bite from each flower. In the case of the other three flowers, he correctly chooses the long tube filled with delicious nectar. But with this mutation, the one that looks like our beautiful flower, where the petals look very much like the long tube, he makes a mistake and harmlessly bites one of the petals instead. Which one of these flowers do you think gets to have children?"

Emma pointed to the flower on the windowsill.

Mr. Englethorpe nodded. "Exactly," he said. "The orchid with the most successful transmutation. What is amazing about mutations is that it is chance, really: there is no brain behind these adaptations, and yet through natural selection over thousands, millions, of years, the selection process makes it seem like there is a grand design behind all of this variation…because she is indeed beautiful, isn't she?"

They all looked at the orchid standing perfectly still in the sunlight.

"Perhaps we could sell those at the flower shop," Elizabeth said. "It really is beautiful."

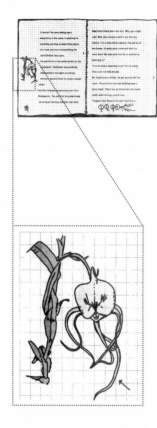

"Well, this central tendril is not like the others."

Dr. Yorn had taught me about this very same flower. He actually had a drawing of a hawk moth in his bedroom in Bozeman.

"And temperamental. *Beauty is fleeting.* I think the proverb goes?"

"What's a transmutation?" Emma asked. Both adults turned to her. She waited for another slap against her thigh, but it never came.

Mr. Englethorpe beamed. He reached out a finger and lightly touched one of the orchid's petals. "That is an excellent question," he said. "But..."

"But what?" Emma said.

"But... we would need the whole afternoon. Do you have time?"

"Time?" Elizabeth asked, bewildered, as though she had not considered the existence of the afternoon that would occur beyond this moment.

They did have time. They spent the rest of the day walking through the garden, Mr. Englethorpe pointing out the related species of flowers and their evolutionary differences, where they were from, what had caused them to develop differently. Occasionally he would become frustrated with himself and go into the carriage house and come out with a map of Madagascar, or the Galápagos, or the Canadian Territories, or a glass case housing a collection of taxidermied finches. He would not bother to put any of these back in the house, and so as the afternoon wore on, the paths became littered with atlases and collecting cases and leatherbound books describing anatomy and explorers' diaries. He brought out two copies of Darwin's *On the Origin of Species* and laid them next to each other on the wrought-iron bench beneath the cherry trees. One book cover was green, the other burgundy. They seemed at home on the bench.

At one point Mr. Englethorpe waved at a figure standing in the window of the main house, but when Emma tried to get a better look through the glare on the glass, the window was empty again.

He gave Emma and Elizabeth each a magnifying glass to carry around with them.

"Take a closer look," he kept saying. "You cannot see much with just your eyes. We were equipped with inadequate tools for this kind of work. Evolution clearly did not foresee us being scientists!"

Elizabeth seemed flushed at the end of the afternoon. Throughout it all, when Emma had not been caught up in the ferocious fun of discovery, she kept glancing at her mother as she hiked her skirts and inspected a bush or listened to Mr. Englethorpe talk of trade winds and seeds. Normally she could read her mother's reactions quite easily: the way her pinky twitched, the color of her neck. But throughout the afternoon her mother had remained strangely guarded and so as the light faded across the magical little garden, Emma feared her mother would never want to see this man and all of his curious instruments again.

But as they were packing up their supplies (the Darwin books, one in each of Emma's hands), Elizabeth touched Mr. Englethorpe's arm. Emma pretended not to watch as she put down the books and busied herself in restoring the drawers of moths to the little cherrywood cabinet.

"Thank you," Elizabeth said. "This was unexpected...and lovely. We learned so much...from you."

"Well, most of it was probably useless anyway. I often wonder about the usefulness of such pursuits beyond the walls of this garden."

Elizabeth seemed not to know what to say. She stood silent for a moment and then said, "Well, I don't think I'll ever look at the flower

Another note in the margin:

Call Terry

Terry? Why did this name sound familiar?

— Terrence Yorn. —

Mr. Jibsen had used the same familiar moniker on the phone. Whenever adults called themselves by their first names I felt like they were speaking in code, referencing a world in which grown-ups did grown-up things that I could not understand.

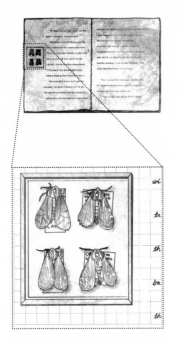

"The little creatures trembled as she slid them back in the cabinet."

I recognized this box of moths. Dr. Clair had the same one. Given that she had already described how little evidence she had to go on, how much of this story was actually true and how much was simply stolen from our own life? As an empiricist, my first instinct was to cling to only that which could be verified, but as I read on, such a disctinction seemed less and less important.

shop in quite the same way. I do want to try and get those orchids, even if they are tempered–"

"Temperamental. Finicky. They prefer Madagascar to New England. So do I," he laughed.

"Perhaps we could...do this again, sometime," Elizabeth said.

Emma could feel her fingers burn as she fumbled with the drawers of moths. The little creatures trembled as she slid them back into the cabinet. One by one they disappeared. "I'll be back," she whispered to them before slipping them into the darkness.

She wanted to return to this garden every day. For the first time in her life she thought of her mother married to another man besides the fisherman she never knew, and now she found herself wishing for this new union desperately, with every bone in her being. She wanted them to get married now, instantly—she wanted to move out of their mildewed basement flat with the dirty windows and into this carriage house with its peculiar knocker and even more peculiar contents. They could become a family of collectors.

They returned the next week, and this time Mr. Englethorpe took them into his study, buried in the back of the carriage house.

"I hate to say it, but this is where I spend most of my time." His fingers were playing with a compass of some sort, nervously, squeezing the metal ends together and then separating them apart over and over again. He had not been this way last week. Emma wanted to go over to him and say, "Don't be nervous, sir, we like you. Very much."

Instead, she smiled and winked at him, which he puzzled at for a second, as though decoding a message, before winking back. He briefly stuck out his tongue at her and then returned his face to neutral as Elizabeth turned to him.

The room was filled to the brim. There were drawers and drawers of birds, fossils, rocks, insects, teeth, hair clippings. A stack of gold-framed paintings lay in one corner. A coil of long rope attached to a mermaid-shaped anchor lay in another. Two walls were covered floor-to-ceiling in bookcases. The books were old, crumbling, some clearly already crumbled, appearing so fragile that if you merely touched their spines the words inside might disintegrate into dust.

Emma buzzed around the room, picking up ornamental knives, sniffing inside old wooden boxes.

"Where did you get all these things?" Emma asked.

"Don't be rude," Elizabeth snapped.

Englethorpe laughed. "I can see that we are going to get along marvelously, Emma. I acquired these things during all of my travels. You see, I have this little—some might call it a *psychological* problem of wanting to know a place through its objects, to understand a culture or habitat through all the millions of little interlocking parts. Dr. Agassiz calls me—affectionately, I might add—'the Walking Museum.' And what you see here is the least of it. The doctor has kindly donated two of his storerooms in his new museum for my collection. Someday I may get to sifting through all of it, but who knows? By that time, I will have collected more. Is it possible to collect all the contents of the world? If the entire world is in your collection is it a collection anymore? A question that has kept me up at night."

"I want to see all of it!" Emma shouted, performing a little leap into the air.

Mr. Englethorpe and Elizabeth both stared at the child standing in the middle of the room, holding a whale tooth in one hand and a spear in the other.

"We have a little scientist on our hands," Mr. Englethorpe whispered to Elizabeth, who looked as if she had been stricken by the flu.

"Perhaps," he said to Emma. "Perhaps I might inquire with Dr. Agassiz about enrolling you in his wife's school inside the main house..."

"Oh, would you?" Emma said. "Would you?"

The contraption inside her head had finally been set into motion, and once the gears began turning, they gained a frantic kind of momentum that nothing, it seemed, could stop.

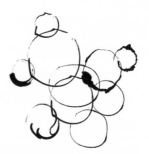

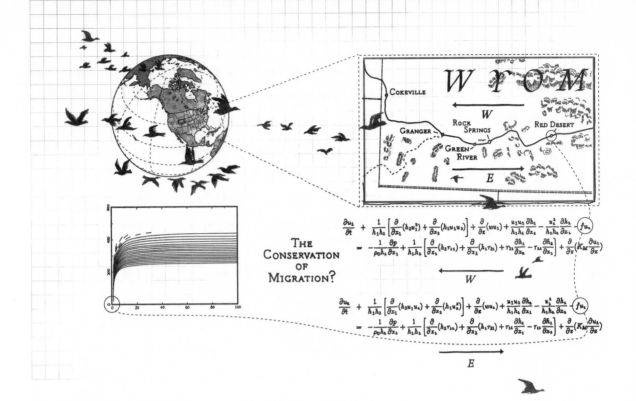

$$\frac{\partial u_1}{\partial t} + \frac{1}{h_1 h_2}\left[\frac{\partial}{\partial x_1}(h_2 u_1^2) + \frac{\partial}{\partial x_2}(h_1 u_1 u_2)\right] + \frac{\partial}{\partial z}(w u_1) + \frac{u_1 u_2}{h_1 h_2}\frac{\partial h_1}{\partial x_2} - \frac{u_2^2}{h_1 h_2}\frac{\partial h_2}{\partial x_1} - \left(f u_2\right)$$
$$= -\frac{1}{\rho_0 h_1}\frac{\partial p}{\partial x_1} + \frac{1}{h_1 h_2}\left[\frac{\partial}{\partial x_1}(h_2 \tau_{11}) + \frac{\partial}{\partial x_2}(h_1 \tau_{21}) + \tau_{21}\frac{\partial h_1}{\partial x_2} - \tau_{22}\frac{\partial h_2}{\partial x_1}\right] + \frac{\partial}{\partial z}\left(K_M \frac{\partial u_1}{\partial z}\right)$$

$\longleftarrow$ W

THE CONSERVATION OF MIGRATION?

$$\frac{\partial u_2}{\partial t} + \frac{1}{h_1 h_2}\left[\frac{\partial}{\partial x_1}(h_2 u_1 u_2) + \frac{\partial}{\partial x_2}(h_1 u_2^2)\right] + \frac{\partial}{\partial z}(w u_2) + \frac{u_1 u_2}{h_1 h_2}\frac{\partial h_2}{\partial x_1} - \frac{u_1^2}{h_1 h_2}\frac{\partial h_1}{\partial x_2} - \left(f u_1\right)$$
$$= -\frac{1}{\rho_0 h_2}\frac{\partial p}{\partial x_2} + \frac{1}{h_1 h_2}\left[\frac{\partial}{\partial x_1}(h_2 \tau_{12}) + \frac{\partial}{\partial x_2}(h_1 \tau_{22}) + \tau_{12}\frac{\partial h_2}{\partial x_1} - \tau_{11}\frac{\partial h_1}{\partial x_2}\right] + \frac{\partial}{\partial z}\left(K_M \frac{\partial u_2}{\partial z}\right)$$

E $\longrightarrow$

CHAPTER 7

I looked up from my reading. The train had stopped. The first rays of sunlight were breaking through over the distant desert hills. I had been on the train for a full day.

I got up from the couch and did some calisthenics. I found another carrot stick that had migrated to the bottom of my suitcase and ate it without shame. I did some vocal warm-ups. And yet, I still could not shake the feeling of dull melancholy that had been lurking since my departure, a kind of persistent hollowness, similar to the feeling I got when eating cotton candy: initially there was so much associated nostalgia, so much promise emanating from those luscious pink threads, but when I got down to the act of licking it or biting it or whatever one did to cotton candy, there was just not a lot there—in the end, you were just eating a sugar wig.

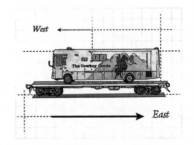

Headed East, Pointed West
from Notebook G101

Perhaps my lingering depression was due to the fact that (a) I had been traveling on a freight train for the past twenty-four hours, and (b) aside from the cheeseburger, I had really not been eating properly.

Or perhaps my condition was subtly influenced by the fact that the Winnebago was actually pointed *west*, in the opposite direction that the train was headed, and so despite the vast tracts of territory that I was obviously covering, I could not help but feel that I was really traveling in reverse.

One should never drive in reverse for long periods of time. All of our cultural language around progress was concerned with traveling forward: "moving on up!" "full speed ahead!" and "onward and upward!" Likewise, "reverse" carried an idiomatically negative connotation: "he backpedaled helplessly," "it was a complete reversal of fortune," and "Johnny Johnson is about as backwards as they come."

My body had grown so used to traveling in reverse that whenever we stopped, I found that my whole field of vision swam at me. I had first noticed this when I was hiding in the bathroom of the Cowboy Condo during one of our numerous station stops. I had become increasingly convinced that the railroad knew my exact location and it was only a matter of time before they sent one of their bulls to come and kill me. As I sat on the toilet in the confines of the tiny bathroom, I suddenly was overcome with the sensation of running into the wall in front of me. It was nauseating to find that your reflection in the bathroom mirror was moving toward you when you were in fact standing still, as though it had managed to break free from the normal laws of refraction and optics. Gradually, through the steady influence of backward motion vectors, my confidence was taking a beating.

➤ This phrase was said out loud by Father to Layton and me as we passed Johnny Johnson carrying his fishing rods on the Frontage Road. Johnny owned a little ramshackle house down valley. I suppose he represented the worst of what rural life can do to a man: he was racist, uneducated, and badly in need of dental work. In that moment of passing on the Frontage Road, I wondered how close the cosmology had come to making me his son. What if the proverbial stork had dropped me off a half-mile too early into the backward arms of the Johnsons? What if...

Then, completely out of the blue, Johnny showed up to Layton's funeral with his wife and sister. It was such a simple neighborly gesture that was also just profoundly nice of him to do. Of course, every time I saw him after that, l felt guilty for judging him. In retrospect, I guess I shouldn't be surprised: over the course of my short life I have learned that more often than not, people turn out to be different from who you originally thought they were.

A Map to the Church of the Big Hole
by Johnny Johnson,
apparently for his sister, retrieved
from her pew after Layton's funeral
from Shoebox 4

And so where did I find solace from this herky-jerky quagmire of momentum?

I knew there was a reason I had packed my studies of Sir Isaac Newton. I searched through my suitcase and grasped the notebook as one grasped an old childhood teddy bear in times of distress.

I had first studied Newton's *Philosophiae Naturalis Principia Mathematica* when I was charting the flight paths of Canada Geese above our ranch, as I wanted a better understanding of the conservation of forces during the act of flying. Later I returned to Newton's work with a more philosophical (and probably inappropriate) approach as I began to conceive of the conservation of migratory behavior. As in: *what goes south will eventually return north,* and vice versa. I had thought about expanding my notebook into a paper on "Theories of Conservation in Migratory Behavior of Canada Geese," but I couldn't ever quite manage to squeeze it (even in an extremely extraneous fashion) into an eighth grade science report on, say, "The Salinity of Coca-Cola."

I opened my notebook on Newton. On the first page, I had written Newton's three laws of motion:

FIRST LAW: AN OBJECT AT REST OR TRAVELING IN UNIFORM MOTION WILL REMAIN AT REST OR TRAVELING IN UNIFORM MOTION UNLESS ACTED UPON BY A NET FORCE.

SECOND LAW: THE RATE OF CHANGE OF MOMENTUM OF A BODY IS EQUAL TO THE RESULTANT FORCE ACTING ON THE BODY AND IS IN THE SAME DIRECTION.

THIRD LAW: ALL FORCES OCCUR IN PAIRS, AND THESE TWO FORCES ARE EQUAL IN MAGNITUDE AND OPPOSITE IN DIRECTION.

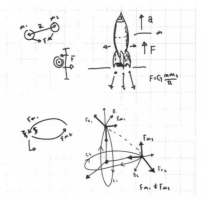

Ah! Here were some laws to help unravel the momentum of my travels. According to Newton, the train was exacting the same force on the Winnebago as the Winnebago exacted on it, but because of the train's much larger mass (and therefore its much larger momentum), and particularly because of the wonderful properties of friction, the Winnebago kindly acquiesced to the train's request to come along for the ride. I, in turn, was equaling the Winnebago's force on me, but also succumbed to its directional inclination due to my slender frame, gravity, and the stickiness of my sneakers.

When Father hit me with the ◀╌ palm of his hand a little too hard in order to say hello, I stepped back a foot, because the differences in our masses (my father was a steady 190 lbs. and I topped out at 73 lbs.) transferred into a more powerful momentum change in my direction. On contact with that slap, I was exerting a change in momentum on him too, just not that much. Similarly, when a school bus hit a squirrel, the squirrel and the bus exerted equal forces on each other, but the vast differences in their masses caused the squirrel to gather a deadly amount of acceleration postcollision.

Equal and Opposite Forces
from Notebook G29

Even if you jumped up and down on the earth, you were knocking it off course a teensy-weensy bit. Mostly it was pushing back at your feet, but your little hop had the smallest effect, like the erosive effect of a wasp's feet on a pane of glass.

Newton's laws of conservation also extended to forces acting upon one another: for every collision or movement there needed to be an equal and opposite counterforce.

But could this philosophy of conservation also be extended to the movement of people? To the tidal shifts of generations across space and time?

I found myself thinking of my great-great-grandfather Tecumseh Tearho and his long migration out west from the cold morainic slopes of Finland. His route to the mines in Butte was not a direct one: first that stop in Ohio at the Whistling Cricket, where he adopted a new name (and perhaps a new history), and then, when his train broke down at a small refilling station in the middle of the Wyoming desert, he would end up staying there for two years as a Union Pacific signalman.

The tracks that my train now followed would pass within twenty feet of where he had once sweated, filling up the great tanks of those locomotives. He must have wondered what kind of country he had come to. The desert was endless, the heat unbearable. And yet, had he come to the right place? Sometime in 1870, amongst all of that red sand and corrugated rimland, between the howl of the steam valves and the rickety call of the turkey vultures that circled the small cluster of buildings, *she* had arrived, surrounded by the twenty men of the surveying party. Perhaps the expedition

174

had arrived by carriage, perhaps by train, but whatever their entrance, the exit was the same: Tearho and Emma had met and felt compelled to never leave each other again. One from Finland, one from New England—they had abandoned their former lives and laid down roots in the New West.

A bell went off in the back of my mind. *I had mapped this history somewhere.* I went over to my suitcase and found the notebook titled "Father and the Curious Variety of His Haying Patterns." My excitement growing, I flipped to the back, and there it was: a Genealogy Placemat that I had made for Father on the occasion of his forty-eighth birthday.

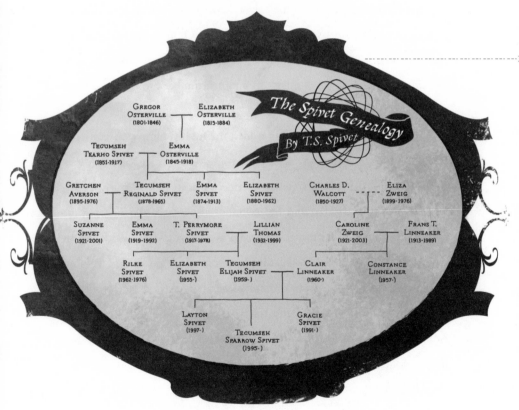

I had hoped Father's aversion to my obsessive mapping tendencies might be tempered by his appreciation for tradition and inherited namesakes (and eating food). After only a glance at the gift, however, he had raised his index finger in a simultaneous gesture of thanks and dismissal—the same gesture he made when he passed nonlocals in the pickup. For six months, the placemat languished in a drawer that also included the turtle paperweights and the number for our pediatrician, who had died two years ago. Eventually, I rescued it and had apparently filed it away in this notebook, as the firing of some subconscious synapse had just reminded me.

Perhaps the family tree was not the best natural metaphor for tracing your genealogy back in time from the single quivering stalk of your existence to the many roots of your ancestors. Trees grow upward, and thus they would be growing back in time as I was now driving my Winnebago backward in time to the site of that fateful convergence. It seemed better to picture the forking and joining of the Spivets and Ostervilles as the forks and splits of a river. And yet such an image raised parallel questions of choice: were the bends of a river guided only by chance—by wind, by erosion, by the fitful heave and sigh of their granulated shores? Or was there a prefixed destination dictated by the sequence of bedrock beneath the riverbed?

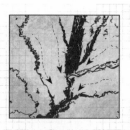

Family Streams and Family Trees from Notebook G88b

As far as I knew, none of the Spivets had ever made it back to Finland, or even east of the Mississippi. Ellis Island, that Ohio frontier saloon, and then the West. Was I naturally counteracting this westward migration? Returning the imbalance of migratory momentum back to zero? Or was I paddling my Winnebago upstream?

Both Tearho and Emma had ridden the freshly completed transcontinental railroad—taking my same exact route—but in the opposite direction. If there had been a time-lapse camera placed by this track, taking a single picture every day, and we rewound far enough, playing back the pictures through a projector that clattered out the years like a stick against a picket fence, there would be Tearho's large-eared face at the train window, quickly followed by the set jaw of Emma several months later, both of them pointed west. One hundred and thirty-seven years and four generations would pass and then there I would be, like an echo. I was pointed west like them, except I was headed east, unraveling time as I went.

I was getting close. I was in the Red Desert and I was getting close to the filling station where Tearho once worked. I knew this from the readings that I had been taking with my sextant and theodolite as well as from some simple fauna and flora observations. I wanted to believe, however, that I could identify the loci of this place not just through scientific observation but through a spiritual reckoning as well, since this place was the backdrop for one of the great meeting points in my family's history.

The Red Desert filling station was the only outpost on the railroad smack dab in the middle of the vast basin that sprawled between the Wind Rivers to the north and the Sierra Madres to the south. Geologists had named this the Great Divide Basin because of its unique position in North America as the only self-contained watershed that did not drain into any ocean. Any rainwater that fell here (and there was not that much of it) evaporated, seeped into the soil, or was lapped up by a horned frog.

From my spot on the train, I squinted out across the vast expanse of red terrain. The tattered foothills gathered together, milling around one another until they reluctantly rose up into the distant mountain ranges that formed the invisible rim of the Basin. I could not help but wonder whether the hearty travelers who had managed to come all the way out here 150 years ago did not in some ways mimic the self-contained hydrology of the Basin. Tearho and Emma could not escape the pull of the vortex. I could almost feel the slow, quiet inward compulsion of the landscape, exerting a certain inescapable force on anything within its boundaries, so that neither water droplet nor Finnish ancestor, once stuck in its concavity, could escape. Perhaps the executives of the Union Pacific Railway understood the nature of this black hole when they were trying to plow their line through, and thus they created the refilling station in the middle of the Red Desert, an outpost of civilization for the thousands of Irish and Mexican workers who laid the tracks day after day amidst the alien scrub brush and the capillary cracks of the desiccated soil.

BLACK GREASEWOOD
Sarcobatus vermiculatus

MORMON CRICKET
Anabrus simplex

~ Life in the Red Desert ~

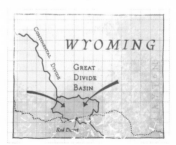

Great Divide Basin as Vortex
from Notebook G101

I opened the hatch of the Winnebago. With both hands firmly gripping the support beam of the flatbed, I gingerly craned my head off the side of the freight train as it barreled its way across the desert. Immediately, I was met with one of the most intense, knifing blasts of air that I had ever experienced.

Let me remind you of a natural phenomenon that you may have forgotten about while sitting in the plush maroon loveseat of your living room: *wind*.

It was one of those things that you didn't think much about until it was upon you as it was upon me now; that you couldn't really quite picture in your mind until it enveloped your entire world; and once you were in it, you could never remember a world where it wasn't the dominating feature of your consciousness. It was like food poisoning, or a huge snowstorm, or...

(I could think of nothing else.)

I inched my head outward, trying to get a glimpse of a jumbled collection of buildings amidst the twisting greasewood that would denote the spot of the old town. I was not expecting much: in fact, I was willing for a single, abandoned ex–depot building to be the only sign of my great-great-grandfather's existence here.

We moved through a gap between two buttes and I looked up at the earth on their shoals: it was red! A deep, blood-colored chalk spilled down the hillside. This must be a sign. Some man a century and a half ago must have seen these buttes as he surveyed the railroad's trajectory, wiped his forehead with his handkerchief, and said to his partner, *We must name this place the Red Desert. You must admit. It is only fair, Giacomo.*

Up ahead, I could see the line of chattering boxcars that culminated in the mighty black-and-yellow Union Pacific diesels plunging us onward into the desert, the thick body of the engine shimmering in the heat. The wind was so vicious against my face that I began conjuring images from a documentary I watched on the History Channel (at Charlie's house) about the genius of Erwin Rommel and his army in the North African theater of World War II. There had been a whole section of the program on the giant simooms of the Sahara and how soldiers protected themselves from the powerful sandstorms.

Suddenly, I was a sniper trying to protect Gazala in the middle of a fierce simoom, weathering heavy fire from the enemy, flak and shrapnel assailing me from all directions. The Nazis must have been everywhere, but I could not spot a single one in all of that endless desert—little particles of sand and grit kept stinging my cheeks and burrowing into my eyes.

Where are you, Rommel? Damn you and damn this simoom! The world blurred. Tears ran down my cheeks. I squinted against the glaring, rust-colored badlands of Wyoming/northern Algeria.

Where was the Desert Fox? [And where was that town?]

I could stand it no more. Acknowledging defeat in both my imaginary ten-second war and my search for the mysterious desert town, I ducked back out of the wind, leaning against the side of the Winnebago, rubbing my eyes and breathing hard. It was amazing the difference the wind made in transforming the scene: out there, exposed to the elements,

*Rommel's Flanking Maneuvers
at the Battle of Gazala*
from Notebook G47

179

it was all Rommel and shrapnel, but in here, sheltered by the curious co-coon of the Winnebago, the world was serene and cinematic.

I rechecked my atlas, took another reading with my sextant and com-pass, and stared out at the desert. The station must be close.

The more I searched the landscape, however, the more I was surprised at the number of *different shades* of reds that were present in the rocks. They were beautifully striated across the topography, like layers of some grand geologic cake. Burgundies and cinnamons tinted the sawbucks at the higher elevations; on the banks of a dry riverbed that wove its way along the railroad line, pink-infused mustard limestone faded into salmon and then luminous magenta at its silty river bottom.

I bit my lip and again craned my head out into the open air, scanning the clumps of sage and bright green jackrabbit weed—*Could we have passed it? Did it no longer exist?* I rechecked my calculations, *No, we could not have passed it...could we?*

And then there it was: no more than an old station sign sticking out of the ground, black lettering on a white background—RED DESERT, it said, like a label in a museum. No depot, no platform, just the sign and a dirt road that ran over the tracks to a distant farmhouse on the flats of a dried-out coulee. The interstate was visible just over the rise, and an old exit pulled into a now abandoned gas station with a crumbled sign that read RED DESERT SERVICE. The gas station had come and gone long after my great-great-grandfather had left; once again people had tried to maintain some kind of service here, only to succumb to the spiralic termination of its surroundings.

This place was where Tearho had decided to stay. Under what cir-cumstances did he meet Emma? What did they say to each other out here amidst the sage? I had to go back to my mother's story. Perhaps she had discovered the secret.

When is a sign no longer a sign?

I sat down at the little table and set up my workstation. As we traveled across Wyoming and then into Nebraska, I entered Emma's world, and when I was moved to do so, I drew pictures next to my mother's text. Someday, we could make a book together.

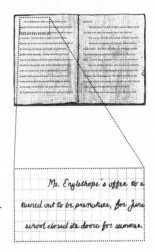

Mr. Englethorpe's offer to enroll Emma in the Agassiz School turned out to be premature, for June was already upon them and soon the school closed its doors for summer. This fact did not seem to deter Emma, however, for as soon as she was free from the clutches of the seminary, she began visiting Mr. Englethorpe's garden nearly every day. During the stiflingly humid days of July, they would sit for hours making sketches of the flora in the garden, and when it became too hot for them to concentrate, they would place cool towels dipped in lemon-scented water on the napes of their necks and lounge in the shade of the weeping willow. As the water trickled down her back, Emma listened to Mr. Englethorpe tell stories about each element found in the earth.

"Phosphorous," he said, "is like a woman who is never satisfied with what she already has in her clutches."

"Oh, but you should make a book of these," she said.

"No doubt somebody will," he said. "Blink and you might miss it. We are in the great age of categorization. This world may be completely described in fifty years. Well…seventy years, perhaps. There are a lot of insects, and beetles in particular."

The two of them did their part, naming and labeling the orchids that Mr. Englethorpe had brought back from his field trips to Madagascar. He taught her how to use the giant optical microscope in his

This is the route that the freight train took as I read my mother's notebook. I would occasionally look up from the page and make notes about our progress. *One should always know where one is at all times* was one of my laminated mottoes.

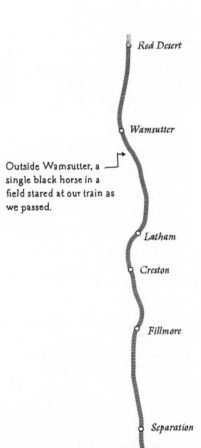

Outside Wamsutter, a single black horse in a field stared at our train as we passed.

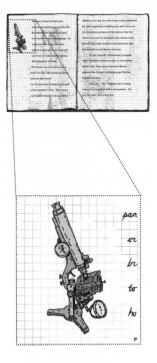

"He taught her how to use
the giant optical microscope in
his study…"

During our first weekend together in Bozeman, Dr. Yorn had shown me how to use the university's electron microscope. What a day that was! When we brought a dust mite into focus we high-fived each other and exclaimed with delight.

Can you imagine Father high-fiving me over a dust mite? Can you imagine Father high-fiving at all? No. He would shoulder-punch you, or once, after Layton had felled a coyote at great distance with his Winchester, Father was so happy that he took off his hat and slapped it on Layton's head, saying, "Attaboy—sonfabitch ca-yote done breathed his last." This spontaneous transfer of Stetson from father to son was a beautiful thing to witness, even if a similar transfer would never come my way.

study and even how to record new species in the big, official book on his desk.

"This book is as much yours as it is mine," he said. "We cannot be stingy with our discoveries."

For the most part, Elizabeth approved of her daughter's visits. There was a noticeable change in the way Emma walked, in the way she came home to their basement flat after suppertime, bubbling over with stories of the reticulation patterns of leaf veins or how the anther at the tip of a particular lily's stamen looked exactly like a fuzzy version of the canoe that they had paddled around Boston Common.

"So you enjoy Mr. Englethorpe's company, then?" Elizabeth asked one night as she braided Emma's hair. They sat on her bed in flannel pajamas, the crickets chirping outside in the New England humidity.

"Yes…oh!…yes!" Emma said, sensing some kind of question within the question. "Do you like him? He is a fine man."

"You spend so much time over there."

"Well, it is just that I am learning so much. You see, Darwin came up with this idea of the natural selection of species and many people like the idea, like this very nice fellow who came over named Mr. Gray, but then many people still think that he's wrong and… You aren't angry with me, are you?"

"No, of course not," Elizabeth said. "I want most of all for you to be happy."

"Are you happy?" Emma asked.

"What do you mean?"

"I mean since he was…since he went into the sea…" Her voice trailed off. She looked up, fearful that she had crossed some line.

"I'm content, yes," Elizabeth said, breaking the silence. They suddenly both become aware of the two Gullivers sitting on the shelf, above their heads. "We are so lucky, you know. We have much to look forward to. We have each other."

"What do we have to look forward to?" Emma asked, smiling.

"Well, our friendship with Mr. Englethorpe, for one," she said. "And, we can look forward to you growing up into a beautiful young lady. A *smart* and beautiful young lady. You will be the catch of Boston!"

"Mother!"

They giggled and Elizabeth traced a finger down her daughter's nose, plucking at the tip. Emma's nose was her father's nose: on him it seemed altogether too tender for such a hardened man of the sea, but on Emma, it had the opposite effect—the slightly tapered bridge, the gentle flare of the nostrils, gestured at a hardened resolve that lay just waiting beneath the surface, ready to pounce.

Elizabeth watched her daughter. Time had slowly worn away the seams of her memories. How far she had come since she was that puddle of a child on the houseboat in Woods Hole. That first year Emma's tiny body receded from the world as if she did not belong, as if her time had come too soon, and perhaps it had. Now, however, that image was unraveling, gradually replaced by the sharp-eyed girl lying across her lap, her arms playfully raised, fingers outstretched in the air and undulating like the tentacles of a jellyfish. Elizabeth squinted at the fingers wiggling above their heads.

I am here now, they said. *I have arrived.*

The summer came to a slow, winding end. With the waning of each day, Emma could feel a panic rising inside herself.

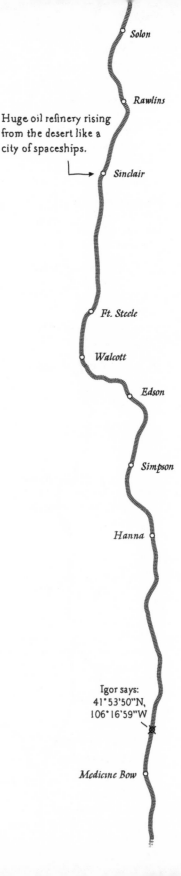

Huge oil refinery rising from the desert like a city of spaceships.

Solon

Rawlins

Sinclair

Ft. Steele

Walcott

Edson

Simpson

Hanna

Igor says: 41°53'50"N, 106°16'59"W

Medicine Bow

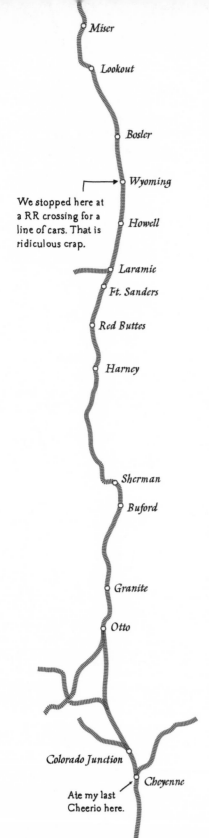

Miser

Lookout

Bosler

Wyoming

We stopped here at
a RR crossing for a
line of cars. That is
ridiculous crap.

Howell

Laramie

Ft. Sanders

Red Buttes

Harney

Sherman

Buford

Granite

Otto

Colorado Junction

Cheyenne

Ate my last
Cheerio here.

Finally, as they sat on the wrought-iron bench one late August afternoon, Emma gathered up her courage.

"Mr. Englethorpe, will you ask Dr. Agassiz again about the possibility of…me attending his school?" she asked. The prospect of leaving this magical garden behind for the hush of those dreadful cold stone hallways and the damp guiding touch of a nun's fingers against the back of the neck was almost too much to handle.

"Of course!" Mr. Englethorpe said quickly, sensing the onset of her tears. "Fear not, Miss Osterville. In the mornings, you shall study in the main house with the other girls. You shall be tutored by a carefully handpicked group of knowledgeable scholars as well as the esteemed Dr. Louis Agassiz himself. In the afternoons, well…you can come out to my humble shelter and teach me everything you learned that day."

Emma smiled. It was all fixed then. She could not help herself, she jumped up and hugged Mr. Englethorpe. "Oh! Thank you, sir," she said.

"Sir?" he tisked her. He made a hollow popping sound with his tongue and patted her long brown hair. At that moment, she was glad for everything that had come before—all of it—because she could not imagine a more perfect world than the one she would soon find herself in.

But it was not all fixed. Josephine contracted tuberculosis and Emma was suddenly needed in the flower shop, so it was a week and a half before she was able to return to the garden, a spell which seemed like a perfect eternity. She finally managed to implore her mother for an afternoon off and slipped away to Quincy Street. When she arrived at

Mr. Englethorpe's carriage house, she found that the door was already open.

"Hello?" she called. There was no answer.

Tentatively, she made her way inside. Mr. Englethorpe was seated at the desk in his study, writing furiously. He looked shaken and pale. She had never seen him in such a state. For a brief instant she wondered if he had contracted tuberculosis just like Josephine, whether everyone in the world had suddenly become sick with the terrible hacking disease. Her mouth went dry.

She stood in the middle of his study and waited. He paused, made a gesture as if he were going to return to writing, then put down his quill.

"He is a madman! How can such a..." He looked at Emma. "I tried."

"What do you mean?" Emma asked. "Are you ill?"

"Oh, my dear," Mr. Englethorpe shook his head. "He said the school was full. I don't believe him, mind you. I don't believe a word he says. I asked him in the middle of an...altercation about this, this... it was an oversight on my part, and I'm sorry. I really am."

"What do you mean?" Emma said, her arms going limp.

"You can of course still come in the afternoons if you like—"

But Emma did not hear the rest. She ran out of the garden, past the group of girls talking surreptitiously on the front steps. As she rushed past them, they stared, momentarily surprised, and then began to laugh at her. It was too much. Emma ran through the hushed pathways of Harvard Yard and out into the bustle of the Square, dodging streetcars and vendors. The tears flowed freely. They ran down her

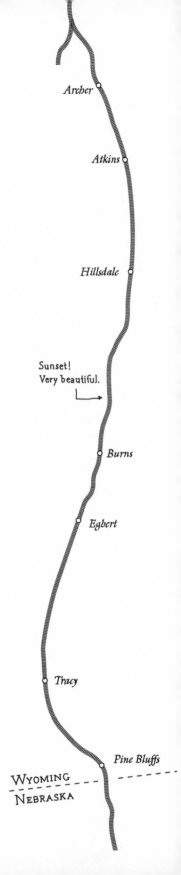

Poor, poor Emma. Could the seminary really have been that bad? My own relationship with religion was like that of a reluctant satellite. Though Father would have loved for us to attend Bible study, Gracie protested so violently (the Conniption of '04) that he was forced to relent. The Spivets were regular churchgoers, but aside from Father's strange habits of touching his crucifixes and butchering Scripture when he was trying to learn us a lesson, our formal Christian commitments didn't really extend beyond Reverend Greer's sermons Sunday mornings at the Church of the Big Hole.

That's not to say I didn't like church. Unlike the nuns of Somerville Girls' Seminary, Reverend Greer was the nicest man you could ever find. At Layton's service, he talked of Layton's death in such a gentle and comforting way that I looked down in the middle of his sermon and saw that Gracie and I were holding hands without even realizing it. At the reception afterward, he let me win at a game of crazy eights. When the receiving line was finished, he took my mother into a corner to have some words. She came back red-faced and crying, but leaning on Reverend Greer's shoulder in a trusting and relaxed kind of way that I had never seen her do with Father.

Father, for his part, used Greer in our house as a sort of fourth axis to the Holy Trinity. As much as Father himself was uneven and selective in his religious practice, whenever he wanted to call up a moral coordinate system, he used Reverend Greer and Jesus interchangeably. One day it would be, "Layton, would Jesus steal a cookie?" and then the next it would be, "Layton, would Reverend leave his unders in the kitchen? Ain't no way in hell, son. Clean those up 'fore I whup ya into Tuesday."

chin and collected in the pocket of her throat, seeping into the pink purled hem of her dress.

She vowed never to visit the garden again.

Her studies at the Somerville Girls' Seminary began the very next week. The school proved even worse than she had remembered. A summer of curiosity and real scientific discovery (Mr. Englethorpe had let her name her own species of orchid, *Aerathes ostervilla*!) was replaced by the droning lectures of aged sisters who seemed to care little for what it was they were droning on about.

All September, Emma moved through the world as if in slow motion, raising her hand when prompted to, lining up when the other girls lined up, and mouthing the hymns in chapel three times a day (though in fact she was actually just whispering the word *watermelon* over and over). She ate less and less. Elizabeth became worried. She asked Emma why she was not going to see Mr. Englethorpe anymore.

"He says he is sorry," she said. "And he has offered to meet with you after school. You mustn't be rude to him, you know. He doesn't owe us anything and yet he is acting so gracious."

"You've been seeing him?" Emma asked, alarmed.

"He's a good man," Elizabeth said. "And he genuinely cares for you. What more do you want from him?"

"I don't want...I...I...," she said. But her resistance was fading.

Mr. Englethorpe called on them the next evening.

"Emma," he said. "I am sorry about Agassiz's school. But perhaps it is just as well. And for this, I give you my word: I will do an even better job than he could in training this little scientist. We are better off this way. Now he won't have a chance to infect you with his stubbornness. Why don't you come by tomorrow afternoon?"

"I can't," Emma said, staring down at the table. "We have activities in the afternoons."

"Activities?"

Emma nodded. The afternoon activities at Somerville Seminary consisted of Bible study, the culinary arts, and "physical education," which seemed to be nothing more than a group of girls strolling around the grounds with badminton racquets in hand, gossiping and giggling under the disapproving eye of Sister Hengle.

"There are always ways around institutional rules, believe me," Mr. Englethorpe said. "I have made a habit of bending the rules."

The next evening, Mr. Englethorpe returned to their residence with a doctor's note diagnosing Emma with a strange disease called osteopelenia, or "Tricky Bones," which precluded her from prayer and any kind of physical exertion. "It's frightfully dangerous," he said in a deep, medical-sounding voice, holding his serious expression until he could not help breaking up into laughter.

Emma was fearful that the seminary would consult an outside doctor on the diagnosis, but Rector Mallard called her into his office, offered his sincere condolences for such a debilitating condition, and sent her on her way—straight to the secret garden, as it turned out.

"Tricky Bones?" Mr. Englethorpe clucked when he opened his door to see her standing there. "My, they really don't do their homework, do they?"

"Can I...?" Emma stammered. At night, she had been having a variation of the same dream: she would come through the gate on Quincy Street only to be surrounded by a pack of girls from the school,

Bushnell

Oliver

Kimball

Owasco

Very bored.

Dix

Jacinto

Potter

Brownson

chanting her name: *Emma, Emma Osterville. Nobody wants her, she makes us ill.*

"Yes?"

"Is there a...back entrance that I can come through?"

Mr. Englethorpe looked at her a moment, confused, and then a wave of understanding swept across his face. "Ah, of course," he said. "Great minds think alike. I have devised just such a trapdoor in the back fence for the times when I...am not faring so well with my host."

And thus their studyship resumed. Nearly every afternoon she slipped through the hinged board in the fence and into the quiet solitude of the garden. Mr. Englethorpe showed her how to use the compass and the collecting net and the specimen jars. They made an extensive display for her natural science class of all the beetles found on the edge of a fallow New England field. The display brought her praise from Sister McGathrite, the science instructor, and long strange looks from her fellow classmates. It was quickly becoming clear that Emma, with her Tricky Bones and love for twigs and creepy-crawlies, was not one for giggling about boys.

Mr. Englethorpe taught her Linnaeus's classification system and told her to pay attention in her Latin class as this was where all the scientific names came from. Together, they closely studied several families of finches. This seemed to be Mr. Englethorpe's specialty, although Emma soon realized that Mr. Englethorpe did not really have a specialty—he dabbled in just about every discipline, from medicine to geology to astronomy. Apprenticing with such a Renaissance man shaped Emma's view of science not just as a collection of disciplines from which one chose a field of expertise, but rather as a holistic way of seeing the world that permeated every part of one's consciousness. Mr.

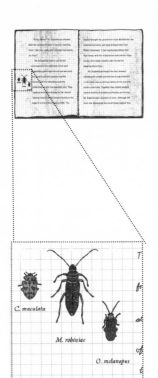

"The display brought her praise from Sister McGathrite and long strange looks from her fellow classmates."

Oh, I knew these looks so well. They came in bunches, as if when one kid made them (Eric, usually), this suddenly gave permission for everyone to start glaring, and then it became a contest for who could come up with the best farting gesture or insult to impress the girls. In many ways, we are not that much different from animals.

Englethorpe possessed a scientific curiosity that was with him always, from washroom to laboratory, as if he had been instructed by some higher power to unwind the great knot of existence. In fact, the devotion with which Mr. Englethorpe approached this unwinding did not seem all that different from the religious devotion that Rector Mallard called upon his young ladies to display, "so that young men may know you to be a good Christian woman—of sound mind and sound body— whom he may offer his hand to in marriage."

In essence, her life was cleaved by the question mark of religion— her daytime activities, regulated as much by the sisters' individual superstitions ("Never bathe with the light on," claimed Sister Lucille) as by the teachings of the Good Book, often felt antithetical to the exactitude of Mr. Englethorpe's tight, cursive observations in his field journal. To point to a filament and describe its properties seemed to her so different from the grandiose proclamations of the Lord: "Every swarming thing that swarms upon the earth is an abomination," He said to Moses in Leviticus 41. "For I am the Lord who brought you up out of the land of Egypt, to be your God; you shall therefore be holy, for I am holy." How could He claim that every swarming thing was an abomination? What was His evidence? Where were His field notes?

Despite this gulf, the lingering presence of faith in their lives was clearly never far from Mr. Englethorpe's mind either. She would watch him emerge from the main house completely flustered, walking in circles and gesticulating like a puppeteer before finally joining her in the carriage house again. They would sit in silence for several minutes, but then, unable to withhold his frustration, he would launch into a rant on natural selection and the unflagging stubbornness of Agassiz, on the

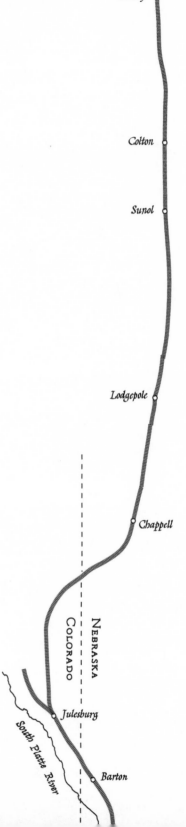

conflicts between "pure science" and Agassiz's own brand of *naturphil-osophie*, tentatively based on the guiding hand of the Deity.

"In theory, both fields—religion and science—are adaptive by na-ture," he said, digging his toes into the gravel. "This is why they are so successful at propagating, because they make room for new interpreta-tions, new ideas. At least this is how I see religion working in an ideal world. Of course, if some people I know heard me saying this, they would label me a heretic and call for a mob to come string me up. But my question is, how can you have a single text and not keep editing it? A text is evolutionary by its very nature."

"But what if you get it right the first time?" Emma asked. "Sister Lucille says the Bible is right because it comes from the word of God. He spoke directly to Moses. And how could God be wrong when he is the Creator?"

"There is no such thing as right. There is only closer," Mr. Engle-thorpe said. "I am sure Sister Lucille is a kind woman who means well—"

"She doesn't," Emma said.

"Well, who at least believes her words to be true," he said. "But to me, there is no higher honor one can give to a text than to return to it and re-examine its contents, to ask of it, 'Does this still hold true?' A book that is read, then forgotten—that is a mark of a failure to me. But to read and reread...that is faith in the process of evolution."

"Well, why don't you write one? Why don't you collect all of your works together and write a book?" Emma asked, almost exasperated.

"Perhaps," Mr. Englethorpe said thoughtfully. "I am not sure which of my works to select for this book. Or perhaps I am just scared no one will read it...let alone *reread* it and deem it worthy of revision.

How do we know which texts will shape our future understanding of the world and which texts will fall into obsurity? Oh no! This is a risk I couldn't take."

Emma did not vocalize her agreement explicitly at the time, for she had too much emotional familiarity with the Church to readily renounce some of its more doctrinal practices. She still drew a kind of subconscious comfort from the stiffness of the seminary even as she resisted many of its declarative principles. But Mr. Englethorpe, who had quietly progressed to the undeclared position of being her best friend as well as her informal mentor, was not without his influence. Slowly but surely, the exposure to his methods, his approaches to problems of inheritance and structure and categorization, gently pushed Emma into the role she was always meant to inherit. She became an empiricist, an explorer, a scientist, and a skeptic.

Indeed, it quickly became clear that Emma, beyond having an undying enthusiasm for collecting just about anything she could get her hands on, had an incredible gift for classification and observation as well. She began keeping a specimen sketchbook that soon rivaled Mr. Englethorpe's in its attention to detail, and Emma demonstrated great patience during the more minute observations that she and Mr. Englethorpe made under microscope and magnifying glass.

Elizabeth, in her own quiet way, began seeing much more of Mr. Englethorpe as well. More and more frequently, she would come to the garden after the flower shop had closed and watch him and Emma at work. As Emma sketched in her notebook, she would notice Mr. Englethorpe drift almost shyly over to her mother sitting on the iron bench in the dying light. They would talk awhile, laughing, the sound

Again, in the margin:

What was with all the phone calls to Dr. Yorn? As far as I knew, I hardly ever heard them speak on the phone. She must have forgotten to follow her marginal reminders. Or maybe she had a secret red phone hidden somewhere with a direct line to Dr. Yorn's house.

I now understood why my mother was frustrated with not having enough historical documents to work from. I wanted to see Emma's childhood sketchbook! I wanted to hold it up against my own notebooks and see if we were sketching the same things.

What had happened to that sketchbook? What happened to all the historical detritus in the world? Some of it made it into drawers of museums, okay, but what about all those old postcards, the photoplates, the maps on napkins, the private journals with little latches on them? Did they burn in house fires? Were they sold at yard sales for 75¢? Or did they all just crumble into themselves like everything else in this world, the secret little stories contained within their pages disappearing, disappearing, and now gone forever.

of their voices lilting through the ferns and deciduous entanglements of the darkened garden. The little pond made its ripples.

He was different around her. "Less like himself," Emma said quietly to her sketchbook. "He is much more nervous around her." *Than around me*, she wanted to say.

When the light had died and she could not continue with her sketches, Mr. Englethorpe would drift back to see her progress. It was strange seeing him shift roles like this, for although she wanted her mother and him to be happy, she also felt a growing ownership of his services that she did not want to share with anyone, including her mother.

He is at home with me and he does not know what to do with you.

She knew that her mother must remain in the picture if these afternoons were to continue, even if it meant watching that smooth, learned voice turn quiet or those hands clumsily drop the pair of dissecting tweezers.

"Thank you...thank you for coming again," she heard him say to her mother. "This is..." The sentence had no end. The straining in his voice pained her, not because of its uneasiness, of the misplaced words, but because of the wellspring of feeling that lurked beneath his utterance. Why was this directed at her mother? What had she ever done to elicit this mysterious and powerful reaction in such a man?

Once that autumn she was sitting alone in the garden, sketching a fallen oak leaf, when she heard someone walking toward her on the gravel path. She looked up and saw her mother carrying a parasol. Since when did she carry a parasol? Had Mr. Englethorpe purchased this gift for her? Emma could feel herself flushing with anger. When she drew closer, however, Emma saw that something was wrong—the woman looked like her mother, except that she was younger, with fuller cheeks and a smaller chin.

Emma sat still and watched the woman approach.

"Hello," the woman said.

"Hello," Emma said.

"Are you Orwin's little protégée?"

"Miss?"

"Dr. Agassiz mentioned that Orwin had a student of his own out here. What's your name?"

"Emma," Emma said. "Emma Osterville."

"Well, Miss Osterville, I don't see why you aren't attending my school, but Orwin's plans are often beyond my comprehension."

They stood looking at the garden. Emma tried not to stare at the woman.

"If Orwin ever becomes too much to handle, please come find me and we shall make other arrangements. Where do you currently study?"

"Miss?"

"School. Which school do you study at?"

"Oh, Somerville Girls' Seminary up near Powder House."

"And how do you find it?"

"It's fine, I suppose." In the face of such scrutiny from this woman, Emma suddenly felt defensive of her little school.

"Hm," the woman pursed her lips. "Well, I hope that you enjoy the fruits of our little garden. Good day."

As the woman walked back down the path, Mr. Englethorpe emerged from the carriage house. They stopped and spoke for a moment. The woman began turning her parasol and then continued on her way.

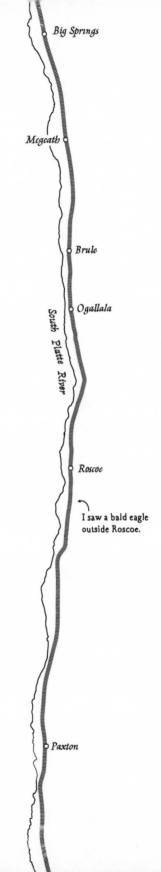

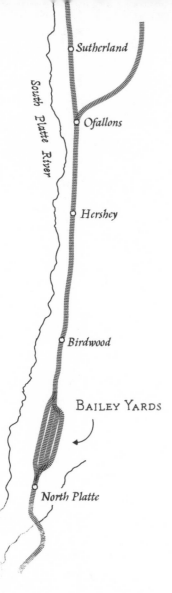

When Mr. Englethorpe joined Emma, she asked, "Who was that?"

"Oh, have you not met Mrs. Agassiz? Lizzie runs the school," he said, almost absentmindedly.

"She said, maybe I could..." but Emma didn't finish the thought.

"I don't think she likes me all that much. She thinks I cause Agassiz a headache, which is no doubt true."

"Well I didn't like her much, either," Emma said.

Mr. Englethorpe smiled. "Oh, you are a good one to have on one's side, aren't you? I mustn't get you angry at me."

For two weekends in a row during the middle of October, Mr. Englethorpe took Emma and Elizabeth out to the hills of Concord to see the turning foliage.

"Look at the anthocyanins doing their work inside the leaves!" he said from within their carriage as they passed the seas of burgundy, maroon, and primrose. "Aren't they a miracle?"

Elizabeth wandered the autumn orchards collecting baskets of apples as Mr. Englethorpe and Emma examined rock strata and measured out soil samples.

"The autumn is when the seasonal cycle most clearly reveals its workings to us," he said. "It is as if you can feel the angle of the earth begin to list away from the sun... and the trees, sensing this shift in the dance, in turn initiate a chemical process so remarkable that modern science still cannot unravel some of its more basic catalysts. My favorite day of the year is the autumnal equinox, when everything hangs in perfect transition, as if you threw a ball up in the air"— inside the carriage he threw up an imaginary ball and all eyes followed it upward—"and then marked its stillness at the exact apex of its ascent. And to think, because nature's ball moves much slower than the twitch of our consciousness, we get a whole day of such celebration!"

"But autumn is when things die!" Emma said. "Those leaves are dead." She pointed to the rush of papery amber beneath their carriage's wheels.

"Oh, but death is beautiful, my dear! Death is the harvest! We could not eat without such widespread epidemics. Evolution depends upon death as much as it does upon life."

Though Elizabeth would bring along her little pick and magnifying glass to these Concord outings, she did not take as much pleasure in the act of collection as her daughter did.

"Is this really useful?" Elizabeth asked at lunchtime once. They were all sitting on a red-and-white-checkered blanket beneath the Concord sycamores, sipping Mr. Englethorpe's homemade lemonade.

"Is what really useful?"

"All of this," she gestured at their notebooks, at the instruments of measurement that sat scattered by the picnic basket.

"Mother!" Emma said. Now it was her turn to scold impertinent questions. "Of course it is useful!" Then, seeking reassurance, she implored her collecting companion: "Isn't it?"

Mr. Englethorpe looked stunned for a moment and then began to laugh. He fell over onto his side, spilling his lemonade all over his trousers, which in turn only made him laugh harder.

Emma and Elizabeth stared at each other, not understanding.

It took some minutes for Mr. Englethorpe to calm down from his hysterics. Every time he straightened his bow tie or smoothed his frock coat, he would begin chuckling again, which would lead to more laughter. Soon Emma and Elizabeth—faced with the ongoing sight

In the margin, my mother had drawn another doodle:

This stopped me dead in my tracks. What did this mean? She didn't love Father? She never had? My eyes grew hot. I almost threw the journal across the room.

Why did you ever get together with him if you didn't love him! I wanted to shout. *You shouldn't produce children with someone you don't love.*

I took a deep breath. They *did* love each other—they *must*, right? In their own peculiar way of not speaking about anything, they loved each other, even if they themselves didn't realize it.

Right?

of such a controlled man reduced to such a state of abandon—began laughing too, as if this was all one could do in this world, at that moment, in that field.

Then, finally, after what seemed like a long, extended dream—basked in the bright light of their collective mirth, in which a certain unspoken intimacy had been passed among them all, the kind of intimacy that could only be attained through unabashed communal laughing—once all was still and they could hear the wind blowing through the sycamores and the horses in the fields ripping at the rubbery grass with their teeth, stamping away the flies with the uneven tamp of their hooves, Mr. Englethorpe said quietly, "Well, I can't be sure that it is useful."

This shocked Emma. "But of course it must be useful? What do you mean?" she said, the tears welling up.

Mr. Englethorpe saw this and turned to the child. "Oh, yes, yes, I mean of course it's valuable, important. But I wonder about the word *useful*, you see. That word has plagued me my entire life. Is travel useful? I am not sure, but it's goddamn interesting, pardon my language, my young seminarian."

Emma smiled beneath her tears. She wiped her face and they listened to Mr. Englethorpe regale them with his tales of travel to eastern Africa and Papua New Guinea.

"I was bitten by a viper in the New Guinea rain forest. I am convinced the only reason I didn't die was because the devil bit me on a new moon and his venom cycle had lessened during this period. This observation was confirmed when I interviewed some of the local villagers, who said the bite of a viper became much 'softer' when the village was in the protection of a spirit dance, which, I found out, corresponded to a lunar cycle."

Some horses ambled by their blanket. Emma was listening, stacking the rocks they had collected.

"I am glad you didn't die from the venom," she said.

He smiled, looking off into the distance.

"Me too," said Elizabeth, almost inaudibly, her hands bound up in the corner of the blanket.

"Well," said Mr. Englethorpe, turning back to them. "Well, well."

It was just about the right thing to say. They sat on the blanket and let these three words orbit around them like the drunken circling of a late summer wasp. Though the subatomic structure of atoms would not yet be discovered for another forty years, each of them, in their own way, sensed they were playing out the most elemental of configurations sitting on this red-checkered blanket. They had no words for this triangulation, they could not describe it in such terms, but here they were, three separate electrons circling a single nucleus, each knowing that soon they would be a real family.

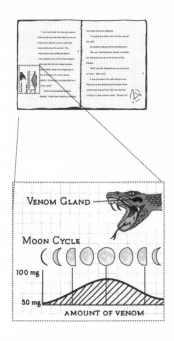

"I am convinced the only reason I didn't die was because the devil bit me on a new moon."

I too was glad that Mr. Englethorpe hadn't died from the viper bite. If he had, the intricate chain of ancestral dominoes wouldn't have toppled and my father wouldn't have been born and I wouldn't have been born, and Layton wouldn't have been born, and Layton wouldn't have died, and I wouldn't have drawn my maps or sent them to the Smithsonian and Jibsen wouldn't have called and I wouldn't have stolen this notebook or gotten on this train or be reading about this viper bite right now. Ow, my head hurt with all the possibilities and non-possibilities.

I had worked extensively with Gracie to categorize and chart the five different kinds of her boredom:

(1) **ANTICIPATORY BOREDOM.** Where the looming nature of something in the near future prevented you from being able to concentrate on anything and thus you became bored.

(3) **AGGRESSIVE BOREDOM.** In this instance, boredom was not so much a state as an act displayed by the sufferer to denote some behavioral message. In Gracie's case, this was often characterized by loud sighs, collapsing on the couch, and the familiar declaration, "Oh my God I am so bored."

(4) **RITUAL BOREDOM.** For chronic boredom sufferers like Gracie, the feeling of boredom in and of itself could be a very comforting, familiar feeling in times of distress or loneliness.

(4) **LET-DOWN BOREDOM.** This was where you expected an event or activity to be a certain way only for it to turn out differently, causing the sufferer to retreat to a (safe) state of boredom.

(5) **MONOTONY BOREDOM.** Sometimes boredom was not an act or due to any disparity of expectations. Sometimes, people just got bored. Many types of boredoms got miscategorized into this kitchen sink category, but I had found that the majority of Gracie's boredoms, upon further inspection, could actually be classified under one of the other four headings.

CHAPTER 8

Don't get me wrong: as much as I was taken with the project of illustrating my mother's story, I did not simply read the *entire* time. I am not a reading nerd. There were plenty of times when my mother's handwriting went blurry on the page in front of me and—all right, maybe I drooled a little as I stared dumbly out the window. Or sometimes I would find myself reading the same sentence over and over for fifteen minutes, like a record player left to skip endlessly in the other room. And sometimes…I even became a little bit *bored*. This was a strange feeling for me. I hardly ever got bored. There was simply too much to map in this world to let yourself slip into the moors of boredom. The same could not be said for Gracie: she was practically a professional when it came to cultivating the five types of boredom.

But now that I had developed a hardy case of monotony boredom myself, I even began to enjoy it a little, to inspect this newfound sensation for its folds and creases: *What was that dull, sinking feeling just behind my earlobes?* And why had I suddenly become mildly schizophrenic? Part of

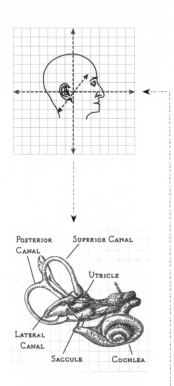

The Twelve-Year-Old Labyrinth
from Notebook G101

I now understood what cowboys felt like when they were off their steeds, how curious the firmness of the ground must feel after the tumbling cadence of a horse's shanks. I could relate to that cowboy with his split lip and his mealy hands, for when the train was still, I found myself simultaneously longing for and dreading that familiar rocking again—desiring the tremble of travel, but fearing what that desire had created inside me.

my brain kept asking "Are we there yet?" and "Well, how about now?" even as the more rational part of my brain distinctly knew the answer to this question.

I willed the landscape to stop, for the miniature men to stop cranking the scenery across my vision with that little landscape machine of theirs. Alas, the landscape continued flowing past with what seemed like an increasingly sadistic determination.

Indeed, after a full day and a half of rail travel, the slow, uneven rocking motion had burrowed its way through my skin into the sinewy tissues around my bones, so that when the train would occasionally come to a jolting halt at some spur or interchange, my whole body continued to quiver in the unexpected stillness. I marveled at how my millions of muscle fibers had been quietly listening to the *thackety-thack* symphony of those rail ties, adjusting to the constant sway and lilt of the car. After a while, some internal system of orientation had concluded that this irregular cacophony of movement was here to stay, and my muscles responded by carefully creating a complicated counterdance of shaking and trembling that attempted to bring my internal calibration back to zero. It was strange to sit at my workstation when the world was still again and have my hands buzz and twitch like this. That tiny labyrinth of fluid in my ear must have been working overtime to keep the ship balanced.

I could just hear the labyrinth conversing with my muscles:

"And it's stopped again!" the labyrinth said. "Keep moving until my command." Despite being only twelve years old, the labyrinth was an old pro at this.

"Should we stop twitching?" asked my left hand.

"And trembling?" asked my right hand.

"No, hold. *Hold, I said*. Wait for it…"

"I grow weary of this game," said my right hand. "I feel like—"

"And we're moving again!" said the labyrinth. "Okay, right three hundred four and two fifths of a degree. *Shake, double shake, back and left*, fourteen and one fifth of a degree. *Double shake, double shake, tremble.* And good, *good*, keep this up."

And so on—a complex series of commands meant to be negatives of what the train was doing, and my two hands wearily followed. It was as if the labyrinth in my ear was attempting to predict the exact contours of the train tracks, of the land we were passing through.

Was it all just improvisation on the part of my internal balancing system, or, as I intuitively believed, was there actually some invisible map of the land buried inside my head? Were we all born with an awareness of everything? The slope of every hillock? Every river's curvature and cut-bank, the rise and fall of the chiseled rapids and the glassy stillness of each eddy? Did we already know the radial shading of every single person's iris, the arborage of crow's-feet on every elder's temple, the ridged whorl of thumbprints, of fence lines, of lawns, and flowerpots, the reticulation of graveled driveways, the gridwork of streets, the bloom of exit ramps and superhighways, of the stars and planets and supernovas and galaxies beyond—did we know the precise location of all of this but ultimately have no conscious way to access this knowledge? Perhaps only now, through my labyrinth's reflexive counteraction to the lilt of the tracks, the dips and pulls in the land, was I getting a glimpse at my subconscious's total knowledge of a place I had never been.

"You are crazy," I said. "This is just because your body is freaked out by all this movement and has no idea what else to do." I tried to get back to my reading, but found myself longing for this hidden map to be true, for us all to have the atlas of the universe preloaded into our synapses, be-

cause somehow this would confirm a feeling I had had my entire mapping life, since I first charted how one could walk up the side of Mt. Humbug and shake hands with God.

I stared out the window at the buttes and vistas and distant canyons that all bled into each other from one valley to the next. If there really was a map of the world buried inside my head, how could I access it? I tried to make my eyes go blurry, like you do with those Magic Eye books, I tried to just let the kinks of the land synchronize to the cortical kinks of my subconscious. I set up Mr. Igor GPS next to my head, and after a minute he managed to locate himself easily: 41°53'50"N, 106°16'59"W. But as much as I squinted and tried not to try, I could not conjure any of the same exactness.

Damn you, Igor, with your satellites drifting above!

We passed through the tiny town of Medicine Bow, and the sprinkle of streets, the parked green Cadillac, the vacant barbershop all looked somehow familiar, but I couldn't tell if this was because I was accessing my subconscious map or if I had just been on this train for a really, really long time and was turning into an unhinged, hallucinatory hobo.

Somewhere outside Laramie our train stopped at a grade crossing to allow a line of automobiles to cross the tracks.

"Are you kidding?" I said to Valero. "This is ridiculous crap."

I mean, show a little respect for the Iron Horse! How were we going to get to Washington when we had to stop for every car, rickshaw, or nun who decided to cross the tracks? As Father used to say about Aunt Suzy when she was still alive, "We was moving slower'n a snail on crutches."

In Cheyenne, we stopped for about six hours waiting for a new engine and crew. I didn't go into my usual hiding place in the bathroom, but rather sat on the floor and peeped out the windows with a blan-

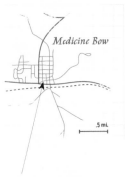

The green Cadillac was parked right here.

ket over my head. If someone came by, I would roll under the table, commando-style.

I watched cars and trucks driving across an overpass that spanned the many railroad tracks of the yards. A couple dressed in oversize leather vests walked along the fence line next to the railroad. They walked without speaking. In their normal lives, when they were talking to each other, what did they talk about? I found it amazing that all these people lived and worked in Cheyenne. This whole time they had lived here! Even when I was in the fourth grade, this town had still existed, right here! This concept of simultaneous consciousness was very difficult for me to wrap my head around: that even now, as I was reaching out for one of my last Cheerios off the tabletop, somewhere at this very moment, seven other boys were reaching out to pick up *their* Cheerios with the same motion. And not just any kind of Cheerio but my kind: a *Honey Nut* Cheerio.

What was confusing to me was that this kind of invisible synchronicity, which could not really be tracked without the benefit of a million billion cameras and a vast, closed-circuit surveillance system, could not be extended across history. Time threw a monkey wrench into the whole equation. Could we even talk about a moment gone past? As in, since their introduction in 1979, there have been 753,362 moments when a boy, age twelve, has reached with thumb and forefinger for a single Honey Nut Cheerio? These moments happened, perhaps, but they were not *happening*, they no longer existed, and so to collect them together seemed to be a bit false. History was only what we conjured it to be. It never just was, like *now* is. Like Cheyenne was in this very moment. The confusing part was that Cheyenne *continued* to be, even after my train departed. The couple in leather vests would live out their lives, alive every moment, the world illuminated from the headlight of their consciousness, and I would

Honey Nut Cheerio Synchrony
from Notebook G101

Location of eight North American boys, age twelve, pinching Honey Nut Cheerios at the same exact moment in time.

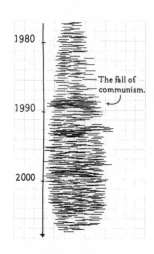

The Inheritance of History:
753,362 Honey Nut Pinches
from Notebook G101

I had checked out my share of books on quantum mechanics at the Butte Public Library (well, I had checked out the three books available), but for some reason they had simply sat next to my bed and then under my bed, still unread. Eventually I lost one of the books and in order to avoid paying the fines, I had to concoct a story for the librarian, Mrs. Gravel (who had a soft spot for literature involving sibling disputes), about how my sister became unhinged and flooded my room with sulfuric acid.

I think quantum mechanics's inherent instability—in that as soon as you added an observer to a theoretical experiment all of the equations collapsed—was just beyond the threshold of my comprehension. Maybe this was because I *was* an observer myself—I wanted the observer to fit into the picture.

While I couldn't quite wrap my head around *superpositions* and *non-locality*, Hugh Everett's Many Worlds Theory was the one idea I could properly sink my teeth into.

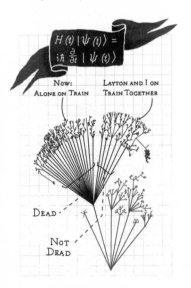

There Might Be Many Parallel Worlds
from Notebook G101

never see them again. We would both be conscious at the same time, but we would be running on parallel tracks that were destined never to cross again.

Late in the evening we pushed through the hills of western Nebraska. I had never been to Nebraska. Nebraska was getting somewhere. Nebraska was flirting with the Middle West, a land of transition and wormholes, a great, flat divide between *here* and *there*—the ultimate terra incognita. In the growing dusk I watched tractor trailers move across a distant highway. For spells there was just the dusk and the fields that merged with the sky into an endless, flat horizon. During these moments of darkness, of earth mirroring sky and nothing more, I imagined it looking exactly like this 150 years ago for both Tearho and Emma, traveling in the other direction. Did they look out the window and wonder what this land would look like in the future? Who would ride these same rails? At that moment in time, were all possible futures located in the same place? Did their unlikely union abut my own existence, which in turn was flanked by a million other possibilities? Were we all waiting in the wings, waiting to see how the performance turned out, to see if our entrance was needed or not? Oh, to be conscious at such a backstage moment! To be able to look around and wonder at the cast of characters that was never to be!

The night slipped by. At around 3 A.M., following several hours of jolting sleeplessness, I made one of the great discoveries in the history of mankind. I was walking around the cabin delirious when I happened to open a cupboard I had previously overlooked. And what was inside?

A game of Boggle.

Oh, the joy! But who would leave such a delectable treat? Surely the Winnebago salesman did not have a clandestine passion for the game, which he kept hidden in order to avoid derision from his colleagues? Or was the

Boggle set pulled out in certain circumstances to mimic the fun that could be had when everyone gathered around in a wordsmith's parlor?

Under the light from my flashlight, I slowly opened the box as one would open the box of some elaborate chocolate cake. As soon as the top was off, however, I was confronted with a tragedy: four cubes were missing. There would be no proper Boggle games played today. Trying to remain positive, I dumped the remaining twelve cubes out at my workstation and they made their little chattering noises, like hens pecking at the table. I turned each cube around and around and slowly spelled out:

It was amazing that I had all the sufficient letters to spell out "the middle" perfectly. Maybe I was luckier than I had thought. But then I realized that even if I had the perfect cube combinations (and what were the chances of this?), I could not actually spell out "the Middle West," as this would require thirteen cubes. I was one short. Everything was ruined after all. For some reason, the impossibility of this task made me sad, far sadder than I should have been considering the ultimate inconsequence of Boggle in our lives.

All at once, I was struck with a very simple modification. With excitement brimming across the pads of my sleepy fingertips, I turned the B cube around in my hands, hoping against all chances that tonight, somewhere in Nebraska, was my lucky night.

It was.

Ah! Life was all about minor victories such as these. Why make a whole new word when you already had plenty of material to work with?

I surveyed my work just like Governor Kemble or Fremont or Lewis or even Mr. Corlis Benefideo might have surveyed their great creations. The light seemed to grow and pulse around this entanglement of three words.

Then I looked out the window and noticed that the triple track we had been following for a while had doubled into six lines and that we were approaching bright lights ahead. The stark floodlights cut against the uncertainty of the night. It appeared as if we were headed directly into an operating room. If this was what the entrance to a wormhole looked like, I wasn't sure I wanted any part of it.

I quickly turned off my flashlight. My first instinct was to run back into the bathroom, but I stifled this impulse (one cannot spend one's entire life running into bathrooms when danger calls!), took a deep breath, and peered out the window.

Up and down the tracks, multiple signals blinked red, white, and red again. We passed a coal train standing motionless on the tracks and then another. More tracks appeared beside the six. Where were we? Some kind of hive for all trains in the universe?

I turned my flashlight back on, and, cupping my hand over the light so that it produced only a half-moon glow, I carefully consulted my railroad atlas. Ogallala, Sutherland, North Platte... In a large, bold font, BAILEY YARDS was printed in the middle of the map. Of course! Bailey Yards was the largest train yard in the world.

I watched as all around our own train more and more cars appeared. We slid by a hump, where a command center at the top of a small hill was sorting through a line of freight cars using the simple effects of gravity. Amazing! In this age of technology, here was an example of how one could use a basic principle of force that was free and infinitely available to sort through cargo. No electricity bill. No fossil fuels. The efficiency of the humping appealed to both the luddite in me and to the twelve-year-old used to living off a weekly allowance.

We slid through the yard. I was waiting for us to stop at any moment, to wait here for a day, perhaps even two. Hundreds of cars were waiting around us. As we passed each car, there was a brief instant when its air brakes hissed the loudest, as if expressing discontent at the delay.

Oh, we must get going, we must get going. What, pray tell, is keeping us? a car hissed as we passed it. And then the sound faded, only to be replaced seconds later by the next car hissing its own set of complaints.

Now that I had formed my Boggle words and resisted that initial impulse to hide in the bathroom, I felt slightly invincible (as boys tend

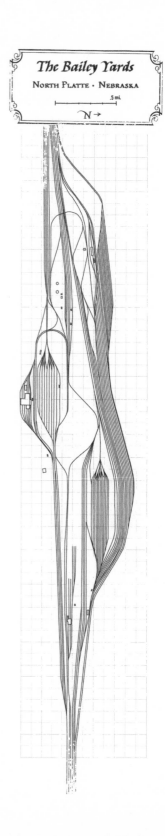

The Bailey Yards
NORTH PLATTE · NEBRASKA

.5 mi.

N →

I think Layton lived his life in a perpetual confidence of small victories. Not that he appreciated and savored every detail; he simply thought he was doing a really good job all the time. After completing a task, or even in the middle of a task, he would often pump his hand from the top of his head down to his knees, going almost a little too far with the arc of this movement, but then Layton pushed everything a little too far—not quite to its breaking point, but almost.

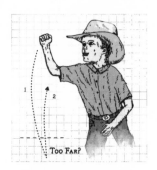

Layton's Extended Fist Pump
from Notebook B41

His tendency to celebrate was one of the few differences between Layton and Father. Father never celebrated a moment in his life. He complained, he pined, he pounded, but he never reveled. Layton was a reveler. Where he got this gene, I don't know. Most Spivets were too busy studying, corraling, moaning, or mapping to enjoy the ride they were on.

to feel after they achieve a series of minor victories). Not bothering to conceal myself, I boldly moved back and forth through the cockpit of the Cowboy Condo as if I owned the yards and was merely surveying them from my own private Winnebago in my nightly 3 A.M. ritual. Out the right-hand side of my cockpit I saw welding sparks flying in the darkness out of a huge cavernous structure. Inside, white and blue lights were pointed up at the ceiling and the shadows of fifty or so yellow UP engines crowded together.

"Good work, workmen," I said aloud in my deep, chief executive voice. "Keep those engines in tiptop shape. They are the workhorses of my fleet. Without them there wouldn't be a rail network. Without them there wouldn't be America."

Silence after this as the line tried itself on and didn't quite succeed. Slightly embarrassed, I let the silence continue, marked only by the chatter of the rails and regular hissing beats of the cars we passed.

"Gracie," I asked. "What would you do if you were here with me?"

"Who's Gracie?" asked Valero.

"Hey, Valero!" I said. "Where the hell have you been this whole time? I've been here like two days! We could've talked a little, passed the time!"

No answer. *Chatter   chatter.   Hiss   hiss   hiss.*

"I'm sorry," I said. "I'm sorry. Okay. It's your prerogative when you want to pipe in. I'm glad to have you back."

"Well? Who is she?"

"She's my sister. My only sister. Well, my only brother or sister right now." I was silent, thinking of Gracie, Layton, and me. And then just Gracie and me. "We're different, you know. I mean, she's older. She doesn't like maps or school or anything like that. She wants to be an actor and move to L.A. or something."

"Why didn't she come with you?"

"Well," I said. "I didn't invite her, really."

"Why not?"

"Because…because this was my trip! The Smithsonian invited me, not her. She's got her own thing with acting and…and she wouldn't like the museum. She'd get bored after a couple hours, and then she'd go into deep Dork Retreat and I'd have to go find her candy.…I mean, she would've gotten bored on this train before we even got out of Montana. She probably would have jumped off the first time we stopped way back in Dillon.…No offense, Valero."

"None taken. But you still love her?"

"What? Yes, of course," I said. "Whoever said anything about not loving her? She's Gracie. She's great." I paused and then warbled: "Gracie!"

"I see," Valero said.

"If we stop here for a long time do you want to play twenty questions?" I asked, but even in asking this question I knew he was gone.

And yet we did not stop. In this locus of training, where all lines converged, where every train was picked apart, sorted, and then sent on its way, we did not even blink. Our train was not sorted. Maybe here, in the heart of it all, we had been granted some kind of hotshot status by the powers that be, as if they knew that time-sensitive cargo was hunkered away in Valero, the Winnebago. We burned straight through the major Union Pacific sorting center and out the other side. Bailey could not touch us.

"Oh, thank you, Bailey, for giving us the green light," I said, executive-style, thumbing at the blinkers from the driver's seat of the Cowboy

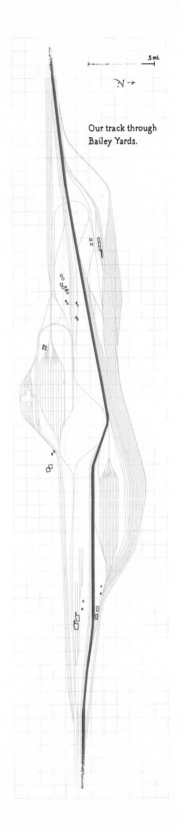

.5 mi.

N →

Our track through
Bailey Yards.

Condo. "You of course know I have to give a speech at the National Academy of Science dinner in D.C. on Thursday evening."

After I said the words, I realized what they meant. Thursday? *This was in three days.* I needed to cross half the country in that time, get to the Smithsonian, introduce myself, and prepare my speech all before Thursday evening. The familiar feeling of panic welled up. I took a deep breath and quieted myself. *A train is a train is a train.* "I can go no faster than this line will allow. I will get there when the train gets there," I said resolutely.

But in case you have never noticed, it is very difficult to *tell* yourself to calm down once a kernel of worry gets lodged in your mind. I tried to sit in my Cowboy Condo and act nonchalant, whistling, sketching images of cowboys and beetles and Tab soda cans in my notebook, but all I could hear was the beating of the tracks whispering, *Thursday Thursday Thursday Thursday.* I would never make it.

Sometime later, after we were clear and back out on the Nebraskan prairie, I looked at the Boggle pieces again. The chatter of travel had loosened them from their grid of meaning. The key to the magical door had disintegrated. They now read:

With my head on the table and my eyelids growing heavy, I pushed the cubes around in circles, listening to the sound of their polished surfaces rubbing against the wooden tabletop. The bright blue capital letters were so precise in their printing, so completely assured of their existence, as if they were unaware of the five other letters surrounding them on all sides. Each time you turned a cube, a new letter came into view and enveloped your world, erasing the letter before it. Turn it this way, your world was a *W* and all things *W* seemed very relevant. Turn it this way, and your world was now a *B*, the world of *W* already a distant memory.

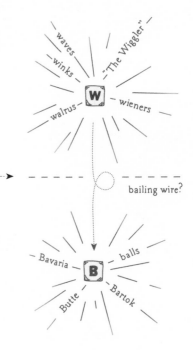

I slept for forty-five minutes on the Teton Bed, woke up, and could not go back to sleep. The cartoon cowboy decal on the television screen looked creepy in the darkness. I groped for my flashlight and flicked it on. The spotlight danced across the false comforts of the Winnebago—the fake wood, the linoleum ceilings, the polyester blankets.

"Valero?" I said.

No answer.

"Valero? Do you know a bedtime story?"

Only the clattering of the train.

Did Father even care that I was gone? Did he want me gone?

I picked up my mother's notebook and held it to my face. It smelled faintly of the formaldehyde and lemony scents of her study. I suddenly wanted to see her face, to touch the lobes of her ears and her green sparkly earrings. I wanted to hold her hand and apologize for taking this book, for leaving without asking her permission, for not saving Layton, for not being a better brother, or ranch hand, or scientist's assistant. For not being a better *son*. I will do everything better next time, *I promise*.

I looked up, and by the light of the flashlight I could see that my tears had made two pear-shaped stains on the binding.

"Oh, Mom," I said. I opened the book.

The orbiting electrons finally found their nucleus.

Two years after that cold April morning in front of the flower shop, Elizabeth Osterville and Orwin Englethorpe were married in a small outdoor ceremony in Concord. Selections from both the *Origin of Species* and the King James Bible were read. Dr. Agassiz, whom Emma had still not officially met, did not attend—in protest, Mr. Englethorpe claimed, over the fact that the wedding was not taking place inside a church.

"A curious protest for a naturalist," Mr. Englethorpe chuckled, though Emma could tell that Agassiz's absence deeply upset him.

Soon after the marriage, Mr. Englethorpe officially moved out of the carriage house, and it was good timing: he and Agassiz had stopped speaking altogether.

A team of Italians was called in to load his thousands of books and specimens out of the carriage house into a large wagon normally used for carting hay. Mr. Englethorpe buzzed around them, plucking at his mustache, imploring the men to be careful. But then he would snatch something from out of their hands and become completely absorbed in the forgotten object.

"Oh! I had wondered where this went," he said to no one in particular, holding a large cross-section of a tree trunk. "It really provides a fascinating peek into this medieval period of abnormally warm temperatures…"

During the move, Emma sat on her iron bench in the middle of the garden and watched them empty the house of its contents. Though she wanted to display an air of maturity and accept such passage as the inevitable way of things, after a while she could not contain herself

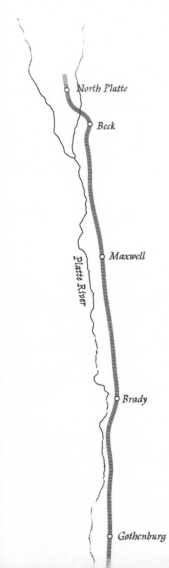

I was so tired and became so absorbed in the story that, as much as I am embarrassed to admit it, I slowly lost my bearings as to my exact location. This, I would come to regret.

North Platte

Beck

Maxwell

Platte River

Brady

Gothenburg

and began to weep at the dismantling of this world, her world. Mr. Englethorpe came over to her, hovered, placed an awkward hand upon her shoulder, then, unsure of what more to say or do, moved back to tending his collection's migration.

In her pocket, Emma could feel the spiky cube of quartz she had discovered on a field trip to Lincoln. She had decided to bury it in the garden to mark her parting, but the constant coming and going of the Italians, gesticulating and peppering comments to each other in their annoying language, ruined the propriety of the scene. It was her last day in the garden and she couldn't even have this to herself.

She decided to take the path around the other side of the house to a quiet spot where there was a little gravel clearing surrounded by hedges. She would mix her quartz with the other stones.

But when she came around the house, a man was already standing inside the clearing.

"Oh," she said, startled.

The man turned. Immediately, she knew that it was Dr. Agassiz, as she had seen his picture in books and in several photo plates in Mr. Englethorpe's study. With all the stories from Mr. Englethorpe, she had been expecting some kind of wild-eyed monster, set on convincing the whole world of his superiority. It was a moment of awakening for Emma: she saw now that her version of Dr. Agassiz was colored by the fraught relationship of these two men, and was not as how he actually was, contained in the same fragile flesh as she. His eyes were tired, gentle—inviting, even, as though he had spent much of his life constructing a house that kept falling down. His eyes made her want to go over and hug him.

"Hello, Miss Osterville," he said.

She was startled. "You know who I am?"

"Of course," he said. "I may not come out here much, but I am not blind."

"I didn't know that you would be here...today, I mean," she said and then wished she had not said anything.

He smiled. "This is my residence."

She rolled the quartz around in her pocket, unsure of what to do. Dr. Agassiz, his arms clasped behind his back, turned away from her. The gravel shifted beneath his feet. "I come here now and then to remember my parents. They are buried in a small cemetery in the mountains of Switzerland, but somehow they are close to this spot as well. It is peculiar how we collapse time and space in this way, is it not? It is one of our more wondrous qualities."

She waited. And then she asked, "Sir, do you hate Mr. Englethorpe?"

He laughed. The warmth in his eyes was startling, perhaps because she could see the potential for anger within them. "My dear, I am too old too hate anything at this point. The Creator has blessed me with the pen and has blessed the world with creatures so intricate and beautiful it will take us a millennium to describe them all. To dwell over personal disagreements is a waste of time."

"Well, sir," she said. "I believe he loves you, dearly, no matter what he might say or do."

"Thank you, my dear," Mr. Agassiz said. "I admit your words mean something to this old man after all I have done for him."

"Do you hate Mr. Darwin?"

"Ha," Dr. Agassiz laughed. "Have you been coached to ask me these questions?" His face grew more serious. "My personal feelings about Charles do not matter. Brilliant men can become set in their ways, that is all. Their intelligence is matched only by their stubbornness. I am afraid no one, however, can design a theory which completely excludes the hand of the Creator. His thumbprint is simply too great." He paused. "Do you mind if I ask you a question?"

"No, sir," she said.

"You seem as bright as Orwin suggested. Why on earth did you not want to attend my wife's school? We could have used more smart young ladies interested in the sciences."

"But I did!" Emma was confused. "You said that I couldn't—"

"My dear, I said nothing of the sort. In fact, I implored Orwin to enroll you, but he was adamant, as he said you were. You wanted to work with him and no one else."

Emma tried to make space for this new information. She stood there, dumbfounded. Dr. Agassiz seemed to grow impatient.

"Well, it was a pleasure, Miss Osterville, but if you'll excuse me, I must return to that infernal act of writing, an endeavor to which I have apparently signed away the rest of my days."

Suddenly, Emma did not want him to go. "What are you writing, sir?" she asked.

"A comprehensive natural history of this country," he said. "Because no one has adequately attacked the field. In order to really be of a place, we must observe its natural contents completely. This I learned from Mr. Humboldt, a dear friend. But why on earth did I agree to produce ten volumes instead of just three or four?"

"Because there are ten volumes of material?"

"Oh, there are many more than this. Ten just seemed like an ambitious beginning."

"I should like to write ten volumes someday."

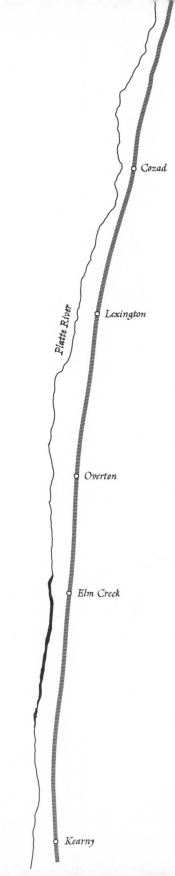

Gibbon

Shelton

Wood River

Grand
Island

Chapman

He smiled. And then his face stiffened. He looked squarely at Emma. "My wife is teaching me that such things—things I would not have dreamed of—might be possible for the other sex, perhaps even in the near future. As much as I would not like to admit it, the field is changing, though I think not for the better. In the pursuit of that serpentine creature that we often label as 'progress,' morality seems to have been lost along the way. May I just say that if you truly want to undertake this profession, you must be ready for the many hours in the field that are required before you may write your ten volumes. One cannot simply pen a taxonomy out of thin air, and truthfully, I remain unconvinced that a woman's delicate constitution is designed for such rigor."

Emma felt her jaw tighten. She gathered herself, puffing out her chest.

"With all due respect, sir," she said. "There you are wrong. And you are wrong about Mr. Darwin, too. You are just scared of evolution. Well, things evolve, sir." She took the bit of quartz from her pocket and dropped it, somewhat ferociously, at the feet of the man who had discovered the last ice age, and then, losing her courage, turned and ran.

The newly formed Englethorpe atom moved into a country house in Concord, just down the road from the Alcotts' new residence at Orchard House. Elizabeth cautiously slid into a friendship with Louisa May, who was temperamental but kind to both Elizabeth and Emma. When she was not away traveling, she would read to them from her latest book beneath the sycamores.

The Englethorpe house was modest but would have been roomy enough were it not for Mr. Englethorpe's vast collections. Dr. Agassiz had requested he remove his inventory from the storerooms at the museum, so his entire collection lay for months packed in boxes around the house and woodshed. Everyone seemed scared to move them for fear of disrupting an order that did not exist.

Instead of inventorying the contents of the house, Mr. Englethorpe set about writing the book he had always wanted to write, a New World companion volume to *On the Origin of Species*, which looked at evolutionary principles through the lens of both native American and invasive species of grasses, sparrows, and shorebirds.

He and Emma sat in his new study, repairing a taxidermied house sparrow that had been damaged in the move. "I intend to spread Mr. Darwin's word to the American Thinking Man. It is no easy task bringing ideas over the ocean. Mr. Darwin needs a good translator who can interpret his message into a form that this country will grasp completely. This book will be a great success, my dear, and we will be able to purchase a much larger house with grounds that will stretch as far as the eye can see. Can you imagine this?"

"You will be remembered by so many!" Emma said, carefully fastening the wing back onto the delicate creature.

"I will not be remembered, but the theory will. The pursuit of natural truth, this matters most. Much more than you or I."

"There it is," she said, standing the little bird up on the desk.

"An industrious little fellow, isn't he? Arrived only a couple of years ago from the Old World and already he's made this country his home," he said, tapping the bird on the head. "Soon you will rule the roost."

. . .

I•ndeed, things were looking up for Mr. Englethorpe: he seemed poised to create something important, something magical, and there were certain days when Emma could almost feel the important ideas floating around the house.

Others sensed it too: through Louisa Alcott, Mr. Englethorpe was introduced to the eminent Ralph Waldo Emerson, who also lived down the hill. The famous (and ornery) transcendentalist took an immediate liking to the thin man who surrounded himself with all manner of birds and beasts, and the two of them could often be seen taking long walks around Walden Pond. Emerson, already an old man at the time, apparently did not care for children, and so much to her chagrin, Emma was rarely invited on these outings.

At the beginning of an unseasonably warm March, a new president was sworn in, just as the confused chrysanthemum buds were first appearing in their Concord garden. A week later, it snowed again, and much to Elizabeth's horror, all of her buds froze to death.

"It's awful!" she said. "Awful, awful awful."

One month later, on a rainy morning in April, the man who brought them their milk also brought them the news that Fort Sumter had been shelled by the Confederacy. The War Between the States had begun.

Men all around them enlisted and left their farms as the memories of the Revolutionary War three generations ago still rang loud in the surrounding hamlets. Even from the quiet of the study the thump of local militia boots could be heard from the newly erected barracks over the hill. At first, Mr. Englethorpe devoured the newspapers, but as the war dragged on that summer and into the autumn, he soon returned to studying his prairie grasses.

"This just makes my work all the more important. If this country is set on destroying itself, we might as well know what it is we are destroying."

"Will you join?" Emma asked.

"One can only do what one was meant to do," Mr. Englethorpe said. "And right now I am meant to listen to those boots thump on and wonder about the ferocity of men and then return to my studies. Besides, would you want me blown to smithereens by some fresh-faced youngster from the Bayou who maintains only a hazy idea of what he happens to be fighting for? I would rather show how this boy is directly descended from the apes."

"But we are not apes, Father," she said.

"You are quite correct," he said. "But we are doing our best to prove otherwise."

"I should not want you to die for this," she said, holding his hand.

The seasons turned, the war continued. Though Elizabeth pleaded with her not to go, Louisa May Alcott left Concord to work in a war hospital in Washington. Left without the comforts of her friend, Elizabeth turned to her garden. She tried to forget her chrysanthemum disaster and began growing vegetables, which she sold in the town market on the weekends.

It was strange how it had all turned out. She had left the sea for this, not for the wide, gasping landscapes of the West but for the gentle slopes, light topsoil, and short growing season of a New England farm.

Central City

Silver Creek

Columbus

Schuyler

If anything, it was a compromise. In her second marriage, something had hardened inside of her. She was happier than she'd ever been and yet she could not shake the feeling that she had missed what she had been destined to do. She had not ridden through the Cumberland Gap to the frontier. She had not felt the slopes and ruts of the land beneath a wagon wheel. She had settled for this life, here. And it was a fine life. Her new husband was lovely, if eclectic and incorrigible, and he was learning to hold her in the evenings not like another one of his taxidermied specimens but as a man holds his wife. And yet no more children came.

After a year of writing, Mr. Englethorpe seemed no closer to completing his book than when he began. Emerson wrote to some friends at the National Academy of Sciences and arranged for Englethorpe to give a preliminary lecture on the evidence for natural selection in North America.

The Academy was doing its best to meet regularly and carry on its mission despite the fact that most people's attention was on the gruesome illustrations printed in magazines, of waxen bodies lying on the frozen fields of Virginia and not on the origin of man. Still, there was a certain comfort in the act of debating, to tracing a long line of descendancy from the beginning of life until now, as though calling attention to our simian ancestors might make this war something ordinary, might prevent it from becoming the end of modern civilization that nearly every bespectacled man of the Academy secretly feared it might be.

A week before he traveled, Mr. Englethorpe offered to bring Emma along.

"Me?" she asked.

"You are as much in this book as I am."

As he said this, she realized that the symbiosis of cause and effect was not just bestowed upon her new father, whom she had always seen as a man who naturally affected the path of history. This gift was also within her: she too had the power to change the course of time; her hands could make things that mattered, write words that people would pay attention to.

They rode in a first-class train compartment all the way from Boston to Philadelphia. One attendant gave her sweets and another gave her warm towels in the afternoon, just as the smoke from the locomotive was threatening to trigger another one of her migraines. Mr. Englethorpe looked impeccable in his traveling clothes. His mustache was waxed and impeccable, his hands never seemed to leave their place at the top of his walking cane.

Sometime during the journey, she looked her new father in the eye and said, "You told Mr. Agassiz I didn't want to attend his school."

His face froze. He ran a finger across his mustache. He glanced at her and then out the window.

"Do you regret not attending?" he asked finally.

"You lied to me. Why didn't you want me to go?"

"Can you blame me? Agassiz is ignorant of his own blindness! God bless the man, but you were too important to our cause for me to lose you to such egotism!"

"Our cause?" She was steaming. She wanted to slap him but didn't know how.

"Yes," he said. "Our cause. You know, I have loved and treated you like my own daughter from the moment I met you, but that love has not clouded my objective assessment of your great talents. You happen to be my daughter and my apprentice, but you also happen to be the future of science in this country."

Her eyes burned. She did not know what to do. To leap from the train? To hug him? Instead, she stuck out her tongue. He looked at her, shocked for a minute, and then he laughed.

"Wait until they meet you," he said, tapping his cane on her knee. "The Academy won't know what to think, just as I didn't know what to think. This place will be in your future."

It was the most memorable weekend of her life. She met hundreds of scientists from all conceivable fields, and much to the amusement of the men around her, she introduced herself thus: "Hello, I am Emma Osterville Englethorpe and I would like to be a scientist."

"Well, what kind of scientist do you want to be, little one?" a rotund man prompted her, smiling at the frothy ribbons on her hat, a gift from Elizabeth for the trip.

"A geologist. I am pretty sure. I am most interested in the Miocene and Mesozoic eras and particularly volcanic deposits. But I also love botany and describing the orchid families of the Indian Oceanic Rim. And Father says I have one of the best topographical eyes through the sextant that he has ever seen."

The man took a step back, bewildered. "Well, my child, may I see you out in the field!" he said, and walked away, shaking his head.

Robert E. Lee surrendered at Appomattox in April 1865. Less than a week later, Lincoln was dead. Both of these events fell on dead ears in the house. Mr. Englethorpe had sequestered himself in his study, but it was unclear what he was actually doing, for there seemed to be no method to the madness: six or seven of the big crates were ripped open and specimen trays were strewn about the room. He grew irritable with Emma, something she had never seen before. The first time he snapped at her to leave him alone, she ran crying into her room and did not leave for the rest of the day. Gradually she learned to create projects for herself. She made a geological map of their property and began taking hikes with Harold Olding, their slightly deaf neighbor, who had been wounded in the war and had discovered a love for bird-watching.

She had just returned from one of these hikes when Elizabeth met her on the porch.

"He is ill," she said.

No one could identify the disease. Mr. Englethorpe gave himself a diagnosis that shifted daily, from dengue fever to sleeping sickness. Emerson came over nearly every day, writing to doctors up and down the Eastern Seaboard about his friend's condition. In they came: men with top hats and medical bags who would go tromping up the stairs to his bedroom and come back down shaking their heads. "I have guesses," a doctor from New York City said. "But I haven't quite seen this confluence of symptoms before. I will leave you these. Take two a day."

The bottles began accumulating by his bedside, but the sheer number of different remedies became overwhelming and none seemed effective, so after a time he ceased taking any of them. When he had the energy, he would make his way downstairs to the daybed in the front parlor, feverishly scribbling notes and then sleeping for long stretches at a time. His face was always flushed, his eyes sunken. As he lost weight, his features changed, and he began to look like a different man, though his eyes still maintained traces of that inexhaustible curiosity. Elizabeth fed him squirrel soup and beet juice. Emma tried to help him organize his notes on finches, but he waved her away.

"Emma," he said finally one afternoon. "It is time that we sent you to Vassar."

"To Vassar?"

"It is a college that has newly begun, in New York. Matthew Vassar, an old friend, has finally managed to realize his lifelong ambition, which is all the more remarkable for it is a college completely for women!"

Emma's heart leapt at the notion. She had often wondered where her life would lead her next, whether she would ever fulfill her self-declared prophecy of being a scientist, beyond the bounds of her property, beyond the bounds of an assistantship to Mr. Englethorpe. Lately, perhaps in the dementia of his illness, even this relationship seemed a dimming hope.

The Vassar project renewed their partnership. Together, Emma and Mr. Englethorpe painstakingly put together an application for her admission that included an extensive set of her notes and drawings. It was exciting to see such a fine portfolio of her works collected in one place. This effort proved not to be necessary, however, for all Mr. Englethorpe needed to do was write a letter to Mr. Vassar, which he did, to inquire about the state of the application they had sent several months before. Mr. Vassar responded in due time and declared that he could not think of anything more appropriate than to embark on such an exciting path toward gender equality in higher education alongside his friend's "bright and gifted" daughter. Emma Osterville Englethorpe would be a member of the first class at Vassar College.

But the dream was not to be. On that late August afternoon, after conveying the exciting contents of the letter to both wife and daughter, Mr. Englethorpe fell into a fever that he could not see his way out of. They stayed with him that night, watching as the second man to bind them together slowly disappeared from this world. Emerson came over, and Louisa May too; they said some words to Elizabeth and then took their final leave.

Emma watched her father lying in his bed. She could not imagine what would happen to all that energy. The man who had glided around this earth, from granite ledge to fog-smudged copse, examining every majestic maple and quivering birch, his eyes always open, wondering, questioning, brewing with possible explanations as to how the world had come to be as it was.

Where did this wonderment go? Later, she would ask herself whether it simply evaporated, dissipating through the half-cracked window, into the trees, out across the fields, settling into the grass like droplets of dew.

He was gone by morning.

CHAPTER 9

It happened somewhere in Nebraska.

Or maybe it was Iowa. I couldn't be sure. Oh, if only I had been awake at that moment to record its occurrence (or to even just get a mile marker reading)! Who knows? I might've been instantly famous. But as luck would have it, I had fallen into one of those rare sleeps that had been so hard to come by during this train ride, ensconced in a dream where I was sipping Tab soda while wading through the Lincoln Memorial's reflecting pool—except that it was several miles long and was lined with crowds of people, who were cheering me on.

When I did wake up, however, I immediately felt that something was wrong. You might think this feeling came from waking up with my cheek on the tabletop, soaking in a puddle of my own drool—but that was not it.

I jumped to life, embarrassed, wiping away the drool as if Valero might judge me for my slovenliness.

"Sorry," I said.

Valero did not answer.

And that was when I was filled with this tingling sense of unease. It was quiet. Much too quiet.

I looked down at the Boggle letters. I must have been in a half-delirious state when I arranged them:

The letters seemed strangely two-dimensional. In fact, the entire cabin of the Cowboy Condo appeared flattened. I felt as if I could simply reach out with my hand and touch all objects in sight, no matter their actual distance from me.

Was I drunk? I had never been drunk before, so I couldn't be sure. Had Two Clouds slipped me a mickey? But that had been days ago...

I looked out the window of the Winnebago, trying to get a read on the time. We were moving—this much I could make out by the famil-iar soft quivering of the world—but I couldn't see anything through the windows. No landscape at all. I don't just mean it was dark; this was not the problem. Darkness was all relative. Even in pitch-black one can sense the otherness of things existing *out there*. This was different. There was *nothing* out there, nothing to echo back my thoughts. The silent confir-mation that we were so used to receiving from a world that effectively said,

"Yes, I am still here. Carry on about your business," was no longer being transmitted.

I slowly got out of my seat and walked to the door. I could hear my sneakers squeaking on the linoleum floor of the Winnebago. I would be lying if I said that in those slow, plodding moments, I did not consider the possibility that there was a vacuum seal on the door—that were I to open it, I would be sucked out through the portal into the oxygenless nether-world, like HAL did to that guy in *2001: A Space Odyssey*.

I peered out into the expanse beyond the train. Nothing. Absolutely nothing. Something compelled me to risk it, though. If I was to die, there was no better way to go out than to open the door of a Winnebago that had managed to fly into outer space. Perhaps my body would become a piece of perfectly preserved space junk and would be found by a race of intelligent monkeys one thousand years into the future and I would become the prototypical human specimen. All other humans from that point forth would be compared to me.

The door handle released easily. *Wait for it…*

Nothing. The door made its familiar unsticking noise as the rubber separated from its seal. There was no great rushing of air, no sensation of all my mitochondria imploding at once. I was not sucked through the portal. HAL—as much as I might want to talk to him and bask in the eerie symphonic calmness of his voice—did not exist.

Actually, the air outside was cool and dry, a temperature and consistency you might expect from an early fall evening somewhere in the Middle West. But there was no Middle. No West. No East. No nothing.

I stared out into the ether. Upon closer inspection, there seemed to be a bluish tinge to the darkness, as if someone had been fooling with the color settings on a television. Not only had everything blue-shifted, but the ground was no longer visible! It looked as if the train was simply floating through a great void.

Perhaps most unsettling of all was that I could no longer hear the clackety-clacking of the tracks. The train was still shuddering as though following the uneven curvatures of the line, the dips and pulls of the rail ties and ballast, but there was no hum of contact, no screech of metal on metal, none of the constant, infernal racket that I had come to both love and hate.

"Hallooo?" I called. No echo. Just the flat, bluish darkness. Without such a sonic acknowledgment, the impulse to yell out seemed useless.

I ran back inside the Winnebago and fetched Igor. Technology would help to solve this matter once and for all. Back outside again, I held Igor above my head and willed him to triangulate our coordinates. I held him aloft like this until my arms grew tired and then I laid him beside me on the flatcar and watched as he searched and searched to no avail.

"You are an idiot, Igor," I said, and threw him into the abyss. To tell you the truth, it was strangely satisfying to see him go.

Was I dead? Was that it? Had the train crashed?

Faced with this possibility, I was immediately filled with a deep sense of regret. I would never finish my maps of Montana. I would let down Mr. Benefideo, who, after our brief encounter at the lecture hall, had perhaps been filled with a great sense of hope, such that his fourteen-hour trip back to North Dakota flew by and he didn't even have to listen to a single book on tape, his breath coming slow and easy now that he knew he had found a willing heir to his life's work. And what would he do only six months later when he heard that his future protégé had died? What tired look of resignation would slide across his eyes when he put down the newspaper describing the train accident? His great task of mapping the continent in all its minutiae would slip back into the realm of a solitary dream, an elaborate hobby, a beginning with no end.

Yet I could not deny it: along with the regret and the guilt and the burning sensation in the tongue came a prickling shiver of relief, for I had gotten the icky part of dying out of the way. Perhaps my body was now smashed to a thousand smithereens, and though my parents and Gracie would suffer when they eventually found out my fate, maybe this meant that I would also get to see Layton again. Eventually, the train would stop, and Layton would climb aboard from some old-fashioned train station floating in the middle of the netherworld, the soft overhead lights revealing him standing on the platform with suitcase in hand next to a kind, bearded station agent with a stopwatch dangling from an out-stretched palm.

"All aboard!" the station agent would call as the train came to a gentle, lingering halt.

"Halllooo, Layton!" I would shout, and he would wave excitedly with the suitcase still in his hand and it would swing back and hit him in the face. And the agent would laugh and beckon and then Layton would climb aboard as the train hissed beneath us.

"You won't believe what I've been up to!" he would shout, throwing his suitcase down and tearing it open. "Look what I got!"

It would be like no time had ever passed. We could start out with a couple of rounds of Boggle and I would be able to tell him all the things I had thought about since his death, all the things I wished I hadn't been too scared to tell him had I known how short our time would be together. And then Layton would become very bored with Boggle and would groan and make those little pistol noises with his mouth and then maybe we could decorate the Cowboy Condo together with our Indian maps of Custer's Last Stand or play *We've Shrunk to an Inch, Now What?*

Come to think of it, who knew all the things we could do in this new world? Maybe we could drive the Winnebago right off the train and explore the landscape of the dead together, just two cowboys on the metaphysical range. We could go find Billy the Kid, or President William Henry Harrison. Or Tecumseh! We could ask Tecumseh if he really cursed President Harrison. In fact, we could find out, once and for all, if curses actually existed! We could bring Tecumseh and President Harrison together and say, "See, now that we know the rules of the game, curses don't exist! Let's all be friends and play a couple of rounds of Boggle. You two can even drink whiskey together if you like....What? Oh no, sir... Layton and I may be dead, but we're still too young to drink....What? Just a bit? Well, fine...what harm could it do, really?" God, it would be grand.

After sitting on the edge of the flatcar and kicking my heels back and forth for some time, I knew the death hypothesis was too easy. I was not dead. Maybe I had entered into a parallel Nebraska/Iowa, but I was still alive (and kicking). I swung my feet and looked out into the void.

"Valero?" I said. "Are you here?"

"Yes," Valero said.

"Where are we?" I asked.

"I don't know," Valero said. "One minute we were going along as usual and the next minute we were here."

"So there was no tunnel? No switching of the tracks? No magic cow that we passed?"

"I'm sorry," he said.

"Do you think we'll get back to the real world?"

"I think so," Valero said. "This place does not seem like an end point, more like a waiting room."

"Maybe…maybe we've gone back in time," I said.

"Maybe," he said.

I sat there and waited. I counted to one hundred, then lost track of the numbers and just sat. My breath slowed. The train disappeared. The old Middle West, or wherever we were, enveloped me. I sat. After a while, when I was ready, I slowly got up, went into the Cowboy Condo, and picked up my mother's notebook to finish her story.

Emma no longer wanted to attend Vassar. She saw no reason to go now that he was not with her. It was for him that she did all this. Without him, she would return to what she was supposed to have been doing all along: searching the parlors of Boston for a suitable Christian husband.

At dinner that evening she told her mother that she would remain with her on the farm, that she would marry as soon as possible so as not to be a burden on their finances. "I should have done this a while ago, but I fell under his spell so."

Elizabeth put down her spoon hard, so that both its handle and bowl struck the wooden table with a loud double tap.

"Emma," she said. "I have never demanded much from you. I have been a guiding but gentle mother to the best of my abilities, and ever since your father died in Woods Hole, I have raised you myself, which, despite your benevolence, has been no easy task. You are the joy of my life—to have you leave me now, now that we are alone again for the first time in what seems like ages, I could not stand it. Even the thought of such a thing has kept me up at night. Nothing terrifies me more. Nothing except this: that you would not go. If you do not pack all of your garments and drawings and notebooks and pens by week's end and you do not take that train, I will never forgive you. You mustn't throw this away. To close yourself off to what is possible is to kill part of yourself, and that part will never grow again. You can marry and you can bear many beautiful children, but a part of you will be dead and you will feel that coldness every time you wake in the morning. You are on the cusp of opening up the world—who knows what great and glorious things lie in store for you at that college? This is a world that has never been tested before, never been dreamed of." She was flushed; she had never said this many words in her life. "Honor him and go."

Emma went. It was not for him, however, but for Elizabeth, her mother, who had been the silent navigator this whole time, who had not barked her orders but had nudged the rudder while no one seemed to notice.

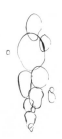

Elizabeth fades from this story like the male wasps that, once they have done their duty of procreation, crawl under a leaf, fold their antennaed heads into their legs, and wait for death to come upon them. Mr. Englethorpe always spoke of these drones with a kind of admiration, as if they were the heroes of the story.

"No complaints," he would say. "No complaints."

Most likely, Elizabeth was not so postulate in her exit stage left. She never remarried, but she captured all that she could in that country house in Concord—she grew the sweetest tomatoes and even penned a couple of ordinary poems, which she timidly showed to Louisa May, who proclaimed them "emotive & telling." But weak lungs kept her from traveling, and she was never able to see the West or her three grandchildren born in Butte. She died a peaceful if lonely death in 1884 and was buried next to Orwin Englethorpe beneath the sycamore trees.

At Vassar, Emma found an important mentor in Sanborn Tenney, her natural sciences and geology professor, but it was Maria Mitchell, the astronomy professor, who offered Emma real academic refuge. Though astronomy was not her chosen discipline, Emma spent many a late night with Mrs. Mitchell studying the cosmos and discussing the composition of the universe.

One night Emma told her all about Mr. Englethorpe. "I would have liked to have met the man," Mrs. Mitchell said. "He has allowed you to see your great gifts despite the voices which may say otherwise. I have battled those voices my entire life, and you will no doubt as well." She swung the telescope over to Emma. "It is the Gemini, the twins."

Through the cold aperture of the scope Emma could see the two parallel lines of stars. And yet how different these twins were! What drove the ancient Greek astronomer to name them as such? Was he looking at the sky and discovered the twins, or was he looking at the sky *for* the twins?

Emma graduated after only three years, writing her thesis on the sedimentary sandstone deposits in the Catskill Mountains. She was the top student in her class, and in her fourth year she expanded her thesis into a dissertation, which was published by the National Academy that September, four years to the day after Mr. Englethorpe died. The following week, Mr. Tenney called Dr. Emma Osterville Englethorpe into his office. He offered her a brandy, which she declined, and then he offered her a professorship in geology at the college. Emma was shocked and flattered.

"Am I ready?" she asked.

"My dear, you have been ready since you first set foot here. Your method even then was more extensive than that of many on this faculty. Clearly, your teachers before your arrival in Poughkeepsie taught you well—I wish that they too could work here, though we are more than happy to settle for you."

Emma returned, triumphant, to the National Academy of Sciences the next year, in 1869, to present her paper and deliver an address, "Women and Higher Learning," which she had co-penned with Mrs. Mitchell over a weekend in the Adirondacks. More than a couple of members from the Academy connected the bright-faced girl they had seen seven years earlier with the confident young woman standing before them now. These men, once amused at the possibility of the girl's ambitions, now turned stony-faced at their colleague's impressive accomplishments. Her reception was cold, if not hostile. Emma noticed but pretended not to care. Maria Mitchell had prepared her for such a reaction.

She finished the last lines of her address:

"...And so let us not ask the sex of a scientist but whether her method is sound, whether she holds fast to the rigorous standards of modern science and whether she is advancing the collective knowledge of the human project. This project matters above all else; above sex, race, or creed. I stand up here not to plead for equal treatment toward women in the sciences on any high moralistic grounds but to tell you this project will be greatly injured without such equality: there is still simply too much to know, there are too many species undescribed, too many diseases to conquer, too many worlds to explore. To sacrifice the female scientist means to deplete the number of minds significantly. My dear teacher once told me that in this age of categorization we would know all the contents of the natural world in seventy years. It is now clear he was off by a factor of ten, if not more, and thus we need the services of every single scientist, regardless of her sex. As scientists in this quest we are defined, of course, by our attention to detail, but most of all by our open-mindedness. Yes, we are nothing if we are not open-minded. With warm gratitude for your acceptance of me into your fold, I thank you from the bottom of my heart."

She made a small bow at the podium and waited. The applause was thin, coming mostly from the wet hand-smacking of a pudgy man who had already made his fancy for Emma known in the hallway before her address. She shook hands with the Academy's president, Joseph Henry, also the first secretary of the Smithsonian, who clearly disliked her. He gave her such a snide smile that she was tempted to rebuff him then and there with everyone watching, but she bit her tongue and quietly left the stage.

The demeaning reception hardened her resolve. She was not to be dismissed—she would not slink quietly into the shadows to make

➤ Here there was a break in the text, and the white space made me suddenly remember that it was my mother who had been writing all of this, that it had not simply happened. In fact, had any of this actually happened? In that first note to herself, Dr. Clair had worried about the extent of her data, and I could see why.... How did she know Emma's interior thoughts? I couldn't believe that the strict, almost paralyzingly empirical woman that I knew to be Dr. Clair would allow herself to take such grand liberties and speculate—no, *invent*—all of these emotions in our ancestors. Though the unstable verifiability of the narrative made me nervous, it also kept me turning the page. I was hooked on both believing and not believing. Maybe I was becoming an adult.

way for the fat old men and their cigars. At a reception the next day, to which she wore a conservative grey dress and a single black ribbon in her hair, someone mentioned to her that Ferdinand Vandeveer Hayden, the famous geologist, was also at the Academy that weekend, drumming up support for his latest expedition to Wyoming. Emma pursed her lips and nodded, sipping her tea as she was supposed to, listening to the next conversation about fossils in Nova Scotia. An idea had been planted in her head, however—an idea that would not go away all that day or the next. She spoke to no one about it until she was absolutely sure of it herself, and then, on her last day at the Academy, Emma boldly arranged an appointment with Dr. Hayden.

To her surprise, he accepted.

They met in one of the elegant parlors next to the gardens of the Academy, presided over by giant portraits of Newton and Agassiz, who appeared much more menacing in oil than in person. Emma, feeling her throat tighten at the beckoning of history, wasted no time in requesting a spot on his expedition.

"In what capacity?" Hayden asked. His face showed no sign of amusement.

"As a geologist. I am also a competent surveyor and topographer. Though I have only one published work, I can show you samples from my collection that I am sure you will find of sufficient quality. I pride myself on my method and exactitude."

Unbeknownst to her, Hayden did not have enough money to hire a surveyor in addition to the party he had already assembled. He sucked at the end of his cigar for some time, staring out at the gardens. What was running through his head, Emma did not know, but finally he turned and agreed to have her, but only after warning her about the perils of such a trip, which she dismissed with a wave of her hand, and also of the unfortunate but unavoidable circumstance that he could not pay her, which she considered, and then accepted. One must choose one's battles.

And so the unlikely pieces were set in place for Professor Emma Osterville Englethorpe to board a train in Washington, D.C., on July 22, 1870—her trunk full of geological surveying devices she had inherited from Mr. Englethorpe and "borrowed" from Vassar's collection—to head out west on the newly completed Union Pacific Railroad and join Ferdinand Vandeveer Hayden and the Second Annual United States Geological Surveying Expedition of the Wyoming Territory. What were the odds that such a woman at such a time would join such an endeavor? It all seemed entirely too improbable. No doubt certain members of the expedition, who most likely were relieved and grateful that they had been chosen to be on the roster of such a unique and important mission, were even more surprised when they discovered that a woman would also be accompanying them in a professional capacity on the groundbreaking adventure through the wide-open territory.

They arrived in wild Cheyenne after two miserable weeks aboard the railroad—their engine had broken down twice in Nebraska and Emma had been plagued by migraines the entire ride. She was grateful to finally greet the open air of the West.

They spent one night in Cheyenne. The town was filled with lecherous cowpokes, eager to blow their trail-drive payments, and all manner of shady characters speculating or peddling this or that once-in-a-lifetime deal. Half the men from the survey, including Hayden, left the hotel to patronize the famous Cheyenne brothels, leaving Emma with only her thoughts and her field notes. After just one night

A photograph, pasted into the notebook, labeled "Hayden's Expedition, 1870"

Though I searched the faces of each figure, I could not find Emma. Perhaps she was off in the fields, making notations in her green notebook. I suddenly hated the men in this photograph. I wanted to kick all of them in the groin.

in town, she was glad to be moving on again. She longed to be amongst the Cretaceous Limestone, to hike the yawning cirques of the legendary Wind River Mountains and see for herself the great tectonic folds and bends that were supposed to dwarf the landscapes back home.

But it did not get easier. For ten days they camped at Fort Russell, the expedition's rendezvous point. On the second night, one of the men drunkenly grabbed her hair and tried to force himself on her. She kicked him in the groin and he crumpled like a discarded puppet, passing out then and there in the dust . The next morning around the coffeepot, he said nothing.

Finally, they headed west. She learned to take her coffee early and then head out into the field before the men awoke. Gradually, she and the men forged an unspoken contract of mutual avoidance.

Hayden was worst of all. It was not what he said—it was what he did not say. He hardly acknowledged her presence. At the end of the day, she would leave her geology notes on the table outside his tent and they would be gone by morning, but he never thanked her, never engaged her on any of her observations. She could feel the muscles in her jaw tighten every time she was near him. These were supposed to be refined men of science, men who could discuss Humboldt and Rousseau and Darwin with ease, men of character, men of observation, but beneath all this they bred a kind of blindness that she found even more distasteful than the lecherous cowpokes of Cheyenne. At least those cowboys would look you in the eye.

Two and half months into the trip, they had traveled the entire length of Wyoming, from Cheyenne all the way to Ft. Bridger and Green River Station on the new Union Pacific transcontinental line, before doubling back along the railroad. William Henry Jackson, the group's photographer, took many photoplates of the UP trains cutting through the high desert country, which he stored in the saddlebags strapped to his faithful donkey, Hydro. Jackson was Emma's only ally on this trip. He did not look through her, did not spit at her feet, did not mutter under his breath as she passed by. In the evenings, her solitary joy was to share a quiet conversation with him, away from the prying eyes of the group. Together they would rehash the day's discoveries, linger on the awe-inspiring views around them. If only she could find her place within this landscape.

In the late afternoon of October 18, they followed the railroad down from the great vista of Table Rock, weaving their way through a valley of bright red buttes to the lonely outpost of Red Desert. They waited as Hayden negotiated with the station foreman, who spoke little English but showed them a sheltered area where they could camp for the next couple of days. A few hills hugged their site to the south, but across the railroad to the north, as far as the eye could see, lay the endless, undulating expanse of the Red Desert.

At sunset, Emma watched while Mr. Jackson set up his camera. Nearby, Hydro pawed at the cooling clay. She heard the men in camp strike up a tune. They must have found some whiskey, perhaps from that brutish station foreman—with this group, singing was always a sign of uncorked spirits. These men desperately cushioned themselves from their own mortality even as they perched precariously on the edge of a cliff to garner vital measurements for the survey. She could not face them again. She left Mr. Jackson to his constant adjustments of the dials and wandered down to the station house. The water tower cast a long, thin shadow across the railroad tracks.

He was asleep when she first saw him. She stood in the doorway, watching him snore, open-mouthed, in his chair. He *was* a brute. She was just about to take her leave when he awoke with a start and saw her at the door. His eyes went wide. He wiped at his lips with the back of his hand in a surprisingly gentle gesture for such an obviously crude man.

"Miss?" he said in a heavy accent, rising out of his seat. He scrunched his eyes closed and then opened them again, as if to clear away a vision. And yet she remained before him.

She sighed. A whirring in her head came to a tired and reluctant halt.

"I'm thirsty," she said. "Do you have any water?"

The writing ended. I flipped through the rest of the notebook. The last twenty pages were empty.

I panicked.

Are you kidding me?

How could she stop writing? This was the whole point! She wanted to figure out why they had gotten together. Why stop now? I wanted the juicy details—okay, I admit it, maybe even some juicy sexy details. (Even I had read page 28 in our school's copy of *The Godfather*.)

"I'm thirsty?" "Do you have any water?" Apparently, this pickup line was all that was needed out west, and then *boom*—she's no longer the country's first female geologist but the wife of a Finn. *What?* Faced with the constant harassment of her fellow scientists on the trip, Emma had simply given up her dream and taken the easier path, abandoning science for the shelter of Tearho's simple embrace?

I knew that two people fell in love not simply due to the confluence of their respective disciplines, but why then in our family, time and again, had a woman of empiricism fallen for a man completely outside her field, a man whose profession was guided not by theories or field data or an artist's sketch but by the heavy handle of a sledgehammer? Was a common disciplinarity actually repulsive, like magnets of the same polarity? Did the true, umbilical love that bound people together for the length of their lives require a certain intellectual dislocution in order to push past our insistent rationalization and enter the rough, uneven space inside our hearts? Could two scientists ever have this kind of natural, *devotional* love?

As I floated in the Cowboy Condo through the netherworld, I wondered if my mother had ever ended up writing the fateful scene where Emma and Tearho actually fell in love. Maybe this was it. Maybe she realized she could no more enumerate the reasons why Tearho and Emma chose each other than she could describe why she had chosen my father. Or maybe the scene was hidden in another EOE notebook, disguised as tiger monk field notes. *Oh, Mother, what are you doing with your life?*

I was just about to close the notebook for good when I glanced at the very last page. At the top, there were some ink scratches as if Dr. Clair had been trying to get her pen flowing. And then, toward the bottom of the page, she had written only one word.

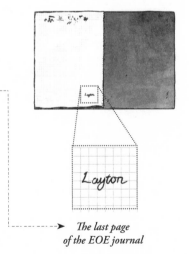

The last page of the EOE journal

Seeing his name on the page caught me completely off guard. *How did she know him too?* My image of Layton in his boots and rifle and spaceman pajamas seemed so far away from the world of Emma and Hayden and nineteenth-century science expeditions, it was as if someone else had stolen this notebook and inserted his name. I looked closely. It was my mother's handwriting.

She had known him too. Not only had she known him, *she had birthed him.* They had a unique biological bond, which I could not even comprehend. Her loss must have been profound—and yet Dr. Clair, like everyone at the Coppertop, had barely mentioned his name since the funeral.

But she had written his name.

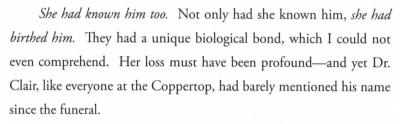

I stared at the clustering of those six letters. I realized my family's denial of Layton's death, indeed his very existence, had nothing to do with Layton. It was a fortification that we were collectively constructing without him. It was our choice; it was not how it must be. Why wrangle all this effort in the pursuit of such a futile task? Layton had existed in the flesh. My memory of how he took the back stairs three at a time or how he would chase Verywell straight into the pond so that for a moment it seemed both of them might run right across the surface of the water before they sank—these memories were real, they were not just present-day acts of creation untethered from our shared experience. Part of me did not want to accept all that had happened up until this moment, and the other part wanted to accept only the past and claim no ownership of the present.

Layton would never have been caught in such a teleological bind. He would've said, "Let's shoot some tin off a that fence."

And I would ask, "But why did you shoot yourself in the barn? Was it an accident? Did I make you do it? Is this all my fault?"

I stared at those six letters. The answers to my questions would never come.

ayton

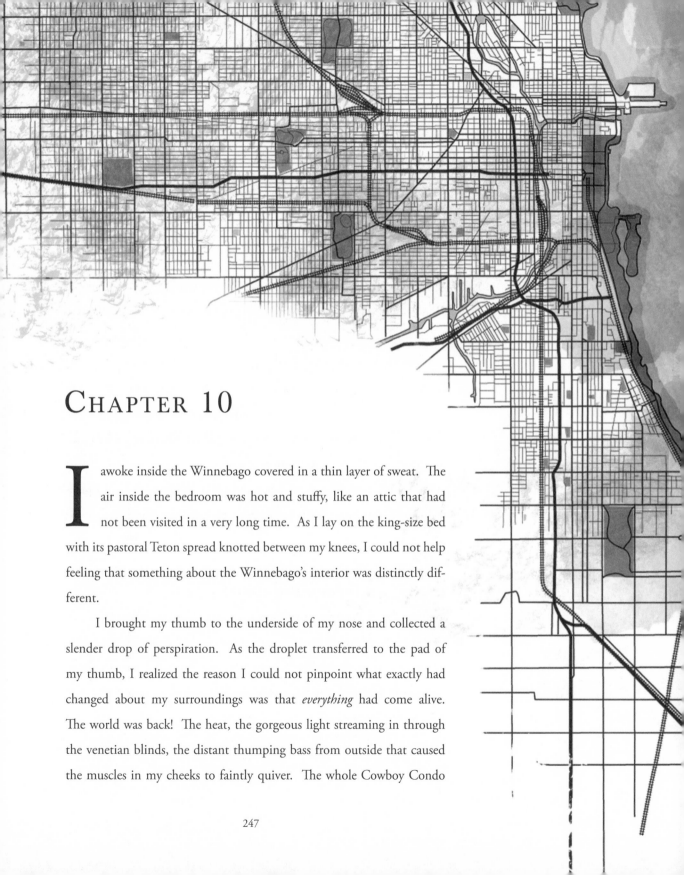

CHAPTER 10

I awoke inside the Winnebago covered in a thin layer of sweat. The air inside the bedroom was hot and stuffy, like an attic that had not been visited in a very long time. As I lay on the king-size bed with its pastoral Teton spread knotted between my knees, I could not help feeling that something about the Winnebago's interior was distinctly different.

I brought my thumb to the underside of my nose and collected a slender drop of perspiration. As the droplet transferred to the pad of my thumb, I realized the reason I could not pinpoint what exactly had changed about my surroundings was that *everything* had come alive. The world was back! The heat, the gorgeous light streaming in through the venetian blinds, the distant thumping bass from outside that caused the muscles in my cheeks to faintly quiver. The whole Cowboy Condo shook with each beat, the plastic bananas shivering in their little bowl. Oh joy of joys! Thermodynamics was back! Cause and effect had returned! *Welcome, boys, welcome!*

At the window, I parted the blinds with thumb and index finger and then made a single, brief groan of amazement.

 A panorama of overpasses.

Okay, okay, I had seen pictures of overpasses before—I had even seen a movie where some guy jumps a bus from one overpass to another—but for a ranch boy like me, this confluence of floating roadways was almost too overwhelming.   Part of my mental paralysis no doubt stemmed from the several days I had spent stuck inside the utter sensory deprivation of a Middle Western wormhole or whatever one called a quantum irregularity like that. Emerging from that experience into *any* sort of tactile reality would have caused a kind of synaptic whiplash—but to emerge into *this reality*! Here was the serpentine geography of civilization: a labyrinth of six overpasses, three layers high, beautiful and beguiling in their complexity and yet highly constructed and practical in their utility, a constant stream of cars weaving above and below one another, their operators seemingly unaware of the synthesis of concrete and theoretical physics that supported them in their turning.

And beyond the overpasses, as far as the eye could see, there were tall buildings and fire escapes and water towers and huge streets that kept fleeing into the distance—a distance apparently composed of more tall buildings and fire escapes and water towers. The depth of field, the number of overlapping lines and materials on display all pushed me to the first stages of hyperventilation. At some point in history, every single one of these tall buildings, every metal railing, every cornice and brick and welcome mat—every one of them had been placed there by someone with his own

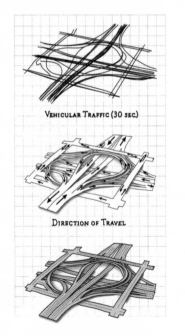

VEHICULAR TRAFFIC (30 SEC)

DIRECTION OF TRAVEL

The Miracle of Concrete ◄- - - - -
from Notebook G101

two hands. The landscape before me was an unimaginable act of human creation. Though the mountain ranges that cradled the Coppertop Ranch were mightier in stature than the sprawl of these buildings, I had always viewed their creation as inevitable, an expected by-product of erosion and plate tectonics. These buildings, however, did not have that easy sense of preordination. Everywhere—in the gridwork of the streets, the telephone wires, the shape of windows, the clusters of chimneys and carefully arranged TV dishes—everywhere there was evidence of a collective obsession with the comforting logic of right angles.

In all directions, the tall buildings cut off the view to the horizon: it felt as if the structures were giant theatrical flats placed strategically to block my line of sight, so that I might forget what the rest of the world looked like.

This is all there is, the buildings called out to me. *All that is important is right here. Where you came from no longer matters. Forget it.* I nodded my head. Yes—in a city like this, Montana did not seem to matter much at all.

In the foreground, a large black SUV idled on a road next to the tracks, and I realized that this was the source of the thumping bass notes. It was producing the strangest music I had ever heard—some hyped-up, masculine version of Gracie's Girl Pop that caused the whole SUV to quiver as if it were composed of firm pudding. The vehicle's windows were also black, so I could not see who was driving. Just as I was wondering how the driver could see where he was going, the traffic light changed and the SUV quickly peeled away. Much to my amazement, I noticed that as it moved forward, it's big silver rims were actually spinning *backward*.

The train slowly pushed through this overcrowded sensory landscape. I opened the door to the Winnebago halfway, ventilating the stuffy

The Car with Black Windows That Drove Backward While Traveling Forward **from Notebook G101**

The paradoxical sum of these vectors made my head spin. I wondered briefly whether the laws of thermodynamics were suspended in a city such as this. Were all bets off? Could urban dwellers simply choose the direction their wheels spun by pressing an Anti-Newton button on their dashboards? Were all cars driven by autopilot so you didn't even have to see where you were going?

cabin. The sun shone against my face—I could tell that it was fairly early in the morning, but already the heat was building up; it was a thick, sticky heat that I had never felt before. It seemed as if little bits of concrete and rubber-coated wires and even some shish-kebab particles had all vaporized into the air, glomming on to the weary urban oxygen molecules.

A clattering of construction rose up nearby. The smells of exhaust and fermenting trash wafted into my nostrils and then were gone. Everything was transitory; nothing lasted more than a few seconds. And the people who moved through this landscape seemed to know this: they moved with a quickness of pace, their arms swung easily by their sides without expectation, as if all that mattered was their destination. There were more people visible at any given moment than I think I had ever met in my whole life. They were everywhere: walking on the sidewalks, crawling on cars, waving their arms, playing jump rope, selling magazines, newspapers, tube socks. More thumping bass came from another passing black SUV (this time, no backward wheels) and then this too was gone, leaving only an echo of *its* echo of the first car, and the two bass-pumping SUVs merged inside my mind to become a single car with both forward- and backward-moving wheels that straddled the space-time continuum. Man, this city was confusing.

Somewhere, a dog started barking—five short barks, followed by a man yelling in what sounded like Arabic. Three black boys on little bikes came whizzing around a corner, all hopping the curb, laughing as the last boy almost crashed before he recovered and joined his two compatriots. Their bikes were so small they had to part their legs in exaggerated V's to keep their knees from hitting their elbows.

In the way you recognize that you have been using a word your entire life without actually knowing its proper meaning, I realized I had never actually been to a real city before. A hundred years ago, Butte might have been a real city too, buzzing with the slap of daily newspapers, the jingle of a thousand transactions, the constant sigh of wool brushing against wool on crowded sidewalks—but no longer. *Here* was a real city. Here—as a large blue *Tribune* billboard announced—here was "Chicagoland."

As I watched, I fell under the city's spell of multiplicity and transience. One could not possibly process an urban landscape like this through the sum of its details. All of my usual abilities of observation, measurement, and visual synthesis began to shut down one after another. Fighting a rising panic, I tried to retreat to the familiar territory of pattern recognition, but with thousands of minute observations to choose from, there were either too many patterns or none at all.

Out west, one could concentrate for days on the particulars of north-south geese migration, but here even just the peculiarly long cut of those three bicycle riders' jean shorts inspired a dizzying array of questions: how close were these shorts to being pants and what was the official length before something became a pant, anyway? How many years had it taken for these long shorts to be culturally acceptable? And what did the variation in length across the three boys suggest? Did the lead boy always have the longest shorts?

I saw a thousand maps rising into the air like ghostly echoes of the twisting city beneath: the ratio of cars to people on each block; the variation of tree species as you moved north through the city; the average number of words exchanged between strangers from neighborhood to neighborhood. I was having trouble breathing. I could not possibly make all these maps. The ghosts evaporated into the air just as fast as the city could produce them. All of these maps wasted, never realized.

AMBIGUOUS CALF ZONE

1980   1987   1994

2001   2007

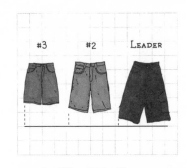

#3   #2   LEADER

When Did a Short Become a Pant? (and Other Modern Dilemmas) from Notebook G101

Without knowing what else to do, I took out my Leica M1, licked my fingers, and removed the lens cap. I began taking pictures of everything the freight train passed: a public mural of a blues guitarist wearing large sunglasses; an apartment building with ten Puerto Rican flags flapping from the fire escape; a bald woman walking a cat on a leash. I took a series of water-tower pictures, trying to capture the varying styles of their conical roofs.

The certainty and framing of these exposures calmed me somewhat, but in a matter of five minutes I was out of film. Perhaps I shouldn't have gotten so hung up on those water towers. I couldn't just take pictures willy-nilly—I had to be much more selective in what I thought was interesting.

"Okay, brain," I said. "Start filtering."

So I opened my notebook. Out of a thousand possible maps, I chose one, which I labeled "The Map of Accompaniment; or, *Loneliness in Transit.*"

Over the course of seven minutes, I recorded how many people were walking or driving down the street alone, how many were traveling in pairs, and how many were in groups of three, four, or five or more. Each time I marked down individual people, there was a brief moment when their world opened up to me and I could feel the urgency of their travels, their feet already anticipating the textured carpets and measured stairwells of their destination. And then they disappeared into the grid and became just another plot on my graph.

Gradually, however, a larger narrative emerged: of 93 people observed, 51 were walking or driving alone. And of these, 64 percent were listening to earphones or talking on cellular telephones, perhaps to distract themselves from the fact that they were traveling alone.

T. S. Spivet
Water Tower #1, #7, #12
2007 (pen and ink)
Exhibited at the
Smithsonian Museum
December 2007

After thinking for a moment, I erased the number 51 and wrote 52, brushing the tiny pink eraser worms off the page with my thumb. I was now one of them.

You are not alone.

Our train pushed away from the people part of town into a grouping of huge cement factories. And empty streets. Homeless people had made little houses out of cardboard. I saw a blue-sock-covered foot peeking out from one of these little cardboard tents. One man had made a small compound in an abandoned, weed-lined lot—he had circled six shopping carts around a tarp and decorated his living quarters with a dozen plastic flamingos. The flamingos looked sad but alert surrounded by all of that concrete, as though they were putting in their hours before they could fly back to Florida and retire to a life of grumbling and complaining about their time roosting amidst this industrial wretchedness. Beneath the distant safety of the palm tree, however, they would eventually become bored, and would secretly long for the immediacy and rawness of their former lives in the dirty lot.

The more I looked around, the more trash I noticed on the ground. It came in every imaginable form: bottles, potato chip bags, car tires, wheelless shopping carts, plastic bags, empty Slim Jim wrappers. All of these items had been produced by factories, probably in China, shipped to the United States on a cargo ship piloted by a sniffling Russian man, handled and discarded by a Chicagoan, and now they lay across the landscape, fluttering in the light breeze (except the tires, which did not flutter). What if you mapped a city only by its litter? What places would be most densely populated?

Concentration of Litter in Chicago

■ >50 pieces of litter (per block)
■ 26-49 pieces of litter
■ 16-25 pieces of l
□ <15 piec

And then we came to a long, hissing stop. A stop! I had forgotten what this felt like. My body stood there, quivering, doing its nostalgic duty to counteract the effects of a trip that, more and more, I could feel was finally over. I had reached Chicagoland, the great Jump-Off, the capital of *la terra incognita,* and now my time in the Cowboy Condo was up. Valero had been a trusty steed. He had gotten me this far, through the Rocky Mountains, through the Great Basin and the Red Desert, across the Plains and the confluent neurocenter of Bailey Yards and into and out of the wormhole and now I was in the Windy City, within striking distance of my destination. All I had to do was follow the advice of Two Clouds and look for those scrumptious blue-and-yellow CSX freighters that would take me east, to our nation's capital, to the president, to a world of diagrams, fame, and fortune. (And also to find some food, as the triumph of eating my last granola bar was slowly being replaced with the dull panic of facing an existence without sustenance.)

"Good-bye, Valero," I said, and waited.

"Good-bye," I said again, louder this time. "I don't know how you got us out of that wormhole or whatever it was. Thank you, sir, for that. I hope whoever buys you is a good person, with a good sense of direction, because they are getting one amazing Cowboy Condo."

Still no answer.

"Valero?" I said. "Friend?"

In the big city, Winnebagos did not speak. Apparently this happened only along the open page of the West. Things were changing.

I tried to clean myself up. Over the course of my journey, bathing had been a bit of a challenge, but there seemed to be a small amount of water in the Winnebago's tanks, so I could at least take dribble showers in the tiny bathroom. Next to the sink, there was another giant decal of the cartoon cowboy, this one saying "Take real showers out on the range!" and mocking me as I scrubbed my body with maniacal speed beneath the thin, freezing line of drool emanating from the showerhead. I was tough, like my father, who hadn't used a drop of hot water in his life. I sang a little pick-me-up beneath the icy dribble and clenched my toes to keep from shivering.

Still, I imagined that even after scrubbing up and changing into a fresh set of clothes, I looked more disheveled than not—maybe not quite like Hanky the Hobo, but certainly nothing like these fashionable city dwellers. I put on one of my grey sweater vests. Right now I needed to do my best to blend in with the Chicagoans. After briefly considering bringing him, I left Redbeard where he was on the dashboard. If Valero ever came back to life, he might need a friend.

Once I had made sure that the coast was clear, I lugged my suitcase out of the Winnebago and gingerly lowered it to the ground. There were hundreds of freight cars around. I looked for the blue-and-yellow engines. There seemed to be a bunch of them a ways up the track.

I tried hauling my suitcase, but the going was slow. As much as I hated to do it, I realized I would probably have to hide my suitcase here while I scoped out the situation. Oh, but how to leave this collection of essential items that I had spent hours assembling? I almost started hyperventilating right then and there, but to stave off a panic attack I quickly pulled out my daypack and loaded it with just the barest of essentials: thirty-four dollars and twenty-four cents, binoculars, my notebooks, a picture of my family, my lucky compass, and, for some reason, the sparrow skeleton.

I began walking up the tracks as nonchalantly as possible, thumbing at my sweater vest as though I belonged in this rail yard, as though I was

This is the only song I know by heart:

LI'L OL' COWBOY

Where have you gone,
My li'l ol' cowboy?
Mama's in the kitchen
And the cows need a'pushin'.

Where have you gone,
My li'l ol' cowboy?
Grass is gettin' high
And winter is a'comin'.

Where have you gone,
My li'l ol' cowboy?
It's lonely out here when
Those ca-yotes start a'howlin'.

Where have you gone,
My li'l ol' cowboy?
I've gone to meet my maker,
Won't be comin' back no more.

–T.Y.

➤ *The horror, the horror!* To leave behind my theodolite and Tangential the Tortoise! I could not think about it too much. I had to learn that I didn't need every device at my beck and call, that carrying an antique theodolite around Chicago was impractical if not an invitation for a beating. I tried not to think too hard what would happen if I got lost and never managed to find this suitcase again. Grown-ups made tough choices in this world all the time and it was time I started thinking like a grown-up.

just taking my usual daily constitutional through the boxcars and signal switches, as though I were not a thousand miles from home and the ranch and the fences and the ignorant goats.

They were indeed CSX engines. I came upon them as one comes upon a large sleeping creature. They were big, beautiful, elegant things. They felt sleeker, more modern than the UP engines I had become so familiar with. Compared with these CSX sophisticates, the Union Pacific crop were like a bunch of rednecks. The CSX engines sat on the tracks, hissing and waiting, as if saying, "You want to ride with us? You have never ridden with our caliber before. Are you worthy of such a trip? We are Easterners. If we were able to, we would wear monocles over our engine eye and talk of Rousseau. Have you read Rousseau? He is our favorite."

I could roll with these engines and their highfalutin ideas. I may be a rancher's son, but I could ruminate on the mixed legacy of the Enlightenment with the best of them—or at least fake it. The real question was: how to know where these dandy-fop locomotives were going? Should I dare ask a rail yard worker? Did I need to come bearing gifts of pornography and beer? Perhaps I could trade them my Map of Loneliness for a railroad timetable? Layton would have had no trouble walking right up to any of these wrenches and striking up a conversation. Hell, after only a few minutes of his charming cowboy talk, they would probably let him drive the train all the way to D.C.

Then I remembered: the Hobo Hotline. This was much less terrifying, as I could avoid conversation with burly railworkers. Although I would need to find a cellular telephone, which would probably mean asking a man on the street if I could use his. I would ask a very nice-looking man with a satin scarf and a small nose and a small dog, the kind of man who enjoyed classical music and public television.

I rifled through my backpack and found Notebook G101. I had taped the Hobo Hotline number to the inside of the front cover. I would use technology as a force of good. All I needed to find was a friendly, silk-scarf-toting resident of Chicagoland to assist a boy from Montana.

First I went about writing down the numbers from boxcars connected to each of the three CSX trains.

Then I tried to find a man with a small dog. This was not so easy in a freight yard that itself was buried within an industrial wasteland. People did not walk their tiny dogs around these parts. In fact, it appeared that no one really walked around these parts, except to perhaps throw their Slim Jim wrappers on the ground and then leave.

I was standing near the gates of the rail yard, debating whether I should just choose one of the CSX trains and hope for the best or whether I could actually work up the nerve to sidle on up to one of the tattooed railworkers, when a black car with tinted windows pulled up next to me. A heavyset man stepped out. I knew it immediately: he was a railway bull. He was the enemy.

"What you up to, stitch? You up to trouble?"

"No, sir," I said. I wondered what a *stitch* was, but dared not ask this of a man with multiple chins who had a two-foot-long club dangling from his waist.

"You're trespassing. What you got in that bag? Spray paint? You vandalizing, stitch? If I find out you touched one of these cars, you're done, you know that? Shit, you picked the wrong day to make trouble, you know that? Come on down with me, we're writing you up, stitch. Wrong day, wrong day, you son of a bitch." He muttered these last words as if he were talking to himself.

CSX 69346 ◄

CSX 20004 ◄

► CSX 59727

Where are ◄
you going?

I panicked. I didn't know what else to do, so I said: "I like Chica-goland."

"What?" he said, shocked.

"Well it's kind of busy, but it's got a nice buzz to it. I mean, it takes some getting used to. I mean, I'm not used to it…at the ranch it's much quieter—just Gracie and her music, you know, but not so much bass. But this place is fine, fine. Yeah, so do you have a telephone I might be able to use?" I was out of my mind; I had forgotten how one speaks English. I had no idea what I was saying anymore.

"Where you from?" he asked, peering at me, left hand working the top of that club.

I started saying the truth, then tried to lie midway through: "Mont… tenegro."

"Well, you little shit, welcome to the great state of Illinois. I'm sure you'll get to know it well, soon as we book you and notify your parents of the charges: trespassing, destruction of railroad property, whatever else you been up to. Oh, boy, you got a pretty sweet introduction coming your way, Mr. Monta-*nee*-gro!"

"Monte-*nay*-gro" I said.

"You are a little wiseass, aren't you, stitch?" he said. "Get in the car."

Once again I was faced with two choices:

1) I could bow to the sweaty double chin of authority and go down to the office to be booked and grilled under bright lights that squeaked when they were adjusted. I would inevi-tably crack and reveal that it was Montana and not Monte-negro where I was from and they would call my parents and it would all be done.

2) I could run. (This seemed pretty self-explanatory.)

I said, "All right, let me just tie my shoe."

He made a gruff sort of nod and then went around to the other side of the car to open the door for me.

Then I began running. The oldest trick in the book. I could hear the sound of my feet against the ballast gravel of the tracks. I ran right out of the rail yards, down a street, and then I took a left, right, left, and another left up some stairs onto a pedestrian overpass—which I ran right over without admiring its utilitarian beauty. I had no idea where I was going—I might as well have been following the broken lucky compass in my backpack. I went left, left, then right through an open grassy field filled with two large dumpsters—one overturned, one upright—over a fence, and finally, just before my lungs exploded, I found myself on the banks of an industrial canal filled with thick yellow milky water. On either side of the canal, smug and sleeping tugboats were tied to great dock cleats with giant ropes as thick as my neck.

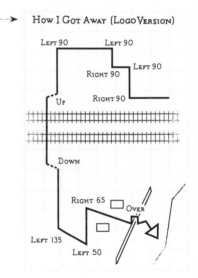

T. S. as Turtle
from Notebook G101

I crouched down on the uneven brickwork lining the canal, breathing hard. It was warm outside. Wafts of gasoline and putrid algae drifted in off the water. Once upon a time, this must have been a small stream or natural drainage—but now? The corseted melancholy, the audacity of man evident in this place reminded me of the feeling I got when I came out of the viewing tunnel at the Berkeley Pit in Butte and encountered the sprawl of metallic eggplant water slowly rising to the brim of that huge hole in the earth. At first there was a blinking, a swiping at the scene as if it were a dream that could be cleared with a closing and lifting of the lids. Then you were slowly filled with a resolute loneliness: the insistence of that pit, this canal, the reality of the water's surface—not a sea of the imagination, but real water that could cover you and enfold you and drown you—the reality of the water's surface forcing you to confront our civilization's choices and inevitably accept them as your own.

I had no idea where I was or what I was going to do. I pulled out my compass from my backpack, unsure of what I was looking for. A miracle, maybe. It was still broken, pointing east-southeast as it always did.

I began to cry. My father was not there to disapprove, so I wept openly at the flawed resoluteness enacted on my compass. The object no longer seemed to hold a secret within its insistence on a singular direction. Now it was simply a broken tool, and I a lost surveyor looking for meaning within its malfunction. Gone was the feeling of determination that I had possessed my whole life: that everything would be all right, that a higher navigational purpose watched over me and guided my hands at the drafting table. This sense of shelter had vanished, leaving a metallic aftertaste: it was just me and the uneven solitude of the endless city.

I was sitting by the canal staring at my sparrow skeleton. He had not survived the journey well: his rib cage was cracked, his head was turned around sideways, one of his feet was missing. His bones looked so fragile, almost watery, as though it was no longer clear where the air stopped and the calcium began.

"Mr. Sparrow, if you disintegrate," I said, "do I still go on living? Do I get to keep my name? What's our relationship like, exactly? As my guardian angel, what kind of contract do we have? Can you fly me out of Chicagoland?"

"Have you abandoned Jeez-us?" a voice said.

I looked up. A giant man in a trench coat was standing over me. His sudden appearance was extremely disconcerting as I had not seen him coming from either direction, and believed that I was utterly alone, so finding him standing over me like that asking about Jesus made me feel as if he had interrupted something very private, which I suppose he had.

The first thing I noticed about the man was the beard. It wasn't one of those long, waterfall beards like you would see on the men coming out of the M&M bar in the afternoon; it was just huge and spongy and wide. The beard made his entire face appear wider than it was long, as if his head had been gently smushed by a giant thumb and index finger. Amidst all this ferocity of hair, one of his eyes was lazy—so lazy that it looked off into the distance of the canal even as he stood staring down at me. I had to admit, I briefly glanced in the direction of where his lazy eye was staring, just to see if I was missing something important.

"Have you forsaken the Lord's word?" he said, raising his voice. He pointed at the sparrow skeleton with a long-nailed finger. "Is this the Devil's form? Leviticus says we detest the falcon. We detest! He who touches the carcass will be unclean, and is an agent of the Devil."

He was dirty, but not too dirty, a bit like me perhaps. The hair on the side of his head was carefully combed all the way over the baldness on top, but it was unwashed and greasy, and curled unpleasantly around his ears. Beneath his trench coat, I could see that he was wearing some sort of old white tuxedo, the lapels of which were stained with what looked like ketchup. In one of his hands he held a Bible—or at least something in the biblical genre. All of his fingers had those long, macabre fingernails. Of all his peculiar features, these made me the most uneasy. If there was one thing that Dr. Clair had taught me, it was that fingernails were meant to be trimmed.

"This is not a falcon," I said defensively. "This is a sparrow."

"When he lies, he speaks his native tongue, for he is a liar and the father of all lies."

THE BEARD

THE LAZY EYE

THE COMBOVER

THE STAINS ON THE LAPEL

THE FINGERNAILS

Fear Is the Sum of Many Sensory Details from Notebook G101

"Do you know where a telephone booth is, by chance?" I asked, try-ing to change this man from a lazy-eyed, long-nailed ketchup-spiller into a classical music lover with a small dog.

I suddenly thought of Reverend Greer—nice, caring Reverend Greer, who spoke in a religious way like this man but did so in such a manner that the muscles in your feet relaxed and you felt safe, safe, safe to let the singing of the hymns wash over you. What would Reverend Greer say to this man?

"You cannot run from Him for He watches with the one eye, al-ways," the man said. "He knows when you have turned to Satan. You must accept His hand to-day, and praise Him to-day, and then the Almighty will save you."

"That's all right," I said. "Thank you, but I need to find a telephone. I have an urgent call to make."

"The temptation and the lies," he growled.

"The what?" I said.

Suddenly he grabbed the sparrow from my hands and threw it against the bricks. The skeleton shattered. "Destroy this evil carcass," he shouted. "Purify your soul! Call out to Him to save you!" The tiny bones parted from one another with great ease, as if they had been looking to split from their brethren for a very long time. They looked like toenails scattered across the bricks, quivering in the canal's warm acidic breeze.

I let out a compact exhalation of disbelief. The bones! Those bones had been intact since my birth. I waited for my body to crumple, for my own bones to shatter.

Nothing happened.

"That was my birth present, you jerk!" I yelled. I got off my bench and pushed the man. I could feel how thin he was beneath his clothes.

This was not a smart thing to do. For a second the man looked surprised at my outburst and then he grabbed me by my collar and literally pulled me up off the ground with one hand. As he pulled me up to him, I could see the man's good eye flicking about, his other eye continuing to drift off into the distance, unfocused.

"The Devil has gotten into your heart," he hissed into my face. I could smell his rancid cabbage breath.

"No, no, no," I said, whimpering. "Sorry I pushed you. Please. There's no Devil here. It's just me. T.S. I make maps."

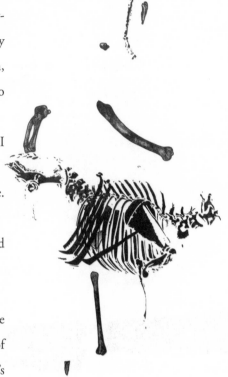

"If we claim we have not sinned, we make Him out to be a liar and His Word has no place in our lives."

"Please!" I cried. "I just want to go home."

"You have been with the Devil, but you will not be fearful, for here is Josiah Merrymore, Reverend of God's Children, Ancient Prophet of the Chosen Israelites, Lord of Lords, and I will save you from the Liar's hold."

"Save me?"

He began shaking again, his good eye joining his bad eye in rolling back into his head. The Bible dropped from his hand, landing on the bricks next to the crushed sparrow skeleton, but his grip on my collar with his other hand remained tight. I couldn't do anything. Despite his grizzled appearance, this man seemed to possess superhuman strength. And then, from the pocket of his trench coat, Josiah Merrymore produced a gargantuan kitchen knife, eleven inches long and filthy, with little bits of food and rust lining the blade.

"High Almighty," he said. "Press out the Devil in this boy's heart, open up his chest and free him of his earthly sin, of his handling of the forbidden carcass, of all his Wicked thoughts, of his fraternity with the

Dark Angel—accept him into your flock, for he is blessed once we rid him of this burden."

He brought the knife to my chest and began to cut open my sweater vest with slow, methodical strokes. He was biting his tongue as he did this, like Layton used to do when he tied his shoelaces using two bunny loops.

So this was how it was meant to be. Every force demanded an equal an opposite counterforce. Since that day in February, I had always had a deep suspicion that for things to be right again, my role in Layton's death would eventually demand my own swift demise. And so here was my counterforce: a crazy preacher opening up my chest cavity on the banks of a Chicago canal. Not quite what I had imagined, but God (or whatever it was) worked in mysterious ways. I closed my eyes and tried to bear it.

This is for you, Layton, I said to myself. *I am sorry for all I have done.* I could feel the cool air on my chest where my sweater and shirt were being cut open and I could feel the wet greasy feeling of blood collecting in my sternum and then running down the surface of my belly. I was dying and now probably dead.

But we are creatures of self-preservation. Pain makes us react in very strange ways. As much as I wanted to endure my unpleasant sentence of death and then join my brother in heaven…*it really frickin' hurt!*

After only a few seconds, I could not help but fight back. Maybe it was just an instinctual reflex. Or maybe it was because I, T. S. Spivet, was not ready to accept this fate—my duties in this life were not yet finished.

People were depending on me; I still had to deliver a speech Washington. I had not even finished the Montana map series for Mr. Benefideo!

I too was an actor on this stage—I could move, speak, react on my own volition. The inevitable counterforce would just have to wait.

Still suspended in the air, I reached into my pocket, pulled out my Leatherman (Cartographer's Edition), flicked open the knife, and stabbed Josiah Merrymore wherever I could, which happened to be in the chest, just below his left arm. I stabbed as I should have stabbed that rattler, as my father shot at coyotes—with great confidence and without hesitation.

He howled and staggered backward. The kitchen knife clattered against the bricks. I brought my hand to my chest and my fingers came away covered in blood. My mouth went dry. I looked up and saw Josiah Merrymore stagger about, trying to locate the source of his pain.

"Why, Devil? Why strike me down when I am freeing you of your burden? God, what mercy have You shown to Josiah? What mercy, when I carry Your Word?"

And then he tripped on one of the staunch metal dock cleats and fell backward over the stone edge into the canal. As he fell, I saw that he was wearing combat boots, and that these boots did not have laces. I ran to the edge and watched him thrash.

"I cannot swim!" he said. "Lord Almighty! Lord, save me!" He was bleeding into the milky water. I could see the pink pools around him, and then he went under the surface, came up, went under again, and then all was still.

I looked down at my chest. It was bleeding pretty good. My sweater vest was growing dark with blood. I began to go dizzy.

"No," I said. "Cowboys don't get dizzy. Jesus didn't get dizzy."

But I *was* dizzy, and not a cowboy, or Jesus, apparently. I fell to one knee. I could feel the blood pooling around my belly button and starting to seep into the waistband of my pants. Despite my effort, maybe the counterforce had occurred after all. However unwillingly, Merrymore and I had enacted the ancient ritual of the duel that had been played out time and time again across the windblown streets and snow-covered fields of history—Pushkin, Hamilton, Clay, and now us. In the course of that timeless dance, we each had inflicted mortal wounds upon the other, completing the honorary handshake of fate.

When I looked up, I saw them coming toward me: in the distance they looked like a swirl of dust, a dense knot of hands opening and closing, humming through the air, skitting across the surface of the water in my direction. I was not afraid. As they came closer, I could see that they were birds, hundreds of them, perhaps thousands, flying so close together it seemed impossible for any single bird to flap its wings on its own. Indeed, the clot of wing and body and beak moved as one unit with one mind, every wing tip fitting into the glimpse of space just vacated by the previous wing tip, and so the mass moved like the oil-softened teeth of many intermeshing gears. As they came down the canal, I could hear the pump of their muscles, the thrushing of feather on feather on feather. Their eyes stared in all directions at once, seeing everything and nothing, wires of comprehension extending outward to every object in space. The sound of a thousand radio stations emanated from their mouths. Occasionally the pack would shiver and jolt to the left or right very quickly, only to come back on course after a second or two. The cloud of sparrows stopped above the place where Josiah Merrymore had disappeared, and I saw the surface of the water part and split as several birds dived down into all that milkiness. Then the birds were all above me. I saw them diving and flecking at the ground where the pieces of the sparrow skeleton still lay. Through the centripetal whirling I caught sight of one bird gobbling up a bone, its throat jerking backward and vibrating as it swallowed the tiny instrument.

I was awash in the white noise of their hushed calls—their voices rippling up and down the frequencies as if they were replaying the sum of all conversations ever spoken throughout history, and I listened and heard my father, and I heard Emma and Tearho's wobbly Finnish echoing across the desert, and I heard Pushkin and Italian lullabies and a young Arab man wailing for his lost son.

Then the sparrows were past me, moving down the canal, the noise of their cackling slowly fading. My head began to pound. My vision swam. The little black flecks were evaporating into the sky. I stumbled after them.

"Where do I go?" I yelled. "Where do I—"

But they were already gone. There was only the silence of the canal and the distant rumbling of the city beyond. I stood there swaying. I was alone.

With nothing else to do, I went in the direction that the birds had disappeared. After what seemed like ages I reached the foot of a stone staircase. My vision swam again; my throat was bone-dry. I grabbed hold of the metal railing with both hands and dragged myself up the steps. With each step, my chest began to throb more and more. My head turned into itself. I reached the top of the stairs, fell to my knees, and threw up into a drain.

I looked up, wiping my lips. I was in some kind of parking lot full of trucks. With great effort, I stumbled over to a man leaning against a purple eighteen-wheeler. He was sucking on a cigarette very hard.

When he saw me, he coughed out smoke, rubbed a knuckle in one of his eyes, and winced. "Hey, little man, what the fuck happened to you?"

"I was hurt by a man."

"Dude, you need to get to the hospital, like now, man."

I knew I was most definitely not okay, but I knew that going to a hospital now meant giving up on my journey. And I had not just potentially killed a man to get only this far. I would reach the Smithsonian if it was the last thing I did.

"I'm okay, I'm okay," I said wincing. "Can I ask you a favor?"

"Well sure, dude," he said. He took another drag from the cigarette.

"Can you drive me to Washington, D.C.?"

"Dude, I'm telling you—you seriously need to see a medic."

"I just want to go to Washington, please, dude."

"Well…" He looked down at his cigarette and knuckled his eye again. I noticed that his arms were heavily tattooed. "You're a tough little fucker, huh? I'm headed out to Virginia Beach, but dude looks like he needs a helping hand and Ricky never ducks away from a battle, you know what I'm saying? We've got a brother down and Ricky's there to drive him wherever the fuck he needs to go."

"Thanks, Ricky," I said.

"Hey, dude, don't even mention it." He took one last hard drag from his cigarette and then carefully rubbed it out on one of the truck's giant wheels. Then he took out a little canister from his pocket and dropped the cigarette butt into it. Ricky must've really cared about the environment. I had never seen anyone dispose of their cigarette in that way.

"Yo, Rambo," he said. "Can I at least get you some Band-Aids or something?"

"I'm cool," I said. I held my breath so I would not start crying.

"Well," he said. "Let's get you home. Hop into the Purple People Eater."

I tried to hop up into the cab but fell back onto the pavement, gasping.

"Dude got hit *hard*," Ricky said. Humming what sounded like "The Battle Hymn of the Republic," he gently lifted me up and placed me in the front seat of his cab.

"There's a war out there, but you're safe now, little man," he said, and then shut the door.

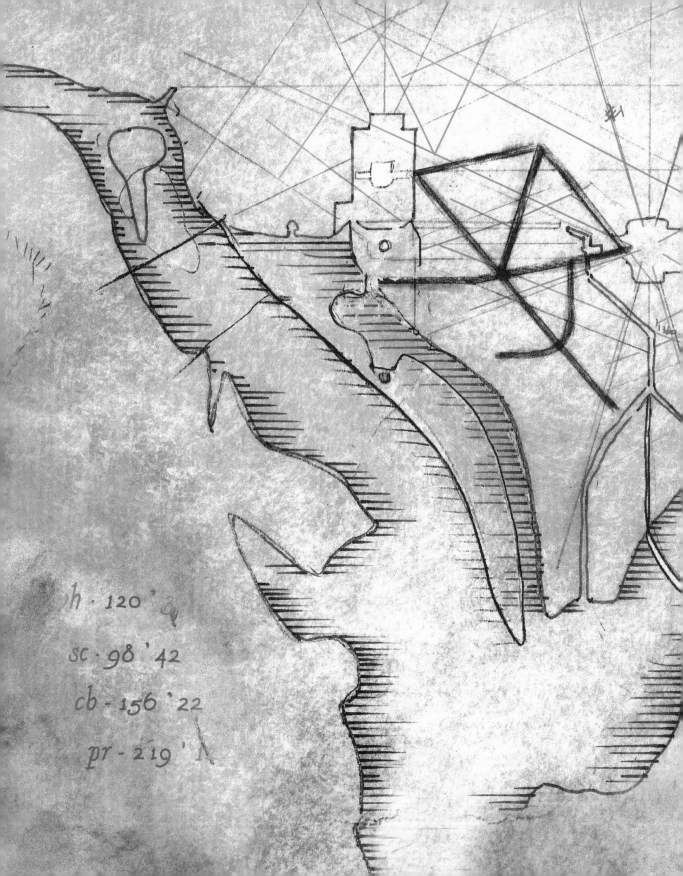

h · 120 ° ⌐

sc · 98 ' 42

cb - 156 ' 22

pr - 219 ' 1

PART 3: THE EAST

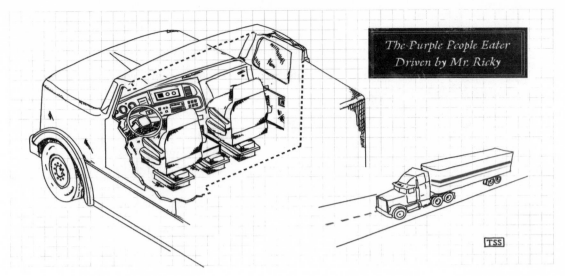

This illustration was left in the glove compartment of the P.P.E.

*The Purple People Eater
Driven by Mr. Ricky*

TSS

Chapter 11

The way I see it," Ricky was saying. "And I'm dead serious here, dude—is you find out who your friends are and then you say *fuck you* to everyone else. I mean, you got to—the world is so fucking big and getting bigger every fucking day, and there's been so much crossbreeding among the racials that pretty soon you ain't gonna know who to trust. I mean, we got Orientals coming up here, we got Arabs and Mexicans and fuck knows what other countries and I'm sitting here, like, *I fought for this bullshit? This* is the American way? No way, bitch." He spat into his Flintstone thermos. "Hey, dude—you okay?"

My head nodded against the seat. It was nighttime. I had been sleeping most of the way, jogged in and out of consciousness by the occasional unbearable throb of pain in my chest. Mostly my whole body just ached. I felt feverish.

"You want some jerky?" Ricky asked, offering me the package.

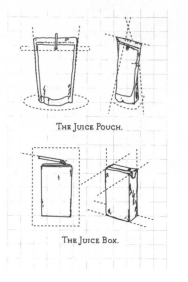

THE JUICE POUCH.

THE JUICE BOX.

Pouch vs. Box ◄
from Notebook G63

I had had many debates about which was the better design. Each had its own merits: the box was sturdier on its feet, but the pouch could fit more easily into the pocket.

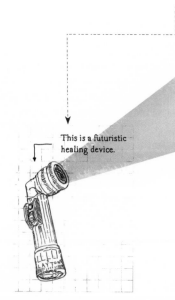

This is a futuristic healing device.

"Thanks," I said, taking the jerky out of politesse. Father said you should never refuse an offering of food, even if you hated the food being offered.

"Capri Sun?"

"Thanks," I said, taking the silver juice pouch. "Where are we?"

"Beautiful, flat-ass Ohio," he said. "I was born here, you know that? But it never felt like home, 'cause my dad was a real fucking prick. Broke my nose with a bat. That kinda shit'll make you run straight to boot camp, do not pass go." He patted the dashboard. "P.P.E.'s home now, ain't she?"

I tried to picture Father hitting me with a bat. I couldn't.

"But listen, T.S.," Ricky was saying. "Let me tell you this theory I've been working out about the Mexicans, because I see them every day in this business and they wouldn't be that bad if it weren't—"

And so it went. Through half-closed eyes I saw the glow of the dashboard and the wisps of red taillights passing by. I imagined I was in the cockpit of a spaceship ferrying me to a distant space station, where they would heal me in two seconds with a futuristic device that looked like an L-shaped flashlight.

When I woke again, the horizon ahead of us had begun to soften with the first strains of dawn. Two hours had gone by, but Ricky was still jawing on as if I had never been asleep: "I'm not trying to be a dick here, dude, just a realist. If you let *some* of them in, then how you gonna know who to trust, you know what I'm saying? Pedro will say one thing to get what he wants, but then he'll turn around and stab you in the fucking back. Oh no, you gotta put up those fences to keep 'em out and don't even look back." He was gesturing at the windshield with another one of those cigarettes.

He turned to me. "How you doing, dude?"

I put my thumb up, but even this simple gesture tugged painfully at my chest.

"You know what, T.S.? I've been in the shit and I can honestly say you're one tough motherfucker," Ricky said. "Seriously, army'd be lucky to have you."

I smiled through the pain. I pictured Ricky walking up to Father, giving him one of those rigorous handshakes, telling him that his son was "one tough motherfucker." Father might politely smile back, but he would never believe him.

I was sleeping again when Ricky jabbed me in the shoulder. "End of the road, dude."

I lifted up my head and stared out at the big cement buildings.

"This is D.C.?" I asked.

"Capital of this great country. What's left of it."

"Where's the Mall?"

"Two blocks that way. Feds won't let P.P.E. get too close," he said. "Wait—hang on a second." He disappeared behind the seats for a moment and then came back with a camouflage handkerchief.

"I wore this in combat. It's for the blood." He made a circular wiping motion in front of my chest. "Can't make a scene in front of the civilians, you know what I'm saying?"

I looked down. My sweater vest was stained brown with dried blood. The skin across my rib cage felt hot and swollen.

"Thank you, Ricky," I said. I didn't know what else to say to him. How did two soldiers part on the battlefield?

I am embarrassed to admit this, but even though I was pretty sure most of what he was saying was very racist and very bad, I kind of liked Ricky. For a man with such menacing tattoos, he was surprisingly attentive: he kept asking how I was feeling, all the while offering me a steady stream of beef jerky, Capri Sun, and Advil. There was something comforting about the constant, husky prattle of his voice, punctuated by spits into the Flintstone thermos and the occasional self-induced guffaw. I wasn't listening to his words, I was just clinging to the saferoom-feeling of the cab. Was this bad? What happens when the words are bad but the feeling *around* the words is good? Maybe I should've told him to shut up and gotten out of the cab right then and there, but I was so tired and it was so warm inside...

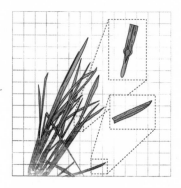

Kentucky Bluegrass Blades Give Me ◄---
a New-Place Feeling
from Notebook G101

When you enter into a new place and get that new-place feeling, it can be difficult to pinpoint what exactly contributes to that subtle, liquidy sense of the unfamiliar. Rather than originating from the big monuments or museums or cathedrals, this feeling arose from the sum of many little things that made me feel like a stranger in a strange land: the textured palette of the Kentucky bluegrass; the way the thousands of American elms mushroomed lazily outward as compared to the stern rectitude of the jack pines back home; the slightly darker pigmentation of green in the street signs; the sweet, melancholic smell of nuts roasting inside those little wheelie carts.

"I hope you find your pine tree," I said and winced at how bad it sounded. Before he could laugh at me, I grabbed my backpack, opened the door, and painfully shimmied down the ladder onto the sidewalk.

Ricky stuck his head out of the truck. "I love you, little man," he said. "Eyes open, head up. A mongoose always recognizes the cobra." Then he yanked on the horn, threw the truck in gear, and drove off.

It was drizzling. I tried to dab at my chest with the handkerchief, but every time I touched the wound the pain was so intense I felt as if I would pass out, so I just tucked the camo hanky into my collar like a bib and let it hang down in front of the wound. It probably looked a little silly, but at this point, I really didn't care. I just wanted to get there.

I limped past what seemed like a never-ending procession of windowless government buildings. Just when I thought I had taken a wrong turn, I rounded a corner and was suddenly confronted with a huge rectangular swath of glorious grass, right in the middle of the city. The National Mall.

The grass was different here than in Montana. From afar, it had the usual grassy green demeanor, but when I stooped down and actually examined the shape of the blades and ligules, I could tell that this was *not* the same beardless wheatgrass that father insisted on using in our bottom fields. This was sweet Kentucky bluegrass.

Two thousand miles later, I had finally made it.

And there *it* was: jutting out into the Mall, somehow perfectly structurally balanced despite its uneven symmetry of turrets, the sprawling burgundy castle was as grand and complex as I had imagined in the blueprints of my mind. As I suspected, there was nothing that could substitute experiencing the Institution in person. One needed to feel one's molecules vibrate in close proximity to red bricks in order to understand

The Smithsonian Castle:
How Asymmetric! How Beautiful!
from Notebook G101

the room feeling of the place. And I was filled with an utter warmth, a gratitude for the insistence of history, a gratitude for attics, for collecting cases, for formaldehyde, for Mr. James Smithson, the English bastard son who donated his entire estate to the adolescent United States of America in order to further the "increase & diffusion of knowledge" in the New World.

I stood in the rain, looking up at the octagonal tower with the American flag hanging limply on the end of its pole, and imagined all that had transpired within the eight walls of that tower, every moment of reckoning, of love, of naming, of disagreement and discovery.

A Chinese man shuffled over to me. He was awkwardly pulling a basket of umbrellas down the gravel path.

"Umbrella?" he said. "Very wet today."

He offered me a huge umbrella, entirely too large for someone of my stature.

"Do you have anything else?" I asked. "This is very big and I am a child. Do you have something in the size that a child might want?"

The man shook his head. "Child. Very wet today," he said. "Thank you."

It was a preemptive thank-you, but I paid him anyway, which left me with only $2.78 in my pocket. If they charged an admission fee at the Smithsonian, I would not be able to pay it. Perhaps I could barter with them, and trade my broken compass for entrance into their temple of knowledge. We would have to see.

Taking a deep breath, I began walking up to the main entrance of the castle with my huge umbrella. Tourists were shuffling along the wide gravel paths. A manic child holding a stuffed tiger pointed at me and said something to his family. I looked down at myself. I was dirty, dressed in

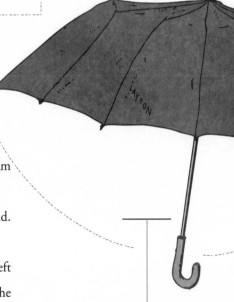

I AM THIS TALL.

a torn sweater vest and camouflage hanky covered in blood, and holding a massive umbrella. It was not quite the entrance that I had planned in my mind: the accompanying servants, the parade of elephants, the unfurling of ancient maps, everyone adjusting their monocles and tapping their canes in a display of appreciation. Perhaps it was just as well.

I rearranged my sweater as best I could to conceal the bloody gash in the middle of my chest.

"A flesh wound," I said, to bolster my spirits and strength. "I was opening a very important letter with my letter opener and merely slipped. Happens all the time, sir. I have so many important letters to open, you know."

The lobby of the castle was impressive. Everything was hushed inside the huge room and you could hear the sound of squeaky feet echoing against the sixty-foot ceilings. Everyone, even the manic child with the stuffed tiger, seemed now to be whispering important conversations about science and history. In the middle of the room, there was an information desk with many pamphlets for the visitor to peruse. The rest of the room was filled with old pictures and maps and time lines of the Smithsonian's history. There was also a diorama of the National Mall with buttons that you could press to light up various points of interest. The manic child had discovered these buttons and was now lighting up each building and then trying to lie down across the buttons so that he could light up everything at the same time. A part of me wanted to join him in his gleeful button pressing.

I walked up to the information desk. The old lady at the desk, who was engaged in a conversation with her colleague, turned to me and stared. I realized I had not folded up my giant umbrella.

"Sorry, bad luck," I said, and struggled to contain it, but the umbrella kept popping open. My camo hanky fell to the ground. I felt like I was enacting a comedy routine in a silent film until a visitor next to me gently took the umbrella from me, clicked it into a closed position, and then handed it back.

"Thank you," I said. I picked up Ricky's hanky and pocketed it and then turned back to the lady at the front desk, who was now staring at my chest.

"Honey, are you okay?" she asked. "Are you injured?"

"I'm okay," I said. On her lapel, the woman wore a name tag that said Laurel and a large red button that said Do you need information?

My mind went blank so I said: "Laurel, I need information."

"You look like you need some medical assistance, can I call someone for you?"

"No, that's okay," I said. The room swam a bit. Everyone was whispering about science. I fought for control. "Thank you. But I would like to speak with Mr. G. H. Jibsen."

The lady sat up. "Who?"

"Mr. Jibsen," I said. "He is head of illustration and design at the Smithsonian."

"Where are your parents?" she asked.

"They're at home," I said.

She looked at me, then over at her younger colleague (name tag = Isla) who also was wearing the oversize button offering information, although she had chosen to attach it not to a her lapel but instead to a lanyard, so that she might more easily take it off and not offer information at certain times. Isla shrugged her shoulders.

She will give you information.
She is a helpful lady.

She will not give you information.
She is not a helpful lady.

➤ *Lanyards Allow Us to Navigate*
Through Our Lives
from Notebook G101

Laurel looked back at me. "Are you sure you're okay? You look like you've hurt yourself badly."

I nodded. The more she said I had hurt myself badly, the more I believed this probably to be true. My chest began throbbing again.

"Do you think you could ring Mr. Jibsen and let him know I'm here? I'm supposed to give an address tomorrow evening."

Laurel's world was clearly rattled. She made a silent whistle through her lips, and then said, "Just a moment, please," in a professional kind of voice. She glanced through some papers behind the counter and then picked up the phone. "What is your name please?" she asked, with the phone tucked beneath her chin.

"T. S. Spivet."

She waited and then turned away from me as she spoke softly into the phone. I picked up a pamphlet about an exhibition on the Blackfeet Indians.

When she turned back to me, her eyebrows were scrunched together, as if she was trying to solve a difficult math problem. "You are T. S. Spivet? Or is your father T. S. Spivet?"

"I am T. S. Spivet. My father is T. E. Spivet."

She turned back to the phone. "Well, I don't know," she said loudly into it after a while, and then hung up.

"Well, I don't know," she said again, not really to me, but to the general collective. "He's coming here anyway. He'll figure it out. You can wait there. Do you need anything? Water?"

"Yes, please," I said.

Laurel came back with a tiny Dixie cup of water. I could see that she was staring at my chest again. She returned to the information desk and muttered something to Isla, who adjusted her lanyard nervously. A group of Japanese people shuffled up to the desk and the two women disappeared behind them.

I found a bench and sat down, looking through my pamphlet on the Blackfeet Nation, with my huge umbrella by my side. To tell you the truth, even though I was normally very interested in all things Blackfeet, I had a lot of trouble trying to follow the pamphlet and found myself drifting off.

"I'm Mr. Jibsen." A voice emerged from out of the ether, the *s* in Jibsen curling around itself like a cat, stirring familiar synapses in my brain. I suddenly missed the smell of my kitchen back home, the long stretchy cord, the chopsticks, the sound the lid of the cookie jar made when you tried to open it quietly.

"Can I help you, young man?" he asked.

I looked up. Mr. G. H. Jibsen looked nothing like I had imagined him over the phone. He was not tall and graceful with a three-piece suit, a Vandyke beard, and a cane. Rather, he was squat and bald, and had on a pair of thick-rimmed designer glasses that made him look nerdy yet at the same time just self-aware enough to maintain an aura of coolness. He wore a black turtleneck and a black jacket, and his only gesture toward the age of antiquity that I had apparently placed upon him was a strange hoop earring in his left ear, as though he had just come from a pirate ball and had removed all traces of his costume except this.

"Can I help you?" he asked again.

When a moment of highly anticipated convergence such as this actually arrives, I have come to learn that the brooding over what might inevitably outweighs the gravity of the actual moment itself. I had tossed and turned through many sleepless nights before a cavity filling or a final test only to be met with the anticlimactic muted whine of Dr. Jenks's drill

1. MR. JIBSEN

2. MR. STENPOCK

Fashion Is Difficult
from Notebook G101

Mr. Jibsen's glasses performed the magical double gesture of conveying equal parts obsessiveness and nonchalance (Fig. 1). I, on the other hand, like Mr. Stenpock, was never able to maintain this level of self-awareness for more than a couple of minutes at a time. For me, calculated consideration of my appearance took a tremendous amount of concentration that inevitably sucked my brain power away from my mapping or whatever I happened to be doing at the time (usually mapping).

Gracie, somewhat sweetly, gave me a pair of green cargo pants for Christmas that had fourteen straps of fabric hanging off them. She said this was the latest style, and when I asked her why there were so many of these straps just hanging there, she rolled her eyes and then said: "Well, not to get too psychological, but maybe it's meant to be like, wow, I've got a lot of straps here because what I normally do is skydive or something really intense, but right now I'm just hanging out, with all my straps undone....But they're just cool, okay?"

I wore them for a day, but became so distracted by all the things one *could* do with the undone straps that I ended up buckling them all. When I came down to dinner like that, Gracie yelled at me for looking like a "mental patient." My place in the world once again confirmed, the pants went into my closet and did not come out again. Gracie has never fully trusted me since.

or the dull look of boredom on Mr. Edwards's face as I drew my intricate diagrams of westward expansion in the margins of my bluebook.

Why did I work myself up into such a froth about this? I would ask myself, and yet when the next test came around, there I would be at 3 A.M., sleepless and frothy again.

Time and time again on my endless journey eastward, trapped in the dark clutches of that wormhole purgatory and left to my own doomsday scenarios, I had thought about what I would say in this circumstance, the countless ways I might convey my expertise through offhand references to glycolysis or controversies concerning the metric system. But I did not put any of my elaborate explanations of accelerated cognitive development, stunted growth, time travel, or powerful breakfast cereals into action.

I simply said, "Hello, I'm T. S. Spivet. I made it." And then I waited for the world to catch up.

Mr. Jibsen cocked his head to the side, looked back at Laurel behind the desk, and then turned to me again. His thumb and finger went up to his earring and he began nervously twisting the hoop round and round. "There must be…" He stopped, looking down at my chest.

"Are you injured?" he asked.

I nodded, on the verge of tears.

He looked me up and down. I had never felt so openly scrutinized in my life. Father scrutinized me by never directly looking at me.

"We spoke on the phone last Friday?"

I nodded.

"T. S. Spivet?" he said, as though trying on a new coat. He put his hands on his face, scrunching up his nose between his palms, and then exhaled out his nostrils very loudly. He brought his hands down to his sides again.

"You drew the bombardier?" he asked, very slowly.

"Yes."

"You drew the bumblebee social schematic? The sewer triptych? The timeline of flying machines? The...the horseshoe-crab blood schematic? The curliest-rivers overlay thing? You drew all of these?"

I did not have to nod.

"Jesus," he said, and then walked away. More playing with the earring. I thought he might go to the dioramas and start willy-nilly punching the buttons that light up things, but he came back after a moment.

"Jesus," he said again. "How old are you?"

"Thirteen," I said. And then: "Well, twelve, really."

"Twelve?! Well that's..." He stopped on the lisp of the *s*, shaking his head.

"Mr. Jibsen, I don't mean to be rude, but I don't feel so well. Perhaps I could just get looked at and then we can talk about tomorrow night?"

"Ha! Are you kidding? That won't...*oh!*" he stopped himself. "Of course, let's get you some attention."

He smoothly slid over to Laurel at the desk and then presently returned. He was staring at me.

"We've got someone coming," he said, still staring in that strange way.

"Thanks," I said. "I'll feel better soon. Then we can talk about..." I was suddenly met with a shooting parcel of pain that began in my sternum and then wrapped around my forehead like a headband. It was quite unlike any pain I had ever felt, more intense than the time Layton accidentally threw a dart into my head or when we sledded into a tree and I broke an arm while he walked away unscathed even though he had hit the tree first. No longer concerned with the world of Jibsen and polite decorum, I let out a low groan.

Jibsen did not seem to notice. "T.S.!" he said. "Twelve years old! Where'd you learn to draw like that?"

I had no answer for this question. Instead, I passed out.

When I came to, an EMT man was examining me. I had on one of those oxygen masks, which smelled very plasticky. They wheeled me out on a stretcher to an ambulance that had driven right up to the entrance of the castle. When I saw the idling ambulance, its lights still whirling, its back doors thrown open, I felt a little proud that I had disrupted the flow of the capital in my own small way.

It was raining harder than before. Mr. Jibsen held my large umbrella over me as I lay on the stretcher, which was very nice of him. He got in the ambulance with me and squeezed my hand. "Don't worry, T.S.," he said. "I'm fast-tracking you to the Smithsonian's own special doctor. We won't have to deal with any of that red tape or wait in line. We'll take care of you."

As we drove through the streets of the capital, they put an IV in my arm. I watched the IV bag dip and sway. Even though the bag was clear, I knew there were all kinds of delicious little nutrients dissolved in there that I was eating up through the hole in my arm. That was pretty cool.

At the Washington Hospital Center, Dr. Fernald, the Smithsonian doctor, examined me. He had two of his assistants stitch me up. They clucked and shook their heads when I told them about what had happened to me in Chicago. I left out the part about me stabbing Josiah Merrymore and him falling into the canal and how he maybe/probably was dead. Some things were better left off the map.

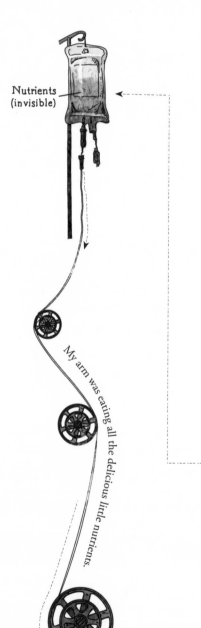

Nutrients
(invisible)

My arm was eating all the delicious little nutrients.

As they were doing their work, Mr. Jibsen was pacing out in the hall, talking into his cell phone. In my haze, I became convinced that he was having a long, disapproving conversation with Dr. Clair about me and my tendency to leave Cheerios in my pockets. I knew that soon she would show up at the hospital to take me back to Montana. I was prepared for this. Hey—at least I had made it this far, and that was pretty far for a twelve-year-old.

After they had performed a round of tests to make sure I did not have any major internal issues (that was how they said it: "major internal issues"), they gave me a tetanus shot and two different kinds of antibiotics. Finally, around midnight, Jibsen and I left the hospital. I wondered if he was driving me to the airport.

"I'll drop you off at the Carriage House," he said, and patted my leg. "You're safe now."

"Thank you," I said, though I had no idea what this meant.

As soon as my head hit the pillow, I fell into one of the deepest sleeps I had ever had. It was the first night in a long while in which I was actually lying still.

When I woke up the next morning, my chest ached. I blinked, half expecting to be back in my room in Montana, to be emerging from the most elaborate dream in my life, but three of the walls were not covered in notebooks and I did not see the familiar outlines of my mapping equipment. Instead, I was in this unfamiliar room, where everything was very clean and ornamental and oaken. There were lots of chairs everywhere. The walls were covered in paintings, including a large, dramatic one depicting some battle by a river. I think George Washington was standing

THE CARRIAGE HOUSE

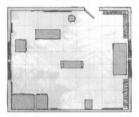

OAK FURNITURE IN THE ROOM

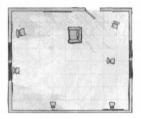

ALL THE CHAIRS IN THE ROOM

ALL THE PAINTINGS.

Views of the Carriage House
from Notebook G101

amidst all the fighting, but to tell you the truth, at that moment I didn't care if it was George Washington, or about any of it really. I felt terrible.

I tried to sit up in bed and immediately felt the tightness in my chest. It was as if I'd been kicked in the chest by a mule, a phrase often used by Father, who had actually been kicked in the chest by a mule. I never understood the pinpoint appropriateness of the analogy until this moment.

"You damn mule," I said, and felt tough for saying it. "It done kicked me good, Father."

After contemplating how painful it would be to get out of bed, I eventually just pulled back the cover and did it. It felt as if I were wearing a breastplate that had been nailed into my skin. I scuffed around the carriage house like a nutcracker, with my torso upright and my arms hanging stiffly by my sides. I had begun examining the oaken contents of the room, getting a little bit of my old curiosity back, when there was a knock at the door.

"Yes?" I said.

Mr. Jibsen came in. His flusterings of yesterday were gone. His gracious Old World lisp had returned.

"Ah, T.S., you're up! My God, we were worried last night. I can't even begin to tell you. Such a nasty thing that happened to you. Sorry about that—didn't know Chicago had gotten that bad—must've been a terrible shock coming from the Elysian fields of Montana."

"I'm okay," I said, though I was suddenly struck with the desperate desire to say *I killed a man and he is dead in a Chicago canal and his name is—*

"Listen," Mr. Jibsen said. "I wanted to apologize for my behavior yesterday—you see, I had no idea about your age. Absolutely none. I spoke with your friend Terry last night and he explained everything to me. At first, I daresay, I was a bit put off by all this chicanery, but I now realize the unique nature of the situation, and, well, the award of course was given strictly on the quality of your work." He paused and shot me a look. "It is your work, isn't it?"

"Yes," I said, and sighed. "It is."

"Good, excellent!" he said, bouncing back to life. "So while we all had one kind of fellowship in mind before…usually the Baird Award goes to…*an adult*, you see—but, I think this all might work out just perfectly. And my only other question is…your parents? I am embarrassed to admit that in my haste, I forgot to tell Dr. Yorn to contact them—may I ask why they did not accompany you on your trip out here?"

Though my head was still foggy, I could not blame my medical condition for what I said next.

"They are…dead," I said. "I live with Dr. Yorn."

What?! Was I out of my mind?!

"Oh my," Mr. Jibsen said. "Oh, I am sorry to hear that."

"And Gracie," I said. "I mean, Gracie and I live with Dr. Yorn."

"Well, this is all the more remarkable isn't it?" Mr. Jibsen said. "I daresay Yorn did not mention this, but he's a…modest man, I suppose."

"Yes," I said. "He's a fine foster father man."

Mr. Jibsen seemed to grow uncomfortable. "Well, you must still be recovering. I'll leave you to rest. This carriage house serves as the quarters of the Baird fellow, so it is at your disposal. Sorry for the lack of accoutrement and somewhat hideous"—he nodded at the painting of Washington or whoever it was—"decoration. But it should meet all your needs."

"Thank you," I said. "It's very nice."

Yes, it was confirmed: I was out of my mind. But part of me had always wished this to be true, and saying it now, in this world, almost made it true.

"If there is anything that you would like to request, please do not hesitate to ask me, and I'll see what we can do to make you more comfortable."

"Well," I said, looking around for my backpack, which I was grateful to see sitting on a chair next to the bed. "I ended up losing almost all my instruments in Chicago. Does the museum have any drafting materials?"

"I am sure we will be able to procure whatever materials you need. Just give us a list and we'll have them by this afternoon."

"This afternoon?"

He gave out a short laugh. "Of course! Remember, you are America's illustrator now."

"I am?"

"Though attendance and budgets may not reflect this, we must never lose sight of the fact that we are a one-hundred-fifty-year-old institution that represents the history of this country's rich scientific tradition. Yet," he said, "even as we admire our rich past, we must always be looking forward to the future, which is why I am very excited about your somewhat dramatic entrance last night. Who would have thought?"

"I'm sorry," I said, suddenly feeling very tired. "I didn't mean to—"

"No, no, no, on the contrary, this whole boondoggle may prove just perfect for the Institution in the long run. I've already mentioned your age to a few colleagues and they've just gone gaga, so you see you may be the ideal instrument to draw us plenty of attention and get people all jazzed up about the Smithy again."

"The Smithy?"

"Yes. You see everyone loves a child, that's what they say. Not that you are entirely a child—I mean, I still see your work as the work of a scientist...it's just..." He seemed to run out of words again, his tongue lingering on the *s* in *just*. His fingers went back to his earring.

I thought of Dr. Clair sitting in her study, writing about Emma's speech at the National Academy of Sciences almost one hundred and fifty years ago. My mother, sitting in a room full of her own work, conjured the world of another: the curl of Emma's spine as she must have stood at that lectern; Joseph Henry's eyes burning a hole in her back; the hostile expressions of the men in the front row as she spoke those words that she had concocted with Maria Mitchell in a cabin in the Adirondacks one night, the stars rotating above them:

"...And so let us not ask the sex of a scientist but whether her method is sound, whether she holds fast to the rigorous standards of modern science and whether she is advancing the collective knowledge of the human project. <u>This</u> project matters above all else, above sex, race, or creed..."

And yet in the end, these were neither Maria Mitchell's nor Emma Osterville's words.

Oh, Mother. Why did you invent this? What did you hope to achieve? Did you just give up your career to study another Spivet whose own aspirations had faded away into the dried, cracked honeycomb buttes of the West? Was I, too, doomed to such meta-reciprocal failure? Was it simply in our blood to study another while we neglected ourselves?

I took a deep breath.

"What do you want me to say tonight?" I said.

"Tonight?" he laughed. "You of course don't have to speak! That was all arranged before…before this happened and…"

"I would like to speak."

"You would like to speak? You would…? But do you feel up to it?"

"Yes," I said. " What do you want me to say?"

"To say? Well, we'll…we'll cook something up. Unless of course you want to write it yourself?"

Each tray passed around the ballroom by the white-gloved waitstaff was filled with a rotating cast of scrumptious little concoctions, the likes of which I had never seen. Despite the lingering pain from my injuries, I was

Recipe for ◄┄┄┄┄┄┄┄┄┄┄
Gracie's Wintertime Special
from the Coppertop Recipe Book

1. Slice up a hot dog.
2. Overcook one cup of green beans.
3. Delicately place limp green beans and hot dog slices onto a bed of ketchup and mayonnaise.
4. Lightly microwave two slices of Kraft Singles. (25 sec)
5. Place cheese on top of hot dog slices and green beans.
6. Serve warm.

enthralled with this opulent display of gastronomical access and excess. It easily trumped the usual fare at the Coppertop—the Next Best Thing or Gracie's Wintertime Special.

For instance: the waiter with the white gloves would pause in front of me and very politely say, "Good evening, sir, would you like some Tuna Tartare on Grilled Asparagus sprinkled with Balsamic Reduction?"

And I would say, "Yes, please," and want to say something about his white gloves, but I would resist the temptation, and then he would place a little napkin in the palm of my hand and then in turn place this scrumptious concoction on the napkin, using a pair of miniature tongs.

"Thank you," I would say.

And he would say, "You are welcome."

And I would say "Thank you" again, because I really was thankful.

And he would make a little bow and move along.

I wanted to taste everything that came my way, but then I began feeling very tired and I had to sit down. Just before we came to the reception, Mr. Jibsen had given me some painkillers from an unmarked bottle.

"That's my boy," he had said in a very gentle way as I downed them with a glass of water.

For a moment, I wondered if the pills were actually truth serum and he would immediately begin asking me all kinds of probing questions, but Mr. Jibsen only smiled and said. "Miracle drugs, they are. You should be bright-eyed in no time. It's your big night tonight. We can't have you hurting on your big night."

Mr. Jibsen had also arranged, on quite short notice, to rent me a fancy-shmancy tuxedo. A tailor had come in at around 2 P.M. and had gingerly taken my measurements. He was a nice man, and he touched my arm and talked about his cousin who lived in Idaho. I asked him if I could have a copy of my measurements, and he said sure and then wrote them all out on a piece of paper, along with rough little sketches of my body. It was one of the nicest things anyone had done for me: an impromptu map of my dimensions.

When we arrived at the dinner, Jibsen sat me down at a table in the front and said, "Just meet and greet, T.S. The speeches won't begin for a half hour or so. Don't worry, you won't have to do too much. If you're ever feeling overwhelmed, just tap my shoulder twice, like this." He tapped me on the shoulder twice.

"All right," I said.

My place setting had an incredible number of tools carefully arranged around my plate. It reminded me of the layout of my mapping tools in my bedroom. I suddenly got a pang of the missing feeling, that painful yanking against the present. I wanted to smell my notebooks, to trace my fingers along the outlines of my instruments.

There were: three forks, three knives, four glasses (all of slightly different shapes), a spoon, two plates, a napkin, and a thingy-bobby. Behind my plate, a place card read, *T. S. Spivet* in copper cursive.

The ballroom was big and echoey, with fifty or so tables, with three forks, three knives, four glasses, a spoon, and a thingy-bobby at each place setting. About twelve hundred forks. And four hundred thingy-bobbies, though I was not sure what these were for. To prevent an awkward situation, I casually slipped my thingy-bobby off the table and put it into my pocket. If it wasn't there, then I couldn't use it incorrectly.

I sat by myself for a while, drawing little maps on a sheet of notepaper of how people moved through the room, as I tended to do when I was nervous. No one seemed to notice me. I could have been the unfortunate child whose parents had not been able to secure the services of a babysitter.

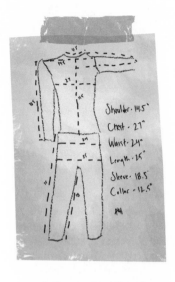

An Impromptu Map of My Dimensions
Taped to Notebook G101

Impromptu maps were among my favorite things, as they were all improvisation and discovery and came out of a direct need at the time. I put the little map of my body into my pocket with the intention of framing it and keeping it for the rest of my life.

Diagram of a Place Setting, or,
"I Am Now a Part of This World"
from Notebook G101

The place card was one of the most amazing things I had ever seen in my twelve short years. Someone had purposefully used a gold cursive script machine to write out my name on a little foldy card with bumpy trim. (*My name!* T. S. Spivet! And not the name of some other famous person like a dancer or a blacksmith who also happened to be named T. S. Spivet!) And then this party organizer had placed this foldy card next to all those glasses and cutlery, expecting me to sit down and use all the glasses and cutlery. I am now a part of this world.

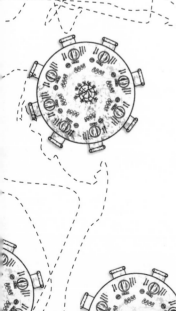

At the front of the ballroom, there was a big stage with a podium on it. Some of my diagrams and illustrations had been mounted on the walls, and I had to admit they looked very nice up there—way nicer framed with lights trained on them than on the floor of my bedroom. Groups of adults were walking around the room chatting, pausing in front of the diagrams and smiling, and suddenly I wanted to go up there and explain each map to them, but I was also terrified of adults, particularly when they clustered and smiled like that and held their drinks very casually and almost haphazardly, as though everyone wanted to spill one drop and only one drop.

Jibsen came over and pinned a name tag to my tuxedo jacket. "Forgot about this! Can you believe it? People would have just thought you were some kid," he said. Then he saw someone across the room, clapped his hands, and disappeared into a crowd of people.

I was just considering bringing out the thingy-bobby from my pocket so that I could perhaps figure out its function when an older blond woman came up to me and said, "I just wanted to be one of the first to congratulate you; we are so lucky to have a boy like you. So lucky."

"What?" I said. Her face looked strange and leathery, like the belly of one of the goats after it had just given birth.

"I'm Brenda Beerlong," she said. "I'm with the MacArthur Foundation. We've got our eyes on you...give it a couple more years..." She laughed. Or: her face was laughing, but her eyes were not.

I smiled, not knowing what else to say, but she was already melting back into the crowd and someone else was coming up to me.

"Fine work there, son," an old man said. He smelled of rotting twigs. As he shook my hand, I could feel that his whole arm was quivering uncontrollably. He looked a bit like Jim, one of the drunks in Butte, except that this man was wearing a tuxedo.

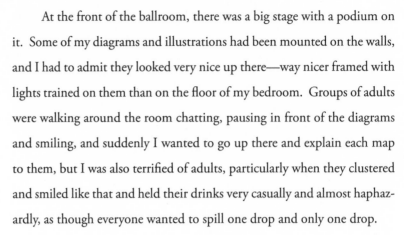

"Really, really quite fine stuff there. How'd you learn to draw like that in Montana? Something in the water? Or just nothing to do but draw?" He chuckled and surveyed the room. His hands were still quivering.

"The water?" I said.

"What?" he said. His fingers shot to his ear; they twiddled with a hearing aid.

"What about the water?" I said loudly.

"The water?" he said, confused.

"What about it?" I asked.

He smiled at me, his gaze unlatching and wandering to my map of the cutlery. "Yes, I suppose so," he said distantly, as though recalling memories from some war.

I waited.

"Damn," he said, and walked away.

After that, a steady stream of people came up to congratulate me. Their smiling remarks began to bleed together and I never quite knew what to say at any particular moment. Jibsen seemed to sense this, because eventually he planted himself beside me and began answering everyone in that performatory voice of his.

"Well, when I heard he was younger, of course I was skeptical, but we thought we'd give it a shot, and can't you see how charming he is? I mean, the potential is really there."

"We didn't know exactly, per se, but we had an idea…and we just thought we'd take a risk."

"I know, we are all excited. The possibilities are endless. Education department? Well, give me your card, and we can chat on Monday."

Bathroom = Safety ◄------------┐

After it had happened, I stared at his head bleeding into the winter hay and then I ran down to the bottom field to get Father. His face locked up when I said Layton was hurt badly, shot even, and he began running in the direction of the barn. I had never seen him run before. He was not a graceful runner. I stood in the field, not knowing where to go. I squatted where I was and I picked at the grass and then I ran to the main house and hid in the bathroom. I stared at the black-and-white postcards of steamships that I had pasted onto the walls and waited for the familiar roar of Georgine's engine so that I could know Father was taking Layton to the hospital. It did not start up. After a while I heard feet on the porch, and then I heard Father using the phone in the kitchen. I squinched my eyes and imagined the steamships floating not across the ocean but across land, across the high country to our ranch to pick us all up and take us away to Japan. One by one, we would struggle to pull our luggage up the steep gangway onto the spacious decks of the big ship.

Finally, I heard the crunch of dirt beneath wheels and I looked through the frosted glass to see the blurry outline of a police car. My father was talking with two policemen. And then an ambulance came snaking down the driveway. Still, I stayed in the bathroom with the steamships, even after the ambulance had left without its lights on. I thought they would come to ask me questions, but they never did. Only Gracie came in after a bit and she was crying and she just came and sat down with me and hugged me and we lay on that floor for a long time, and we did not say anything, but it was the closest I had ever felt to anyone.

"Yes, yes, that's how we've always seen it....I was sitting in my office before I called him on the ranch, and I said to myself, 'He's twelve, but let's still do this!' And clearly the risk paid off..."

As I listened, the story of what had happened began to morph into something completely different. I began to grow uncomfortable. *My* story was quietly becoming *his* story. It was like someone was slowly turning up the volume on a very annoying tone, little by little, until by the end I felt like I had lockjaw. Even the white-gloved waitstaff began to take on a sinister air. When a woman came to refill my water glass I waved her off, suspicious that she was attempting to poison me.

At one point, Mr. Jibsen leaned down and whispered, "They're eating you up..."

I felt ill. I tapped on his shoulder twice, but he patted my arm and went on talking to a very attentive woman wearing an eye patch: "Oh, yes, yes, of course—outside events, the works. He's here for at least six months, but everything's negotiable."

I got up and walked stiffly to the back of the room. I could feel people watching me. As I passed their little pockets of conversations, they stopped talking and pretended they weren't looking at me, even though they were practically staring. I tried to keep smiling. I could hear the groups of people turn back into themselves once I had passed and animatedly begin talking again. If this has ever happened to you, you will know what a strange, out-of-body experience this can be.

"Where is the restroom, please?" I asked one of the waitstaff. She seemed nice, even if she was standing against the wall with her hands folded behind her back, hiding those white gloves.

She pointed to a pair of double doors. "Down the hall to the right."

"Thanks," I said. "Why are you standing like that? Are you hiding your white gloves?"

She looked at me strangely and brought out her hands from behind her back. "No…," she said. Then returned them to their original position. "This is how we're supposed to stand. My boss'll fire me otherwise," she said.

"Oh," I said. "Well, I like your gloves. You shouldn't hide them." And then I left the huge room.

Two men were laughing loudly in the hallway; they looked like old friends who had not seen each other in a long time. One of them pointed at his crotch and the other punched the man in his shoulder. They cackled and rested their heads against the wall, trying to catch their breath. They were having a great time. Luckily, they did not look at me as I passed.

As it turned out, the bathroom had an attendant. I had never encountered a bathroom attendant before as they were not very prevalent in Montana. I had only seen one on a television show where a spy was posing as a bathroom attendant and he assassinated this man by giving him a breath mint that was actually poison.

This bathroom attendant looked college-age and slightly bored. He did not look like a spy who would try to poison me. On his lapel, there was a tiny red M pin. When he saw me come into the bathroom, his eyes brightened.

"How is it out there?" he asked in a slightly conspiratorial style.

"Pretty bad," I said. "Adults are weird sometimes." With this pronouncement, I took the risk of excluding him from the "adult category," but by excluding him, I was also bringing him into the camaraderie of non-adulthood, and I got the feeling that this was where he wanted to be, whether he was technically an adult or not.

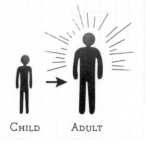

CHILD   ADULT

When Does a Child Become an Adult?

Clearly, this was a diagram I could not yet draw as I was not an unbiased observer. But it was a question that often bugged me: there were plenty of young men in Butte who looked even older than this bathroom attendant but who I would not characterize as adults. Like Hankers St. John. There was *no way* he was an adult yet, even though he must have been, what— thirty-five? So if it was not age per se, then what was it? I was not sure, but I knew an adult when I saw one. You could identify them by their behavior.

You were an adult if you:

1. Took naps for no reason.
2. Didn't get excited about Christmas.
3. Were very worried about losing your memory.
4. Worked very hard at your job.
5. Wore reading glasses around your neck but often forgot that you were wearing reading glasses around your neck.
6. Said the phrase, "I remember when you were this big" and then shook your head and made an AU-1, AU-24, AU-41, which roughly translated to the *I'm so sad because I'm already old and am still not happy* look.
7. Paid income tax and enjoyed getting angry discussing "what the hell they were doing with all of your goddamn change."
8. Enjoyed drinking alcohol in front of the television every evening by yourself.
9. Were suspicious of children and their motives.
10. Didn't get excited about anything.

"I know," he said, confirming my suspicions as to his allegiances. "How did you get dragged along to something like this, anyways? Don't you know any better? Those guys survive on sucking your life force from you. No wonder people think science is dead and gone."

After briefly considering lying to maintain a level of coolness with this guy, who I increasingly wanted to grow up to be, I decided against it.

"Well," I said. "Actually, I am one of the guests of honor. I just won the Baird Award at the Smithsonian." Hearing myself talk, I suddenly became bored with myself, and realized that this young man probably had no interest in hearing about the Baird Award or anything I had to say about sewer systems or wormholes or climate change. He was just making small talk, what bathroom attendants were supposed to do.

But his eyes lit up. "Oy," he said. "Mr. Spencer Baird, our fearless leader." He made a strange mock salute in which he first pointed at his head, and then up to the ceiling with three fingers. "Congratulations. What do you do?"

I was so taken aback by this that for a moment I was not sure what to say; I just drooled inside my mouth. But seeing he was still waiting for an answer and had not just asked the question out of politesse, I said: "Well, I suppose I make maps."

"Maps? What type of maps?"

"All types, really...maps of people chopping wood...maps of chopping..." For some reason, all I could think of was people chopping wood.

"Maps of chopping wood?" he raised an eyebrow.

"No, no, no....I mean I also make maps of McDonald's locations in North Dakota, and the curvature of creeks and drainage patterns, maps of a city's electricity grid usage, maps of beetle antennae..."

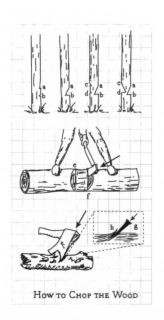

How to Chop the Wood

from Notebook B43 ◄╌╌╌

I actually had drawn a diagram about how to chop wood after watching Father expertly fell the pines down the hill for a day and a half. Boy, could he chop wood.

"Oy," he said. His expression had suddenly become very secretive. He went to the door and looked out in the hallway, one direction, then the other. Maybe he *was* a spy. Maybe he was about to kill me, finish the job started by the Rev. Merrymore, who was also a spy, working undercover as a bum crazy preacher. And now that I had killed one of their own, this ring of spies was furious and would finish the job in a bathroom, by suffocating me with a plunger.

The bathroom attendant turned the bolt in the door and came back to where I was standing. I had to admit, I was terrified. I searched in my pocket, but realized I had left my Leatherman (Cartographer's Edition) at the scene of the crime on that cold and lonely canal in Chicago.

"Well," he said in a half-whisper. "Have you ever heard of the Megatherium Club?"

"The...the Megatherium?" I was shaking.

He nodded and pointed to the shelf below the mirror, where the little hand towels and cologne and potentially poisonous mints were arranged. Next to the bowl of mints stood a miniature creature that looked like a prehistoric sloth. This, I realized, was a Megatherium.

Made in China

The Megatherium Figurine

"Made in China," he said. "But, according to fossil data, surprisingly accurate."

"Of course," I said, exhaling. "I always wanted to join the Megatherium Club, until I realized I was born about a hundred and fifty years too late."

"You are not too late," he said. And then in an even lower whisper. "We still congregate."

"The Club still exists?"

He nodded.

"And you're a member?"

He smiled.

"But how come I haven't heard of this?"

"Oy," he said. "There's lots of things in this town that you've never heard of. If you or anyone else heard of them, they would cease to exist."

"Like what?"

"Follow me," he said. He pocketed the Megatherium figurine and  put a fancy little card on the counter.

"Sometimes the sign works better than having me here," he said. "People like the idea of giving, but they don't like the actual *act* of giving."

We left the bathroom together and walked down the hallway. The two laughing men had apparently returned to their seats.

I said, "I think I have to go give a speech very soon."

"This won't take a minute. Just wanted to show you something."

"Okay," I said.

We followed the hallway to the end and went down a flight of stairs into the basement.

"What's your name?" I asked.

"Boris," he said.

"Hi," I said.

"Hi, T.S." he said.

"How did you know my name?" I asked suspiciously.

He pointed to my name tag.

"Oh," I said, and laughed. "Okay. Name tag, duh. I don't usually—"

"What does it stand for?"

"Tecumseh Sparrow."

"Nice," he said.

In the basement, we walked past several boilers and then came to a janitorial closet. Again, visions of murder and buried bodies flashed in my head.

Boris looked at me and smiled. But it wasn't a *I'm now going to kill you* smile, it was more the kind of conspiratorial smile that Layton would throw me just before he unveiled his latest aerial trick or homemade explosive device.

Then Boris clapped his hands twice, like one of the top-hatted magicians at Gracie's old birthday parties, and opened the closet door. I looked inside tentatively, expecting to see a live alligator or something of that nature. But the closet seemed to be in order. There were the mops. There were the buckets.

"What is it?" I asked.

"Look," he said, pointing to the back of the closet. I looked, and in the gloom I spotted a four-foot iron door with a large handle, like the door to a large, old-fashioned oven. We pushed past the mop handles and knelt in front of the door. Boris spat on his palms and put some weight against the handle. You could tell he was really giving it some torque. I heard him softly grunt and then after a moment the handle made a low moan before turning counterclockwise.

Boris swung open the iron door, revealing a small tunnel that sloped steeply down into the darkness. The tunnel was a little too small for an adult to walk through comfortably, though I could have managed quite nicely. I leaned forward. The wafts of cool air coming from the tunnel were surprisingly dry, not musty as I might have expected. I closed my eyes and tried to parcel out the componentry of the smell: a twinge of rusted iron and the cushioned coolness of old soil and perhaps the burnt aftertaste of a kerosene lamp. And now that I was smelling with such con-

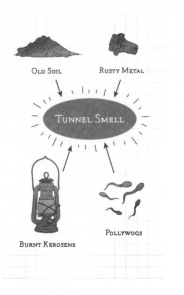

Smells Are Evocative but Hard to Describe from Notebook G101

I wonder if there was ever a smell *in and of itself* or whether all smells could in turn be broken into their smaller component parts, ad infinitum. The olfactory system seemed the trickiest of all our senses, because we lacked a real language for it. My family always spoke about smells in terms of tastes or memories or metaphors. Once, when one of Dr. Clair's toasters was burning, Father came into the kitchen and said, "It smells like the fourth circle a'hell in here. Woman, you asleep at the wheel?"

And Layton screamed from upstairs, "Yeah, it smells like burning poop!"

And Gracie looked up from her toilet seat computer and said, "It smells like my childhood." And she was not wrong.

centration, I did sense a touch of moisture, a sprinkle of pollywog. All of these smells came together to form the smell: *tunnel.* I breathed.

"What is—" I asked after a second.

"A system of tunnels," he said, sticking his head inside. "They date back to the Civil War. We found a pair of cavalry boots in one of them. They go from the White House to the Capitol to the Smithsonian." He traced a little triangle on his palm. "They were built in order to allow an easy escape for the big guys in case the city was besieged. The idea was that they could take refuge in the Smithsonian and then get the hell out of the city before the Rebs could find them. The tunnels were sealed off soon after the war ended, but a Megatherium found them in the forties and we've been using them ever since. Of course, it's a secret. So if you tell anyone, I'd have to kill you." He grinned.

I wasn't scared anymore. "But I did a map of the Washington sewer system and pored through all the old underground maps and never saw these tunnels."

"I'm sorry to say, my man, but there's a lot that doesn't show up on maps. And that which does not show up is precisely what we are most interested in."

"Do you know anything about wormholes, by chance?"

His eyes narrowed. "What kind of wormhole?"

"Well, on my way out here, I think my train went through some kind of wormhole thing—"

"Where was this?" he asked.

"Somewhere around Nebraska," I said. Boris nodded knowingly. I continued: "I mean, I can't be sure, but that's what it seemed like, because the world disappeared for a while and then all of a sudden we were in

Chicago. I remember reading something about some study of wormholes in the Middle West once…"

He nodded. "Mr. Toriano's report?"

"You know it?"

"Oh yeah—he's famous in Megatherium circles. A real legend. He disappeared about fifteen years ago, trying to document the instability of the space-time continuum in Iowa. *Got caught and never came out,* if you know what I mean. But I can get you a copy of the report, easy. Where do they have you staying?"

"The Carriage House."

"Oh, the Carriage House…where all of our distinguished guests have stayed. You know, you are sleeping in the same bed as Oppenheimer, Bohr, Sagan, Einstein, Agassiz, Hayden, and William Stimpson, our founder. You've joined a long line."

"Agassiz?" I said. I wanted to ask *and Emma Osterville?* but was scared he had never heard of her. No one had. *She was a quitter.*

"We'll get you a copy of the Toriano report by tomorrow morning. A guy named Farkas will deliver it. You'll know him when you see him."

I wanted to ask a bunch of questions about tunnels and wormholes and who Farkas was and how I could get one of those M pins, but an alarm bell went off in my head.

"Thanks," I said. "I should probably go. I need to explain what I'm doing here to them."

"Knock 'em dead," he said. "Just remember: no bullshit. Don't get sucked into their games. Even though they would never admit it, they brought you here to spank them around the room. They want to have their eyes opened."

"Okay," I said. "How do I find you?"

"Don't worry," he said. "We will find you." And then he gave me that little salute again, finishing with pointing three fingers at the ceiling of the janitor's closet. I did my best to give it back to him, though I knew I must be getting some element wrong.

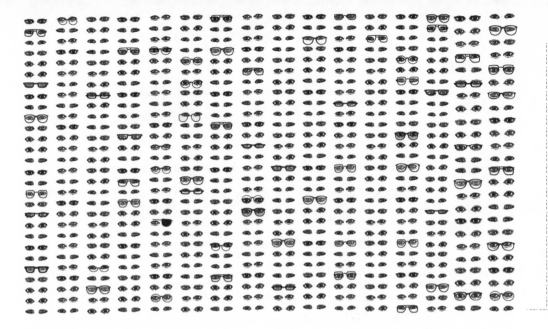

This Is the Room-Feeling of 783 Eyes Staring at Me
from Notebook G101

CHAPTER 12

When I got back upstairs, the lights had already dimmed. The last few people were making their way to their seats. For a second I became disoriented—I was so overwhelmed with the conflagration of black sleeves and wedding rings and halitosis that I forgot where I had been sitting.

Someone grabbed my elbow and jerked me backward. A shot of pain went through my entire body—it felt as if the stitches had suddenly ripped open in my chest.

"Where have you been?" Jibsen hissed into my ear. I winced in pain.

"*Where have you been?*" he repeated. His eyes were transformed; I searched his face for Nice Jibsen but could find no remnant of his old self.

"I was in the bathroom," I said, feeling the tears well up. I didn't want to disappoint Jibsen already.

He softened. "I'm sorry," he said. "I didn't mean to…I just want this to go well."

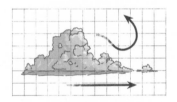

The Transience of Anger, Thunder Boomers
from Notebook G101

I had never heard this tone of voice before. It was a kind of focused anger that Father never displayed—his was a silent, diffused resentment at the inadequacies of the physical world. This resentment manifested itself in grumblings, dismissals, and an occasional tongue-lashing that was done as soon as it had started, like the passing thunder boomers in early spring.

He smiled, but his eyes maintained a trace of all that anger. I could see it lingering just beneath the surface. Watching his eyes, I suddenly had an idea of how adults can hold on to a feeling for very long periods of time, long after the event is finished, long after cards have been sent and apologies made and everyone else had moved on. Adults were pack rats of old, useless emotions.

"How are you feeling?" Jibsen said.

"I'm all right," I said.

"Good. Let's take our seats," he said. His voice was syrupy now, cajoling. He loosened his grip on my arm and guided me back to our table. Our tablemates half-smiled at me as I sat down. I half-smiled back.

My plate had a tiny salad on it. There were tangerine slices in the salad. I looked around and saw that everyone had already been picking at theirs, like little birds. One woman's salad was missing all the tangerine slices.

Then a man from a nearby table got up and walked onto the stage, to light applause by all. I realized he had shaken my hand earlier during the scrum of introductions, but now I recognized who he actually was: the Secretary of the Smithsonian. *Here he was, in the living flesh!* Somehow seeing him up there, his hair combed, his pudgy face and slackened jowls bobbing as he smiled and nodded for silence, made my entire expedition across 2,476 miles of U.S. soil a tangible *fact*. I was here. I grabbed my pinky and licked my lips in anticipation.

As soon as he began speaking, however, my brain began creaking, and without knowing it, I began distancing my esteem and conception of the Smithsonian from this pudgy man with the insincere smile. His speech was astoundingly mediocre: it floated into the room and then out, making everyone feel fine but nothing more.

A Small Note on Mediocrity

Dr. Clair hated mediocrity. And as far as I could tell, she thought most things were mediocre.

One morning she forcefully folded up our copy of the *Montana Standard* and said, "Oh, mediocre, mediocre, mediocre, mediocre."

"Mediocre, mediocre, mediocre," Layton promptly began to repeat over his breakfast cereal. I soon joined in.

"Cut it out," she said. "This is serious. Mediocrity is a fungus of the mind. We must constantly rally against it—it will try to creep into all that we do, but we must not let it. No, we must not."

Layton continued to repeat "mediocre, mediocre" under his breath, but I could no longer join him, for I believed what my mother said. I was silently pledging my allegiance to her cause, even in the way that I ate my Honey Nut Cheerios with careful, determined bites.

304

A Log of the Secretary's Very Boring Speech

Time	The Secretary Said This:	The Old Man Next to Me Did This:	My Interest Level (1 to 10):
0:05	"We are so pleased to have… "	Smiled; Sipped his drink	8
0:32	"the current state of science is exciting…"	Took a bite of salad	7
1:13	"…at the Smithsonian we are expanding our horizons...	Stared at the ceiling; patted his wife's leg	5
2:16	[more words]…		2
3:12	"…and this reminds me of a story..."	Smiled at his wife (I hope it is his wife)	4
3:45, 4:01	[joke]… [another joke]...	Laughed (but more at the 2nd joke)	5
4:58	[more words]...		2
5:48	[practiced pause]...	Wiped his nose with a hanky; sipped his drink	3
6:03	"…Ladies and Gentlemen, the future is indeed now. Thank you."	Applauded; smiled at his wife/woman	4

Jokes

MY INTEREST LEVEL

TIME →

0

After only a minute of this, I wanted to see if I could flick a limp carrot stick into my wineglass. I had trouble listening to adults who didn't really mean anything that they said; it was as if their language poured into my ears only to drain right out a little spigot in the back of my head. But how could you tell when someone was being insincere? This, like my father's expressions, was something I would never be able to map. It was a mixture of many things: disembodied hand gestures; hollow smiles; long, crinkly pauses; inopportune eyebrow raises; a shifting tonality to the voice that was very measured and calculated. And yet it was none of these things.

I began to grow very nervous. I had written a speech that was tucked in the inside pocket of my tuxedo, but I had never actually given a speech before, I had only imagined that I had given a speech, and so I wondered if I would be able to pull off any of those smooth half-smiles and eyebrow raisings.

Then the President of the National Academy of Sciences leapt up out of his seat and shook the Secretary's hand with an expression of polite enthusiasm wrapped carefully around a core of mild disdain, which was

Disembodied Hand Gestures
from Notebook G101

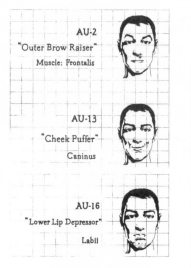

AU-2
"Outer Brow Raiser"
Muscle: Frontalis

AU-13
"Cheek Puffer"
Caninus

AU-16
"Lower Lip Depressor"
Labii

Components of the
"*Thanks, Please Leave*"
Smile-Grimace

an expression (an AU-2, AU-13, AU-16, to be exact) that Dr. Clair gave when Aunt Hasting had come over to comfort our family this past spring with a Tupperware container of her famous squirrel soup.

The NAS President greeted the podium by grabbing it with two hands and ducking his head up and down to acknowledge the applause. He was bearded and his eyes were totally different from the secretary's. In fact, the more he nodded and bobbed around, the more his face began to resemble the mannerisms and sparkly twitchings of Dr. Clair. In his eyes, I recognized the same hungry impulse that I had seen in Dr. Clair's eyes during her most vociferous moments of inspection, when you could not pull her from chasing down the taxonomic conundrum of a question mark in a cilium or an exoskeletal pattern. As in: the world had shrunk to unraveling a certain problem and every mitochondrion in your being depended upon its unraveling.

He bowed, embarrassed at the extended applause. I applauded along with everyone. It seemed we did not know why we continued to applaud, but we knew that it felt good: to bestow our appreciation on another human being whom we perhaps knew or didn't know but who we could tell deserved our appreciation.

When the room had finally quieted down, he said, "Thank you very much, ladies, gentlemen, our honored guest." He looked right at me and smiled. I squirmed.

"Ladies and gentlemen, I would like to tell you a little story. This story is about our friend and colleague Dr. Mehtab Zahedi, one of the world's leading researchers on the medicinal uses of horseshoe-crab blood. Just yesterday I read in the *Post* that Dr. Zahedi had been stopped by airport security in Houston for having fifty horseshoe-crab specimens in his luggage. The specimens and equipment were all legal to transport, but Dr.

Zahedi, who happens to be Pakistani-American, was held on suspicion of terrorism and then questioned for *seven hours* before being released. His specimens, representing six years of work and nearly $2 million in research money, were confiscated and then 'accidentally' destroyed by the airport police. The next day, the local paper's headline read ARAB MAN STOPPED AT AIRPORT WITH FIFTY CRABS IN LUGGAGE," he said. The room chuckled.

"Yes, put that way, it's a humorous anecdote that no doubt elicited laughs from several couples on their way to church. But please, colleagues, note the flattening: Dr. Zahedi is one of the most important molecular biologists in the world, whose research has thus far saved thousands of lives, and as we come in contact with more diseases resistant to penicillin, it will perhaps save millions more in the future. Here, however, he is just an *Arab man with fifty crabs* who is harassed and whose life's work is then destroyed.

"Lest I risk burdening this story with too much import—and I will be honest, after reading this, I threw my newspaper across the room, nearly hitting my wife in the head—let me just say that Dr. Zahedi's ordeal touches upon many of the complex obstacles that we are up against today. Indeed, *obstacle* is no longer the right word: in the current climate of xenophobic pseudoscience, we are actually under attack from all sides. And it is not just in the Kansas schoolroom—all across the country there are subtle and not-so-subtle jabs at the scientific method from right, left, and center, whether it is from animal-rights groups, oil executives, evangelicals, special interest groups, even, dare I say, the big pharmaceuticals." There was a grumbling and shifting in the room.

The man at the podium gave a knowing smile and waited for the rustling to die down before continuing: "I hope that the Smithsonian, the National Academy, the National Science Foundation, and the entire

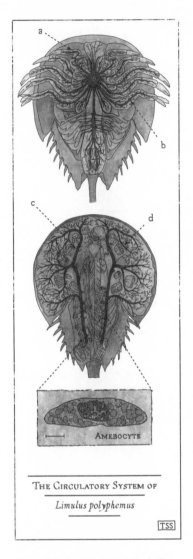

THE CIRCULATORY SYSTEM OF
Limulus polyphemus

TSS

Dr. Mehtab Zahedi?! I had illustrated one of his articles last year! We had corresponded for several months through the mail, which both Dr. Zahedi and I seemed to prefer, and once I had sent him the final proofs he had written back, "These are beautiful. Like the images from my dreams. When I am next in Montana, I shall buy you a drink, T.S. —M.Z." And I remember thinking that M.Z. was the coolest initial pairing I could think of.

scientific community can work together to fight this hostile landscape of derision and simplemindedness. As much as we would like to retreat to our laboratories and field sites, we can no longer sit back passively, for it is indeed—and pardon the misuse of this often misused term—a *war* in which we find ourselves. Make no mistake about it: we are at war. To think anything less would be to fool ourselves, and at this point in time, such blindness is criminal, for they are working as we speak.

"Recently, scientists made a key discovery, a *monumental* discovery, of the gene that might connect our evolutionary brain development back to the great apes. And yet what does our president do the day after this discovery is made? He urges Americans to remain skeptical of the 'theory' of evolution, as if *theory* were a dirty word. I am afraid that we must learn to fight fire with fire and enter into the arena of public relations, of media savviness; we must convincingly present our message or it will eventually wither and be cast aside in favor of slicker messages, catchall explanations based solely on faith and on fear. This is not to say faith is our enemy— many of us here are believers, and many of us have cast our faith not in a higher power but in double-blind testing." There was a general chuckling in the crowd. We were all laughing. I was laughing with them. It felt good to laugh with them. *Double-blind testing. That is hilarious!*

"Yes, colleagues, faith itself is a beautiful thing, perhaps *the* beautiful thing, but it is faith run amok, faith that clouds judgment, faith that dispels rigor and encourages mediocrity, faith that has been abused and misused and which has brought us to this dangerous crossroads. We all thrust our faith into the inevitability of the scientific process, of the great march toward truth, through hypothesis, testing, and reporting, but this is not a given—this is a creation, and, like all of man's creations, our methods and belief systems can be taken away from us. There is no inevitability in human civilization save eventual destruction. Accordingly, if we do not do something, the field of science in America will be vastly different for the next generation and perhaps unrecognizable in a hundred years, that is, if our civilization does not collapse before then from the impending fossil fuel crisis."

He gripped the podium. This was the kind of man I wanted to be.

"This is why I look forward to meeting our guest of honor tonight, a member of the next generation, a person whom we are all—whether we like it or not—putting our faith in. And as you can tell by his extraordinary ability to illustrate what is often so difficult to convey, this little man is doing more than his part to keep science alive and well, quite well, it appears."

There was clapping and the president held his hand out to me. The audience shifted in their seats and I felt the winsome sensation of all the eyes in the room upon my back, which immediately made me want to hyperventilate. The lights irised in and out. I gripped my pinky.

Jibsen leaned over and touched my shoulder. "You feeling all right?" he asked.

"I'm okay," I said.

"Knock 'em out," he said, and punched me in the shoulder. It hurt.

As the 783 eyes (by my rough count) collectively watched, I slowly rose from my seat and then wove my way around the tables with the dozens of still unused thingy-bobbys lying in wait. I took the stairs up to the stage one at a time. Each step-up motion felt like it was tearing open my chest one more centimeter. As soon as I stepped out onto the stage, the rest of the room disappeared beneath the glare of the lights. I blinked. Behind the lights, I could hear a great silence of anticipation.

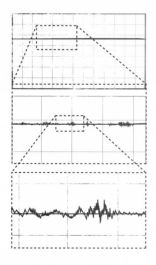

The Sounds of Silence

There were many types of silence in this world and almost none of them were actually silent. Even when we said a room was silent, what we actually meant was that no one was talking, but of course there were still the tiny sounds of floorboards warping, or clocks ticking, or the rattling of stray water droplets in the radiators, the velveteen brush of cars outside. And so as I stood on the stage looking out into the wash of bright lights, what had started out as silence parted into the whine of the spotlights above me, the auditory collage of 392 people trying to be quiet, even as their feet nervously tapped and their arms quivered from various neurological diseases and their hearts contracted beneath their lapels, their breath wheezing gently out through the pinch of their nostrils. I could hear tinkering and voices from the distant kitchen, the suck and swing of the kitchen doors as someone burst through them, the kitchen voices momentarily louder and then muffled again. And then, beneath it all, came the low-grade hum of the fans from above, which I had not noticed before. For a moment, I wondered if the quiet, persistent *hoowooowooo* was actually the sound of the world spinning around itself, but no, it was just the fans.

Squinting and trying to smile, I shook the hand of the president of the Academy, just as Emma had done with Joseph Henry.

"Congratulations," he said softly, and it was the first false word he had said all night. He gave me an AU-17. This man liked the idea of me, but now that we were standing face-to-face, I no doubt reminded him of a twelve-year-old.

I could just barely see over the podium. The president noticed this and produced a small footstool, which caused a rustling and some laughter from the audience. I dutifully mounted the footstool and took out the crumpled piece of paper from my pocket.

"Hello, everybody," I said. "My name is T. S. Spivet. I am named after Tecumseh, the great Shawnee general, who tried to unite the tribes of all Indian nations before he was gunned down by the U.S. Army at the Battle of the Thames. My great-great-grandfather Tearho Spivet, who was from Finland, adopted this name after his arrival in the U.S., and someone from every generation has been named Tecumseh since…and so sometimes when I say T.S., I can feel my ancestors inside there. I can feel T.T. and T.R. and T.P. and even T.E., my father, who is very different from me—I can feel them all in my name. Maybe even Tecumseh himself is bumping around in there, very confused as to why this lineage of Finnish-German farmers has co-opted his name. But of course I don't think about my ancestors every time I say my name, especially when I am just saying it quickly, like when I say, 'Yeah, it's T.S.,' in a phone message or something. If I was always thinking about my ancestors—my God, this would become ridiculous." I paused. "But I guess you are probably wondering what my other initial stands for."

I got down off the little footstool and walked to the screen behind me that had the giant Smithsonian sun projected on it. With my thumbs locked together, I did my best to re-create the sparrow shadow puppet that Two Clouds had shown me.

"Can you guess what it is?" I said, unmicrophoned. I heard people shuffle about. I squinted and saw Jibsen shifting uncomfortably in his seat. His eyes were pleading: *What are you doing? Please, dear Lord, do not screw this up.*

I looked back at the shadow and saw that it didn't really look like anything. It lacked the quivering aliveness of the creature that Two Clouds had conjured against that boxcar in Pocatello.

"It's a kind of bird," I said, growing anxious.

Someone shouted: "It's an eagle!"

I shook my head. "That doesn't start with *s*. Unless you mean a Sulawesi Hawk-Eagle. But, no, my other initial does not stand for a Sulawesi Hawk-Eagle." A woman laughed. People relaxed.

"It's a sparrow!" someone said from the back. The voice sounded incredibly familiar. I tried to squint past the glare of the lights but could only see a great crowd of tuxedos and gowns sitting in the darkness.

"Yes," I said, racking my brain as to how I knew this voice. "Tecumseh Sparrow Spivet. Good guess. I guess the sparrow is my guardian animal. Probably some of you are ornithologists and could tell me a lot about the sparrow, and I'd like that."

I took a deep breath and continued: "You are all probably very smart people who have earned their Ph.D.s and whatnot, so I will not try to tell you things you do not know about, because I have only graduated seventh grade and do not know as many things as you. But, besides my name, I would like to tell you three things tonight."

I held up my first finger. I squinted down at the front row and showed them my finger. I could see Jibsen. He smiled and held up his

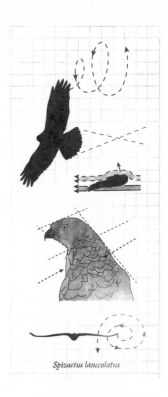

Spizaetus lanceolatus

▶ *The Sulawesi Hawk-Eagle Enjoys Flying* from Notebook G77

finger. Something caught, and then everyone up front held up their fingers. I could hear a great shuffling as I imagined 392 fingers collectively held up in the air. "The first thing I want to say is thank you for letting me speak and thank you for not canceling my fellowship because I was younger than you might have expected. Often, I am younger than I might have expected, but this does not stop me from doing my work. But it is a dream come true to be at the Smithsonian. I have always wanted to feel its room-feeling and now I am here. I will try to work very hard to show you that you did not make a mistake in choosing me for this award. I will spend every second of the day mapping and making new diagrams for the museum, and hopefully everyone will be happy with my maps and diagrams."

I held up a second finger. This was keeping me on track. Jibsen and the audience dutifully followed suit. Twos abounded. "The second thing I would like to tell you is why I make maps. Many people have asked me why I spend all my time drawing maps instead of playing outside with other boys my age. My father, who is a rancher from Montana, does not really understand me. I try to show him how maps can be useful in his line of work, but he doesn't listen. My mother is a scientist like you people, and I wish that she could be here tonight, because I think that even though she says the Smithsonian is an old boys' club, she would have many interesting things to say to you and also she might learn how to be a better scientist. Like, for instance, she might learn that she would be better off not chasing after the tiger monk beetle anymore, that there are actually a lot of other useful things to do besides search for something that doesn't exist. But you know what is strange? Even though she is a scientist, she still doesn't understand me. She doesn't really see the purpose of mapping all the people that I meet, all the places I see, everything that I have ever witnessed or read about. But I don't want to die without having taken a crack at figuring out how the whole thing fits together, like a very complicated car, like a very complicated car in four dimensions…or maybe six or eleven, or I forget how many dimensions there are supposed to be."

I stopped. There were probably many people in the audience who knew how many dimensions there were. They had perhaps even discovered these dimensions. I swallowed nervously and looked at my notes. I realized that I did not have a third point written down. This must have happened when the tailor came in and Jibsen gave me those unmarked painkillers. Everyone waited, their two fingers in the air.

"Um…," I said. "Are there any questions so far?"

"What's the third thing?" someone asked.

"Yes," I said. "What is the third thing?"

"T.S.!" a man called from behind the glare. This was that same familiar voice. "Don't worry about dying! You've got about fifty years on us! We're the ones who should worry about getting our work done. You have your whole life in front of you."

His words caused a stirring in the room. People were whispering.

"Okay," I said. "Thank you."

"Okay," I said again. People were still whispering. I looked down at Jibsen, who was shifting uncomfortably. He made a motion with his hands for me to keep going. I had lost them. I was a failure. I had no idea what I was doing. I was a child.

"My brother died this year," I said.

The room went silent. True silence.

"He shot himself in the barn.…That sounds weird to say out loud, because it has never been said like that. No one ever said, 'Layton shot himself in the barn.' But that is exactly what happened. I didn't mean

313

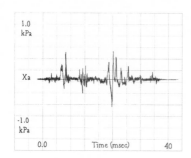

1815 Flintlock Musket .72 cal.

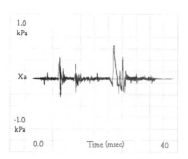

1860 Kentucky Style Double Barrel .40 cal.

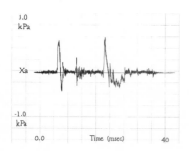

1886 Winchester Short Rifle .40-.82 cal.

for it to happen. We were working together on a seismoscope diagram. I was so excited. You see, he collected guns and we had such a hard time playing together….I think he thought I was so weird, always drawing and recording, and he would punch me and say, 'Stop writin' it down!' He never understood. He wasn't like that…he, he just tackled everything without blinking. He loved his guns. He would spend all day shooting empty bean cans off the jack boulders or go hunting voles down in the gulches. So I came up with this idea…we could play with his guns together. I would make a sound-wave map for each gun, and I could overlay all kinds of information in these sonic displays, like gauge and accuracy and distance, and I thought this would be a way for us to just be doing our things together. To be both comfortable and be brothers. And it was great. We worked together for three days. And he loved to shoot his guns for me and I was getting really great data. You would never believe how different gunshots can look from one another….And then one of his Winchesters jammed while it was loaded. He was cleaning the top or something, just checking the muzzle, and I went to hold the bottom, just to steady the base, you know? And I didn't even touch the trigger. But there was this explosion. And he flew across the room. I looked and then I…He was bleeding and his head was turned away from me but I could feel he wasn't my brother anymore. He wasn't anyone anymore…I could tell just by my own breathing that there were two of us and then there was one of us. And I…" I let out a tight, thin gasp. "I didn't mean to do it. I didn't, I didn't."

The room was still silent. Everyone waited. I took a deep breath. "And ever since that moment of looking and feeling my breath and then his breath gone, I've been feeling like something's going to happen to me. It's the way of things. Sir Isaac Newton says that every force demands an equal and reactive force. So I am waiting. On the way out here, I almost died, maybe to balance things out. Because Layton shouldn't have died. Maybe I should have. Because that ranch was going to go to him. He was going to make that ranch beautiful. Can you imagine Layton running the Coppertop?"

I imagined, and then began again:

"When that knife was cutting open my chest in Chicago, I thought, 'T.S., here it is. You're finally getting it. This is how it ends.' And I thought I would never get a chance to talk to all of you like I am doing right now. And that's when I fought back. And I made the Reverend the equal and opposite force. He fell into the canal, and the balance returned. Or…is everything more unbalanced now? All I know is that it felt like I was meant to be here. My ancestors were meant to go out west, and I was meant to be here. Does that mean Layton was meant to die? Do you know what I mean?"

I paused. No one spoke. "Can you tell me how pervasive cellular cause and effect is? How much does nanochance dictate the course of time? I just get a feeling sometimes that everything is predetermined, and I am going through the motions of tracing an existence that will be what it will already be." I paused again. "Can I ask you a question?"

I realized this was silly to say to 392 people, but it was too late now, so I went ahead. "Do you ever get the feeling like you already know the entire contents of the universe somewhere inside your head, as if you were born with a complete map of this world already grafted onto the folds of your cerebellum and you are just spending your entire life figuring out how to access this map?"

"Yes, how do we access it?" a woman asked. It was startling to hear a woman's voice. Suddenly, I missed my mother.

"Um," I said. "Well, I am not sure, ma'am. Perhaps if we sit still for three or four days and really concentrate. I tried doing this on the way out here, but I got bored. I am too young to pay attention that long, but I just have this tiny feeling that is always present—like a low humming tone that continues beneath everything—that we know everything already, but that we've just somehow forgotten how to harness this knowledge. When I make a map that exactly captures what it is trying to map, it is like I already knew this map existed; I was just copying it. And this gets me to thinking: if the maps already existed, then the world already exists and the future already exists. Is this true? Those of you with Ph.D.s in future science, has this meeting already been predetermined? Is what I will say already a part of the map? I am not sure. I feel like I could've said a lot of different things from what I am saying now." Silence. Someone coughed. They hated me.

"Well, all of this is to say that I will do my best to fulfill your trust in me. I am just a boy, but I have my maps. I'll do my best. I'll try not to die and I'll try to do everything you want me to. I can't believe I am finally here; this is like a new beginning, a new chapter for my family. Maybe I can decide. And I am deciding to continue Emma's story. I am very happy to be here. Maybe they are here too—all the Tecumsehs and Emma and Mr. Englethorpe and Dr. Hayden and every other scientist who has ever picked up a rock and wondered how it got there.

"That is all I have to say. Thank you," I said. I folded up the piece of paper and stuck it in my pocket.

There was no silence this time. People clapped and I could tell by the way they were hitting their hands together that their applause was genuine. I smiled and Jibsen was standing and everyone in the first row was standing. It was a great moment. The Secretary of the Smithsonian came onto the stage and grabbed my hand, and as they cheered more, he roughly raised my arm into the air and I heard some ripping and gasped as my chest exploded. People were cheering and he was holding my hand in the air like a boxer and I could hardly breathe and my feet were giving way beneath me. Then Jibsen was at my side and supporting me. With his arm around me, he guided me off the stage. I was incredibly dizzy.

"We've got to get you out of here before there's a scene."

"What's happening?" I asked.

"You're bleeding again, through your tuxedo. We don't want to scare them."

I looked down and saw a patch of blood just above my little belt thing. Jibsen ushered me through the crowd. Everyone was swarming us, talking loudly.

"Call me," someone said.

"Sorry, sorry, we've got somewhere to go," Jibsen said.

People were handing him business cards and he was collecting them with one hand, stuffing them into his pocket as he shielded me from the crowd with his other arm. From beneath his arm I looked up and saw a sea of terrible smiles, and there was the flash of a camera, and then, in the briefest of instants I thought I saw Dr. Yorn in the crowd, but then Jibsen was pushing me along, smothering me. I realized this must have been an illusion, because plenty of scientists had huge glasses and large, unaddressed bald spots. Besides, Dr. Yorn would never wear a tuxedo.

Finally we were through the swinging doors and out in the empty hallway. The echoes of the party drifted away behind us. Several members of the waitstaff stood nearby, watching us leave. They were still wearing their white gloves.

As we fetched our coats in the lobby, I was so wobbly that Jibsen had to prop me up against a large palm planter. I saw Boris on the other side of the lobby. He was alone, leaning against the wall. I smiled at him weakly. He saluted me, but I was too exhausted to return the gesture.

Once we were both coated, Jibsen carried me outside into a light rain. I was glad for the squeaky interior of the black car that was waiting outside the hall. I liked being a guest of honor and having things like cars just waiting for you. Listening to the soothing slap of the car's wipers, I watched water droplets on the windows curl back into themselves. A water droplet was an admirable thing: it always followed the path of least resistance.

Fig. 1

Fig. 2

Fig. 3

Fig. 4

CHAPTER 13

The next morning, I awoke to find that someone had already snuck into the Carriage House and left a breakfast tray on the desk. The tray's contents: a bowl of Honey Nut Cheerios, a little porcelain pitcher of milk, a spoon, a napkin, a glass of orange juice, and a copy of the *Washington Post,* neatly folded in half.

This inventory immediately made me wonder how the anonymous breakfast courier knew about my almost philosophical obsession with Honey Nut Cheerios, but I admit, I did not ponder this mystery for long. A dry bowl of cereal has a way of calling to you. I doused the Cheerios with milk and dove headlong into the delicious world of tiny crunchy doughnuts. When I was done, I performed my favorite part of the ritual: the drinking of the leftover milk that had become lightly infused with sweet strains of honey, as if a magical honey cow had dispensed her milk right into my bowl.

I then propped myself up in bed and settled into the job of "finishing" the morning comics, which always lifted my spirits.

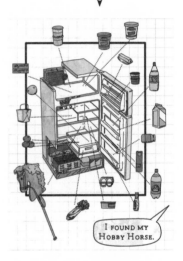

→ *The Fifth Panel*
from Notebook G101

Right after Layton died, I started drawing fifth panels for the morning comics. Somehow, the exercise comforted me. I liked how I could enter these imaginary worlds and always have the last word, even if my efforts diluted the humor of the original strip. The boundedness of a comic frame was satisfying, as nothing could penetrate the insularity of that world. Except the boundedness was what always left me feeling a little hollow, even after fifth-paneling a whole paper. And yet the next morning there I was again, drawing away.

319

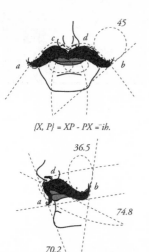

$\{X, P\} = XP - PX = ih.$

The Strangely Attentive
Mustache
from Notebook G101

At some point during my labors, I remembered last night's events. The image of me addressing a ballroom filled with hundreds of fancy people seemed so foreign that I began to consider whether the entire thing had been a painkiller-induced hallucination, whether my subconscious had in fact invented Boris and the one-eyed woman and the white-gloved staff.

I spotted my tuxedo lying on the floor with the ruffled shirt still inside it. Embarrassed, I hung them up and attempted to conceal the bloodstains on the shirt by crossing the sleeves of the jacket across the chest and then over the shoulders. I took a step back. It appeared as if an invisible man inside the tuxedo was hugging himself.

I was still admiring the invisible man's loving self-embrace when someone knocked at the door.

"Come in, please!" I said.

A young man with a strangely attentive mustache pushed opened the door. He was carrying several large boxes.

"Hello, Mr. Spivet," he said. "These are your supplies."

"Oh," I said. "How'd you know…what I needed? I didn't write anything down yet."

I did not mean to sound snobby, but I was very particular about my mapping tools. Though grateful for their effort, I doubted they would be able to guess at my peculiar preference for certain pens and sextants.

"Oh, we had a pretty good idea. The Gillot 300 series? Berger theodolite? We've seen you at work before."

My jaw dropped open. "Wait a minute," I said. "Did you bring me the Honey Nut?"

"What?"

"Uh…nothing," I said. I suddenly remembered I only had $2.78 in my trousers pocket. "You know, I'm not sure I can pay for all of this right now."

"Are you kidding? Smithy's footing the bill—at least they're good for that," he said.

"Really?" I said. "Wow! Free stuff."

"Best things in life," he said. "If there's anything else you need, just write it on this order form and we'll jiff it over."

"What about candy?" I asked, testing the limits of my power.

"We can do candy," he said.

He finished stacking the boxes by the desk and then brought in several portfolios. "Here's your work from out west," he said.

"Out west?"

"Yeah," he said. "Dr. Yorn just sent them across the divide."

"You know Dr. Yorn?" I asked.

The man with the mustache smiled.

I began looking through one of the portfolios. My most recent projects were inside. I thought no one had seen these but me. There was the beginning of my great Montana series: old migration trails of the bison herds overlaying the interstate system; elevation and topsoil reliefs; an experimental flip chart showing the slow transformation of small farms and family ranches on the High Line into behemoth agribusiness plots.

These were my maps. This was my home. I touched the overlays, traced the tight pen lines with my fingertips, rubbed my thumb over a place where I remembered erasing a false stroke. I recalled the *he-haw* squeak that my drafting chair emitted whenever I bent forward. *Oh, to be home again!* I could smell my father's stiff coffee percolating downstairs, the richness of the beans mixing with the few stray scents of formaldehyde from Dr. Clair's study.

"You all right?"

I looked up and saw the young man staring at me. "Yes," I said, embarrassed, hastily wiping at my cheeks and closing the portfolio. "Fine, these look good and fine."

"Well," he said. "I'd hate to see you when they bring in all of your notebooks."

"My notebooks?"

"Yeah," he said. "Yorn's arranging for them to be shipped out here. Including the bookshelves and all the rest of your equipment."

"What?" I said. "My entire room?"

"I've seen pictures of your room. Pretty cool. Feels like headquarters. Careful, though. Before you know it, Smithy will want to make an exhibit out of it. I'd tell them to fuck off. They're hungry for anything that has a pulse. Somewhere along the line they forgot that science was about pushing the envelope, living dangerously, not kowtowing to the masses."

I was quiet. I tried to imagine how Dr. Yorn had emptied my room without my parents noticing. *Surely they had noticed. Surely at least Gracie had told them about the note in the cookie jar!*

"Just a couple of letters for you here," the man said.

He handed me two regular-size envelopes and a larger manila envelope. The first envelope was addressed to:

> Mr T.S. Spivet
> Smithsonian Institution
> Carriage House, MRC 010
> Washington, D.C. 20013

I recognized Dr. Yorn's handwriting. I also noticed that the letter was postmarked August 28, the day I left Montana. I was about to rip open the envelope when the man handed me a silver letter opener.

"Thanks," I said. I had never used one of these before—somehow it made the whole act of letter opening very official.

Dear T.S.,

I know this may have all come as a shock to you. I was going to tell you that I had submitted your name for consideration of the Baird Award, but I didn't want to get your hopes up. Most people apply for this award for several years before they even begin to consider you. But so it goes, and they contacted me just after they contacted you and when I called your house, you had already left!

Can you imagine! What a fright you gave your parents. I talked with your mother for quite a while. I think she was in shock, and I was too, I must admit, because by this point we had heard nothing from the Smithsonian as to your arrival. Tell me, is it really true you rode a train across the country? How dangerous! Why didn't you come talk to me? We could have arranged your transport. Of course I feel responsible. And your mother will not speak to me anymore. I had to tell her about all of our work together and she felt understandably betrayed, jealous, or protective—sometimes I am not sure with Clair. I just wish she could see what an extraordinary opportunity this is for you...

I will call you soon. Congratulations and best of luck.

Best,
Dr. Terrence Yorn

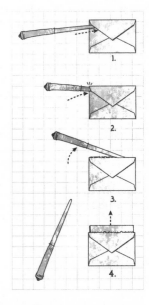

*How to Open a Letter
with a Letter Opener
from Notebook G101*

The real sense of glee came not at step 3 but step 2, when you had the blade of the knife poised against the crease of the envelope and you were anticipating the certain path of your incision.

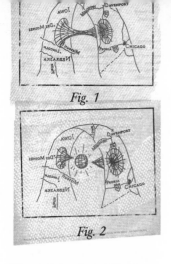

Fig. 1

Fig. 2

Wormhole Pinching-Off in Iowa ◄

From Toriano, P. "The Preponderance of Lorentzian Wormholes in the American Middle West 1830–1970." p. 4 (unpublished)

As far as I could tell, the report was a layman's article adapted from Toriano's dissertation at Southwestern Indiana State, though for reasons unknown, the dissertation had not been accepted. In his report, Mr. Toriano claimed that over the course of 140 years, close to 600 people had disappeared in the Mississippi River Valley between the 41st and 42nd parallels, including eight whole Union Pacific trains. Included were excerpts from internal Union Pacific memos, which urged the company to avoid a public relations nightmare by dismissing the disappearances as "various acts of God."

What interested me the most, of course, were the incidences of accelerated travel of certain western-bound parties. Mr. Toriano had relatively few of these documented cases, which was surprising, for I would've expected anyone who had been in and out of a wormhole to begin hooting and hollering about their experience to anyone who would listen. In the nineteenth century, I suppose no one would believe you. Heck, in the twenty-first century, no one would believe you. I guess I was a case in point—I had kept mum about my experience. There was just something about being in a wormhole that was a little embarrassing.

So she did know.

I looked up. The young man was still standing in the room, smiling at me. He seemed to have no intention of leaving. I tried not to betray any sign that the entire plan might be ruined, that my mother might be on her way at this very moment to ground me forever. I instead turned my attention to the larger manila envelope. A red M was stamped on the front of it. I realized that the letter opener was engraved with the same initial.

"Are you...?"

"Farkas?" he said. "I thought you'd never ask. Farkas Estaban Smidgall, at your service." He gave a little bow and plucked at one end of his mustache.

I tore open the envelope with the letter opener. I was becoming quite adept at this. Inside was Mr. Toriano's report, the same report I had discovered in the Butte archives, but then lost in the bathroom: "The Preponderance of Lorentzian Wormholes in the American Middle West, 1830–1970." It was a copy that had clearly been xeroxed many times over.

"Thank you," I said.

Farkas looked around the room, and then motioned for me to come closer. "We can't talk safely here," he whispered. "You never know when Smithy's listening in...but I'd love to talk with you more in depth sometime. Boris said you were inside a wormy on your way out here?"

"Yes," I whispered, enjoying the secret feeling of our conversation. "I mean, I think so. I can't be sure. That's why I wanted to read this report. Why are they concentrated around the Middle West?"

Farkas glanced suspiciously at the painting of George Washington. "I'll catch you up on everything we know, but not here," he whispered. "I've been picking up where Toriano left off...he never got to the bottom

324

of why the Middle West. His hypothesis was that the unique bend in the continental plate beneath the Mississippi River Valley created a kind of hiccup in the space-time continuum. The theory is that the particular composition of the bedrock in the region, combined with a number of other complicated subatomic factors create this abnormally high concentration of quantum foam between the 41st and 42nd parallels…which of course leads to more frequent pinch-offs and singularities. The real question is where the *negative matter* comes from and how it manages to hold these wormies open long enough for anything to pass through them. Let me tell you, a wormhole is not an easy thing to create."

"Is Toriano dead?" I whispered.

"No one knows," Farkas whispered. And then, in a louder-than-normal speaking voice: "Well, Mr. Spivet, it's a pleasure to have you here."

"Oh, you can call me T.S., please."

"How, how, T.S." Farkas said, quietly again. "We've been waiting a long time for you to get here."

"You have?" I said.

"You'll find instructions on the back of the sparrows," he whispered.

"What?"

He gave me the salute and slipped out of the room, closing the door behind him.

Confused, I opened the manila envelope again and discovered a second packet of paper inside: "Swarming Behaviors of the House Sparrow" by Gordon Redgill. Again, the article had been photocopied several times, and certain pages were already extremely faded.

"Farkas!" I yelled.

How had they known about the swarming sparrows that saved me in Chicago? I hadn't told anyone about this. If they knew about the spar-

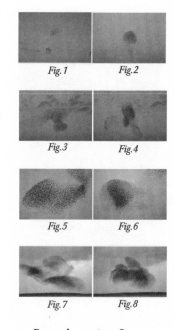

Fig. 1   Fig. 2

Fig. 3   Fig. 4

Fig. 5   Fig. 6

Fig. 7   Fig. 8

Passer domesticus *Swarms Outside Davenport, Iowa*

From Redgill, G. "Swarming Behaviors of the the House Sparrow" (unpublished)

rows did they also know about Josiah Merrymore? Did they know I was a murderer? Would they blackmail me?

I flipped to the back of the report. Someone had written:

Monday, Midnight
BIRDS of D.C. Hall.

"Farkas!" I yelled. I ran over to the door and opened it. At that exact moment, Mr. Jibsen was reaching for the doorknob on the other side.

"Oh, T. S., you're up! Splendid! And I see that they've delivered your things."

"Where's Farkas?" I asked.

"Who?"

"Farkas," I repeated impatiently, trying to see around him.

"The courier? Well, I just saw him leave. Why? Is there something else you need?"

"No," I said. "No."

"How's the pain, my boy?"

I realized that with all the hubbub over the delivery of the portfolios and the reports and the letters I had completely forgotten about my injury. Now that Jibsen brought it up again, my chest began to throb quietly.

"It hurts," I sighed. *Birds of D.C. Hall? Midnight?*

"Well, I figured as much," Jibsen said. "So I brought you some more magic pills."

I dutifully took two more pills and lay down on the bed.

"Well," Jibsen said. "It was really a fantastic job last night." The words came out smooth and nearly lipless. His speech seemed calmer in the mornings. Perhaps his jaw muscles responded to the gravitational pull of the moon, like the tides.

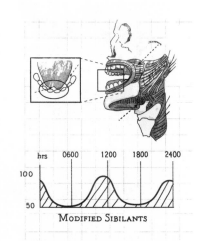

hrs 0600 1200 1800 2400

100

50

MODIFIED SIBILANTS

The Muscles in ◄------
Mr. Jibsen's Jaw Are Tidal
from Notebook G101

How many things in life were actually dictated by the pull of the moon?

"I really could not have dreamed for anything better," he said. "They loved you. Granted, they are a bunch of scientists, but if this is any indication of the public's reaction, we've got a gold mine. I mean to say, you are a gold mine. I mean, I'm so sorry for what happened to you. It must have been…"

He sat down on the bed. I smiled weakly at him. We smiled at each other. He patted the bed and stood up again.

"But what a story! My cell phone's been ringing nonstop. They love, just absolutely love, this stuff! Grief, youth, science. Oh, it's the trident!"

"The trident?"

"The trident," he said. "People are so goddamn predictable. I should write a book about how to suckerpunch people into caring." He walked over to the George Washington painting and stood musing in front of it. "Washington had his trident and look how that turned out for him."

"What was his trident?"

"Oh, I don't know," Jibsen said, irritated. "I'm not a historian."

"Sorry," I said.

Jibsen seemed to soften a bit. "Now, I don't want to overtax you… Are you sure you're up for this?"

"I think so," I said

"Splendid," he grinned. "CNN wants first crack. The press release is out and Tammy just got a call…and I don't want to get your hopes up… but the White House is sniffing around."

"The White House?"

"State of the Union is next week and they love to have his talking points in the audience. Not that our fearless leader's ever given a damn about science, but you have to admit, you are too good to pass up. I can

The Trident
from Notebook G101

And how many tridents were there in this life? Why do we always group things in threes? (The answer was probably deeply neuro-cognitive and could be traced directly to a part of the cerebrum that had three loading docks for big ideas.)

just hear him now: 'Look, the American education system is working! Our heartland is creating little genius children for the future!' Oh, we'll let him have his scientific moment in the sun. Who knows, he may even raise our budget."

"Wow," I said. For a second, I forgot who the president was. I tried to imagine what it would be like to shake his hand.

"Well, I suggest you telephone Dr. Yorn, your foster—your…well, I suggest you telephone Dr. Yorn and your sister and tell them to come out here at once."

"Gracie?"

"Yes, Gracie. We also need some photographs of your parents, and of…your brother. Do you have any family photos of them?"

I realized I had saved the Christmas card of our family from being lost in Chicago by placing it in my day pack. It was still there right now, hanging in the corner of this room. But suddenly I did not want to give this photo to Jibsen or to anyone at the Smithsonian. I did not want people to see my family in newspapers and on television, thinking they were all dead. Gracie would come, of course, she would gladly pose on the scientific red carpet, or any carpet that was red for that matter, and she would probably happily go along with the "Spivet family is dead" story line, but I could not follow through with this quagmire of deception.

"No," I said. "I had a picture but I lost it in Chicago."

"Shame," he said. "Well, when you speak with your…Dr. Yorn, tell him to FedEx some photos out to us. We'll pay for everything. And remind them to send a picture of your brother in particular."

"Oh, Dr. Yorn doesn't have any photos," I said, my molars aching.

"Nothing?"

"No, he thinks they are too painful to have around, so he burns them."

"Really? A shame. What I wouldn't do for a photo of your brother, preferably with a gun, and you in the background. Oh, it would be too much, too much! What was his name again?"

"Layton."

We sat looking at each other.

His cell phone beeped.

"Have many famous people slept in this room?" I asked.

"What?" Jibsen said, fiddling with his phone. "Perhaps. Other Baird Fellows, to be sure. Why?"

"No reason," I said, sitting up in bed.

"Hello? HELLO?" he said into his phone. "CAN YOU HEAR ME? Oh, yes, this is Mr. Jibsen of the Smithsonian."

He jumped up and began pacing.

"Yes…what?! But you said…that's ridiculous!" He looked at his watch. "Tammy said…yes, I understand, but…yes, but…we can't just…"

I watched this funny little man pace back and forth, gesturing animatedly, plucking at his earring.

"Oh, okay, *fine*…yes, yes, no, I understand. Now is *fine*. Fine…I see…Good-bye, ma'am."

He turned to me. "Get dressed. They switched the times…they want to interview you live in two hours."

"Should I wear the tuxedo?"

"No, *you shouldn't wear a tuxedo,* just put on something respectable."

"I don't really have anything else."

"Nothing? Well, fine, put on the tuxedo, but—" He inspected the suit, uncrossing the arms. "Oh, Lord, it's all…well, put it on, and we'll see what we can find on the way over there."

Parallel Longing Brings Us Closer Together

In fact, there *was* such a photo, taken by Gracie for her photography class, a nice departure from her string of 125 belabored self-portraits. I was only able to briefly catch a glimpse of the snapshot when Gracie was arranging her portfolio on the dining room table. At the time, I asked her if I could have the photo after she was finished with it. Of course, as with everything that Gracie does, promises were made and promises were broken, and the photograph disappeared into the general malaise of her closet. Now, alongside Jibsen, I found myself longing for the return of the actual image just as he longed for the imaginary image. Together, we pictured the blurred abstraction of my figure contrasted with the sharp focus of Layton's determined grip on the gun barrel. Our parallel longing actually made me feel close to Jibsen for the first time.

• • •

I was in another black car. This one was being driven by a man who appeared as if he had just stepped out of a film noir. As he held open the door to the backseat, I caught a whiff of his cologne. It was so overwhelming that for a second I thought he was trying to chloroform me. I had to breathe through my mouth and ride with the window cracked open.

"Where to, champ? Vegas?" he asked, giving me a wink in the rearview mirror.

"CNN, Pennsylvania Avenue, please," Jibsen said.

"Thanks, guy," the driver said. "I know where you twos is going. I was trying to lighten up the kid."

Jibsen shifted uncomfortably in his seat. "CNN, please," he said again. "Oh, and we need to stop and get T.S. a suit."

"Ain't nothing on the way, carries his size. Hollaway's closed two years ago and Sampini's northwest."

"Nothing? What about Kmart or something?"

The driver shrugged.

Jibsen turned to me. "All right, T.S., you're just going to have to wear the tux. But keep it closed, all right. Keep it closed."

"Okay," I said.

"So just to CNN then," Jibsen said loudly.

The driver rolled his eyes and winked at me again. He wore a lot of shiny pomade in his hair. He looked a bit like Hetch, our barber back in Butte. The driver had expertly shaped the front of his hair so that it was frozen in a cascading wave across the top of his forehead. It was as if he were daring wind, gravity, or any force of nature to try and pull down the wave.

As we drove, he started humming along to the radio and tapping on the dashboard with his index and middle fingers. I liked this man. He was a navigator.

I watched the cement buildings go by. *We were going to a cable television station*—a place where the television signal was created and then broadcast all across the country to hungry satellite dishes and little black cable boxes. *Oh, to have cable television.* It was one of Gracie's lifelong dreams. (And I have to admit, one of mine as well.)

"So, you understand?"

"What?"

"Pay attention. This is important. I want you to get this right." Jibsen's lisp was back in full force. He started coaching me on how I should answer the interviewer. These were small lies, he said, but they would make it much simpler to tell the story.

"These media types, they oversimplify everything anyway," he said. "We might as well give them the simple version that *we* want."

So this was how it went, he told me: the Smithsonian knew about my age all along. After my parents died…

"When did they die?" Jibsen asked.

"Two years ago," I said.

After my parents died two years ago and Dr. Yorn took me in, I began a long relationship with the Smithsonian, in which I had really blossomed under their guidance. My dream had always been to work there. When Layton died, I was devastated, and decided on a whim to apply for the Baird Award so that I could get out of Montana, despite never really believing that I would receive such a prestigious honor.

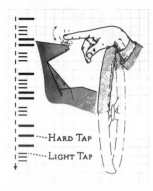

The Driver Taps His Little Beat; He Is a Navigator.
from Notebook G101

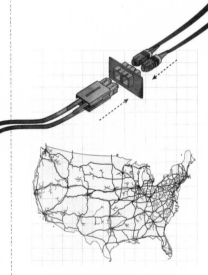

The Fiber-Optic Network in America
from Notebook G78

Though we had only westerns to satiate our hunger for media at the Coppertop, Charlie had DirecTV. (Charlie! My only friend in the world! How I missed his cowlick and goatlike qualities!) The first time I went over to his house, I held down the channel changer button and cycled through all 1,001 channels three whole times, paralyzed by my options.

➤ And now to think, in only an hour and fifteen minutes, Charlie and his lazy mother could be watching DirecTV in their little trailer and *BAM!*—there was his friend T.S. on TV. I made a mental note to say hello to Charlie just in case he happened to be watching, although his mother never watched CNN. She usually watched those judge shows. I hated those judge shows. There was nothing to map.

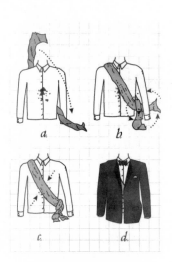

How to Tie a Sash So as to Cover a Bloodstain in the Middle Chest Area **from Notebook G101**

Looking at myself in the mirror made me want to meet this woman's grandfather. He must have been an army man, a religious man, or an actor. I wondered if he was proud of his granddaughter and her amazing makeup skills. I would be.

"And one more minor thing: until we talk to our lawyers, you need to steer away from any sort of culpability in regard to your brother's death. We don't want any complications. You witnessed the shooting and ran to get help. Okay?"

"Okay," I said.

We pulled in to the underground parking lot of a big cement structure.

"Here we are," the driver said, chuckling. "The factory of lies. Or maybe that's further down Pennsylvania Avenue."

"Thank you," Jibsen said, getting out of the car quickly.

"What's your name?" I asked the driver as I was leaving.

"Stimpson," the man said. "We've already met before."

They gave me a lollipop and then they put me in a barber's chair and started hurriedly painting my face with makeup and eyeliner. Gracie would have died laughing if she could have seen me. They styled and combed my hair and then the woman took a step back and said, "Adorable, adorable, adorable." Very fast, many times over. She seemed not to be from this country, but when I looked in the mirror, I had to admit, she was good at what she did. I looked like a character on TV.

When she saw my bloody shirt, she clucked her tongue and yelled for one of her assistants to find me a change of clothes. They came back a few minutes later empty-handed.

"We have too little time," she said, shaking her head. She took a piece of blue cloth and wrapped it around my shirt like a sash, and then slipped the tuxedo jacket over me. She nodded. "Like my grandfather used to wear."

People kept coming up to me and squeezing my arm just above the elbow and then rubbing the back of my head. One woman with a clipboard and a headset came over to me and hugged me, then started crying. She moved away, wiping her face with the back of her hands.

I heard her say, "I could just eat him."

At first there was some controversy about whether Jibsen should be sitting next to me when the interview happened, but the host of the show vetoed this idea. He wanted me alone, "in the raw" he said, which made Jibsen nervous and fired up his lisp again.

"When someone says that they could eat you—" I began to ask Jibsen, but then there was some yelling and a hand painfully grabbed my elbow and ushered me onto the stage.

I sat in the large sofa chair across from Mr. Eisner's desk. He was the host. The lights were extremely bright. Before the cameras began rolling, Mr. Eisner asked me what my favorite movie was. I got the feeling this was a set routine he did with any sort of child that came on his show. I told him about the Sett'ng Room and then I drew him a map of my top-nine favorite movies. Mr. Eisner seemed to like this.

A man with a clipboard and a spiky hat said, "And we're on…in five, four, three, two, one," and as soon as the red light went on above the camera, Mr. Eisner changed into a TV creature. His voice went plastic and he sat up very straight in his seat. I tried to do the same.

"My first guest this morning is the newly announced Baird Fellow at the Smithsonian, Mr. T. S. Spivet. Mr. Spivet is a very accomplished cartographer, illustrator, and scientist, and had been producing illustrations for the museum for a year before he was awarded this high honor. His pictures are highly detailed and incredibly impressive—one glance will prove this to be true. But the most remarkable piece of this story is that T. S. Spivet is only twelve years old." The camera panned over to include me in the frame. I tried to smile.

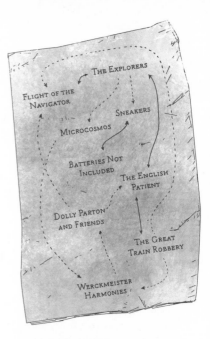

➤ *My Top-Nine Favorite Movies and Their Thematic Relationships* **On a Napkin** **(Property of Mr. Eisner)**

We ran out of time before I could come up with a tenth movie, but in retrospect, I would have to say it was Herzog's *Aguirre, the Wrath of God.* I guess the same part of me that was fascinated with the tragedy of the Berkeley Mining Pit was also drawn to Klaus Kinski's deeply flawed conquistador.

Dr. Clair almost didn't let me rent the movie on account of the violence depicted toward animals, and she had a point. There was one scene in particular that I have never been able to shake from my mind: the group of conquistadors, led by an increasingly maniacal Kinski, are floating down the Amazon river when suddenly one of their terrified horses falls overboard. While the horse swims to shore, the expedition continues to drift down stream. The horse is just left standing there in this massive jungle, staring out at the disappearing rafts with a mournfulness that even Herzog's camera could not have faked.

"What happened to that horse?" Dr. Clair yelled at the television. And then, less explicably: "I hate these Germans!"

Three Rituals ◄- - - - - - - - - - - - -

It was true: if I never saw my father again, I think I would remember him by his rituals. There were many. Perhaps the entirety of his day was spent simply performing a series of elaborate rituals; but I will remember these three the most:

1. Every time he entered the house, he would touch the cross next to our front door, twice, bring his thumb to his lips, pause, and only then get down to the business of unlacing his boots. *Every time.* It was not the singular act but the accumulation of the acts, the metronomic timing and utter consistency with which he enacted this entrance that gave the ritual its meaning.

2. Every Christmas, he would write each family member the briefest of letters, usually referencing the cold weather and "how quickly another year has passed us by"—a line he had culled from one of his Westerns. I never questioned how strange it was to write letters to people who lived in the same house as you; growing up, the presence of those envelopes on the tree was just another Pavlovian visual cue that gifts would be forthcoming.

3. Before each meal (at least for those where he was present), Father had us pray. He would never say anything; his head would just tilt down, and we would know to tilt our heads down too, to close our eyes and listen for that quiet, gruff utterance vaguely resembling an "amen" so that we could safely begin devouring our chow. When Father was not at dinner, Layton would lead this ritual, but after he was gone, Gracie, Dr. Clair, and I quietly abandoned the act.

"T. S., an orphan, who also just tragically lost his brother, joins us today to kick off a three-part series we are doing on child prodigies—where they come from and what they will go on to do in our society."

He turned to me.

"Now, T. S., you grew up on a ranch in Montana, is that right?"

"Yes."

"And your father—I'm very sorry—how old where you when he died?"

"I was…nine or ten," I said.

"I understand he was a cowboy of sorts?"

"Yes," I said.

"He once turned your house into a Western movie set."

"Well, that's—" I could feel Jibsen's eyes on me. "Yes, that's true," I said. "I think he wanted to live inside the world of *Stagecoach* or *Monte Walsh*."

"*Monte Walsh*?"

"It's a Western with what's-his-name…it's actually one of the—"

"So what's the most important thing your father taught you before he died?" Mr. Eisner interrupted

I had the feeling I would get this wrong. It was not the kind of question you could just give the right answer to the first time. But as I sat there and stared into that red light above the camera I knew that just staying quiet was not an acceptable course of action. I said the first thing that came to my mind: "I think I learned the importance of ritual from him."

"No, wait, can I give another answer?" I said.

"Sure, sure. You can say whatever you like! You are the Baird Fellow."

"I think he taught me why family is so important. Our ancestors, I mean. Our name. Tearho Spivet."

The host smiled. I could see he didn't know what I was talking about, so I said, "My great-great-grandfather was from Finland and it was really a miracle that he made it all the way to Montana and married my great-great-grandmother, who was on an expedition to Wyoming—"

"Wyoming? I thought you were from Montana."

"Yes, well, that's right. I suppose people migrate around."

Mr. Eisner looked at his notes. "So…growing up on this ranch with cattle and sheep and everything, how on earth did you get into scientific illustration? It seems the furthest thing from milking cows in the barn!"

"Well, my mother." I paused.

"I'm so sorry," he said.

"Thank you," I said, growing red. "My mother had a hobby of collecting beetles. So I began drawing those. But my great-great-grandmother was one of the first female geologists in the entire country. So perhaps it was just in my blood."

"In the blood, eh?" Mr. Eisner said. "So you always wanted to be this little mapboy?"

Little mapboy? Mapboy was not even a word. "I don't know," I said. "Did you always know you would be a television host?"

Mr. Eisner laughed. "No, no. I thought I was going to be a country music star growing up…*Hey li'l darlin'…*"

When I did not react, he stopped himself and rearranged his note cards. "You see, one of the questions we're asking in the next couple of days is how do prodigies come to be? Did you have an innate predisposition in your brain, or did you learn all this from someone?"

"I think we are born with a map of the entire world in our heads," I said.

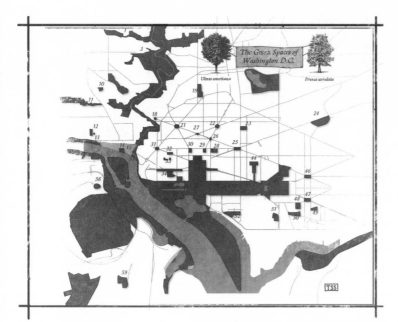

The Green Spaces of Washington, D.C. from Notebook G45

This was part of an exhibition to commemorate Earth Day at the Natural History Museum. It was one of the first maps that I ever did for the Smithsonian.

"Well, that certainly would be convenient, just don't tell the GPS companies," Mr. Eisner said. "Although, I think it's perhaps more accurate to say that *some* of us were born with a map of the world in our heads, and my wife is not one of them. Speaking of which, I've brought a couple of your maps." He held up a map on his desk and pointed it toward the camera. "And this one is…a map of D.C. Parks?"

"Yes. And Northern Virginia."

"First of all, a bang-up job here.   Simple and elegant."

"Thanks."

"I look at this map, and I say to myself, There are fifty parks in downtown D.C.? And it makes me see this place a little differently, which I suppose is what you're trying to do here. But my question is, how do you figure out how to make something like this? I mean, my brain just does not work in this way. I get lost coming to the studio in the mornings." He laughed at himself. I tried to laugh too.

"I'm not sure," I said. "I don't feel like it's anything that I do. The world is out there, and I'm just trying to see it. The world has done all the work for me. The patterns are already there and I see the map in my head and then draw it."

"Wise words indeed from a young scholar. We are lucky the future of the world rests on your shoulders."

I was suddenly very sleepy.

"Later in our program we talk with Dr. Ferraro about her findings from studying MRIs of child prodigies, and I'm sure she's going to want to take a peek inside your head to try to find that map that you're talking about."

After the CNN interview I ate doughnuts backstage while Jibsen scheduled an MRI with Dr. Ferraro for the following day. Then I talked with a nice man in headphones for a while about how to operate the teleprompter. Mr. Eisner walked by and ruffled my hair, although my hair did not really ruffle, because it was frozen into place with hair gel.

"If you ever want to hang out with my children, give a call," he said.

The rest of the day was a whirlwind. I did four more interviews on television. Stimpson shuttled us across the entire D.C. quadrant and then to a Northern Virginia television station.

At the end of the day, on our way back into the city, we were all exhausted, even Stimpson, who had stopped winking hours ago.

"Welcome to the District," he said as we crossed the Potomac. "Where they can never get enough of you even when they've got enough of you."

"How are you feeling?" Jibsen asked, ignoring him. "We only have one more stop today. It's a shoot for the magazine. You've got the cover story next month. We've got some ideas, but I wanted to give you a chance to give some input too. Where would you like to have your picture taken?"

Where to have one's picture taken? In some ways, this was a dream question, but it was a hard question, for essentially Jibsen was asking: of all the places in the world, where would you like to visually locate yourself in

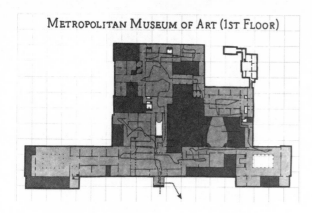

FTMUFMBEF Map #4:
Clara and Jamie's First Day
at the Museum
from Notebook B45

It was every child's dream to linger as the crowds disappeared, to hide under a bench as the guard turned the key in the lock. I had read E. L. Konigsburg's *From the Mixed-Up Files of Mrs. Basil E. Frankweiler* in one day beneath the cottonwood tree. As I flipped the last page and was met with only the stiffened cardboard and cloth of the back cover (it was a library book from the Butte Public Library), I was stung with the realization that this was a work of fiction, that no such events had ever taken place as described in between the bounds of that cloth.

So I drew a series of maps documenting Clara and Jamie's travels. At first I was filled with that empty feeling that often accompanies the invented landscape (the same feeling I experienced when I tried to map *Moby-Dick*), but then it slowly dawned on me that Ms. Konigsburg's novel was actually completely free from the burdens of the mappable world. I could draw this made-up map in a thousand different ways and never be wrong. Unfortunately, this freedom of choice paralyzed me after a while, and I eventually returned to my lifelong task of mapping the real world in its entirety.

a photograph that is meant to be most representative of your hopes and dreams and the architecture of your life project. Part of me wanted to fly back home, to be photographed on the fence post, or in the doorway of Dr. Clair's study, or at the stairwell leading to Layton's attic abode. These would be good photographs. But I was not in Montana. I was circling an institution of representation.

"How about the Hall of D.C. Birds?" I said. "In front of the house sparrow?"

"Oh, that's brilliant," Jibsen said. "I get it. Sparrow. That's subtle and brilliant. Better than anything we could've thought of. That's why we have you around."

I looked up and saw Stimpson smiling at me. "Good choice," he said. "But the bird has flown the coop."

As we waited for the photographers in the lobby of the Natural History Museum, a funny thing happened: the museum closed. Everyone started migrating out the front entrance and I looked up at Jibsen, but he seemed not to notice this fact and we stayed where we were.

Two young black girls clutching matching stuffed egrets dashed away from a woman in a red jumpsuit. Even as they left through the great double doors, I could hear the sound of the woman's yelling echoing off the ceiling high above. Finally, after everyone had left, it became quiet. Only the security guard lingered in the great lobby. Jibsen went over to talk with him and then came back. We were safe.

The full wash of deliciously naughty feelings caused by staying in a museum after hours was tempered because I was being escorted around the museum by adults in charge: I was supposed to be here. However, thanks to Boris, I did know there was an entrance to a secret tunnel somewhere, although my chances of spotting said secret entrance were slim, I realized.

The two photographers finally showed up with their big shoulder bags and the four of us went downstairs to the hall. Well, the Hall of D.C. Birds was not actually a "Hall" in the uppercase sense; rather, it was really just a *hallway* tucked behind the Baird Auditorium.

"Where is that sparrow? Where is that sparrow?" Jibsen muttered up and down the glass cases of birds. "What? It's not here."

"But the house sparrow is a bird of D.C.," I said.

"No, I mean the spot is here but the bird is missing."

Indeed, he was right. There was a little marker that read: HOUSE SPARROW (*Passer domesticus*) but the pedestal was empty. "Of all the times to repair the animal. I mean, really—what luck. Well, we'll just have to shoot you in front of something else. Back to plan A. We'll have you looking up in amazement at the elephant in the main lobby, sketching in your notebook."

"But I don't have my notebook," I said.

"George," Jibsen said to one of the photographers. "Give him a notebook."

"But this isn't the right color. I wouldn't draw in this kind of notebook."

"T.S.! No one cares," Jibsen said, his lisp lurking among the frozen fowl. "It's been a long day. We'll take the pictures and then we can all go home."

. . .

On our way back to the Carriage House, Jibsen's phone rang again. He answered wearily, but after only a few seconds his face lit up. I tried to follow the conversation but was too tired. I had decided I did not like this place anymore. Perhaps if I was able to set up my studio in the Carriage House and get back to the work of mapping, things would change, but so far this award seemed to be about everything but the maps.

Jibsen hung up.

"We're on," he said.

"What?" I said.

"That was Mr. Swan, staff secretary at the White House. We're the seventh and sixteenth slots in his speech, mentioned twice—in the education *and* homeland security sections. National camera will pan to us *twice*. Oh, it's sweet, T.S., it's so sweet. You might think this always happens in this town, but it doesn't—*you* arrive and doors start opening up all over the place."

"The president is bullshit," Stimpson said from up front.

"No one asked you," Jibsen snapped. He turned to me. "I know this can all be a bit much, but you're doing great things for us. And after this week I'm sure it will all calm down."

"It's fine," I said. In the rearview mirror, Stimpson stuck out his tongue and mouthed "It's bullshit." Although, it could have also been "He's full of shit." Either way, I smiled and turned red at the use of the cussword. Like Ricky, these were real adults who cussed whenever they liked.

Just before I retired to bed, I remembered the third letter that Farkas had delivered this morning. The envelope was still sitting on the desk. It was sealed, but there was nothing on the outside—no address, no handwriting, no stamps.

I fetched the letter opener and pressed the blade to the crease. The
envelope parted.

Inside, I found a short note:

Dear T. S.,
I am glad you found the journal.
I forgive you.
          - Mom

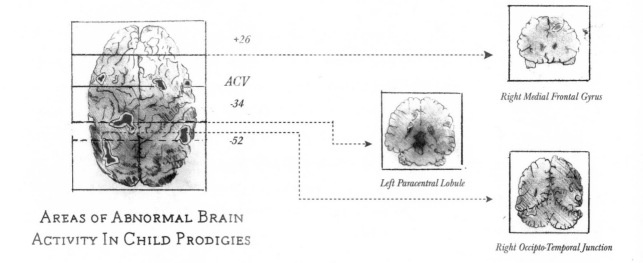

AREAS OF ABNORMAL BRAIN
ACTIVITY IN CHILD PRODIGIES

+26

ACV

-34

-52

Right Medial Frontal Gyrus

Left Paracentral Lobule

Right Occipto-Temporal Junction

CHAPTER 14

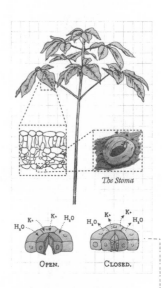

The Stoma

K. H₂O   K. H₂O H₂O K. H₂O

OPEN.   CLOSED.

▶ *The Opening and Closing
of the Stoma*
from Notebook G45

This weekly cycle of urban silence and renewal reminded
me of the opening and closing
of a plant's stoma, which I had
mapped in science class during
our unit on photosynthesis.
Mr. Stenpock had given me a C
on the project for not properly
following his instructions, but
I was later given some vindica-
tion by publishing the illustration in *Discover*.

On Saturday afternoon, Stimpson drove us back to the
Washington Medical Center so that Dr. Ferraro could
perform her MRI scans on me.

Downtown Washington was almost completely deserted. A scraggly
man with a long beard stood on a red Indian rug in the middle of one of
the sidewalks, his hands on his hips, as if he were about to perform some
trick, though no one was around to be tricked. As we drove through the
empty streets, plastic bags blew about, latching themselves onto parking
meters and traffic lights. It was as if everyone in the city had just dropped
what they were doing and commenced a two-day hibernation.

"What happened to all the people?" I asked Jibsen.

"Don't worry—it's just the calm before the storm," he said, fingering
his earring. "They'll come back. Every Monday, they always come back."

This is American urban silence on the weekend.

Adult Women and Coffee

I wondered if Dr. Ferraro would get along with my mother, whether there would be enough mutual intellectual respect between them to sustain a relationship. I desperately wanted my mother to have friends, female colleagues with whom she could share a coffee, laugh about the finicky nature of mitochondria, and complain about the political hoop-jumping of peer review. Perhaps Dr. Clair could unpack the nature of her husband's silence with Dr. Ferraro or do whatever adult women do behind closed doors. But would Dr. Ferraro's brows furrow when she realized that my mother wasn't actually going anywhere in her career? She would put down her mug of coffee and nod vacantly, waiting to get away from this washup of a scientist. She would stop returning my mother's calls. It occurred to me that this collegial rejection had probably already happened; scientists had already put down their mugs and deemed my mother a washup.

X CHROMOSOMES

We met Dr. Ferraro in her office and then headed down to the MRI suite in the basement of the hospital. In the elevator, I kept stealing glances at her. I couldn't help it. There was something about her presence that reminded me of Dr. Clair. Dr. Ferraro wasn't wearing any jewelry and her exterior was a little more composed—a little meaner, perhaps, in the way she kept frowning at everything: the elevator buttons, her clipboard, my tuxedo—but the jut of her jaw, the half-cocked twinkle in her eye recalled my mother's most serious moments of scientific enquiry. Dr. Ferraro clearly meant business—she was engaged in something *real*—and standing close to a scientist engaged in the real world conjured a new kind of excitement in me that I wasn't used to.

Once in the MRI suite, Dr. Ferraro gave me a pad of paper and a pencil. I noticed that the pencil was missing its eraser and that grooved metal ring, so its top just ended in a little naked wooden square.

For the first test, Dr. Ferraro said she wanted me to imagine a place that I knew well and then to draw a map of that place on the pad. I decided to draw a map of our barn, because even though I knew it well, it also felt very far away, and I suppose this was part of the reason I drew my maps in the first place: to return the unfamiliar to the familiar.

I thought this was going to be a pretty simple exercise until Dr. Ferraro had me lie down on the MRI table and then proceeded to strap me down. I mean, how was I supposed to draw *anything* when (a) I could hardly move my arms, and (b) these two plastic pincer plates were pressing hard (and then harder) into my temples?

Dr. Ferraro said something to the technician and then the table started sliding into the machine. As I was disappearing into the white tube, Dr. Ferraro told me the most important thing was not to move my head, *not even a millimeter, or I could ruin everything.*

Despite the fact that my upper arms were strapped down, I managed to lift the pad so that it was resting against the ceiling of the tube, which was really only about six or seven inches above my chest. I could just see the paper in the bottom of my vision. It was not going to be my best map, but I could do what she wanted. I tried to move my head not even a millimeter.

The naked wooden square made me feel uneasy, though I could not say why.

Then the machine turned on and began to let out a very annoying array of loud, high-pitched tones that then repeated, like a car alarm cycle. *Oh let me tell you, it was annoying.* The endless, repetitive racket completely threw me off the task of drawing my barn map—instead, I found myself wanting to draw a diagram of a car alarm and sound radii showing how very high-pitched noises could destroy the tender synapses in our cerebrums.

After a very long time the machine stopped. I came out of the white tunnel feeling as if I had already gone crazy, as if I were emerging back into reality as a deeply changed boy, without any sort of grip on accepted social customs. Dr. Ferraro did not seem to notice what must have been an unhinged look in my eyes; she took my pad, smiled, and put me back in the machine.

This time she asked me to solve a series of very hard math problems in my head. I could not even *begin* to solve these problems. I had only completed seventh grade. I hadn't even taken Algebra I. She seemed disappointed.

"Nothing?" she said from outside the machine.

I felt terrible. *But come on, lady,* it's not like I'm a freak math genius or something.

Then she told me to just lie there and think of nothing, although I of course thought of car alarms. I hope this did not screw up her data sets:

Car Alarms and
Their Effect on Our Brains
(an Unscientific Diagram)
from the files of Dr. Ferraro

she would unknowingly show an MRI of "Boy Contemplating Nothing" to her colleagues at a big conference when in fact it was actually an MRI of "Boy Contemplating the Terrible Nature of Car Alarms."

Before I could warn her that I was actually having a lot of trouble thinking of nothing, she handed me back the pen and paper and told me I could draw whatever I liked, so, in the end, I got to draw my little diagram of the car alarm and its effect on our self-perception.

Afterward, Dr. Ferraro thanked me for my work and even gave me a smile.

I was about to ask her if she would like to meet my mother, when I realized that my mother was supposed to be dead, so I said, "My mother would have liked you."

"Who is your mother?" Dr. Ferraro asked.

"His mother and father have passed," Jibsen said quickly. He pointed at my drawings. "Can we have copies of those?"

"Of course," Dr. Ferraro said.

As they were talking, I went over to the MRI technician. Her ID badge said JUDI.

"Thank you for scanning my brain, Judi," I said.

She gave me a strange look.

"I have a question," I said. "It seems that…what with our technology these days, that we could figure out a way to scan people's brains without the car alarm part of it."

She stared at me blankly, so I pointed at the machine. "Why does it have to make that crazy noise inside there? You know: *erh erh erh erh erh we woo we woo weo woo…*"

Judi seemed almost insulted by the question.

"It's the *magnets*," she said slowly and with exaggeration, as if she were talking to a child.

That Sunday, it rained the entire day. I sat at my desk in the Carriage House and tried to resume my work. Jibsen had requested a molecular diagram of the H5N1 strain of avian influenza. Without anything better to do, I started drawing the H5N1 molecule and how the resulting cytokine storm quickly destroys tissues in the body, which, across certain population densities, could trigger a mass pandemic. But I soon found that I didn't want to make this diagram. I was not interested in pandemics right now. I was not interested in anything right now.

I stared at the page, and then I picked up the phone and dialed Dr. Yorn's number in Bozeman. I couldn't tell you why I did it—it wasn't like I was a good phone-talker—but suddenly the receiver was in my hand and it was ringing.

Much to my relief, he didn't pick up. The phone rang and rang, and then, for the second time in a little over a week, I found myself leaving a message for an adult clear across the country. Except this time I was calling from the East—the land of ideas—to the West—the land of myths, drinking, and silence.

"Hi, Dr. Yorn, it's T.S."

Silence. There wasn't anyone on the other end of the line. I needed to keep talking. "So…I am in Washington, but I think you already know this somehow. Anyways, thank you for submitting my work for the Baird Award. It's pretty fun here, I guess. Maybe you can come by sometime. Well, I got your letter, and I wanted to talk to you about Dr. Clair, because…well, because I told them some things here that are not true…"

More silence.

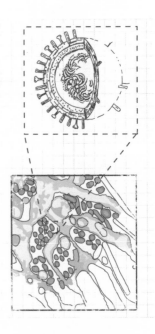

Avian Bird Flu H5N1 Virus

This diagram was never completed. Like the second Death Star, it was later destroyed, though unlike the second Death Star it was destroyed by accident, by a cleaning lady with a generous definition of what qualified as rubbish.

"Well, specifically, I said that my parents weren't exactly alive anymore and that I was living with you. And Gracie. I'm not quite sure why I said this, but it seemed maybe like a better story than the real story and I didn't want the Smithsonian to call Dr. Clair or my father and get them involved in everything here, because it's crazy here. It really is. I'm not sure I..."

I took a deep breath.

"Well, okay. Sorry that I lied. I didn't mean to, but maybe you can give me some advice as to what I should do, because I really have no idea—"

The phone beeped and the machine cut me off.

I thought about calling him back and leaving another message in which I said a formal good-bye, but then thought better of it. Dr. Yorn could fill that part in himself.

I turned back to my diagram of the H5N1 influenza virus. After sketching only a few more lines, I still did not feel right. I looked at the telephone.

I dialed home.

The phone rang ten times, then twenty. I pictured it ringing in the kitchen, the chopsticks vibrating just so with every clamor of the ringer. The kitchen, empty. The house around, empty. Where were they? At this point, they would certainly be back from church. Was my father out in the fields, kicking goats, mending fences as though his firstborn had never disappeared? Was Dr. Clair out on one of her hopeless field expeditions? Or was she writing more of Emma's story? Why had she wanted me to have her notebook? And what did she forgive me for? For leaving? For getting more recognition than her? For killing Layton?

My last hope was for Gracie to remove herself from her cocoon of Girl Pop and monologues and nail polish and come down to answer the phone. *Gracie! Get down here! I need you right now. I need you to bridge the space between us.*

The phone continued to ring. We had no answering machine.

I waited. As with the MRI, I could feel the synapses in my auditory cortex begin to mold themselves to the repeated beat of the phone's ring:

rinng   *rinng*   *rinng*   *rinng*

(I was being hypnotized.)

rinng   *rinng*   *rinng*   *rinng*

I felt a kinship with that distant kitchen, as if I had somehow commandeered the space with my constant barrage of sound, the chopsticks quivering in their little jar.

And then, finally, I hung up. They would not be coming.

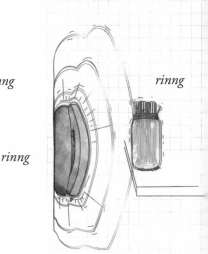

rinng   *rinng*

rinng

➤ *The Jar of Chopsticks Quivers;*
the Telephone Commandeers
the Kitchen
from Notebook G101

On Monday, the day I was to have my secret meeting with the Megatherium at midnight, Jibsen bought me three suits. "We're going to have three press conferences today—"

"And I need a different suit for each?"

"No. If you would let me finish, I was going to say that we have three press conferences today, State of the Union tomorrow, then we'll fly up to New York on Wednesday and Thursday for *Letterman* and the *Today* show and *60 Minutes*, although they're being a little wishy-washy right now, which is just bullshit, because I don't have time for them. If they snooze on this, it's their fucking loss. We've got requests a mile long and they're just lucky I'm playing ball with them for this long. *Pretentious bastards.*"

As he talked, I realized that I didn't actually want to do any of this. I did not want to do any more press conferences. I did not want to go on television, to sit in bright rooms and to banter with strange men in makeup. I did not even want to meet the president anymore. And I did not want to sit in this Carriage House drawing maps for the Smithsonian. I wanted to go home. I wanted to cry and I wanted my mother to come and pick me up in her arms and I wanted to feel her earrings against my eyelids and I wanted us to drive up our road to the ranch and I wanted to see Verywell under the apple tree, gnawing at some little bone he had found. How lucky I was to have grown up on such a ranch, such a castle of the imagination, where hounds gnawed on bones and the mountains sighed with the weight of the heavens on their backs.

"You know what?" Jibsen said. He had been staring at my wardrobe. "Let's forget the suits. Let's just go with the tuxedo. For everything. Yes, it's a better image for you. Always formal. We'll get you two more sets."

If there was any good news in all this, it was that my wound seemed to be slowly healing. Those moments of utter pain—where I would turn my body a certain way and feel as if I was going to black out—those had become much less frequent. I would not be dying of gangrene. I suppose one could always take comfort in overcoming the perils of gangrene.

At the press conferences, I smiled and nodded. Jibsen would have me stand up and bow as he introduced me and then he would tell an increasingly warped version of the events that had occurred: he was born out in Montana; he always had an interest in the area and its people; he had discovered me during a talk he gave at Montana Tech; he had become my mentor from across the country; he had flown out when my parents had died in the car crash; he had found Dr. Yorn; he had really turned my life around, *thank you very much.*

I didn't care anymore. I nodded. With every new flash of the bulbs, every disembodied hand gesture, I wanted to leave this place more and more.

The journalists took pictures and asked me questions and I looked at Jibsen before each one of my answers and it was as though he was telling me exactly what to say with his eyes. I had learned to read his eyes; I could almost hear his lispy voice in my ear and so I repeated what I knew he wanted me to say, and people seemed to believe this, and my parents remained dead. After a while, I could picture the car crash that had killed them both. Georgine, flipped upside down on the side of I-15 just south of Melrose, the taillights illuminating the soft wash of junipers in the early morning darkness.

Jibsen was pleased as punch.

"You are a true genius, T.S.," he said afterward. "We're going places, you know that? We're really going places."

Finally it was evening. I kept urging the clock to move itself closer to midnight so that I could meet with the Megatheriums. Something told me they were the last people in this world who would actually look after me.

But first I had to suffer through a long dinner at a fancy restaurant with a gaggle of adults including the secretary of the Smithsonian, who was jowled and boring as usual. He pinched my chin when he first saw me and then didn't say another word to me the rest of the night.

I ordered lobster. This was exciting: I cracked open every part of the body (even the parts that I didn't need to crack) and I was able to use the thingy-bobby to scoop out the meat as if I had been using it my whole life. It was satisfying to match a tool with its very particular use.

Back in the Carriage House after dinner, I turned on the television in order to pass the time. I watched a show about Civil War reenactments. These people really loved the Civil War. They ran across fields in

This is where my parents died.

Cartography Is Useless

When you drew a map of something, this something then became true, at least in the world of the map. But wasn't the world of the map never the same as the world of the *world?* So no map-truths were ever truth-truths. I was in a dead-end profession. I think I knew I was in a dead-end profession, and the dead-endedness was what made it so attractive. In my heart of hearts, there was a certain comfort in knowing that I was doomed to failure.

Was I Evil or Just Prepubescent?

When I was done with my lobster, I sat listening to the men talk and laugh and ignore me and suddenly I had a very strange sensation that I had never had before: I wanted to take my thingy-bobby and stab it into the Secretary's jowls. I was surprised at the innocent urgency of the impulse as compared to the inevitable carnage such an action would elicit.

Did this urge indicate I had become a fundamentally evil person, or was it just a random passing thought, a harmless symptom of prepubescent cerebral growth? (Oh, but those jowls.)

These six minutes took twelve minutes.

The Passage of Time
from Notebook G101

Time passes at a relatively constant rate (at least when your speed was less than the speed of light), but our perception of *how* time passes was most certainly *not* constant.

full costume, they fell to the ground twitching, pretending they were dead. My father would have hated these people. I kind of hated these people. I turned off the television.

> 10.30 P.M. 10.45 P.M. 11.00 P.M. 11.05 P.M.
>
> 11.09 P.M.
>
> 11.12 P.M.
>
> 11.13 P.M.
>
> 11.15 P.M.
>
> 11.23 P.M. It was time to go.

I realized I did not have my hobo-ninja outfit anymore; this, like nearly everything else in my life, was lost in some rail yard in Chicago. I only had three suits and my tuxedo. I donned the darkest of the suits and wrapped the blue CNN sash around my head.

In the garage attached to the Carriage House I found an old, dusty bicycle with a basket. The bicycle was much too large for me, even after I had lowered the seat as far down as it would go. It would have to do. I left to meet the Megatheriums.

As I cycled through the deserted streets of Washington, I realized that I had forgotten to look at a map of the city to see exactly how I would get to the museum. I had assumed it would be easy, as most streets in D.C. are lettered or numbered, but then my brain froze and I couldn't remember if the letters went north or south or east or west. In the dark, the real world had become distorted.

I rode in circles until I ended up in a parking lot. I got off my bicycle and approached the attendant booth, the inside of which was lit with a single lamp. The parking attendant was asleep. As I drew nearer, I noticed the same prehistoric sloth figurine in the window of the booth that

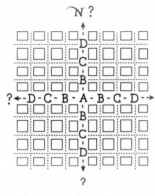

If you were the alphabet, in which direction would you head?

I had seen in Boris's bathroom. My heart leapt. I knocked on the window. The attendant awoke with a start. He glowered at me.

Without knowing what else to do, I made my version of the Megatherium salute, probably butchering it to pieces. His entire faced changed.

"Oy," he said. "Longevity and recursion. What are you doing out here?"

"I'm T.S.—"

"I know who you are. You should be at the meeting."

"How'd you know about the meeting?"

"Word travels fast underground," he said. "What are you doing here? Why the head scarf?"

I put my hand to my head. "I'm lost," I said sheepishly.

"Oh, the little mapboy is lost."

"I don't think *mapboy* is a word."

"It is now. That's the beauty: you say it, and it's a word."

I pondered this but decided not to get into an argument with this man. I made up words all the time—except: I was a child.

Instead, I said, "Nice booth."

"Well it's a way to keep the eyes aboveground. See who's coming and going. A lot of powerful people park their ride in here." He gestured to the parking lot behind him with his tongue, which was a strange thing to do.

I looked down at my oversize bicycle, with its basket and seat lowered down as far as it would go. This was embarrassing.

"But you've got to get to the museum!" he said suddenly. He gave me directions to get back to the Mall. "Don't be late," he said, and made that strange gesture with his tongue again.

I turned to go, then asked, "How many Megatheriums are there in this city? You guys seem to be everywhere."

"Not many. We're just in the right places at the right times. We like to keep our ranks low. People aren't good at keeping secrets."

At approximately seventeen minutes past midnight, I rolled up to the grand entrance of the National Museum of Natural History. I stood with my bicycle in front of the giant stone stairway that swept up to the grand, columned entrance. High above, banners promising exciting exhibits on Vikings and valuable gemstones hung limply in the darkness. A car drove past.

How was I going to get inside? It wasn't as if I could just simply walk up and ring the bell: *Yes, hello, thanks for answering. My name is T.S. and I am here for the secret meeting at midnight...*

Just when I was about to commence some kind of embarrassing break-in attempt involving climbing and then probably falling out of a tree, I saw a small light flash twice near a statue of a triceratops head. I propped my bicycle against a tree and followed the light. A set of stairs led down into a parking area. When I was at the bottom of the steps, another light flashed, this time from inside a little tunnel beneath the huge stone staircase. Someone had propped open a service door with a rock (or a valuable gemstone?).

Once inside the museum, I crept through a darkened hallway, past a bathroom with a Wet Floor sign guarding its entrance, and then, just like that, I emerged into the rear of the Hall of D.C. Birds. The rows of display cases were dimly lit, casting strange avian shadows across the walls. There was no way around it: large numbers of taxidermied birds were just plain spooky.

In the gloom of the bird shadows I spotted a figure at the other end of the room. The figure beckoned me to join him. When I was halfway across the hall, I saw that it was Boris. I sighed in relief.

He was standing with four other people, and as I drew closer, I realized they were congregated around the place where the sparrow had gone missing, although as I came upon them, I could see that the sparrow had returned.

"How, how, T.S.!" Boris saluted me. "Longevity and recursion. Glad you could join us."

I tried to salute him.

"Three fingers," he said.

"What?" I said.

"Three fingers: start at the heart, then eyes, then mind, then sky."

"Why three fingers?" - ➤

Boris pondered this for a second. "I'm actually not sure," he said. He turned to those assembled, "Anyone?"

"Kennicott came up with it. We should ask him," someone said, stepping into the light. It was Dr. Yorn. "Although he's been dead for a while. A suicide, poor bastard."

"Dr. Yorn?"

"Hello, T.S. Nice turban."

"Oh, thanks," I said. "I just left you a message on your machine in Montana."

"Did you, now? What did you say?"

I looked around at those assembled, suddenly self-conscious. There was Boris, Farkas, Stimpson, a young man with a beard whom I didn't recognize, and Dr. Yorn. They were all smiling at me, sipping some drink from matching mugs. This must be the spiked eggnog! I wondered if the

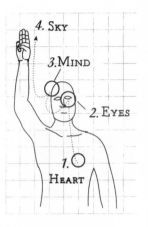

The Megatherium Salute from Notebook G101

But why three fingers?

delicious

The Holding of the Mug
from Notebook G101

One always held particularly delicious beverages with two hands. Maybe this was in case the mug failed in its duties of containment; from this position, one could cup the hands together quite quickly and save what you could manage of the precious liquid.

My Mother as My Mother

I felt my mind creak and shift trying to make room for yet another version of Dr. Clair. Not only was she a *writer* in addition to being a *scientist*, but perhaps she was also a *mother* with real designs for her children's future. She had known all along? She had wanted me to succeed? To become famous in her stead? Even as I felt my mind shifting to accommodate this new version of her, I was not sure I liked the idea of Yorn and Dr. Clair developing an elaborate plan for my future, particularly because it didn't seem to be doing much good for me. Now, hearing of her surreptitious plotting, I found myself longing for the comfort of my old mother: the distracted, beetle-obsessed mother who did not ask who was calling her children on the telephone. That was the mother who had raised me into the person I was now.

eggnog was delicious. It seemed delicious, just by the way they were holding the mugs close to their bellies with two hands.

Dr. Yorn cleared his throat. "T.S., I owe you an apology of sorts. You see, I haven't been entirely truthful with you…though it was for your own good."

"I've been lying," I said.

"*Lying* is a strong word," Dr. Yorn said. "A lie depends on motive. We lied when we submitted your work, but with good intentions. Most things in this world would not get done without a little bending of the truth."

"But I said—"

"Listen: your mother has known the entire time."

"What?"

"She knew what we were doing. She knew about all of your work in the magazines. She has a copy of everything in her study. All of it—the issues of *Science, Discovery, SciAm*…. You think she wouldn't know? She was the one who suggested the Baird Award—"

"Why didn't she tell me?"

He put his hand on my shoulder and squeezed. "Clair is complicated. I love that woman very much, but she sometimes has a problem translating the thoughts in her head into actions."

"But why didn't she—"

"It got out of hand. I didn't know that they would call you first. I don't even know how they got your number on the ranch. I thought if you won the Baird, it would be a good time for everyone to come clean and we could all fly out to Washington together."

My eyes had become hot. I blinked. "Where's my mom?" I asked.

"She didn't come."

"Where is she?"

"She's not here," he said. "I *told* her she should come. You know, I told her to come…but she got that *look* on her face and…and she said it would be better if I came instead. I think she doesn't consider herself a good mother."

"*A good mother?*"

He stared at me. "She is so proud of you," he said. "She loves you and she is so proud of you. Sometimes she just doesn't trust herself to be the person I know she can be."

"I told them my parents were dead," I said.

He blinked. "What do you mean?"

"I told the Smithsonian they were dead."

He tilted his head to the side, looked at Boris, looked back at me, and then nodded.

I tried to read his face. "You aren't mad?" I said. "Isn't that bad? Shouldn't I tell them I'm lying?"

"No," he said slowly. "We'll see how it plays. It could be better this way."

"But I told them you were my foster father and Gracie was living with us."

"Okay." He smiled and made a little bow. "I'm honored. What else did you tell them? I want to be sure to get my story straight."

I thought about this for a moment. "I told them that you hated pictures of people and burned all of them."

"I do dislike pictures of myself, though I tend to keep everything in triplicate. But I can embrace the pyromaniac angle. Anything else?"

"No," I said.

→ This would not be the first club that I had joined, but it would be the first club I had joined in person, and somehow that made it more clubby.

List of clubs, groups, and societies of which I was a member:

- Montana Geological Society
- Montana Historical Society
- Montana Society of Children's Book Writers and Illustrators
- Entomology Society of America
- North American Cartographic Information Society
- Northwest Tab Soda Appreciation Society
- National Beekeepers' Society
- International Steamboat Society
- Monorail Appreciation Society of North America
- Leica Fans of the USA!
- The Young Scientists' Club
- Ronald McDonald Club
- Western Film Society
- Museum of Jurassic Technology (Youth Membership)
- Butte Middle School Science Bowl
- Butte Ladies' Birdwatchers' Club
- Nature Lovers of Montana
- Youth Rawhide 4H (Southwest Montana Division)
- Continental Divide Trail Alliance
- Tiger Beetles of North America
- National Geographic Kids' Club
- Mag-Lev Enthusiasts
- Dolly Parton Official Fan Club
- National Rifle Association (Youth Membership)
- Spivet Family

"Well, then...*son*, let's call this meeting to order."

"Wait, you're Megatherium too?"

"Western Chapter chief," he said, and clucked his tongue. "Longevity and recursion."

"Welcome, all," Boris said, and rapped on one of the glass display cases. "We've called this emergency meeting due to the arrival of our friend here. And we'd like to begin the meeting by formally inviting you into the Megatherium Club. Normally, the induction ceremony is a little more...rigorous, but given the timing of recent events, it seems appropriate to make an exception this time around and forgo the potato-sack races."

"Potato-sack races?"

"Well, we can schedule them for later," Boris said. "I have to warn you, you would be our youngest member, but you have Megatherium written all over you."

"I do?" I beamed, wiping my nose, nearly forgetting about my mother and her absence.

→ I puffed out my chest. "I accept your invitation."

"Excellent," he said. He produced a book from his pocket. I caught a glimpse of the spine: Alexander von Humboldt's *Cosmos: A Sketch, or A Physical Description of the Universe, Vol. 3.* "Please put your left hand on the book and raise your right hand."

In my nervousness, I initially put my right hand on the book. Boris patiently waited until I corrected myself before continuing: "Do you, Tecumseh Sparrow Spivet, pledge to uphold the spirit and tenets of the Megatherium Club, to question what cannot be questioned, to chart the Terra Incognita of Existantia, to honor our forebears and bow in the face of no state, organization, or man to uphold the secrecy of our fellowship, but never lose sight of the mug's embrace, to pledge your faith to longevity and recursion?"

I waited, but he seemed to be finished, so I said, "Yes, I do."

Everyone burst into applause.

"How, how, T.S., welcome," Stimpson said. Each man patted me on the back. Dr. Yorn squeezed my shoulder.

Boris continued: "Welcome, welcome, you are a Megatherium now. It seems that since your arrival in D.C., interest in you has grown exponentially. You are on your way to becoming quite a little—*pardon*—celebrity in this town, and no doubt very soon a household name in the entire country. Being as you are a new member of our club, we feel it is our duty to protect your interests. Please let us know how we can assist you at any time."

"How do I get ahold of you?"

"Well, we'll be around, but if you need to get ahold of us immediately, use the Hobo Hotline."

"The Hobo Hotline?" My mouth fell open.

He handed me a card. "Yes, it goes to our headquarters, which is actually a parking booth northwest of here. Always manned, 24/7. Call them with your question or query and whoever's on duty should be able to direct your call."

"Except if it's Algernon, and then you're fucked," the man with the beard said.

Stimpson slapped him on the back of his head. "The kid's ears, Sundy, please. We ain't savages."

Everyone laughed and took a sip from their mugs. This seemed the proper way to do things: laugh, then sip the deliciousness from the mug.

"Can I have some?" I said, pointing to Dr. Yorn's mug.

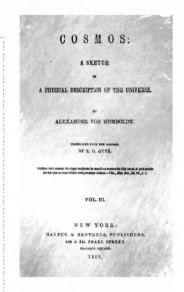

Cosmos: A Sketch, or A Physical Description of the Universe by Alexander von Humboldt

I liked the subtitle of Humboldt's masterwork—it implied a kind of modesty to this herculean task... perhaps it was *just* a sketch...or perhaps it was a Description of the Universe. *Cosmos*'s impact cannot be underestimated: it was the first empirical scientific attempt to describe the universe in its entirety, and though it was a failure in many ways—Humboldt didn't have access to all of the unifying theories at that point—its influence was lasting and pervasive. Humboldt was largely responsible for all of the systematists out there, all of the Dr. Clairs trying to describe the world through every one of its beetle antennae.

— *The Hobo Hotline* —

((308-535-1598))

"Yeah, give the kid some magic juice," Sundy said.

"What's magic juice?" I asked.

"Are you crazy?" Stimpson shook his head at Sundy. "I pray for your children."

"Is magic juice spiked eggnog?" I asked, feeling proud that I knew a word like *spiked*.

"Tell me what you know about children," Sundy said to Stimpson.

Farkas leaned over, thumbing that terrific mustache of his. "Yeah, it's Sundy's eggnog with a touch of the Pirate's Drink in it," he said to me.

"A touch?" Sundy looked over at us, suddenly veering away from Stimpson, who looked like he was going to hit him again. "I would like to formally protest Mr. Smidgall's characterization of my beverage's alcohol content. I mixed these myself, and I happen to know for a fact—"

"Please shut up, Mr. Sunderland," Boris said calmly. He turned to me and smiled. "Perhaps we'll bring more drink options next time. What would you prefer?"

"Well...Tab soda."

"Tab soda it is," Boris said.

"Did you know a computer invented that name?" Farkas said. "The IBM 1401. Way back in 'sixty-three. Coke wanted to come up with a diet soda that was *different*, so they asked the computer for the answer. Back then, they believed these new computer devices held all the answers. They asked the computer for all possible four-letter combinations with one vowel, and the IBM 1401, which was the size of a small car, spat out 250,000 possible names, most of which were utter crap." He made a computerlike noise with his tongue and waved his fingers, which I think was supposed to be the sheets of paper coming out of the IBM 1401. "The sheer effort of computing this raised the room temperature by three degrees. So the team members, who were probably sweating at this point, pored through these names and narrowed the list down to twenty, which they gave to the boss. And he chose *Tabb*. With two *b*'s. The second *b* was later dropped for the incredibly efficient three-letter beauty we have today: uppercase *T*, lowercase *a*, uppercase *B*."

"It's evolution," Sundy said.

"It's *not* evolution," Dr. Yorn said. "It wasn't natural selection. It was some guy in a board—"

"It *was* evolution! It—"

"Thank you, Farkas, for that fascinating bit of information," Boris interrupted. He turned back to me. "So, T.S.—just as we are here for you, there is something you can do for us."

"Okay," I said. I would do anything for these guys with their mugs full of magic juice and their stories of ancient computers.

"You are a Megatherium now and so you have already agreed to our bonds of secrecy, but I would like to reiterate: what is said here must not be repeated to anyone else. You understand?"

I nodded.

"One of our principal projects right now is called *Eyes Everywhere/ Eyes Nowhere*—"

"*The Homeland Security Project*," Sundy interjected.

"Or…*The Homeland Security Project*. We've got a member in Nebraska who's coordinating the feeds, but in a nutshell, it's a guerrilla performance piece that will go live on September 11th. We're going to project it onto the side of the Lincoln Memorial from Stimpson's MCPM van."

"Two Denver Boots on the back wheels. Very difficult to move," Stimpson said.

SWOT
SWUB
SWUD
SWUG
SWUK
SWUL
SWUM
SWUN
SWUP
SWUR
SWUT
SWUZ
SYNC
SYPH
TABB
TABU
TADD
TADA
TAFF
TAFT
TAHR
TAIL
TAIK
TAIN
TAIQ
TAIT
TAGS
TAKA
TALC
TALF
TALK
TAME
TAMM
TAMP
TANK
TANG
TANN
TARN
TARP
TART
TASE
TASK

TaB

The Locations of the
16 Most Restricted Facilities
in America
from Notebook G101

The original map was later
confiscated by the FBI.

"Yes," Boris said. "For as long as it is up, the picture will be composed of sixteen feeds streaming directly from inside the bathrooms of the most restricted facilities across the country: San Quentin, Los Alamos, Langley, Fort Meade, Level Four Lab at CDC, Fort Knox, Mount Cheyenne, Area 51, STRATCOM, Dulce Base, Greenbrier, Ike's bunker beneath the White House…we're smuggling webcams into the men's rooms of all of them."

"How'd you do that?" I asked.

Boris pondered for a moment. "Let's just say people enjoy the challenge of planting tiny cameras in places where tiny cameras are not supposed to be. As long as no one's going to get hurt, the right people don't need that much convincing. A couple of beers, a night out, and we're all on the same team."

"Why are you doing this?"

"Well," Boris said. "That's open to interpretation."

Sundy laughed. "No, it isn't. It's a commentary on our ongoing complicity in propping up a totalitarian state that purports to be a free and open democracy. It's a visual depiction of the boundaries that exist in this country to separate the public from the secret machinations of its own government, and it's a way of saying that we can tear down these boundaries if we want to, but despite our better judgment, we are actively choosing not to, and this choice is what is saddest of all. We would rather watch the shadows of the puppets in the cave than let the sunlight hit our faces."

"Well, some of us, apparently, have very strong opinions about how to interpret the piece, but that does not mean you have to buy in to their version, right, Sundy?" Boris said.

Sundy glared at Boris, looked at Stimpson, who still seemed as if he wanted to punch Sundy in the face, and then shrugged. "Yes, fearless leader, it means whatever you want. All hail relativism's nimble embrace!"

I did not really understand what was going on, but my own understanding did not seem to be an important part of the equation.

"So here is our small request: tomorrow, at the State of the Union, we need you to get the president to wear this pen in his pocket while he delivers his address." Boris produced a pen and handed it to me. "It has a tiny wireless remote control camera on top. If the footage is good, this could be the centerpiece for *Eyes Everywhere*—"

"*The Homeland*—" Sundy corrected.

"—*Eyes Nowhere*," Boris hissed.

The two men stared at each other. Boris sniffed.

"But how would I get him to take it?" I asked quickly, trying to dispel the fight that seemed imminent.

"Oh, *come on*, just make something up…" Sundy said. He put his hands beneath his chin and tilted his head to one side, speaking in a very high, girlish voice: "'Um, can you please wear this, Mr. President? It's my dead father's…and it would mean so much…and he was just your biggest fan…he loved the war in Iraq…blah, blah, blah.' They'll eat that shit up."

"They *do* eat that shit up," Farkas said.

"How! How!" Sundy called.

"How! How!" Dr. Yorn said.

"How! How!" Farkas said.

"*Oh howdy how how!*" Sundy whooped again and then he began to dance very strangely, moving his hips around and around in slow motion as if he were pretending to use a hula hoop. Soon the others joined in, and

In sixth grade, we did a unit on underground caves and spelunking and we all had to write a report on a famous cave of the world, so I chose Plato's cave. In retrospect, I'm not sure this was a good choice, as I believe all children spend some necessary time down in the cave on their way toward intellectual thought and reason. You shouldn't beat yourself up for lingering in the cave as a child. Heck, even to this day I'm not sure I've made it out to see the sunlight. I wouldn't even know what the sunlight would feel like against my face. Would everything just be different? Would it be like emerging from a wormhole?

Children Should Not Read Plato (from Notebook G26)

1.

2.

3.

Grown Men Dancing
from Notebook G101

It was exhilarating to see grown men dance like this, but it also made me feel a little uncomfortable and embarrassed, like when you saw a second grader innocently pick his nose while waiting in line for the bathroom.

I AM A:

THIEF—
  I once stole $21.75 from Gracie's Change Cow to buy a kaleidoscope. (I paid her back eventually, though the damage was already done.)

LIAR—
  Over the past week and a half, I had lied about my age, about where I was from, about my parents' death—was there anything left to lie about?

~~MURDERER—~~
  ~~(Josiah Merrymore? Layton?)~~

BAD PERSON—
  When I was five years old, I hid my father's boots in the basement. He searched for a whole day, grumbling, periodically lashing out and breaking things in the house. I was not sure why I did such a thing, but for some reason it was intensely pleasurable to be the only one on earth who knew where those leather creatures were hiding.

---

everyone was doing this slow-motion hula-hooping, coming up to me and shaking their head back and forth like they knew something I didn't.

Boris was the only one not dancing. "Here," he said. He dropped something into my palm. It was a tiny red M pin.

"Wow, thanks," I said, and pinned the M onto my lapel. *I was one of them now.*

Boris pointed at the House Sparrow. "We've even got a camera inside there, recording everything he sees."

We looked at the sparrow, who sat frozen on his twig. The sparrow looked back at us.

"The report that Farkas gave me," I said. "How did you know about the swarming sparrows in Chicago?"

"Eyes everywhere," Boris said, still staring at the sparrow.

I scrunched up my nose and blinked away the tears. "Do you also know about...?"

"Merrymore?" Boris said. "He's alive. It would take a lot more than a dunking to bring that man down."

"Oh," I said.

He looked me in the eye. "It wasn't your fault," he said. "It wasn't."

"Oh," I said again. My eyes began to water. I took a deep breath. *At least I could cross off "murderer" from the list.*

"Is my mother really not coming?" I asked.

"Wish she was, my man," he said. "She hasn't been to a members' meeting in ten years."

We were waiting, Jibsen and I, in the Carriage House. I was lying on the bed, wearing one of my new tuxedos (with the M pin on the lapel).

Jibsen was pacing the room like a madman. I had never seen him quite so keyed up. His lisp was in full force, and for the first time he seemed to be self-conscious about his speech; he would try to cut off his mishandled words in mid-lisp, which left him constantly out of breath.

He kept turning on the television, furiously flipping through the stations, and then turning it off in disgust.

"What do you want to find out?" I asked finally. "If the speech has been canceled?"

"Like you know *anything* about this town," Jibsen said, turning off the television again. "Things change very quickly around here. This is something you have to learn. Some story breaks, and—*boom!* We're off the schedule. Kids die, someone's been put on life support, and suddenly science doesn't matter anymore. You have to take your shots when you can get them."

Then Jibsen got a call. He was so worked up about it being "the call" that he dropped his cell phone in the process of trying to open it. In fact, it did turn out to be "the call." Jibsen yelled at me to get up and get going, and I thought this was unfair of him, because I *was* getting up and going—human muscle fibers just didn't respond that quickly. Jibsen was an asshole.

Outside, Stimpson was waiting for us in the car. As I was getting in, he motioned to his breast pocket and put his fingers to his lips. I nodded. Inside my pants pocket I gripped the camera pen. At least I would try to do the Megatheriums proud. They were the last people I had on my side. Even though I didn't really understand their project, I would still try to make *Eyes Everywhere/Eyes Nowhere* a resounding success.

We passed through two police checkpoints, Stimpson muttering a few words each time, showing a pass, and the policemen waving us on.

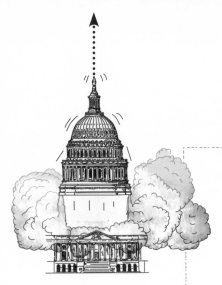

The Capitol Dome Blasts
Off into Space
from Notebook G101

This would actually
be very difficult.

This is How You Use a Large
Dentist's Mirror
from Notebook G101

The police had closed off a huge area around the Capitol. The giant dome was lit very dramatically, like how they lit spaceships in movies, and I wondered how difficult it would be to engineer it so that the dome could actually blast off in times of war.

Finally we pulled up to a scary-looking gate south of the Capitol guarded by two men wearing bulletproof vests and brandishing very large guns. Seeing those big black guns, of course, made me think of Layton. He would have loved these men. In fact, he would have loved this entire experience: the guns and domes that might blast off into the sky and the president eagerly awaiting our arrival. How I wished he could've been sitting right next to me.

Stimpson rolled down the window and spoke with one of the gun-toting men. Stimpson seemed very calm and collected, not at all perturbed by the sight of these guns so near his face. Another guard with a large dentist's mirror checked for explosives underneath our car. Someone checked the trunk. After a minute, they waved us on and we drove up to a side entrance of the Capitol Building.

Upon exiting the car, we were immediately greeted by a man with a clipboard. This was Mr. Swan. He stooped down next to me and said in a Southern accent, "Well, welcome to the United States Capitol, little man. The president is very glad that you could join him as his honorary guest for the two hundred seventeenth State of the Union." His smile was nice but very fake.

Mr. Swan was nodding vigorously at something Jibsen was asking and said, "Right, right, right," and as he was doing this, he put his clipboard against my back and gently ushered me toward the entrance. This pissed me off. I knew exactly where the entrance was, thank you very much.

We had to go through a metal detector before they would let us into the building. I took the pen out of my pocket and placed it into a little plastic tray, which they ran through the X-ray machine. After it had gone through, one of the guards in the bulletproof vests picked up the pen. My heart dropped. He was probably going to accuse me of being a spy and take me to jail and *The Homeland Security Project* would fail and Sundy would be very angry that people wouldn't realize they were living in a cave and I would not live up to any of Boris's expectations. *He had such promise,* Boris would say wistfully of me years later. *But he wasn't cut out for this kind of work. He wasn't who we thought he was.*

The guard twirled the pen around in his large fingers.

"Nice pen," he said, and then gave it back to me.

"Pen is nice," I said stupidly, and hurried along.

Jibsen didn't have as much luck. He kept setting off the machine. He emptied his pockets and he even took out his earring, but the machine still kept howling each time he went through.

"Oh, Jesus Christ, are you kidding me!" Jibsen said. The guard had to hand-search him, and Jibsen was angry about this and the guard had to keep explaining that it was standard protocol. I hoped the guard hated Jibsen.

As I waited for them to finish, I looked at the box of items that had been confiscated from visitors. The items didn't look that dangerous: hand lotions, soda cans, a peanut butter and jelly sandwich. But I suppose it was a terrorist's job to come up with crafty ways of making bombs out of hand lotion.

Jibsen, red-faced and still muttering under his breath, finally emerged from his session with the security guard. We then followed Mr. Swan through several long hallways. He would point out certain rooms as we

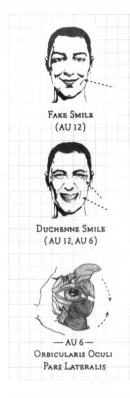

FAKE SMILE
(AU 12)

DUCHENNE SMILE
(AU 12, AU 6)

— AU 6 —
ORBICULARIS OCULI
PARS LATERALIS

How You Can Tell When
Adults Are Faking It
from Notebook B57

Way back in 1862, a Frenchman named Guillaume Duchenne discovered the difference between fake and genuine smiles, and he did it by electrifying a patient's cheek muscles so that only the zygomaticus major muscles contracted. Duchenne noticed that in genuine smiles, the eye muscles also contracted as an unconscious reflex of enjoyment, lifting the cheeks, lowering the brow slightly, and creating crow's-feet at the outside corner of the eyes. Dr. Paul Ekman would later name a genuine smile, which demonstrated both the AU-12 (zygomaticus major) and AU-6 (orbicularis oculi, pars lateralis), a "Duchenne Smile."

Mr. Swan had little to no orbicularis action at the corners of his eyes. He, like most adults I had met on this trip, was all zygomaticus.

What's the Deal, America?

This map was part of my final project for a unit we did on world religions last spring. After doing my research, I had thought about cutting out the Americas from the map entirely; they simply were not supplying many major religions for the world. But I like the map better this way—the Americas represent the open frontier that has been conquered from these simple birthplaces so far away. My seventh grade social studies teacher, Ms. Gareth, did not appreciate the empty Americas. She was a Mormon.

Birthplaces of the World's Major Religions

passed them, but he was always walking, walking, walking. Everyone we passed had on a lanyard and was carrying a clipboard. So many lanyards and clipboards. So much scurrying to and fro. Everyone looked unhappy. Not with an intense misery, more of a mild disdain that they had grown used to; Dr. Clair often looked this way at Sunday church service.

And then we were shown into a room, and Mr. Swan said we would wait here for about forty-five minutes and then the president would come by and meet us. The room smelled of cheese.

"*Well, la di da,*" Jibsen said. "Our little holding cell."

More people began to filter into the room. In came two black women, both wearing T-shirts that said 504 on them in big white letters. Then six or seven men in army uniforms, one of whom was missing both legs. Then a reverend, a rabbi, a Muslim cleric, and a Buddhist monk, all talking animatedly about something important.

The room began to look like the backstage for a very long play about war and religion. The air in the room became hushed and tense. I began to feel ill. My chest started to throb again.

"Do you want some sandwiches?" Jibsen asked, pointing to the food table, which did indeed offer an array of triangular sandwich halves on several large silver platters.

"No, thanks," I said.

"You should eat some sandwiches. I'll get you some sandwiches."

"I don't want any sandwiches."

Perhaps my tone was overly harsh, because Jibsen put up his hands defensively and walked over to the sandwich table by himself. I really didn't want any sandwiches. I didn't want to be here. I didn't want to give the president Boris's camera pen. I wanted to curl up into a ball in some corner and go to sleep for a very long time.

I wandered over to the corner and sat down in a chair next to the army man with no legs.

"Hello," he said, and offered his hand. "Vince."

"Hello," I said, and shook it. "T.S."

"Where are you from, T.S.?" he asked.

"Montana," I said. And then: "I miss it."

"I'm from Oregon," he nodded. "I miss it too. Home. Ain't nothing like it. And you don't need Fallujah to tell you that."

We got to talking, and for a moment I forgot where I was. We talked about his dogs back home in Oregon and I told him about Verywell and then we talked about Australia and whether the toilet water flushed backward down there. He didn't know. Then I got up the courage to ask him about phantom-limb syndrome and whether he could still feel his legs.

"You know, it's kinda funny," he said. "I know my right one's gone. I mean, I can feel that it's gone for sure—my body knows it, I know it. But my left one comes back to me. It feels like I'm a one-legged man, and then I look down and it's like, *Oh shit, I don't even have that.*"

There was some yelling out in the hallway.

"Would it be bad of me if I didn't do this?" I asked.

"Do what?" he asked.

I pointed at the room, at the snack table. "This," I said. "The president, the speech, everything. I want to go home."

"Oh," he said, and looked around the room. "Well, there are plenty of times in life when you can't think about just yourself, you know. Whether it's your country, your family, whatever. But if I learned anything from this whole goddamn experience, it's that when the chips are down, you have to look out for *numero uno* in the end. You know what

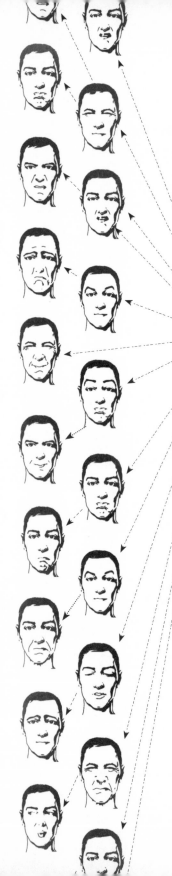

I'm saying? Because if *you* don't, who the hell will?" He took a sip from his drink and looked around the room. "God sure ain't."

At that moment the door to the room burst open and in came a fiery-eyed Jibsen. Apparently, he had migrated away from the sandwich table. A few steps behind him, holding his cowboy hat in his hands, was my father.

He was the most glorious sight I had ever seen, and in that single instant, my conception of my father was forever changed, forever inflected with the expression on his face as he walked into that room inside the U.S. Capitol and spotted me sitting in that chair. A thousand diagrams of Dr. Ekman's facial units could not capture the relief, the tenderness, the deep, deep love, bound up in my father's face. And not just that: I realized that these emotions had *always* been there, they had just been hidden behind the curtains of his silent akimbo. Now, in a single moment, his cards were on the table and I knew. *I knew.*

Jibsen walked right up to me.

"T.S., is this man your father? Just say the word, T.S., *just say the word,* and I'll have him arrested for trespassing and impersonation and whatever else they can slap on him," he was yelling, and people were staring. "I should have known people would try stuff like this, but I had no idea they'd be this insi...insisididios..." He couldn't quite get the word out in its entirety.

The rabbi and the Muslim cleric were staring.

I looked at Father. He looked at me. His expression had retreated back into its normal weary silence; he shifted uncomfortably from one boot to another as he always did indoors, but it was not enough to erase what I had seen before. I beamed. I was crying perhaps; it didn't matter anymore.

"...I mean, he confirms thingsss that we have not released to the public," Jibsen was lisping. "But your father is dead, yesss? So thisss is ss-some cruel and ssssick joke this...thisss imposssstor is playing, yesss?"

"He's my father," I said.

Jibsen was speechless. He was swaying.

"Dad," I said. "Let's go."

Father nodded slowly. He shifted his hat and held out his hand to me. I could see his bum pinky. I took it.

Jibsen's eyes bulged. "What?" he cried. "Your father...is...what? Wait...*Going where? Where could you possibly go at this moment in time?*

We walked toward the door.

He ran in front of us and grabbed Father's arm. "Sir, I do apologize, I do apologize, but you can't leave now, sir...uh, Mr. Spivet. Your son is attending the president's—"

I didn't see it coming. Neither did Jibsen. Father laid him out good, "ass over teakettle," as he used to say, when teaching Layton how to wrestle. Jibsen reeled, crashing into the food table, sending the little triangular sandwiches flying. I think he fell to the floor, but I couldn't quite see, we were already at the door.

My father nodded at the priest before exiting: "Father." The priest smiled meekly back at him.

We were out in the hallway.

"How we gonna get outa here?" I said, resuming the comfort of my father's vernacular.

"Reckon I ain't a'clue in hell," Father said. *Oh, it was like slipping into an old familiar coat.*

And then there was Boris in front of us, dressed to the nines in a tuxedo and white gloves. I must have looked surprised to see him, because

Boris made a little bow and then said, "Even congressmen must make their shits now and again. And where there is shit, there is a bathroom attendant. Gentlemen, may I be of assistance?"

"This is my father," I said to Boris. "Dad, this is Boris. Don't hit him. He's with us."

"A pleasure," Boris said, shaking Father's hand.

"Um, Boris, we need to leave," I said. "Quickly." The door behind us opened. I saw Mr. Swan with his clipboard. The three of us began hurrying down the hall together.

"I'm sorry, but I can't do what you want," I said as we walked.

"Are you sure about this?" Boris asked calmly.

"Yes," I said. "I want to go home."

Boris nodded. "Then follow me," he said.

We walked to the end of the hall and then took a narrow set of stairs down three flights to the basement. Down another hallway, past boilers and a control panel, to an inconspicuous doorway. Boris produced a set of keys. I glanced behind us, but no one seemed to be following us. Boris opened the door and we walked into what looked like a storage room for lumber, paint buckets, and drop cloths. A few stray desks were stacked in the corner. It smelled stuffy.

We walked to the back of the room. Boris pushed away a wheelbarrow. The wall was made out of brick. He grabbed ahold of something (I could not see what), gave a tug, and the whole wall began to swing outward, making a grinding noise as it opened. In a moment, we were staring at the entrance to a tunnel.

Boris handed me a flashlight. "In about two hundred meters the tunnel forks. Take the left fork. From there, it's fifteen hundred meters to the Castle. The tunnel ends in a janitor's closet in the basement. You'll be able to slip out through the southern exit. Don't take the right fork. It takes you to the White House, and I can't guarantee your safety that way."

Father leaned into the tunnel, skeptical. "This roof stable?" he asked.

"Probably not," Boris admitted.

Father poked at the tunnel wall and shrugged. "Hell, I was buried up near Anaconda for day'n a half—ain't that bad."

"Boris," I said, and produced the camera pen from my pocket. "I'm sorry—"

"No worries," he said, taking it from me. "We've got others to help us. A nice man named Vincent. Hell of a pool player. The pen can now belong to *his* father. A good story always translates."

I began taking off the Megatherium pin from my lapel, but Boris shook me off. "Keep it," he said. "Lifetime membership."

"Thanks," I said. I flicked on the flashlight. Boris gave us the salute, and then slowly closed the door behind us. It latched shut. We were alone.

Together, Father and I set off into the darkness. It was deep and earthy down there. Things dripped onto our heads. For a moment, I was afraid that the tunnel would collapse on us then and there, but as we started walking, the world fell away.

For a while, we didn't speak. The only sound was the crunch of our footsteps.

Then I asked, "Why didn't you stop me that morning I was leaving the ranch?"

I waited. Perhaps I had overestimated the deeply caring nature of his expression when he had first seen me in the Capitol. Perhaps it was a fluke. Perhaps he did not really love me and never had. And yet: he had left the ranch and come all the way to Washington. For *me*.

And then he started speaking: "You know, that whole situ-ation was yer mother's. I thought it was horseshit, but that woman seems to know more about these things than me, so I let 'er have at it. I was s'prised as hell to see you early up, crawlin' down the road with Lay's wagon, but I s'posed it was all some kinda plan I wasn't privy to. Woulda liked to at least wish'd you a good trip 'n all that—seeing as my boy's headin' out into the world, but…I didn't want to blow it fer your mother. She cares a hell'a lot, ya know that? May not show it… hell, neither us is much fer jawin', but that woman's devoted to you somethin' powerful. 'Cept now I'm seeing this things'a load horseshit, your mother's been cheatin' me and they ain't done right by you. So here we is three hundred miles 'neath War-shing-ton, trompin' long like a' bunch Rebs fixing to blow up Lincoln. But you all right…You all right, and that's my pri-ori-ty at this here moment in time. My boy's all right."

In my twelve short years of living, this was the longest speech my father had ever given.

Then he licked his fingers and took off his hat and put it on my head. He punched me in my shoulder, a little too hard. I marveled at the weight of the hat on my brow, the cool feel of his sweat on the brim.

We walked the rest of the way in silence, the light from the flashlight bobbing ahead in the darkness, our footsteps loud and crunchy on the floor of the tunnel, but it didn't matter. Nothing mattered anymore. We were off the map.

As the tunnel began sloping upward, I found myself longing for this subterranean world to never end. I wanted to walk side by side with my father forever.

Then my hands were on the door. I hesitated. My father clucked his tongue and gave me a nod. I pushed open the door and walked into the light.

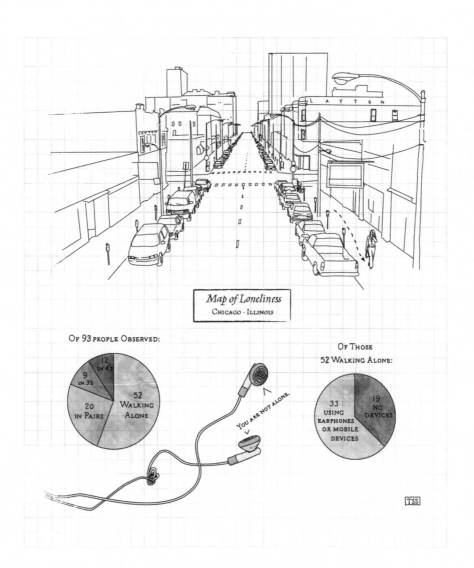

Map of Loneliness
CHICAGO · ILLINOIS

OF 93 PEOPLE OBSERVED:

12 IN 4'S
9 IN 3'S
20 IN PAIRS
52 WALKING ALONE

YOU ARE NOT ALONE.

OF THOSE
52 WALKING ALONE:

33 USING EARPHONES OR MOBILE DEVICES
19 NO DEVICES

TSS

T.S. would like to thank:

Jason Pitts and Laurence Zwiebel for their help with *Anopheles gambiae* proboscis research. Dr. Paul Ekman for helping him understand the ways of adults with Dr. Ekman's Facial Action Coding System. Ken Sandau at the Montana Bureau of Mines and Geology for providing aerial maps and surveys of Butte. The Minneapolis Institute of Arts and the Christina N. and Swan J. Turnblad Memorial Fund for allowing him to reproduce a detail of One Bull's "Custer's War" in the back of Georgine (even if he never completed it). The Missouri Water Resource Center for their diagrams of water tables and also for their general love of water. The Syndics of Cambridge University in faraway England for letting him use a page from Darwin's transmutation notebook B. Raewyn Turner for her patience with his mispellings in their pen-pal correspondence and for letting him use her "Sound Drawing of Brahms's Hungarian Dance No. 10." Mr. Victor Schrager for his beautiful photographs of birds and hands and birds in hands, including "Canadian Warbler" © Victor Schrager. Max Brödel for his vestibular drawing, the original of which is housed in the Max Brödel Archives, Department of Art as Applied to Medicine, Johns Hopkins University School of Medicine, Baltimore, Maryland, USA. Scotts Bluff National Monument, for William Henry Jackson's photograph of Hayden's 1870 USGS expedition. The Autry folks for allowing T.S. to use Gene Autry's Cowboy Code © Autry Qualified Interest Trust, reprinted with permission. Martie Holmer for her maps and her wisdom and her sketches of formal place settings from Emily Post's *Etiquette*, 17th Edition, by Peggy Post. Paccar Inc. for the diagram of a truck cab and for general knowledge of things that move forward. Bjarne Winkler for his magical photos of Black Sun Starlings in Denmark. The Marine Biological Laboratory Woods Hole Oceanographic Institution Library, and Alphonse Milne-Edwards for his wondrous anatomical drawings of *Limulus polyphemus*. Publications International Ltd. for the diagram of how a refrigerator works, © Publications International Ltd. Rick Seymour at Inquiry.net and Daniel Beard's *Shelters, Shacks, and Shanties* for providing much guidance and diagrams on how to chop the wood. And of course Dr. Terrence Yorn, for putting together his selected works.

Thanks to all sentient beings, but more specifically, thanks to the very generous and helpful crowd in Montana: Ed Harvey, Abigail Bruner, Rich Charlesworth, Eric and Suzanne Bendick, and those diligent souls at the Butte-Silver Bow Public Archives.

Thanks to Barry Lopez for creating the character of Corlis Benefideo.

Thanks to the teachers and students of the Columbia MFA program for their endless wisdom and tireless work. Special thanks to Ben Marcus, Sam Lipsyte, Paul La Farge, and Katharine Webber for their invaluable feedback. I feel very lucky to have worked with all of you.

I am also fortunate to have a brilliant compagnie of readers: Emily Harrison, Alena Graedon, Rivka Galchen, Emily Austin, Elliott Holt, and Marijeta Bozovic. An army, they are—do not mess with their kind.

I am profoundly indebted to my agent, Denise Shannon, perhaps the best agent in the world, who always kept her steady hand on the tiller in fair and foul weather. And to the incredible Ann Godoff, who has taught me so much throughout this process. Thanks also to Nicole Weisenberg, Stuart Williams, Hans Juergen Balmes, Claire Vaccaro, Veronica Windholz, Lindsay Whalen, Darren Haggar, Tracy Locke, and Martie Holmer. I am grateful to all of you for your patience and your grace. And perhaps the biggest thanks of all to Ben Gibson, who worked so tirelessly on this project, made it look beautiful, and put up with all of my nitpicky nonsense.

Thanks to Lois Hetland, my seventh grade teacher, for teaching me (almost) everything I know.

And: Jasper, Mom, Dad, & Katie—thank you. I love you. You made me happen.

Gasho.

EVERYTHING IS FICTION.

10.